ALONG THE COAST ROAD

D.G. CRAIG

To the A team.
All is for you.

CHAPTER

1

C ome on in! You're most welcome. Many times in life, we start at a beginning. When we meet a significant other for example. Or when we find a new job, or on January first each year, when we begin a new promise to ourselves for a little while, then oft return to where we were before.

For Gerry, our beginning would be right here in this quiet pub, where the whiff of stone walls and the forever wood fills the senses. Where the rain batters against the roof, and the log on the corner fire burns its way through winter's cold.

In this place, no matter how many beginnings, nothing ever seems to change.

No matter how much one may need to . . .

———— • ✳ • ————

"Jimmy, they say death changes people?"

"Well, time won't leave us as we are, Gerry."

"Sorry again, fellas. He was a fine player in his day, a big lump of a man if ever there was one. A great man too," said Teddy McCarthy, another from the town, seventy-something and related somehow, but not *that* related: Pa's second or third cousin.

"Thanks for coming, Ted," said Gerry, watching Teddy's eyes flicker down at the handshake. He wasn't the first and wouldn't be the last either. Gerry's hands were the size of shovels, and if you hadn't shaken them in a while, they'd shake you.

Teddy left for one of the sandwiches that Aunt Cara had cut with care into triangles, and for a chat with another second or third cousin who was there. There were others there too, non-cousins, those who had played football with Pa all those years ago. Others from the farming community had known him as a fair man, the kind who wouldn't sell you a calf with three legs, at least not without letting you see it for yourself.

"I'm tellin' you, what's left for us here now?"

"Jaysus, Jimmy. He's only gone." Gerry's voice was loud enough and bereft enough to bring the wake to a standstill. He glanced across the bar to see John McHugh — his best pal — and the Connelly brothers, amongst those staring in his direction.

"Sorry Gerry, you're right," said Jimmy.

Gerry looked down at the bags beneath his brother's red eyes. *If grief were a sight,* he thought. Gerry had been better at hiding it until then, he supposed, but sure, a few pints had been had since the coffin had hit the six-feet mark a couple of hours ago. A few pints more would be had yet too. The night was young, after all, and the house would be as cold as it had been last night — and it wasn't due to the crisp, mid-February wind.

"I'm going for another pint," Gerry said.

He stepped around the plates of sandwiches before missing the small step that had been missed by many a person in O'Brien's pub, stumbling into the table that held the photograph of Pa with the small quote from the Bible, the excerpt that Jimmy had selected.

Gerry lifted the card and peered into Pa's blue eyes, the same eyes he saw in the mirror, reading the words again:

Patrick 'Pa' McCarthy, Ballyduffy, 1910-1975. May he rest in peace.

His hand began to shake, and he swallowed the lump in his throat before placing the card back on the table and walking towards the counter.

"Your money's no good here, Gerry; not today," came the voice of Toe

O'Brien from behind the bar as he put another glass under the Guinness tap. "So don't ye be tryin' to pay fer it."

"Thank you, Toe," said Gerry, taking a seat on a high stool. "I know he didn't come in here often — "

"But when he did, sure, didn't he bring the craic?" said Pat Storey, a regular of the high stools of O'Brien's, and of many of the other pubs in Ballyduffy. "Pa sold me a cow once, you know. Had her up in that top field o' yours, the one with the auld thatch cottage that he grew up in at the top of Drumbarron Hill. Used to take an auld rickety bike down that hill on his way to training, so he did, and after many pints in here when we were younger. *And* in McMurphy's, and O'Neill's, I suppose. That was many years ago now."

"He was some man, Pat," said Gerry. "Right enough, he was."

"Joe," shouted Pat across the bar, "Do ye remember Pa's rickety auld bike?"

A smile came across the face of Joe, an elderly fella who never missed a football game for Ballyduffy, sitting at the corner of the bar.

"Ah yeah, the camel? Wasn't that what we called it? He'd be bent over it with that lump of a back of his up in the air. Stubborn auld hoor, he was. You'd never see him walkin' dat bike up a hill even if he thought it might kill him to ride it," said Joe.

"He was stubborn all right, Pat," said Jimmy. He took a stand behind Gerry. "A pint for myself too please, Toe."

Gerry thought back to all the arguments in the house between Pa and his brother. Two stubborn men more like each other than they'd ever admit, although Jimmy had more of Ma in him. "Your half-cooked dreams of travellin' across that feckin' ocean," Gerry often remembered his father saying to Jimmy, "and you think you'd have it better over there, boy, than the smell of the fresh green grass and the feel of a ball in your hands down at McHugh Park."

And Gerry also recalled Jimmy's arguments back: "Ah, there's more to life than Ballyduffy, Pa. Ma knew it, but you... If ye didn't have to go to the cattle market in Tralee, you'd never leave the length of your trousers."

The glass of the black stuff landed in front of Gerry and brought him back into the room.

"Here you go," said Toe O'Brien.

"Thanks, Toe. Father Michael did a good job, didn't he? I'd say Pa would've enjoyed those words," said Gerry.

"Certainly, sure, he was a good man in the community, deserved everytin' Father Michael said," replied Toe.

Gerry smiled for a second before drinking the foamy top of his pint.

"You two boys want of anything now, there's plenty of us around. I'm sure you might need a hand with the new lambs come the spring; still a few weeks off yet, it feels," said Toe.

Gerry nodded, then he glanced at Jimmy's distant stare over the top of his glass of Guinness.

The evening continued with stories and songs and handshakes, and stares at the size of Gerry's hands before he could take no more. With a belly full of stout, and a couple of the final triangle sandwiches in his hands, he and Jimmy put on their coats and headed off down the main street, away from the faint streetlights where the stars would light their way home.

The brothers had walked this many a time together, up past the O'Neills' farmhouse, with their sheepdog that would bark no matter if it happened to be the brightest day or two in the morning. However, tonight, the sheepdog was silent, and the lads too were quiet, not a word or a song between them. The wind was still and the clog of their good shoes on the road — only worn at funerals or weddings — was the only sound to grace their ears.

"So, will you be around for lambing season then?" said Gerry.

"Jesus, Gerry, what do you think I am?" said Jimmy, an air of drunken disgust in his voice.

"I saw you when Toe mentioned it earlier, but it'd be useful to know as I'll have to get someone else if you're not."

"I'll be feckin' here. So, don't give me that shit."

"What shit?" said Gerry. "I only asked."

"I know what you're doing; you sound like Pa, always wanting me to have a life like his, afraid of the world, where fifteen drunks in a pub sing you off, and the next morning everyone wakes up and it's like you were never here and no one gives a shit," said Jimmy.

"Pa would've liked it today," said Gerry.

"Would ye feck off?"

"He feckin' would have."

"And that's what you want, too, you big hoor? You've no idea what's out there," said Jimmy.

"Would you ever stop with your shite? For one day at least," said Gerry.

Jimmy turned and stumbled across the grassy patch in the middle of the road, swinging a fist just wide of a stumbling Gerry.

"What are you doing, you gobshite?" said Gerry, who swung a leg in return, kicking his brother in the stomach. It sent Jimmy reeling back a step, the pints and the whiskey knocking him back another. They were not a good combination.

"Come here you big hoor," said Jimmy. He lunged and wrapped his arms around Gerry's torso. Gerry fell back onto the side of the road, and they both began to roll down the grassy hill, coming to a stop only where the bank took a momentary break. And they continued to wrestle before Gerry put his brother in a headlock and held him tight there.

Jimmy flipped and flung his arms about.

"Calm down, or I'll spank you like Pa used to," gasped Gerry.

The sound of laughter escaping echoed in Gerry's ears.

Jimmy stopped flinching and relaxed, Gerry beginning to laugh now too.

"I was nineteen when I realized I couldn't beat you anymore, you big hoor," said Jimmy once he'd rolled over onto his back and regained his breath.

Gerry remembered the day too, the day a sheep had left the bottom field, and it took Gerry half the day in the pouring rain to find it whilst his brother sat reading some book in front of the fire, his feet up on the coffee table because Pa was out and couldn't tell him off.

Gerry stared at the stars above; they were out in force tonight, the air crisp and cold. The wet dew of the grass licked at the backs of his head and his legs.

"I miss him too," said Gerry.

A bleat from a sheep somewhere, not too far away, broke the silence.

"He was a good man," whispered Jimmy. "Even if we didn't see eye to eye."

The ducts behind Gerry's eyes filled; however, Pa had always taught him to 'leave the water to the wells.'

"We'll be all right, you and me. But I think you should go," Gerry said.

A silence came over the lads. A silence that said all those words they couldn't find the voice to speak to each other. A silence that said it was better to take good wishes when you went, despite how much you'd miss each other. Despite how much you needed each other.

"Thanks, Gerry."

———— • ✳ • ————

The head weighed like a ton of bricks the next morning, but nothing a twenty-one-year-old couldn't handle after an extra couple of hours lying in. Gerry blinked, then rubbed his eyes. *Lying in,* he thought; he'd never had much chance of that before because Pa just wouldn't allow him so much as ten more minutes. The memory of Pa's voice sounded clear in his mind.

"Get up out of that bed!"

Pa would always have made sure his son was up at an early hour; there were sheep and cattle to care for, no matter how much of the black stuff was still roaming Gerry's veins from the night before. But now, Pa was gone.

Gerry looked across to Jimmy's empty bed. *He's probably out checking the fields, or on a run, trying to clear the head,* thought Gerry. The fresh Kerry air would do that, and at this time of the year, could wake even the deadest of men. Gerry walked into the kitchen, lifted the light kettle, and placed it under the tap. Not a normal morning task for him, just another thing he'd have to learn. There seemed to be a lot of them, and Pa had barely been gone a few days as yet. One thing about Pa was if he woke you up, at least the water for the tea would be there.

Gerry reached into the cupboard and his hand wrapped around a cup before he paused. Pa's green and gold cup sat still and empty, looking forlorn on the shelf. Abandoned.

Gerry lifted the white mug — his usual one — to the side, and after he'd thrown a tea bag into it, he took a seat at the kitchen table, putting his feet onto the chair opposite since again, there was no voice to stop him doing it and no slap of the newspaper to make him shift them. *He really is gone.*

The tick of the clock and the whistle of the kettle were the only breaks from the thoughts that came racing through Gerry's mind, the many memories that would linger for a moment before he threw them out. After that would come all the thoughts of the sheep and the cows to be fed, and the lambing season only weeks ahead. Had they enough feed for the animals for the next few weeks? More thoughts rampaged through his mind, thoughts of the markets, and of the silage later in the year. Not to mention the football and the training. That would be starting in a couple of weeks, and maybe this year, they'd have a go at the championship. Although, with Jimmy going, it would all be harder. A knock on the door provided the chance to escape the silence.

"Only me, Gerry," came the voice as the back door opened.

In this part of the world, doors didn't need to be locked, something that had more to do with a close community than having nothing much worth stealing.

"How's it going?"

"Not so bad Gerry, but it's me who should be asking that question."

"Not so bad here either, Cara. Do you want a cup of tea?" said Gerry, rising from his seat. He hoped she might join him; it would stop his wayward thoughts racing away with him.

"Sit you there, I'll get it myself."

Aunt Cara, a woman of sixty, walked over to the silver kettle sitting atop the old black stove. She reached for a cup as she often did, pausing just as Gerry had done moments earlier.

She brought down her brother's green and yellow cup and ran her finger along the old chip around the top. "At least there'll be more tea in the house now," said Cara. "Your pa must've got through a tin of the stuff a week. Didn't he?"

Gerry said nothing, just smiled and nodded, picturing Pa's tea-stained brown teeth.

Cara swapped cups for another before she opened the small fridge. "Not much milk left; you're in charge of that now, I suppose, Gerry. When will ye be replenishing the fridge?"

"I'll go today."

Cara nodded at him, opening her mouth to say something. Then sighed.

Gerry nodded back and slurped his tea, the sound reverberating around the kitchen.

"How's the head? Your brother's out in the field, says he'll be home in a bit. How's he doing?" said Aunt Cara.

"The head's grand and he will be too. He's heading off after lambing, he says. Nothing to keep him hanging about here. So he says."

Gerry heard the sound of Cara's cup landing on the countertop. Not in anger, more a realization of something that had been coming a long time.

"So, I thought. And what about yourself?" said Aunt Cara.

"What do you mean what about me?"

"Have you thought about things? It's a lot around here. A lot to do, Gerry. Pa had you and your brother. You have —" Cara held her tongue, bringing silence to the place.

"This has been our family's farm for how many years? Look, I'll be fine," said Gerry. "Someone has to keep this place going." He walked towards the kettle and passed Cara who had taken a seat. He stared out the window and up the lane. The rain was starting to spit.

"Your pa loved his tea. You know, at one point, he had talked of turning that auld cottage at the top of the hill into some sort of tea shop," said Aunt Cara. "Can you imagine that?"

"Jaysus," said Gerry. He slammed the kettle and cup down and rushed to the sink. Cold water swept over his burning thumb.

Cara laughed when she saw the smile pass over Gerry's face.

"I never heard of that. What the hell's a tea shop anyway?" said Gerry.

"I don't really know myself. A place where people come in and have a drink and a chat, I suppose."

"You mean a pub?" said Gerry. "Well, like a pub. Can't see that catching on."

Cara's laughter filled the room. At that moment, the door opened, and a wet Jimmy entered.

"What's all the laughs about?" said Jimmy with his smile.

The smile that could always light up a room, thought Gerry.

Jimmy slipped off his green wellies and placed them on the mat, then hung his coat on the back of the door. The place was eerily quiet, as if everyone was trying to conjure words to say.

"You ever heard of a tea shop?" said Gerry, still shaking his burnt thumb.

"A tea shop? A coffee shop, you mean? I have, they're big in France. I think America has a couple of them too."

"Of course, America would have them," Gerry said. He rolled his eyes at Cara.

"Why'd you ask?" said Jimmy.

"Your pa wanted to open one once before," said Cara. "Not a coffee shop though. Tea shop. Same thing, but for tea. Big pots of tea on the go all day."

Jimmy glanced at Gerry, and then back at Cara before a fit of laughter filled the room. He bent forward and tears fell, and not only his own. Tears of hilarity, and of grief.

And Gerry pictured his father — the camel — behind the bar at O'Brien's pub handing out pints, never mind cups of tea. His pa had been a community man through and through, but his farm and football were all he knew. Opening a coffee shop, or a tea shop, or whatever this was, seemed absurd for Pa McCarthy. *Well, let's be honest, it's absurd full stop,* thought Gerry.

"That must've been the one time in his life he let himself dream," said Jimmy once the commotion calmed down. His chair squeaked on the old tiles as he took a seat beside Cara.

"He was all for it. Then, sure, your mother passed, and I suppose he had the two of ye to look after then; and let me tell ye, ye weren't the easiest pair to look after either," said Cara with a twinkle in her eyes, the remnants of a tear shining in the light. "He'd have had no time to think after he was landed with you two, all on his own like that. It's a cruel world, sometimes."

With his thumb now cooled, Gerry poured some more water into his cup, watching the tea bag dispensing its swirling blackness. Whatever had happened to the silver teapot they used to have? The one his mother used to leave on the stove in case any visitor came into the house, like Aunt Cara or Uncle Brendan? Those were the days in which there was always the odd blow-in walking the hills and taking a stop along the lane, knowing that Geraldine and Pa McCarthy would always be good for a cup of tea.

Gerry recalled the voices of the visitors but not their stories — likely chatting about some piece of land, or a sheep for sale. Or about the football, an up-and-coming player, the next star for the Kerry seniors or perhaps for Ballyduffy.

For a time, Jimmy was thought to be the next star, but an injury here and there, and then his dreams of pastures new, and then of America, would get in the way.

Gerry knew that to play at the top level, you needed to think about football and nothing else, although he was more than happy turning out in midfield for the Ballyduffy team on a Sunday. Yet, Pa and his tea shop. What a laugh that was. As odd a story as he'd ever heard.

Pa would've needed that silver teapot, he supposed.

"I hear you're off to America, so?" said Cara.

Gerry caught eyes with Jimmy, seeing the surprise in his demeanour, then his shrug.

"I am. I'll be headin' out after lambing season. Johnny Ryan has an uncle out there who'll be letting me stay with him for a bit," said Jimmy.

"That's good; nice to have one of your own around just in case. You're always hearing about them murderers and psychopaths and whatnot out there on the television. Mad for their guns they are. I heard they carry two, one in each pocket, just in case the other doesn't work," said Aunt Cara.

"Sure, there's a gun under Pa's bed," said Jimmy.

"But that's different; that was to ward away the wild dogs. Pa didn't think he was Clint feckin' Eastwood now, did he?" said Cara. "Didn't go around saying, 'look at my gun!'"

"You're watching too much of that television, Cara. There's a reason Pa never had a television in this house," said Gerry, turning to take a slurp of a tea as he stood against the counter.

"Maybe we should get one, Gerry? Might be useful to have when I'm away," said Jimmy.

"Didn't you hear me? I said there's a reason Pa never had one in this house," said Gerry.

"Can't keep away from the world like he did. Times, they're a changin'. And I'll tell you another thing, there'll be coffee shops all over Ireland at some point too," said Jimmy.

"Jaysus, you talk some shite too, Jimmy. You must've taken after Pa more than I realized. If that's so, why don't you open a feckin' tea shop?" said Gerry.

"It's a coffee shop," interjected Jimmy. "I'm going to America, Gerry. If you've no time for that then you can feck off like the rest of them."

"Lads, Jaysus Christ! Will ye just feck up, the both of ye," said Aunt Cara.

The room fell silent, the gentle whistle of the kettle and the slurp of the tea from Gerry's cup all there was to be heard for a moment.

"And I couldn't listen to feckers like you slurpin' their tea all day either," said Jimmy.

Gerry caught the wry smile and the eyes flicking up on Jimmy's face before a raucous laughter filled the small kitchen again.

CHAPTER

2

Through the spring, the weeks around the McCarthy farm would go fast and slow. Fast when Gerry was out in the fields, pulling the two front legs from the behind of a sheep or a cow, sometimes at ungodly hours. Fast when he was running lengths of McHugh Park after a ball or a player on the opposing team. A couple of games had been played, a win and a loss to start, but it wasn't looking like a championship year based on how things had started, and the goals that Jimmy scored. Gerry swore Jimmy was trying harder than he had in many seasons, only so that everyone would miss him more when he left. *The gobshite,* thought Gerry.

The weeks went slow too. Slow in the evenings when the two lads were in the house by themselves. The first couple of weeks, a visitor would pop by every second night or so — Cara or another relative, John McHugh or the Connelly brothers, different lads from the team.

However, life had slowly settled back to the norm. Everyone had their own trials and tribulations that would demand their attention. Their own ewes to lamb. Their own fields to attend to. Their own mouths to feed.

For Gerry, too, the nights were quiet, and he made himself useful by fixing a leg of a table or cutting some firewood for next year. He had spent a few evenings rebuilding the old stone wall which had fallen down last autumn, out the front of the house. Anything to keep him from Jimmy's planning and his constant stories of America.

"Boston, that's where the Irish go, Gerry. Ma told me that a long time ago. Sure, himself was from there: JFK, President of America."

"I feckin' know who JFK is."

When news like that went off in America, the rest of the world murmured. *Maybe Cara was right,* thought Gerry. There hadn't been any man shot in Ballyduffy that he could remember.

On Fridays, the lads would head into O'Brien's for a couple, then on to McMurphy's, where Seanie O'Shea would play the fiddle and others would sing.

There'd be a few of the girls from the town as well. Yet, despite Gerry's chiseled jaw, bluest of eyes and six-feet-four-inch frame which drew quite the attention, when it came to chatting about anything other than cattle or football, he proved to be more like his father.

On the other hand, the odd night, he would walk home alone under the stars or the rain to find Jimmy with one of the O'Connor sisters in the kitchen. And again, the odd morning, he'd wake to find the other O'Connor sister leaving by the back door.

Jimmy's tall tales of America and coffee shops were apparently the perfect main course for those local girls who had their appetizers from the images on their televisions.

One morning, Gerry would overhear Dymphna, the older sister, asking Jimmy, "Why don't you have a television?" This was Gerry's cue to head up Drumbarron Hill to check the cattle in the top field.

Gerry took the bike up that day, a solid frame that he'd picked up a couple of years back for cheap change off Jim O'Brien whose son James Jr had left for Dublin, and auld Jim hadn't as much use for it. It wasn't anything flashy, nor was it a rickety auld thing like the camel, but it was a grand bike, and took him up and down that bastard of a hill that was Drumbarron much quicker than his spindly legs could. At the start, it had been hard work. Pa would laugh when he'd catch up as Gerry would hop off a quarter of the way, pushing it the remainder. Even now, if Gerry got three-quarters of the way up, that would be as far as he could go.

"Used to do this with only half a bike. Look at the size of you; you're a whole inch taller, and a couple wider with hands like shovels, and you can't

ALONG THE COAST ROAD

get yourself up this ant hill here? Jaysus lad, at your pace we'll never get home for a cup of tea!" Pa would say.

In this part of the world, the bonds between a father and his son ran deep, although Pa's and Gerry's words would only ever skim the surface.

Gerry placed the bike up at the gate, then strolled across the grass as the rain began to fall. Not heavy rain, or sideways rain, but spring rain — gentle on the face and good on the grass. Today, his green wellies avoided the cow shites littered across the field.

Other days, when the wind blew hard and cold, and the rain squeezed through every crevice of your coat, those cow shites weren't worth worrying about.

He checked the brown cow with her hanging belly and big udders. *No sign, but she's close,* he thought. She'd be the last of it for this year. Gerry watched the seven calves dance their way to the other side of the field with their mothers, his stare staying a little longer than usual as the youngest calf — the white one — of which he had become quite fond in the past couple of weeks, tried to bury his head under the mother for a suckle. But the mother was in a walking mood right now, and the young calf bleated out in frustration.

After he checked a few of the others for signs of lameness and lay out some feed, Gerry turned, his gaze darting down the hill and across the valley, all the way past the O'Neills' farmhouse and down into Ballyduffy town before meandering out along the green fields that surrounded it. They continued past McHugh Park, where he could see a couple of small figures were out kicking a ball in the distance. And he looked out along the coast road.

This was the road that led down towards Tralee, the largest town in these parts. Then his eyes darted out towards the dark blue ocean that today looked grey under heavy blanket of clouds above. Right out to where the sea met the sky.

The line of no return, he thought. *Where so many crossed the Atlantic, never to come home.*

The old songs of the famine that were sung in the pubs had first taught this, and now many a young man or woman darted off for promises new, a different life to the smell of cow shite around these parts. They all said they'd only be gone for a while, hardly anyone thinking they'd be staying in America for good. But once they were there, they forgot about this place.

13

"I'll save some money and take it home," they'd pledge.

"I'll save some money and buy my auld ma a house," said others, before disappearing.

John McHugh's older brother had left nearly a decade ago now, and there was still no sign of him. Except for the odd Christmas card. There were plenty of other stories like that from villages in other parts of Kerry. And Jimmy was to go too, in the morning. The previous night, half the town had been in O'Brien's, and then in McMurphy's, to see him off.

Gerry sighed, then headed back towards the gate.

There was no calf today, but he'd be back tomorrow just in case it'd put in an appearance overnight as they often did. He took a breath in. The wind blew through his dark hair, and the squelch of the grass underneath his feet gave plenty of spring as he walked across the field. It was a fine field too, just as fine as the other at the bottom of the hill with the sheep. And in a fine place of the world. He turned again to take a look down the valley.

Sure, what the hell do you need television for? he thought.

He closed the gate behind him, and looked at the old, abandoned building a few metres ahead, the house where Pa grew up. Gerry's eyes then darted farther up along the road; another hundred metres or so where you'd reach the peak of Drumbarron and could see Limerick on the other side. But you didn't have the view of McHugh Park and Ballyduffy, or the Atlantic Ocean.

For a building which must have been close to a hundred years old, it was in remarkably good shape save for the thatch on top, gone rotten after years of rain and without any care. There were still some shards of glass in the holes for the windows, where years ago, bored youths had likely thrown a few stones before getting bored again, ambling away to create havoc somewhere else.

Gerry bent down and stuck his head in through one of the windows where the youths had gotten better luck with their stones, no more glass remaining. The inside was filled with dust and shards of broken wood, where someone had taken the good parts of a table or a chair and left the rotten ones behind. The stone floor still remained, of course, unmoved after all these years.

The cottage was split in three, though really, it was one big room, with the main room split and a bedroom on both ends. *With a few months of work, Pa could've turned this into a tea shop no bother,* he thought. *Although, what equipment do you need for a tea shop? Few chairs and tables,* he supposed. *A stove to heat the tea. Plenty of cups and teaspoons. A counter maybe.*

It was a shop after all and it would need a till, and that would have to be on the counter as that was where the shop, and the butchers, and the pubs of Ballyduffy had theirs.

The churns of an auld green grocery van came over the hill as Gerry stepped back from the cottage and headed towards the bike. The rain had started to fall heavier now, and he took out his light woolly hat from his coat's pocket before the sound of a handbrake demanded his attention.

A man, perhaps a couple of decades older, rolled down the window, flinging his ginger-topped head out the side.

"How are ya now?"

By his accent, he was a Midlander, Mullingar or Tullamore maybe, Gerry guessed.

"Not so bad," replied Gerry, tall enough that the man didn't have to glance down from his seat in the van.

"Here, I'm looking for Tralee; don't know if I took the wrong turn a while back there, but by Christ, what a view this is up here," said the man.

Gerry looked over his shoulder and down the valley before turning back to the van.

"You should've taken the turn back there, but it's about the same from here." Gerry pointed down towards the village before continuing, "Head through Ballyduffy, and take the coast road down into Tralee. Takes you right there."

"Good man yourself. Moving in, are you? Thatch needs a bit of work," the man said with a nod towards the cottage.

"It does, all right. Good luck to you now," said Gerry, who turned back towards his bike.

The handbrake clinked as it was released, and the engine chugged again as the van rolled off down Drumbarron as Gerry had instructed.

———— • ✳ • ————

The smell of grilled meat hit Gerry's nose as he arrived through the door. Taking off his hat and his coat, he glanced toward the kitchen table where two plates had been laid out, together with a pot of potatoes with the steam rising off them, sitting in the middle.

"Sit down now, you big hoor," said Jimmy as he walked in from the living room. "I was just throwing something in the fire there."

"What's all this then? Think you're Christ himself with the last supper, is it?" laughed Gerry.

"Something like that. Sit down there now; this is nearly ready."

Jimmy lifted a steak from a frying pan and threw it down on Gerry's plate before turning back to another saucepan. He arrived back, threw some gravy over the steak, before setting some on his own. Gerry picked a few potatoes and placed them on the plate before dipping one into the gravy.

The taste brought him back to a place from long ago.

"This is Ma's auld gravy, isn't it?" said Gerry.

"It is, Gerry. She showed me a few things back in the day, whilst you were out cleaning the sheep's shite with a toothbrush," said Jimmy with a smile.

"Not bad — not quite like hers, but not bad," said Gerry.

"How could it be like hers?" asked Jimmy nonchalantly.

Gerry knew he was right. It had been years since he'd tasted this, but he couldn't forget those odd occasions they'd have it. The day after his confirmation for one.

"Last time was your confirmation, I think, at least from what I remember," said Jimmy. "You had to borrow a pair of my trousers; you were too feckin' tall for the outfit I'd worn not three years earlier. You came out with the ankles showing, and Ma and Pa were in tears laughing, saying you were like one of those boater boys Ma had seen in Dublin one time."

Gerry laughed. It wasn't the only time he'd worn something too small back then.

"At least the shoes fit," said Gerry.

"They were mine too," said Jimmy. "You were always catching up quick. Maybe in a year, you'll catch me up in Boston."

Jimmy took a seat and picked a few potatoes, landing them on his plate.

Gerry cut into a bit of meat and threw it in his mouth. He'd enjoy this meal, even if it was their last for a while. *For how long, who knows?*

"You didn't have to do this, you know," said Gerry.

"You're my little brother, and you'll always be. Don't care if you stand over me or not," said Jimmy, never lifting his eyes from the plate.

"What time do you go?" asked Gerry.

"I'll be away when the cock crows."

"You flying from Shannon?"

"Only the odd flight goes to Shannon, Gerry. Dublin is the main airport."

"Take you a while to get up there, so."

"You're right, a few hours, so when the cock crows," said Jimmy, still looking at his plate.

"You'd crow louder; no bigger cock than yourself," said Gerry. "I heard Dymphna O'Connor's voice this morning in here. Kathleen will have your balls for breakfast when she finds out. That's the reason you're going when the cock crows."

The laughs echoed around the house when Jimmy started to choke and cough on an errant potato that had lodged itself in the wrong tube. The water fell from Jimmy's eyes as he finally hacked the wayward spud into the correct pipe, and the two lads sat for a moment in the silence that had become too common around the house.

"I shouldn't have," said Jimmy.

"Takes two to tango," said Gerry.

"True that. I shouldn't have done that either, but I meant with Pa. All those years arguing about here nor there, pointless stuff; and you know what? I miss his feckin' roars," said Jimmy.

A Kerry man didn't show much, but Gerry could see what was going on behind his brother's eyes. "Pa should've known. Saw it happen to Paudie," said Gerry.

Paudie was Ma's brother. An uncle who was like his sister – Ma — and like his nephew too, Jimmy, not Gerry. A dreamer of far-off places in faraway lands, who happened to grow up in Carrickbay, a village the other side of Tralee that had even less going on than Ballyduffy. Other than a wedding or a funeral, there wasn't anything other than livestock and football. And this drove Paudie mad. Drove him madder when he impregnated one of the local girls of the town, which meant a hand in marriage, bringing a house and a family to provide for.

The only outlet for Paudie had been the black stuff.

Wasn't a bad drunk, just a useless one. Once the family was fed, any spare change and time were spent in the local pub which drove Ma mad, not to mention Paudie's wife.

Ma would try to get through to her brother, saying 'this is the last chance' time after time. But Pa was a bit more realistic in these things, seeing when a man's circumstances were caused by no one but the man himself. In those cases, he could never understand why Ma would put up with Paudie's drunken nights spent on their sofa, and with his sorry tales of lost dreams.

Gerry remembered the one time he and Jimmy had listened through the bedroom door as Ma and Pa had it out.

"He never imagined this life for himself; he wanted to go to America," Ma said.

"Well, he should've thought of that before he got himself a son. He's got to man up, Geraldine."

Over time, there was only so much resentment that could grow, and Pa was a straightforward man like Gerry. Pa would often say, "if you're a young buck, you can have your fun. But when you've a family, you take care of them, no more questions or words needed."

But when Jimmy — after making his way onto a great Kerry minor team — said he wanted to go to America, Pa took it as an insult. Pa would whisper to himself, "have I not been breaking my own back to make sure these boys have everything they need? Food on the table and books for school? And have I not taken Jimmy and Gerry down to kick a ball around McHugh Park for years whenever they wanted whilst they were growing up?

"And now, when he's close to making the Kerry team, and starting to impact the Ballyduffy team, Jimmy goes and throws his hands up in the air like that."

And Gerry could see that point of view too.

Over the years, Gerry watched as they grew apart.

Jimmy would still do what was needed of him when it was needed, but there was that hump on his back. *Maybe Jimmy's more like Pa than he thinks,* Gerry considered for a moment. Their arguments would shatter the walls, come close to fists at times, but Pa would never go that far. Jimmy too, knew where the line was, even if he did stretch it as far as it went.

And after the arguments, there was always that painful silence that would place itself on the chairs of the kitchen, broken only by the men's grunts or a slam of a cup on the table.

And of course, for all Jimmy's mouthing and bollocking of Pa, not once would he defy him and head off to America. But Gerry could see the wear and tear on his brother's face. That locked bird syndrome he'd heard Ma say about Uncle Paudie once was starting to grow on Jimmy. First it was the injuries, a clash of his knee in a game against Carrickbay, of all teams, which would send Jimmy down for surgery in Tralee. But his knee was never the same.

Apart from this year, of course, where he started like a house on fire with five goals.

Maybe he knew they were his last few games, thought Gerry. *When you see the end, perhaps you lighten up and enjoy it more.*

"You know what he said to me the night before he passed?" said Jimmy, his voice sombre. "He said that he and you were like two of the same, but that I had more of Ma in me, and he'd only just understood Ma, and was sorry he couldn't know me better."

Gerry looked up as Jimmy paused, his eyes on the plate of potatoes in front of him.

"Then he said, 'I've some money in that auld teapot of your Ma's for you. It's not much, but if that's what you really want, take it with you to America.'"

Gerry felt a lump — that wasn't a potato — stuck in the back of his throat. The auld hoor had finally given Jimmy his blessing. He had held on until his last breath, but still, he had given it.

"He kept it late," said Gerry slowly, before Jimmy let out a laugh and wiped his hands across the undersides of his eyes.

"He was some bollocks, but I loved him," said Jimmy. "Anyways, I'm not going to eat much more." Jimmy lifted his plate and began to clean up. "You'll have a drink of Pa's whiskey with me, for auld times' sake."

"Jaysus, it's the last supper now, isn't it?" said Gerry.

The fire burned bright into the evening as the two lads sat on the rocking chairs in the living room, listening to the cracks of twigs as they bent amongst the heat. Gerry squirmed as he sipped on a glass of whiskey. He had managed to bury one glass but at twenty-one, he knew it took a man with many more years, or sadly more experience, to truthfully enjoy a glass of the stuff.

Jimmy, tree years older, forced his down. It'd be his last drink on Irish soil for a while.

"I don't want you getting up in the morning, you hear me?" said Jimmy. "I'll write you when I'm there, but tomorrow, I don't want to see your face."

Gerry rocked back and forth. He understood why.

He'd have been the same, he supposed, if roles were reversed. But then again, in what world would they be reversed? Gerry had the farm to look after and that's what his role in life was, and a straightforward role it was too. But he understood.

"I'll write back, so," said Gerry.

"I should feckin' hope you would," said Jimmy. "You know, I'm proud of you, Gerry. You ever need anything, you say it, and I'll be on the next plane home."

They both knew this wouldn't happen. Not that Jimmy wouldn't; of course, he would've. But something would have to be very wrong for Gerry McCarthy, son of Pa McCarthy, to write for help, and if it was very wrong, he'd be in no shape to write a letter.

"Don't worry about me. Plenty around Ballyduffy if I need a hand," said Gerry, his voice low and deep but if he didn't know it, filled with compassion.

And Gerry was right. There'd be plenty around town to give him a hand. He knew that tomorrow before noon, Cara would be knocking on the door, having made her way from the town, whether it was rain, snow, or sunshine, and that the lads from the team would be up a couple of times this week. That's how things went in Ballyduffy, and this was where Gerry felt at home. Yet, that night, after a hug and a pat on the back, the two brothers lay down in their single beds, not six feet apart. Neither had made it yet to Pa's room.

But this would be the last night they'd sleep in the same room, and although neither spoke a word, they both knew sleep would be hard for the other to come by that night.

———•✹•———

When the cock crowed and the first slivers of daylight began to fill the room, Gerry stirred, but didn't roll over. And he heard the footsteps and the close of the bedroom door, and then the close of the front door, and then that was that.

He had livestock to feed and a cow that was about to calf.

CHAPTER

3

After a few weeks, things began to become normal for Gerry. The new normal, we could say, and the weeks passed slowly, but they passed. Gerry kept himself busy with the fields, and the new calf was born, bringing a total of eight for the season. Not bad, all things considered. The football hadn't gone so well; another four games were played, with a singular victory, and the air of inevitability had set in around the club that this would be just another year without a league.

However, as with all teams in Ireland, you still plugged away as the championship would offer a solitary chance, if only a small one, to make things better.

Any goal was a good goal in these parts as time was marked by goals.

A goal of having a successful calving season in the spring.

A goal of winning a championship with Ballyduffy.

A goal of seeing the great Kerry team win an All-Ireland Championship in September.

A goal of having the bales of hay ready for the winter.

Days and weeks didn't mean so much in this part of the world, as you can see. And with Ballyduffy not doing so well, and the calving and lambing done for the year, Gerry needed a new goal. And with the auld cottage at the top of Drumbarron Hill, he had found it.

Weeks passed as Gerry cleared that auld cottage out after a day in the field. He had sledged the auld rotten cabinets that had hung on the walls inside and had turfed out the other remnants of decades passed. The toilet was down in the bottom bedroom where the stone floor continued from the living room. And it still flushed, although the stagnant water that had lain there for many goals and decades had turned the bowl dark, and it would need a paint job.

But by some small miracle, it still flushed and that was what mattered.

Today, the inside was empty, gutted out, the floors brushed, the paint on the walls cracked and missing in places, but the walls were solid and reliable as they ever were.

But in the bottom room, where the thatch was in bad shape, water had run down the side of one of the walls, leaving lines and a shaky stone or two underfoot.

Gerry walked outside and turned to look up at the thatch.

"It's in bad shape all right," he whispered to himself, knowing full well his good work so far could be ruined at any point.

When the time came, that would be the biggest goal, and the costliest. But today, he looked down the valley. The sun was shining, mid-summer, the times when the skies were blue and the grass was green, and the cows would lie down in the field at midday, waiting for the heat in the air to dissipate. And today, the sun was burning.

No worries for the cracked walls in the bottom room.

He walked over to the gate, finding himself laughing when the little white calf, who for some reason he had come to name Penny, rose to her feet and walked towards the gate, sticking her head through the metal.

"You're thirsty, Penny. But there's no milk over here," said Gerry.

The approach of a car rolling gently down the hill caused Gerry to turn around. A silver Datsun, and it beeped at the large man with the dark hair, the youthful looks, and a farmer's tan. Gerry turned, seeing a man with glasses, and his wife in the passenger seat, and three rowdy looking kids in the back.

"How are ya?"

A Dubliner, down in these parts for the holidays, thought Gerry.

"Not so bad," said Gerry.

"We're looking for Dingle. Not sure if we should have turned there a few miles back or not. Wondering if you could help us out?"

The man didn't notice the wife bending back a little further to catch eyes with Gerry, but Gerry did. All the while, the kids in the back fought over who took a magazine or something of the sort, legs and arms flailing everywhere, accompanied by yelling and the occasional scream.

"You should've, but it's the same from here now anyway. Go straight down through Ballyduffy, then along the coast road to Tralee, and you can't miss the signs for Dingle there."

"Good man yourself. Will we take you this year?" the man asked.

The All-Ireland Championship. Kerry and Dublin had been the two previous winners, and all signs pointed again to another final match-up.

Kerry had won the prior year and were favorites again for 1976. But Gerry knew the Dubs always thought of themselves as favorites at anything they did.

Besides, this was a special Kerry team, one Jimmy should've been on.

"We'll take ye all right, I'd say. Good luck to you now," said Gerry, who caught eyes again with the wife with the blonde hair and the red lipstick, and who gave Gerry a smile and a look he'd not known in his life before. And then he turned away.

The man gave a beep, a thank you, as he headed off for Dingle. Gerry closed up the black door, hopping on the bike and heading home.

The man hadn't been the first to ask for directions this summer, and wouldn't be the last, and Gerry continued his work on cleaning up the auld cottage. Also, Jimmy hadn't been the only one left some money by Pa, and although it wasn't much, it was a step towards some fresh thatch to cover the hole in the roof.

----- · ✶ · -----

One night, Gerry heard a knock on the door and the familiar voice of Aunt Cara as she walked in. "How's it going, Gerry?"

"Not so bad, Cara."

"Have you eaten yet? I made some chicken tonight and I wrapped some up in a few sandwiches and have them here for you," she said, sitting down at the kitchen table beside Gerry and taking out four large sandwiches from her bag.

"You didn't have to," said Gerry.

"I wanted to. I heard the Connellys got a right load of hay this year. That'll keep their auld boy happy. He's a hungry hoor, that man, when it comes to the money."

The whole town knew Tom Connelly Sr was a hungry hoor, but it always made Gerry laugh when Cara came out with these kinds of words. Her grey hair bore a strand or two of the black it had once known, and her face had more wrinkles than normal, but that was more to do with the summer tan than anything else.

"Here, I meant to ask; I assume you got the money Pa left you? Your brother found his, I suppose?"

"I did. And he got his as well."

"I know it wasn't much, but we've got to be grateful; your pa wasn't a wealthy man. And what did your brother do with your ma's teapot, so?"

"I don't know; forgot to ask."

Cara stood up from the seat. Despite having very few dark strands of hair, she could still move quickly when she wanted to. *All that walking in and out from town to here,* thought Gerry.

"Must be in your pa's room," said Aunt Cara.

And before Gerry could rise from his seat to say anything, Cara was already opening the door to Pa's room.

"Jaysus, Gerry."

Gerry slowly left the seat, and the sandwiches, and followed Cara into the room.

"You can't leave it like this, Gerry."

Gerry looked at Ma and Pa's bed. Well, it was Pa's bed the way it was now and had been for a decade. And his clothes, and his good suit, were still hanging in the wardrobe.

Ma's stuff was still sitting on top of a dresser – a mirror and a bracelet or two, and a pair of earrings. Not expensive jewelry by any means, but the kind that made her feel worth a little more when she had it on. And in that moment, Gerry remembered her wearing them.

"We have to clear some of this out," said Cara. "You could sell some of this too, Gerry. Every little helps."

Gerry kept quiet as he helped Cara clear out the bedroom that evening and most of the next day. Cara knew not to probe, but at the same time, they both knew it had to be done. Sometimes in grief, one needs a helping hand to get moving along.

Cara had brought a couple of cardboard boxes and they placed Pa's clothes in one, and then the other bits and bobs, including Ma's jewelry and books that had lain scattered at the bottom of the wardrobe, in the other. There were old papers and documents from years gone by: birth certificates for Ma and Pa, and for both Gerry and Jimmy. Plus, there were land leases, livestock records, and tax documents that Gerry didn't know too much about.

I'll have to figure this out now as well, I suppose, he thought.

"Here it is," said Gerry, reaching high into the back of the shelf at the top of the wardrobe. His hand wrapped around the old iron teapot that had been silver once but was now a mixture of black and flaking silvery stuff.

"Jimmy must have left it back where he found it," said Cara.

Gerry nodded, knowing he would've done the same.

"You had a few cups out of this yourself," said Gerry.

"Half the town did, sure. If you were auld enough yourself, you would've as well. Christ, people always coming and going. And now look at you, the man of the house at twenty-two." Cara sighed before turning back to the boxes on the bed.

Gerry placed the teapot on top of the dresser, and they continued with the remainder. He did a final sweep of the top shelf of the wardrobe; right at the back, behind where the teapot had been, he found a book. Its hardback was scuffed, and the edges dented and folded in places, and it was light. Gerry turned it around and read the cover: The Coffee House.

On the front was a strange looking cup that was very small, and one of those fancy plates underneath. *You'd be needing that plate,* Gerry thought, *as that cup wouldn't hold much tea.*

He flicked through the pages.

It turned out to be a picture book of different coffee settings and cups and small descriptions, merely a line or two long, some saying 'Espresso, Milano, Italia', others with strange machines behind counters in Paris and Bordeaux, with taps that looked like those in O'Brien's pub, but different. And they weren't tills either, as Gerry could see those to the side on one picture with a grey-haired man and glasses, a white apron folded like a skirt around his waist and a tea towel in his hand. All very strange and unusual and European, Gerry thought. Not Kerry-like. Anyways, he put the book down on the dresser, beside his ma's auld teapot.

"And what about this, Gerry?" said Aunt Cara down on her hands and knees, peering underneath the bed.

Gerry got down too and looked at Pa's auld rifle.

"We'll leave that there, so," said Gerry, because he knew that as a farmer, it was always handy to have a gun around the place.

Then, he stood up and helped carry the two boxes out into the kitchen.

"That looks like it all, so. Have you training tomorrow night? You think you can get one of the lads to throw these boxes down my way, and I'll get them sold in Tralee someday? I have to go down that way soon enough to help Father Michael with some collections for the Church, so I could do it then," said Cara.

"Can do. As always, thank you for —"

"Don't thank me, Gerry, you'd do the same. I'll see you during the week. Good luck to you."

With that, Cara headed off and in front of the fire later that evening, Gerry pondered. A restlessness had come over him that was unusual. *Perhaps the dust appearing from the movement of things and objects that have sat in their place for years can do that,* he thought.

Gerry went into Pa's room and lifted the teapot from the dresser, putting it back on the stove in the kitchen. He would have a cup from it tomorrow. But he still felt restless. He went back to the dresser and lifted the strange book, beginning to flick through the pages in front of the fire. And his mind searched. So, Ma's was the teapot and Pa's was the book, and Pa had decided he wanted to open a tea shop, or coffee house, and then that dream had all disappeared. And Gerry thought about his mother's dreams and his father's straightforwardness, and it clicked.

Pa must have come around to Ma's idea to open a tea shop, and with her death — and with Pa not having the wherewithal or the humility to ask for help — their dream had withered and died. The arguments of Pa and Jimmy echoed in Gerry's ears that night.

Jimmy, who still hadn't written, and about whom Gerry had tried not to think in the meantime, had Ma's personality. Pa had missed it, and he needed it, but never had the balls to say anything about it. *Jaysus, Pa,* thought Gerry.

He laid the book down on the small table, just as he had done to many a teacup — and he smiled. Because he knew he had the biggest goal of all: the McCarthys' goal.

CHAPTER

4

"I've something for you, Gerry," shouted Cara.

Gerry, clean shaven and washed after a long day in the field, put on a shirt and left the bedroom. He walked by Jimmy's neat and tidily made bed with its empty pillow, which Gerry now had on his. It was the first time he'd ever had two pillows, and sure, Jimmy wouldn't mind.

Cara was sitting at the kitchen table and had two cups of tea poured as Gerry took a seat.

"I got rid of most of the boxes. Have a couple of things still to go, but here you are," said Cara, laying out a number of notes and coins on the table.

Gerry lifted his cup and took a drink, his eyes counting the money to the nearest penny. Plenty for some bits and bobs for the cottage, but the thatch and the hole in the roof would be out of reach, and with winter approaching and the monsoon-like rains that could come with it, Gerry knew it could knock him back months if the place got flooded again.

"Thank you. Must've taken you a bit of time to shift that lot," said Gerry, once he put the cup back down. "Do you want a biscuit?"

"Go on then, why not? And it wasn't so bad. Kelly's in Tralee took the bulk of it, and knowing them, they'll sell it on for double, if not triple," said Cara as Gerry rose and went to take a packet of biscuits from the cupboard.

When Gerry turned back to take a seat, there was an envelope on the

27

table, white and regular, except the words on front were addressed to *Gerry McCarthy, Drumbarron Hill, Ballyduffy, Co. Kerry, Ireland.* Gerry felt himself pause for half a second, before ushering his ass to the seat.

"I guess we both know who that's from. I was in the post office earlier and Patricia asked if I would take this out to you. Save Gerard the walk," said Cara. "Don't worry; I didn't open it."

Gerry's eyes rose to meet his aunt's. *Well now, that's something,* he thought. Cara was like many of those in small towns, enjoying any bit of news that came her way, but she knew better when it came to her nephews. And Gerry looked down again at the letter. It had a stamp in the top corner, depicting an odd-looking statue with a crown on its head, and it looked as though it was holding an ice cream cone to the sky.

The stamp was small and not too easy to make out.

"Only one person this could be from, so," said Gerry.

"You can open it later when I'm not about. So, I hear ye were beat again on Sunday, Gerry? Will ye be relegated now? Missing Jimmy's goals, it seems. Uncle Brendan says ye are doing all right at the back, but getting the scores are like hen's teeth, hard to come by," said Cara.

Gerry knew the hen's teeth saying. And he knew Uncle Brendan was right too. It had been a season to forget for Ballyduffy. And a first-round knockout in the Championship to add to it all.

"Shite enough to be honest. But we won't get relegated; Drumboe haven't won a game all year, so they'll go down. We'll scrape by for another year."

"Always next year. And those clowns, Kerry, got taken to the races by the Dubs. First time since 1934 that Kerry lost to Dublin. Sure, Jaysus, Gerry, if they wanted to get taken to the races, they should've gone to the horse track at Tramore," said Cara, pursing her lips.

Gerry blinked as he took a drink. What Cara hadn't heard yet was that there were rumours the Kerry team had actually been caught with too many Guinness at Tramore racecourse, right before the game. He always thought Cara had superstitious thoughts, and here was another. Old women, 'closer to God' they said; maybe He left the back door open for them.

And Kerry had been useless in the game last Sunday. O'Brien's had been packed with those who hadn't gone to Dublin, and chairs were nearly thrown at the small television in the corner, which Gerry and the others had all squeezed around for the game.

Gerry listened to Aunt Cara eat her biscuit and tell him some more chat about the goings on in the town: a baptism for Sue Feeney's child; the schools in Tralee now putting tirty in the classes instead of twenty-five as they always had; and the price of milk, of which Cara had put another carton in the fridge. But through all that, there was only one thing on Gerry's mind, and that was the spare seat at the table where Jimmy would always have sat.

Gerry looked at the white envelope on the table.

Gerry McCarthy, Drumbarron Hill.

The first letter he'd ever received in his life. When you were twenty-two and from a village like Ballyduffy, sure where, and to whom, would you be sending letters?

And after Aunt Cara left, he began to potter around. He cleaned the dishes, of which there weren't too many, swept the floors, and then lit the fire.

He watched the flames as the autumn rain began to caress the windows. He picked up The Coffee House book again and flicked through its pages. Although he was good with his hands, breaking and making things, he hadn't a clue about design, and Pa and Ma would've wanted a nice tea shop for people to sit inside. Here was where he'd have to let the book provide some guidance. The picture of the Parisian man behind the nicely shaped counter was what he thought a good coffee house might look like. Then there was another picture of a round table and two chairs from a cafe in Milano. These were the two he had his eyes on.

As yet, he hadn't made his mind up as to which. Albeit he'd still need to come up with money, despite the amount Cara had left on the table.

Gerry's head turned back towards the small kitchen, to where the letter sat unmoved. He rose from his seat and walked over and filled a cup of tea before taking the cup, and the letter, back with him to his seat by the fire. He ripped open the letter as delicately as a man with shovel-sized hands could, lifting the singular sheet of lined paper and unfolding it as if handling a delicate silk handkerchief for the first time in his life. He held it between thumb and forefinger, by its corner.

July '76

Well, Gerry,

How's it going? Not so bad over here. The birds of summer are in full flight beneath the sky of blue above. Been a week now since I saw a cloud, and by Jaysus is it hot! Ninety degrees so it is, that's thirty something back home. The farmer's tan is on show right now, I tell you.

Staying with Fergal Ryan (Johnny's Uncle), down in the south side of Boston for now. He's got me some work on a building site there too, loads of work Gerry, plenty much for a big hoor like yourself should you fancy it. Fergal's married to a Boston woman, Rebecca, lovely woman. Reminds me of Ma, but a right bit younger, and they've taken me under their wings, thanks be to God. And they've twin daughters with the blondest of hair, born the same month as you, would you believe? But never you mind about them, Gerry!

I'm playing football too. They've six teams out here; I'm playing for St. Mike's. Fergal is involved with them, played for them when he first came over all those years ago. Mix of lads, few from up the country, few Dubs, two Kerry boys, from down Killarney way. I even scored myself a few goals. Good craic now, plenty of beers to be had, and plenty of bars to have them in.

It's a different world, Gerry. Non-stop, always something to do. They've these towers downtown they're building that are reaching into the sky. As high as Drumbarron Hill itself. And sure, they're friendly folk, doesn't everyone wish you a nice day, Gerry.

Was a bit odd at the start, on those days when you're still figuring the place out, you know, wondering why is this fella eyeing me up, telling me to have a nice day? Does he know something I don't? But sure, I say it now, myself. Different food out here too. They've these places for breakfast, like the coffee houses we were laughing about, but you sit at the counter, and they come out with plates the width of tyres, and they may be stacked with five or six pancakes high and whatever else. Although I can't get a good cup of tea anywhere. That's the one downfall.

How's all back there? I hope you're keeping out of trouble and keeping the head down. I forgot to tell you, that auld teapot of Ma's is up on the top shelf of Pa's wardrobe. And you know, there'll come a time when that room

ALONG THE COAST ROAD

would be better off cleaned out, Gerry. I think about Ma and Pa most days but sure, I'd say it's the same for you.

Managed to find a bar not too far away called O'Ryan's, and a crowd go in and listen to the games on the radio on a Sunday. Don't know how they manage to get a signal this far away, but where there's a will, there's often a way. What you make of Kerry this year? I thought they look a bit full of themselves in what I've listened to so far. Not what you need to win back-to-back titles. The Dubs will be waiting in ambush, Gerry. How's Ballyduffy doing?

I've no doubt ye are missing my goals; sure you can only catch the ball in the middle, ye still have to score it!

All the best and chat soon,

Jimmy.

James McCarthy
15 Euclid Ave,
Boston, MA 01125
USA

Gerry put the letter down and smiled as he took a cup of tea. *That bastard always called the Kerry team right,* he thought. *It must take a while for letters to arrive from America.* Then again, Kerry wasn't Dublin, and things moved slower down here. For all Gerry's silent worries, it sounded like Jimmy was the cat he'd always been, landing on his two feet. Job and football. Not to mention the twins! Gerry shook his head and laughed again. Sure, at the pub on Sunday wasn't Dymphna O'Connor and her sister Kathleen, both asking Gerry how Jimmy was getting on.

"He's some gobshite," Gerry said quietly to himself.

Gerry glanced up towards the closed door of Pa's bedroom, then back at the letter. If only Jimmy knew what Gerry had been up to and what his plans were. They'd have to wait for now. Gerry wasn't a man of many words, and he didn't need to be shouting about plans when they were only just that: plans. Gerry looked at the letter again. *Boston, MA 01125.*

Maybe that was Jimmy's number in America. Odd way to be handing out letters, he thought. For tonight, he put the letter back in the envelope, and placed it in the small box that he kept in the top shelf of his dresser. It'd take a few days to figure out what to write back.

———— • ✸ • ————

As summer turned into autumn, Gerry spent his days in the fields and his evenings up the top of Drumbarron. The wall separating the bottom bedroom and the main room had been knocked down by now, and Gerry had painted the inside walls of the top room a light yellow, just like the image of the Milano coffee shop from the book. However, there was still a hole in the roof, and he was still short of the money to cover it, and winter was looming on the horizon. Then one day, as he was out in the top field laying feed down for the cows, an idea popped into his head.

Borrowing an auld tractor and trailer from Uncle Brendan, Gerry made the trip along the coastal road, and down outside Tralee to the market that was held the first weekend in September each year. Gerry had pondered, like people often did over decisions like these.

It was, 'Will I? Won't I?' before concluding that there was no other way to do it. However, he also knew that a farmer selling off a couple of his prized sheep and cattle – whilst not uncommon – attracted questions. Not so much from those in Tralee, but from those around Ballyduffy, where Aunt Cara, amongst others, didn't miss a beat.

After an hour in which the constant beeps of people in much too much of a rush for Gerry's liking echoed in his ears, he parked the trailer up.

To his defence, the coastal road to Tralee was awful bendy, not an easy place to pass a tractor and a trailer of livestock. They should've gone to Mass last night, Gerry said to himself, when one fella sped by him in a Datsun and threw the middle finger out the window.

Gerry had been here a couple of times before with Pa, when they'd been doing a bit of trading. Trading a few sheep for a cow. Or on the lookout for a new bull that year when Barney died. *Nice bull,* Gerry thought, although it would see red if you hung around long enough.

Barney had once chased Gerry out of the top field. Gerry had dropped his hat behind him as he leapt over the fence, only to turn and see a raging bull drop a shit on top of it, to the howls of laughter from Pa and Jimmy.

"Gerry McCarthy," said a voice as Gerry got out of the tractor, a light drizzle sweeping his face.

"Well, Thomas, how's it going?"

"Not so bad, Gerry; grand soft day. Come here, I'm awful sorry to hear about Pa. He was a great man. Great cattle too. What do you have with you there?"

Thomas Murtagh was the manager of the Carrickbay football team. He had three sons on the team, and off the pitch they were all as nice a man as you could meet. On it, the biggest bunch of feckers you could ever get; they would drive right over you if it meant they'd win the game. Gerry had gotten in a scrap with one – Johnny Murtagh – in the final game last year. Boxed the head of each other, they did. The game nearly had to be called off.

Then, in the bar after the final whistle, Johnny bought him a pint to pay his condolences about Pa, and for the black eye that Gerry would be wearing for the next week. But then again, Johnny was wearing two himself at that stage.

"Few sheep and a couple of cattle, Thomas, if you want to have a look?" said Gerry.

"I will indeed Gerry. That last cow your father sold me, has me a calf every year and not a moo out of her. Ye were lucky to stay up this year, Gerry. Missed that brother of yours, ye struggled to get scores. We did all right ourselves now. Johnny got man of the match in the Championship final, despite the loss," said Thomas, walking over to the trailer as Gerry led the animals out into a pen.

Carrickbay had nearly won the Championship, and any year that they did well, and Ballyduffy did poorly, was an especially bad year.

"But we stayed up, Thomas, and we'll be back again this year," said Gerry with a wry smile that caused Thomas to laugh.

"Just like your pa. You know me and him would bait the shite out of each other on the pitch in our day. He was a good player now, but it was a great team he was on. Toe O'Brien and auld John McHugh, great players in their day. Anyways, I'll take the two cattle. What do you want for them?"

Gerry paused. His eyes lit up. He didn't expect to sell the two cows this fast. If he got them sold in the one day, he'd have been happy enough. However, this would be more than enough to cover half of the thatch, the bad thatch.

"You know the price: one-fifty."

"Jaysus, Gerry, is that a sheep or a calf in there?"

Gerry turned to see what Thomas was looking at. Hidden in the dark of his trailer was a little bit of light. *Penny! How the feck did she get in there?*

"That's one of the youngest calves for this year, Thomas."

"Jaysus, she is a picture. A prize calf. Much you take for her?"

And Gerry's eyebrows raised, and he rubbed his hand through his hair. He knew the little white calf was a picture, and she could get a good price, maybe sixty pounds. And that would leave him with more thatch, perhaps enough for tree-quarters of his roof.

"I'll give you one hundred for her," said Thomas, and he took out a roll of notes from his pocket and began counting them in his hand.

Jaysus, thought Gerry. Between the lot, he'd have a new roof. And he pictured how the tea shop would look with a lick of paint and a full roof of brand-new thatch.

"So, you'll take it?" said Thomas.

Gerry turned again to Penny. And there she was, standing quiet and alone at the back of the dark trailer, surrounded by all the noise of the market. Much more noise than her field at the top of Drumbarron Hill, where nothing much happened.

And Penny turned and looked at Gerry and she swished her tail. *Ah would you look, she's scared.*

"I – I can't Thomas. The calf's not for sale."

"What do you mean, Gerry? One hundred not a good offer?"

"Oh, it's a fantastic offer, it's way too—"

"Well, how about one-fifty for her then?"

Jaysus! Gerry rubbed his head. One-fifty for a newborn calf was extraordinary. Unheard of. He pictured what he could do to the tea shop with that money. He could buy tables and chairs, maybe a counter. He'd have it finished in no time. But for some strange reason, be it Pa's death, or Jimmy leaving, or whatever it was, he was fond of the calf.

"I'm sorry Thomas, she's just not for sale. Now if it were any other... Just not this one."

"Well, Gerry. Fair enough. One-fifty for a calf is unheard of, but I hear you."

The men traded, and wished each other luck for the football this year, which neither of them meant, and Gerry found another buyer for the sheep. Within a couple of hours, he and Penny were on their way back on the coastal road, and he knew she'd be much happier out in the top field beside her mother. As the sun shone across the Atlantic Ocean with not a cloud in the sky, Gerry chugged along in the tractor, knowing that a good day's work lay behind him. Not even the constant honks of the cars following, or the Datsun that spun by with the horn held and four middle fingers, one out each window, could wipe the wide smile off his face.

CHAPTER

5

"Now we're in business," Gerry whispered to himself.

He stood back and looked across the room. It had taken him all winter to get here. He looked at the light-yellow walls where he had hung an auld photo of the Kerry team, and another picture that Ma had down in the house of a map of Ireland, with all tirty-two counties, 'as it was supposed to be', just as Pa would always say.

And he looked at the four round timber tables that he had made and sanded himself, with two wooden chairs positioned at each one. *So that's eight,* Gerry thought, *nine including the stool at the counter.* Then his eyes carried down into the auld bottom room, although there was nothing to distinguish it now, all open and one big space with the picnic table; that was a little longer than a typical picnic table, one where eight could sit handily enough, and then two more of the small round ones. Plenty of seats for twenty or so. Gerry shook his head.

What a silly thought!

He hadn't even a single customer yet and didn't know if any would fancy coming along. This thing was going to be a tea shop, after all; it was an absurd idea, always had been. But then he looked up at the pictures on the wall again. This had been Ma and Pa's dream, and it was nearly there. It was his job to make it happen, to bring to fruition that which Ma and Pa couldn't.

In another man, in another part of the world, this would be the point where some emotion would be released, perhaps even a tear might roll down the cheeks, but the minute Gerry felt a tickle in his throat, he walked behind the counter and pressed against it.

Seems sturdy enough, he thought.

He had designed it just like the Paris Café, wide enough to showcase some buns or cakes. He still hadn't figured out where those buns would come from, but it was good to have goals.

All in good time. Keep it simple, Gerry. Pa's dream would have been simple too.

Languishing behind the counter, was an old fridge Uncle Brendan had been about to throw out before Gerry stopped him under the watchful eyes of Cara. He'd cleaned that old thing up and there was nothing amiss with it. If you were making tea — lots of tea, gallons of the stuff — then you'd need milk.

Then there was the gas stove that Gerry had purchased from the McHughs.

It was second hand and needed a lick of paint and a shine, but it worked, and it had four rings which could hold plenty of teapots. He could keep the tea coming all day on that stove. *Keep it simple, Gerry.*

Just then, Gerry heard a loud bang on the front door; he almost jumped sky high. Not that he was scared by any means. It was more that the door had never been banged, and no one knew there was anything going on inside. Or let's say, no one *should* know.

Outside, the cottage still needed painting and the half-fresh, half-old line of thatch up top still made the place look uninhabited.

Gerry pulled the door open to see a man with a navy coat and a pair of glasses standing outside. Gerry walked out and saw the green *An Post* van behind. The man was a postman, but he wasn't a Ballyduffy man, or not one that Gerry had seen before anyway.

"How are ya?"

"Not so bad," said Gerry, who noticed the man take a step back when he saw Gerry bending his head a little lower to get out the door.

"I'm looking to make it to Tralee, not sure if I should've taken the turn a few miles back. First day down these parts. Covering for Paddy Sweeney. He's in Spain on holidays for the week."

Paddy Sweeney. Gerry had heard the name before.

Sweeney was a Dingle man and sometimes did the rounds right up to Tralee, whereas Ger O'Shea was the postman for the rest of Ballyduffy and the surrounding area. Gerry could tell this fella was a Limerick man, and not used to this part of Kerry.

"You should've, but you're as quick from here as you would be from there. Straight down the hill through Ballyduffy and along the coast road to Tralee."

"Ah good man yourself. Here, have you any water in there? I've nothing left in my flask. I'm Cillian by the way, from Nenagh."

A Tipperary man. Gerry had guessed wrong.

He glanced over his shoulder and through the door, before turning back to Cillian. He hadn't let anyone inside, but what would be the harm?

"Sure, come on in and I'll fix you up," said Gerry, who headed inside as Cillian went back to the van and brought out a blue flask.

Gerry walked behind the counter and towards the sink that he had cleaned up.

"Jaysus, never would've guessed you'd have a pub in here," said Cillian as he walked in the door. He didn't have to stoop to fit through the low doorway, and Gerry watched over his shoulder as Cillian assessed the furniture and the walls before he walked towards the counter, taking a seat on the stool. Cillian played with the seat as it rocked against the floor below, finding a spot where it balanced as if it really mattered.

"Where's your taps? Can't have a pub without the taps, big fella; I'm sure you know that."

Gerry hid his chuckle. "You talk an awful lot for a postman. I thought you lads just delivered."

Cillian replied, "They also say postmen never get lost. Is that a teapot over there?"

Gerry paused as Cillian's eyes flicked towards the silvery black teapot sitting on one of the rings on the stove. Gerry had brought up Ma's teapot a few months back when he realized he'd be spending more time up here to get the place together.

And many cups of tea were had back then. However, only ever by Gerry.

"It is," he said.

Cillian bent back to look around at the tables and the picnic table at the end of the room. "Strange auld pub this. No taps and a teapot. Ah, you're only just setting her up. Bit of an odd spot though for a pint, right up the top of this hill."

And for the first time so far, Gerry stopped what he was doing, and thought — *what if this doesn't work out?* He'd spent all this time and all his savings, every little penny he had to get the place to where it was today.

"But sure, if someone is tirsty, they're tirsty. Anyways, is there any tea in that?" said Cillian. Those words seemed to kick that inkling of doubt from Gerry's mind, and he stopped thinking, and turned to the task at hand.

"There is; why do you ask?" said Gerry.

"Well, if you've a cup of tea going, I'll have a cup of tea. Bleedin' parched so I am, and my tea got cold quicker than you think in those flasks. Not up to much, they aren't."

"Are you not supposed to be on your way to Tralee?" said Gerry. He stood against the back shelf with a towel in his hand, drying the cup he'd washed earlier.

"I am, but sure I'm late already, and it doesn't matter if you're tirty minutes late or an hour late, you're still late. So, I may as well be late than be late and tirsty," said Cillian. "And if you're opening a pub, you should be more welcoming to your customers than reminding them of work. Only a poor barman reminds his patrons that they have work in the morning."

They laughed as Gerry poured Cillian a cup of tea.

"D'you have any milk there, big fella?" said Cillian.

"I do."

Gerry went into the fridge and poured some milk into the tea, giving Cillian a spoon to stir.

"You think Kerry will do it this year?" said Cillian, looking at the picture on the wall.

"Please God," said Gerry.

"I think they will too. Last year will sharpen ye up. The Dubs ambushed them. Speaking of that, I heard back in Nenagh there, that new American restaurant opens up in Dublin this week. Right in the middle of Grafton Street."

Everyone in Ireland knew Grafton Street, the shopping and trading centre of the country; however, Gerry had never been to Dublin, and he didn't imagine there were many sheep for sale on Grafton Street. But he was curious, and perhaps Jimmy would know about this American restaurant. Maybe he'd have eaten in it before.

"What's this now?" asked Gerry.

"McDonald's, they call it. A new type of food. Non-stop food or fast food, or something like that."

"What the hell does that mean?" said Gerry.

"Not too sure myself, but I hear one's talking about it now. They say it's the future."

"And what do they have in this fast food?" asked Gerry,

"Ah, it's burgers and chips, I believe. But here's the thing, they all start with Mc. You don't have a burger, you have a McBurger, and you don't have chips, you have McChips," said Cillian as he took a slurp of his tea.

Gerry laughed and shook his head. Catchy enough, he supposed. However, he wasn't sure a McCart-tea had the same ring to it.

They chatted some more before Cillian asked Gerry to fill up his flask with some more tea, despite Gerry's point that Tralee was less than an hour away.

"Thanks for that. It was a grand cup of tea. All the best to you now," said Cillian, who hopped into his post van, and headed off down Drumbarron Hill.

Gerry turned to have a look at the counter. There was plenty to be done.

The stool would need to be fixed, and he should build another one. Just in case there were ever two postmen in a van. But he had a spring in his step. It had been his first customer after all. Well, he hadn't asked for money, and neither should he have. But still, it was his first customer, and he left a happy one at that.

"Grand cup of tea," Gerry whispered to himself.

Maybe it was a tea shop. It was getting there.

———— • ✹ • ————

The weeks went fast as they often did in early summer, with the longer nights and football, and Gerry had been busy putting the finishing touches on the outside of the tea shop. By that, Gerry painted the front of the cottage a fresh white, and one day whilst walking back from checking the cattle, he realized that the black door had an air of death about it. And that was the last thing he wanted someone to think. So, he painted the door green, and then seeing as he was a proud Kerry man, and Kerry wore the green and gold, he painted the windowsills yellow, as yellow and gold weren't too far away from each other, and gold paint would cost him.

And standing back one evening, as the sun was making its way west for the night across the Atlantic Sea, he admired the work that he had done. The other half of the thatch would have to wait, of course; but at the same time, it didn't take too much away.

"Adds a bit of character to the place, Penny," said Gerry, looking into the field and over towards where the young white calf had filled out over the past twelve months.

All the tea shop needed now was a sign. And that could be made in no time at all.

Gerry took the bike down Drumbarron Hill and opened the kitchen door, where the familiar sight of Aunt Cara sat at the table. And Gerry had a fair idea what she was here for.

"How's it going, Gerry?"

"Not so bad, and yourself?"

"Not so bad. Are you hungry, Gerry? Brought up some ham sandwiches. I made too many earlier."

Gerry knew this was a lie, but he was grateful all the same. Would save him starting to cook at this late hour and by the time he'd have the potatoes ready, it'd be near nine o'clock.

"Thank you," said Gerry, who took a seat at the table.

"Now Gerry, I've something to ask you."

Gerry tried to hide his smile as he bit into a sandwich.

"Have you been feeling all right? I've been up here a few times in the last couple of weeks and had no sight of you. And then, Brendan had heard you'd sold some good cattle down in Tralee to the Murtagh's. And you know Gerry, we're just a bit worried about you?"

"I'm grand, Cara; nothing to worry about here."

"Now Gerry, you can talk to me, you know, if you ever need anything or have anything going on?"

Gerry nodded and chewed.

"Have you a woman, Gerry? Is that what it is?"

Gerry almost choked before he coughed.

"Or a man, Gerry? You know we'd love you regardless."

This made Gerry laugh some more. Cara was always one for a bit of gossip, and despite her concerns for Gerry, this was why she had really come.

"I've no woman, Cara, and men aren't my cup of tea, although there's nothing wrong with that sort of thing, I suppose. And to your other concerns:

yes, I'm grand. I've just been spending some time at the auld cottage up at the top field."

Gerry looked up as Cara sat back satisfied, but she still had a curious look in her eyes. He had given her a bone, a needed one to stop the questions, *and what comes of it, comes of it,* thought Gerry. Drumbarron was a big hill after all.

"I can still remember that cottage, Gerry. Wasn't too dissimilar to this place, but we didn't have the kitchen or the bathroom. Just the toilet, you know. And your grandmother used to wash us in the sink when we were little. Been a couple of decades since someone lived in that now. What are you doing up there?"

Gerry got up to make a cup of tea, his answer taking too long for Aunt Cara's mind.

"Is that where you took Ma's teapot to, is it?" said Cara.

Gerry smiled as he looked down at the cup of tea. His back was to Cara so she couldn't see. *She's a wily auld one, always was,* he thought.

"It is. You don't miss much," said Gerry.

"Was I supposed to, Gerry? That's the question."

Gerry laughed again. *A very wily one.*

"Anyways, you hear any more from Jimmy? He sent me a letter a while back and I replied, but sure it takes forever for the letters to go back and forth. And sure, Kerry's not Dublin. Probably stuck in An Post in some van up there, it is," said Cara.

Gerry thought of Cillian the postman, his first customer. He hadn't seen him since.

A couple of folks had stopped by as he'd been painting the cottage, others who had got lost on their way. A northern fella looking for Killarney. *He was a long way off,* thought Gerry.

Strange one too, that one. He was driving a white van, but Gerry could tell by the sound of the van that there wasn't much in the back. And the man had a look on him that said he didn't want to hang around too long. Gerry told him directions as best he could. Another fella, in a tractor from Slieve, a town just over the border in Limerick, fancied taking a drive over the hills to enjoy the views. Gerry filled up his flask with water; however, the man didn't want to intrude, and he sat in his seat whilst Gerry went inside. "One of the nicest views I've seen in my day," the man said, looking down Drumbarron Hill and out towards the Atlantic in the distance.

"Sent him one a while back but haven't heard. It's summer over there now, so I'd say he's busy with the football and the beers," said Gerry.

"And the women. Don't think I haven't heard the stories about town," said Aunt Cara. "As long as he keeps himself out of trouble. He was some scallywag when he was younger. Anyways Gerry, I'll be off now."

Later that evening, Gerry took out The Coffee House book, searching for any inspiration regarding the type of sign he could make. He flicked through the pages, surprising himself with his realization that the inside of his tea shop had a French-Italian aesthetic, mixed with a certain Irishness. He shook his head at the thought. It didn't sound like a thought he often had. Anyways, he found no inspiration for the sign, and it would be up to himself to figure it out.

The next day, after the new lambs and the new calves had been checked, Gerry found himself outside the front of the thatch cottage. Should he put a sign above the door? There wasn't much room. Then he looked down the hill towards Ballyduffy. And he looked back up the hill, a hundred yards or so to the peak, where it fell over itself towards Limerick.

Now, he knew what he had to do.

With two spare bits of timber, one long and narrow, and another shorter and a little thicker, he began to hammer nails together. He painted the wood white, and then, with the remaining green paint from the door, he wrote 'Tea Shop' on both sides, also drawing arrows. With that, he lifted his pole with the sign sticking off the edge and stuck it in the ground.

A grand job, he thought. *Now, it's a tea shop.*

Gerry went inside and stood behind the counter.

He had his teapots on the stove, and a small tin box with loose change on a shelf under the counter. There was milk in the fridge and plenty of tea. A bag of sugar was languishing in the cupboard, and even a pack of digestive biscuits. He was ready.

Gerry looked around the room. He had made all this come together. A year and a bit had gone by now, but he knew Ma and Pa would be proud. All he needed were customers. He put on the kettle, and he poured himself a cup of tea. And he waited. Then he poured himself another. Gerry didn't put up a clock, because in his mind, when you're having a cup of tea, you should have it in peace, not looking at the time and counting your minutes. However, he was sure a couple of hours had passed. Then, the door swung open.

"Well Gerry, how's it going?"

Gerry couldn't help but laugh when Aunt Cara walked through the door, a few strands of grey hair stuck to her forehead. It was a big hill after all.

"So, this is what you've been up to?" said Aunt Cara. "But, come with me for a minute."

Cara walked back out the front door and Gerry, his brows raised, headed after her. She walked towards the sign, then passed it, a little downhill in the direction of Ballyduffy.

Gerry followed behind.

"Now turn around, Gerry," said Cara.

Gerry turned and looked up the road towards the peak, not having a clue as to what he was supposed to be looking at. Then he caught it.

"I nearly ended up in the ditch, Gerry," said Cara, who walked straight back towards the tea shop without a stop. The arrow on his sign was pointing to the opposite side of the road and into an empty field, one with a ditch. He shook his head, then followed Cara inside, turning to check if the arrow on the other side of the sign was pointing in the right direction. It was.

He'd fix the wrong arrow later.

"Now, this is quite a sight Gerry," said Cara, who checked out all the chairs and tables and then turned to check the top bedroom. "So, this is where you've been staying?" she said when she saw the bed.

"Do you want a cup of tea?" said Gerry.

"That's the stuff, Gerry," said Cara, her eyes opened wide. "But how much is it going to cost me? That's what this is after all. Pa's dream?"

"Ma and Pa," said Gerry, who explained how he'd come to his discovery.

Cara listened, still looking around.

"You'll need a few buns or cakes I'd say, for this counter here, Gerry. Once customers start coming in of course," said Cara.

"I was thinking that all right." So, now his thought about the buns had been vindicated. Not such a daft idea after all, and he was glad to hear Cara mention it.

"I'll make you some and bring them the next time I come up, how does that sound?"

"That's great. Thank you, but you don't have to," said Gerry, grateful for whatever help he could get. *Now, if she could only help with a real customer,* he thought. But that would be up to him. He paused for a moment. His goal had been to bring this all together but what he had never thought about was what came next: actually running the shop. This was a place where time went slow, and that meant he was prepared for a few quiet months. But with the farm, he'd be busy. He would shift things around, spend most of his time up here and at the top field. And tend to the bottom field first thing in the morning and in the late afternoon or evenings.

As long as it didn't interfere with his football, he supposed.

"We'll have to get it blessed, Gerry. Maybe Father Michael could do it. Can't have a place like this unblessed or it will bring you bad superstitions," said Cara. "They'd be proud of you, Gerry. It really is quite the thing you've put together here. I didn't think I'd be walking into this when I reached the top of the hill. And Ma and Pa will be looking down on you."

Gerry swallowed something, then he shook his head and washed a cup and tended to the teapot. After some more suggestions from Aunt Cara, she left, and Gerry fixed the sign.

The first day of the tea shop had ended. He may have only had one customer, and not a paying one, but she did give him some good advice. Plus, Cara would be good to her word regarding the cakes. However, it was a start. And sometimes, that's all we need — to start.

CHAPTER

6

The first few weeks of the season had commenced and Ballyduffy had started with a couple of wins, including one against Stradbally, a team east of Tralee and who had been relegated from the higher division the year before. Gerry felt very fit, cycling more than halfway up that Drumbarron Hill each day, and his hands were like glue when it came to catching the ball in the middle of the field. *Must be the washing of those slippery teacups,* he thought.

One of the Connelly brothers had been to Dublin to visit an uncle, managing to bring himself to Grafton Street, where he saw the big M hanging out the front of the new American restaurant.

"Sure, it was in my mouth before I'd even ordered," said Tom Connelly, getting a round of laughs at training one night. *Fast food eh,* Gerry thought, *a different world to my tea shop.*

He still hadn't mentioned much about it, although word had begun to get around as it did in these parts. One afternoon, Pat Storey, an auld fella and a regular of O'Brien's pub, walked through the door of the tea shop much to Gerry's surprise. To begin with, Gerry's eyes just went wide as if a ghost had ambled in. It was hard to know quite what to do; many a time, he'd prepared for this eventful and momentous event in his mind. But this was real now. A customer.

Pat Storey took off his hat, the few strands of hair left on his head all sticking to the skin at the top, and he placed his walking stick beside one of the high stools. He's some trooper, Gerry thought. Pat was well known about the town, being a bachelor. He spent his days helping out with the other auld folk, popping in to have chats with those whose sons and daughters, just like Jimmy, had ventured off to places farther afield. When Pat wasn't in a pub, that is.

"Well Gerry, how's it going?" said Pat, in his slow and dry tone.

"Not so bad, Pat, and yourself?"

"Not so bad, but a man needs a drink. I'll have a pint of the black stuff, and — funny auld name for a pub you've got out there. Would you not have gone with McCarthy's?"

Pat's eyes darted up and down the counter looking for a tap, and his hand swept through the remaining strands of hair on his head.

"Pat, I don't have any Guinness," said Gerry, not sure whether to laugh or cry.

"You what? Well, that's a pity. Throw me whatever beer you have; sure Gerry, that'll do grand, man's parched. Mighty auld hill that," said Pat.

"Pat, I don't have any beer," said Gerry, leaning down on the counter with his forearms.

Pat glanced up, and with his eyebrows raised, said, "Not much of a pub without Guinness or beer, Gerry?"

Gerry couldn't keep the smile from his face. "It's not a pub, Pat. You see, it's a tea shop."

Pat rubbed his head again. He put his hat back on, then took it off as he looked at the tea pot at the counter. "So, you've tea, is it? That's an odd thing in a pub."

"Sure, there's plenty of pubs, Pat, but only one tea shop. Will you have a cup?"

"Go on then," said Pat. His bewildered look still hadn't gone away, but he licked his lips and needed a drink.

Gerry laid out a cup of tea for Pat and had a cup himself. The two chatted for what felt like hours. Pat told Gerry stories of the aulden days of Ballyduffy, the matches won and lost, and more interestingly, the late-night gossip, known only by the whispering drunks in these parts of the world. Those fellas who were in and out of the pubs all the time like Pat would pick up on some loose lips of a patron who only appeared late at night here and there, those patrons who couldn't hold themselves like the professionals of the high stools.

"You know, Gerry," he said. "I heard a story one night a while back in McMurphy's about Toe O'Brien. Rumour has it he bought that pub off one of the Connellys a few years back on the cheap. And I heard *how* he got it on the cheap. Auld man Connelly had a few too many in him one night in there whilst he was standing behind the counter working, and Toe O'Brien was in.

"And, sure, Toe's cousin was down from Dublin for the weekend. Now, she was a grand woman with gorgeous red hair. I was in the pub a few times when she was about back then. I'll tell you, not too many like that around these parts. Anyway, sure, didn't they have a lock-in that night, and auld man Connelly lost the run of himself, and Toe O'Brien caught him and his cousin in the back of the bar on a table. Now Connelly begged Toe not to say a word, and when you've got that over a man, you'll keep it that way until you want something.

"And that's the story of how Toe O'Brien got that pub."

Gerry sat and nodded along. *Jaysus,* he thought. *Imagine what else Pat knows. And what he must tell the lads at the bar after a few Guinness, never mind a cup of tea.*

Auld man Connelly had died a decade ago of a heart attack.

No wonder, thought Gerry, *with this hanging over him.* And the Connelly brothers were good friends of Gerry, and they'd hardly know any of this about their father; or maybe they did, and not much was said about it. Sometimes, in towns like Ballyduffy, that was the path chosen. The path of least commotion was to walk the road inside yourself, rather than bring everyone else along with you. But Gerry would know to look at Toe O'Brien with perhaps a little less reverence next time he was serving him a pint.

"Much do I owe you, Gerry?" said Pat.

"Ten pence, please Pat."

"No bother, Gerry, here you go. Not a bad cup of tea; all the best to you now," said Pat, who gathered his walking stick, put on his hat, and walked out the door.

Gerry placed the coin in his silver box. His first paying customer had been Pat Storey. He'd remember that.

———————•❋•———————

Spring turned into the height of summer and one day, Gerry was making his way up Drumbarron Hill, roughly halfway there, plugging away like he usually would, when out of nowhere, he heard a "Watch out!" Gerry jerked the bike into his right, looking over his shoulder to see some fella in light green Lycra gear, on a type of bike that Gerry had seen only a couple of times before, come racing by him on the way up the hill. Gerry had never seen anyone move like it; he had to stop and walk his bike the rest of the way.

Once Gerry turned the corner to the top field and the tea shop, there, sitting on one of the rocks outside the front, was the fella in green Lycra, and against the wall of the shop leaned his bike. Gerry glanced at the man as he pushed his way along.

He looked as light as a feather, but at the same time he had legs like tree trunks, although with the Lycra, Gerry knew it was rude to look at the man's legs too long. To be honest, the Lycra made him look as if he had frog's legs. Skinny body, big thighs.

"Sorry about that. If I'd stopped, I wouldn't have gotten going again," said the man.

A Dublin accent.

"Not a bother. Never seen a man take the hill like that. They say my Pa used to, but I can't get near it," said Gerry.

"It's like anything. It takes its time, just got to keep at it. This your tea shop?"

"It is. Would you like a cup?"

"I would indeed. Jesus, some view. Can see right out to the Atlantic from here," the man said.

"It's a nice one all right, and on a day like today, sure you couldn't beat it. I'll get you a cup here now."

Gerry went inside and poured a cup for the man who followed him.

"Nice spot you have here. Very European. I might take this outside if you don't mind?" said the man.

"Not at all; I'll leave you to it," said Gerry.

The man took his cup outside, and Gerry began to sweep the floors and go through his usual routine of making sure everything was in order. As he swept by the door, he glanced out the window at the man who seemed very content, sitting on the rock with the tea in his hand, enjoying the views of the valley. He had his helmet off, and Gerry could see that he had black hair that looked pretty similar to his own. After a while, the man came back in, and he placed his cup on the counter and paid Gerry, before saying, "If there'd been a cake, I would've bought one." Then he bid his farewell and headed off on that bike. To where, Gerry had no idea.

Gerry laughed at the strange thought that popped into his mind.

"Sure, Dublin's miles away, there's no chance of that," he said to no one.

He lifted the cups and put them in the sink, and then thought, *it might be time to hit Aunt Cara up for those cakes.*

That evening, Gerry returned down the hill to the house, and there, on the counter, was another letter. *Only one man this could be from.* After cooking some potatoes and a couple of pork sausages that had been in the fridge, Gerry sat down at the rocking chair by the fire.

He opened the letter.

June '77

Well, Gerry,

How's it going? Not so bad over here. The summer birds are back, thank Christ. That winter will be hard to get used to, Gerry. Some days, it was minus thirty, snow so deep that when it melted, I needed a pair of goggles and flippers to swim my way out. But like it always does, winter melts away and spring starts, and over here, the summer turns on as if someone flicks the switch, and you're in shorts and t-shirts now for the next few months, and farmers' tans and everything else.

I moved out of the Ryans' house and I'm renting a place in Southie (that's South Boston) with another couple of fellas that play football for St Mikes. A Mayo lad and a Dub. He's not too bad. We'll see later in the year if they do back-to-back titles, which to be honest, I'm afraid of, Gerry. It's a good Dublin team. Anyways, it was sad to say goodbye to the Ryans now, lovely folk. Don't believe too much of what you may hear if you're chatting to Johnny. You know how stories go.

I'm still working the bricks, keeps me busy and gets the money in the pocket. But I might be getting off these soon. Have a fella — American guy, but his grandfather was from Donegal — that might be setting me up with something different soon. Insurance. Shirt and tie and all.

But it depends on getting the right papers. Have another fella helping me get set up with different papers so I can stay a bit longer out here, a green card, that's the colour you want a card to be if you're Irish, Gerry, and I'm hopeful I'll get it sooner or later.

You're right, McDonald's is big over here. I've even had it a few times. The burgers are all right now. They've one called a Big Mc, and after a couple of pints one night, I asked the girl behind the counter was it named after big Gerry McCarthy from Ballyduffy? She was close to calling security, but I talked her down and told her to have a nice day. Burger King is another of these fast-food places, I'm sure they'll end up on Grafton Street next.

How's all back there? How did lambing season go? Hopefully, you were all right to handle it on your own. Aunt Cara wrote me and said there was a right few at the anniversary Mass, and you had a right few pints in O'Brien's after. When I heard that, I missed it now.

Anyways, how's the football going? Hopefully, it will be a better year for Ballyduffy than last year. Joe Connelly wrote me, says you bate the head of Johnny Murtagh from Carrickbay in a game last year? I taught you well, it seems.

All the best and chat soon,

Jimmy.

James McCarthy
12 Wentworth St
Boston, MA 12860
USA

Gerry smiled and put the letter down. Later that night, he would place the letter in the silver box in his top drawer, beside the others. However, sleep was hard to come by, as usual. At times, he would look across at where Jimmy's bed used to be. The house was silent, and he even longed for the snores of his brother. But so life goes. And worst of all, Jimmy said he fancied the Dubs this year, and that was very bad news. He also knew Jimmy would find out about the tea shop soon enough, so maybe it was something for his letter back.

CHAPTER

7

The summer passed and it was a poor one for the Kerry team, with an early exit and no final appearance, and the Dubs strolled to victory, proving Jimmy right again. And Ballyduffy, although not having a terrible year, didn't have a great year either. But one September day, after beating Carrickbay in the final game of the season to prevent them from winning the league, Gerry could barely lift his elbows to put his pint to his mouth as the patrons came squeezing into O'Brien's pub. And the night was filled with celebrations of the little victories, more pints in McMurphy's, and Seanie O'Shea brought out the fiddle and a few others sang the songs. By leaving time, Gerry was a little more unsure of his steps than when he'd first entered.

Standing at the corner of the bar, half-buried in a pint and with another glass of whiskey beside it — never good at those hours of the early morning — John McHugh, one of Gerry's best pals in the town, began to speak, "So, what is it you're doing up Drumbarron Hill? I thought you were refurbishing it to sell it, but I've been hearing rumours about the place."

Gerry slurped his pint. John wasn't the first person to ask him this today.

"What have you been hearing?" asked Gerry.

"Strange things, now. Wasn't sure when I first heard it. Pat Storey was mentioning it one night in O'Brien's, said you've a pub up there for pioneers. But then I figured out what he meant. He was a few pints over the limit like he usually is," said John.

"Well, Gerry," a voice said.

Gerry looked over his shoulder to find Dymphna O'Connor, bright-eyed, playing with her hair.

A flash of Jimmy popped into his mind before Gerry glanced at the television that sat behind the bar. Dymphna was pretty, a couple of years older than Gerry, although her younger sister Kathleen was the real looker of the town. And he knew why Dymphna was here, and it was for nothing of the sorts that you're thinking about.

"Well Dymphna, how's it going?" said Gerry.

"Not so bad. Tell me this, I've heard you've opened a tea shop, and I had to come over and find out if it's true. Can't believe a word that auld Pat Storey says when he's a few pints deep."

Gerry took another sip. Of course, this was what she wanted to know. He supposed she was right about Pat Storey though.

"It is, Dymphna," said Gerry.

Dymphna and John looked at each other. Gerry knew what they'd be thinking too. *Gerry McCarthy has a tea shop?* He also knew he'd have a couple more customers that week.

"Well, that's something, Gerry," said Dymphna, before wishing him good luck and returning to her seat in another part of the bar.

"The news is out now," said John, flicking his head in Dymphna's direction, and Gerry could see her already in deep discussions with Mary Feeney and Mary O'Shea.

Then Gerry caught an angry looking Johnny Ryan stumbling over after one too many pints. For some reason, a flash of Jimmy's letter appeared.

Johnny was another forward on the team, the same age as Jimmy and a quieter sort, keeping to himself. However, Gerry had noticed the odd look he had given him in training that week, and the hefty shoulder tackle that wouldn't have normally been thrown around by a man of Johnny's size against a big lad like Gerry.

But with the tea shop and the farm, sure Gerry hadn't much time to think about that.

"Your bastard of a brother, Gerry McCarthy," said Johnny, as he stood with one hand on John McHugh's shoulder, and the other on the bar to keep himself from falling backwards.

"What's he gone and done now, Johnny?" said Gerry.

The image of a pair of blonde twins crept into his mind for some reason.

"You heard he moved out of Uncle Fergal's in Boston, I suppose," said Johnny.

"I did. He wrote me, said he was sorry to go." And Jimmy *had* written that.

"I'm sure he was, the bastard," said Johnny. "And did he tell you why he moved out?"

Gerry took a sip and looked at John who had a twinkle in his eyes. John knew Jimmy well enough to have known there must be something on the way.

"I didn't, Johnny. He never mentioned that. Just that Fergal and his wife — what was her name again, Rebecca was it — had taken good care of him," said Gerry.

"Ha, he said that, did he? Sure, of course he did. Well Fergal sent us a letter last week. He'd thrown Jimmy out. Sure, didn't he come home from work one day and find Jimmy and Rebecca in the kitchen. The wee snaking bastard," said Johnny.

Jaysus, thought Gerry. He took the rest of the whiskey. "The feckin' gobshite," he whispered under his breath. Then Gerry heard the sniggers of John McHugh beside him. He lifted his head and John couldn't hold the laughter in, full-bellied laughs surrounding Gerry. And then Johnny Ryan, who by now had two hands on the bar to keep himself steady, turned and looked at John, and saw the tears of laughter falling down his face. Gerry began to snigger too. Then he saw the frown turn around on Johnny Ryan's face, and Johnny burst into laughter himself.

"He was some gobshite," said Johnny after the laughter stopped.

"Always was," said John McHugh. "But he was good craic all the same."

And after one more pint and a chorus of 'Black Velvet Band', Gerry took his leave and walked, a little unsteadily, back out to the road, and past that bastard of a sheepdog that ran out and barked as the lights turned on in O'Neills' farmhouse whenever he walked by.

And he thought of that night when he and Jimmy had fought and fallen in the field, not too far from here. He thought of Pa and the quiet house to which he was walking home.

"I miss him. I miss them," he whispered.

Gerry looked up and saw the big hill under the moonlight that lit the fields around him. A sheep bleated, woken from its sleep in the bottom field, and Gerry dropped his head.

At least he had the tea shop.

———•✻•———

Sure enough, that week, Dymphna O'Connor and her sister would make an appearance at the tea shop, and John McHugh and a couple of the others in the team would also drive up in his van and helped themselves to one of Aunt Cara's queen cakes. And Gerry had gotten used to the strange looks, and the questions about why he hadn't any taps, and why he hadn't any Guinness.

"Plenty of pubs, only one tea shop," he would often say. And people would sit for a while, happy for a drink of tea after walking all the way up the big hill.

And other people were starting to come about. Not so many that Gerry ever had more than two customers at a time, but enough. Cyclists were a big draw. The kind with the Lycra leggings and thick frogs' leg thighs. Gerry had found out the fella in the green Lycra, the Dub, was named Stephen, and he had brought a few others with him a couple of times, although Stephen would always arrive first. And if the weather was good, the cyclists would sit out the front on the rocks, their boney arses not minding the lack of cushion, thought Gerry.

They'd look down over the valley, and out towards the Atlantic Ocean. Aunt Cara's cakes were a big hit, and Gerry had even started paying her to bake twice a week, although she wouldn't allow him to pay her much. However, Gerry still hadn't gotten the place blessed. But for a twenty-tree-year-old heading into autumn, it wasn't a bad place to be.

Winter passed with a letter here and there from Jimmy, although Gerry still hadn't told him about the tea shop, just that he'd put in some work to the auld cottage and cleaned it up a bit, and other tidbits about football and cattle and all the things Jimmy would expect him to write.

Podge Feeney, another player for Ballyduffy, had left for San Francisco.

Jimmy mentioned that Podge had written to him, and that Podge had ended up apparently working on that nice bridge, cleaning it or painting it or whatever. Jimmy also wrote in his letter that he'd heard Podge had talked down some man who'd been about to jump off that bridge one day, and the man had ended up asking Podge whether he wanted to learn something called a computer. "The future," Jimmy had said in his letter to Gerry.

And years later, Gerry would hear that Podge had something to do with a social company, whatever that meant, and Gerry thought this was very odd. Because even though Gerry himself was a man of few words, Podge had to be the most antisocial person he'd ever met.

And Jimmy now had the shirt and tie on, working in insurance for cars and whatnot, and seemed to be enjoying it. The Americans appeared to like his charm, and he was doing all right for himself, whether that was money or whatnot, Gerry wasn't sure.

But the tea shop was doing more than all right for himself too, he supposed.

Another year passed, Ballyduffy not doing too bad but getting a little better, Gerry thought; that great Kerry team had finally fulfilled their promise and won the All-Ireland, and all of a sudden, it was new year again. And on New Year's Eve, after a glorious sunny day, as he sat in O'Brien's with some pints and the lads, for some reason, Gerry felt 1979 was going to be a big year. But he didn't know why, though one thing that came to mind was the announcement that the new Pope would be making a trip from the palace in Rome all the way to Dublin.

"The first time in five hundred years," Pat Storey would say in O'Brien's one night.

And even Father Michael seemed to have shaky hands when he was putting the chalice of wine towards the sky on Easter Sunday. That year in Ireland, the place was as alive as Gerry had ever known it. And the tea shop, too, was getting more of the cyclists than he'd ever known.

They had made it a weekly thing where on a Saturday afternoon, if the sun was shining, Gerry would lift out the picnic table and set it down outside, sure that Aunt Cara would have the cakes ready. Like any man behind a counter, he'd often overhear their conversations, and it turned out a few of them would be cycling in Europe, even touring around France at some point.

No wonder Stephen said the place looked very European the first time he was here.

Then one day in early summer, an English fella in a white Datsun came over the hill as Gerry was cleaning some of the weeds growing in the grass out the front of the cottage.

Likely someone who missed the turn a few miles back, Gerry thought as the man pulled up.

"Wow, now this is what I was looking for; the thatch, the colour of the door, the sign," said the man as he stepped out of the car, looking at the cottage and down the valley.

Gerry stood and leant on the shovel as he eyed the curious man who had a blue shirt on, and had wavy brown hair. Then the man looked at Gerry and started walking around the cottage and towards the sign, again staring down the valley. He looked up towards the sky and Gerry heard him whisper, "Perfect," in his English accent. Gerry too looked up at the sky to see what the man was looking for, but there wasn't a cloud to be seen anywhere.

"Hi there, what's your name?" said the man.

"In these parts, we ask how someone is, before we go handing our names out," said Gerry as he looked back at the white Datsun.

The man tilted his head, then said, "Sorry; ok then, how are you doing today, sir?"

"Not so bad, how's it going?" said Gerry, unmoved from his spot, the shovel by his side.

"Oh, I'm great, thank you. What a spot you have up here. It's one of the most wonderful images I've ever seen — a postcard, if I do say so," said the man. "I'm Peter Barrett, and I work with Postal Publishing in London."

"Well, I'm Gerry McCarthy, and I work on the farm and in this tea shop," said Gerry.

"Oh, ok. I tell you what, Mr. McCarthy —"

"You can call me Gerry."

"Oh, right — well, Gerry — what we do at Postal Publishing is make postcards that people like to send when they visit certain places. Hold on, let me show you an example."

The man turned back to the Datsun and returned with a white folder, and he flicked through pages of rectangular cards with all sorts of images. One had a big spire, and had 'Paris, France' written underneath the image. Another had a strange wall with all sorts of graffiti, and the words 'Berlin, Germany.'" There were others, too, of windmills and green fields; however, Gerry looked around, and none were as green as the fields around here.

"You see Gerry, I've been looking for the perfect postcard of this part of the world, and I think I've found it," Peter said.

Gerry turned around and looked at the field behind him where his black and white cows were having lunch — and down the valley, where Ballyduffy was its sleepy self — and out towards the ocean, which was as blue as the sky today. He always knew it was a fine view.

"I see now," said Gerry.

"Would you mind if I took a few pictures of the place?" Peter said as he walked back to the car and brought out a strange black box with a ribbon on it, like those medals Gerry had won when playing football when he was younger. The man put the box over his head, held it up to his eyes, and he pressed a button. Flashes of lights went off, and Gerry realized it was a camera.

"Stand right there please, Gerry; that's it, with the shovel. Don't move a muscle," said Peter as he walked around and bent down and leant back, all with the camera to his eyes.

After clenching his chiseled jaw tight for a while, Gerry finally said, "And, I suppose if you're making postcards of my tea shop, I should probably get a few of those?"

Peter laughed before putting his camera away. He walked back into the Datsun and brought out some pages. "Of course, Postal Publishing is the largest maker of postcards in England, and soon to be in Europe. Our typical rate is fifty pounds for the image."

"You must be mad. I'm not paying you fifty pounds for a postcard of my own tea shop!"

Peter laughed again before shaking his head. "No, we pay you fifty pounds. And in addition, you'll get a pack of the postcards once we have them made."

Jaysus, Gerry thought, *fifty pounds.*

With that, he'd be close to putting the rest of the thatch on the roof.

"All right, what do you need from me?" asked Gerry.

And so, Gerry signed the paperwork and the man passed him fifty pounds, all in notes. And Peter stuck around and took a few more pictures before heading off as happy looking as any man who had ever left the tea shop. And for a while, Gerry forgot all about that day.

———— • ✳ • ————

As summer ended, Gerry had managed to sell another cow, an off-market sale mid-year to one of the Connelly brothers and although he didn't get as good a price as he could have if he had waited for the spring sales, it gave him enough to finish the thatch roof. And now, the tea shop looked as perfect a spot as there had ever been.

Then September rocked around and one day, the only man in the tea shop along with Gerry was Pat Storey, with his walking stick against the counter, and the strands of hair swept back on his head. Pat would come visit once a week, often on a Tuesday, when the hangover of the weekend — if the man even got hangovers anymore — had left his body. "Good for the ticker," Pat said in reference to the walk up the hill; and sure, he wasn't wrong.

Gerry and Pat spent the afternoon with tea and cakes, and Gerry was in a good mood, so he took out the digestives, placing a couple on a plate.

"I don't mind this auld pub, Gerry. Nice change from the others, you know," said Pat.

He's changed his tune, thought Gerry, unable to stop a smile spreading.

"The town's empty, you say, Pat," said Gerry, loudly so Pat could understand him as Pat's hearing had begun to fade this past year.

"All away to Dublin. His Holiness is in the park doing Mass up there. They say there's five million at it, Gerry, would you believe," said Pat, taking a sip of tea. Despite the fact that Gerry didn't know much about anything other than Kerry, he knew enough to know there were only tree million people in all of Ireland. But he nodded along anyway.

"Must be a sight," said Gerry.

"But sure, with that many, Gerry, we're as close to him here as they must be up in that park in Dublin," said Pat. He never batted an eyelid, swigging another sip of tea.

Still, Gerry thought, *it would be something to see him, wouldn't it?*

"All the way from Rome, eh?" said Gerry as he left the counter and walked down the shop and into the bathroom. He urinated, then washed his hands and gave the bathroom a quick clean before coming back out to see Pat, still seated on the stool at the counter.

"Jaysus, Gerry," said Pat, looking out the windows behind him, flapping his hands around for Gerry to come over.

As invited, Gerry scampered behind the counter to see what the fuss was about, then the strangest sight he'd ever seen could be made out through the windows.

There were fancy black cars with blacked-out windows lining up all down the road.

At that very moment, the door opened and in walked a priest in black with a white collar, followed by two more dressed just the same. But these weren't priests at all. These fellas had to bend their heads for their long red hats to get through the door, while their plush gowns were the finest red, reaching right to the floor. Pat started to cough, and Gerry realized one of the priests was holding a set of rosary beads, and another was moving some ornament back and forth. That smell of a church — incense, it was — began to fill the room.

Maybe they're blessing the place.

And then another one in a red gown and those large hats strode in.

What are these lads called again? Gerry thought. *Cardinals, that's the word.*

He had seen bishops once or twice before with Father Michael in Ballyduffy church, but these men walked a bit slower, and quite a lot straighter.

"Good day," the third cardinal said. He had very tan skin and dark eyebrows, and an accent that was very European.

Gerry looked down at Pat, who turned around, raised his eyebrows and shrugged.

"How's it going?" said Gerry.

"Very well, thank you. And how are you today, child of God?" said the cardinal.

"Not so bad! And what can I do for you?" said Gerry, blinking as if to rid his eyes of an apparition.

"We are looking for Shannon Airport. We may have come too far," said the cardinal.

Jaysus, they certainly did, thought Gerry.

Shannon was outside Limerick, and a good bit back along the road. *How did all these people manage to get lost and always end up here?* Not that he was complaining; it brought business to the door, people who'd often manage to fit in a cup of tea or two before getting on their way.

"Ye certainly did. You'll have to turn back and head to Limerick, and there'll be signs there," said Gerry.

"Ah. Well, that clears it up. And what time will that take, would you guess?"

Pat, who had finally lowered his eyebrows, said, "Well, that'll take ye a good hour, I'd say."

"Ah. Thank you. God bless you both. Father Guerrin, please wait here a second," said the cardinal to the priest in the black robes before he walked out the door.

Gerry looked down at Pat, who by now had a twinkle in his eyes at the irregularity of the situation. And Gerry, too, knew this was odd but regardless, he had a tea shop to run.

"Would any of ye want a cup of tea?" said Gerry.

The two cardinals looked at each other, and then at Father Guerrin and towards the teapots sitting on the stove.

"Thank you for your kind gesture," said Father Guerrin with another European accent. "But I don't believe we will have the time."

Just then, the first cardinal came back in the door, followed by two other priests in black. *Jaysus,* Gerry thought, *three priests and three cardinals in my tea shop. Sure, it must be blessed by now.* Then the cardinal spoke, casting his gaze around as if seeking something.

"Child of God, this is your tea shop?"

"It is," said Gerry.

"Our Holy Father would like to know if he could use the bathroom. I'm afraid an hour is too long of a journey for him," said the cardinal.

Jaysus!

Gerry looked down at Pat Storey whose jaw had hit the floor. But it made sense. A journey from Dublin was a long trip for any man, never mind a man of the Pope's age.

"Certainly, he can," said Gerry, and the cardinal ushered one of the priests to go outside.

Then, Gerry couldn't believe his eyes when, with robes as white as a dove, a tea cozy hat on his head, and a set of rosary beads around his neck, the Pope walked in the door. And he didn't walk; he glided into the room, thought Gerry. *Jaysus, if only Ma and Pa could see me now.*

And the Pope smiled at Gerry, and at Pat Storey, and said, "Hello. Bathroom?" with a heavy European accent that didn't sound like it knew too much English.

Gerry, a man of few words, suddenly found himself with none at all, and he pointed to the bathroom. The Pope nodded, gliding slowly across the uneven stoned floor as Gerry's and Pat's eyes couldn't look away. Gerry's heart thundered inside his chest as he heard the latch of the bathroom door close shut, and suddenly, he shook himself. The Pope was in his shop, but sure like anyone else, he'd need his privacy. So, Gerry looked down at Pat Storey, whose eyebrows had raised again, before turning back to the cardinals.

"Are you sure ye won't have a cup?" said Gerry.

The priests and the cardinals all turned to the one cardinal who had retrieved the Pope and was obviously of more senior rank. The cardinal nodded to one of the priests, before turning to Gerry. "His Holiness would like some tea."

The next moment, the priest placed a small red and white flask on the table, and Gerry looked back over to Pat Storey who was staring at the flask, his jaw on the floor again.

"Not a bother," said Gerry, his hand shaking as he lifted the empty flask.

"Please, no milk for His Holiness," said the cardinal, and Gerry turned back to the stove. He looked down and rotated the flask in his hand. On one side it said, 'Polska', and the other had a cross. Gerry blinked. Time stood still. As he lifted Ma's auld teapot and poured the tea into the Pope's flask, he never would've imagined in a million years what was happening.

Jaysus — and Pa and Jimmy, imagine they were here!

As Gerry put the lid back on the flask, the latch of the bathroom door opened, and the bright white radiance of the Pope walked out, heading back towards the counter. The Pope stopped at the pictures on the wall. Then His Holiness walked a little closer for a better look.

Gerry stood silently, his heart still beating hard as the Pope pointed at the picture and turned to Gerry. "Football," he said.

Gerry's jaw hit the floor. *Jaysus,* Gerry thought, *he knows the Kerry team!*

Gerry nodded, then the Pope smiled and walked towards the counter. Gerry reached out and presented the flask which wouldn't stop shaking. The Pope looked down before staring a little longer at Gerry's large hands. "Goalkeeper?" he asked.

Jaysus, he thinks I'm a goalkeeper, Gerry thought.

Gerry shook his head and tried to speak, but only two words would come out, and barely more than a whisper. "Midfielder. Bally — Ballyduffy."

And the Pope blinked, and then he smiled at Gerry and said, "God bless you." Then he took his flask, turned, and glided out the door, followed by the priests and the cardinals.

Gerry moved behind the counter, and he and Pat Storey stood in silence, watching through the windows at the enormous black cars trying to make three-point turns in the narrow road. And just like that, they were gone again, the tea shop silent once more.

Pat Storey turned and shook his head, rubbing his hand back and forth over the few strands of hair he had left on the top of his head. Pat began to open his mouth to say something, but then stopped, and took a sip of his tea.

Then he looked up at Gerry and said, "Do you think he knows the Kerry team?"

Gerry leant on the counter. "I don't know, Pat. I was thinking the same myself."

Pat placed his cup back down on the plate. "Jaysus, I need to use the bathroom after that."

He got off the high stool and grabbed his walking stick, slowly walking across the floor towards the bathroom with much less grace than His Holiness had, Gerry continuing to stare out the windows and trying to wrap his head around what had just happened.

Gerry's heart felt full, and a wry smile came over his face.

Then he started to giggle at the sheer madness of it all. He had plenty of material now for his letters to Jimmy. Just then, he heard Pat's voice,

"Jaysus Christ. Would you come and look at this."

Gerry looked towards the bathroom, where the door was open; Pat was standing there, flapping his hands again for Gerry to come over.

"Would you look in there?" pointed Pat.

Gerry sniffed the air before he slowly edged forward and looked down the bowl. A singular brown log of shite floated in the water.

Gerry ran his fingers through his hair before putting a hand to his nose. Then he heard Pat say, "What are you going to do with it?"

"Jaysus Pat, what do you mean what am I going to do with it?" said Gerry, and he reached forward towards the handle to flush the toilet.

"Wooooow, hold your horses there, Gerry," said Pat, more urgently than Gerry had ever heard before.

"It's a shite, Pat. It needs to go." Gerry stepped back and looked again in the bowl.

"It's not just any shite, Gerry. It's the Pope's shite."

And Gerry stood back and folded his arms. Pat had a point. Sure, people were always selling holy water and rosary beads and whatever else had been blessed by priests and bishops all over the country.

"But it's a shite Pat," said Gerry.

"I know but hold on a minute. Let's think about it before we go rushing it down the toilet." Pat turned, walking back towards the counter. "I'll have another cup of tea Gerry, good man," said Pat as he took his seat again.

"And what am I to do with this, Pat?"

"Hold your horses, come have a cup of tea and we'll put our heads together. Two sharp minds like ours will figure something out," said Pat.

Gerry returned behind the counter and poured them both two cups of fresh tea, and they sat in silence and thought. Just then, the door swung open, and in a hurry and a fluster, Aunt Cara burst in the door and threw a bag of cakes on the counter.

"How's it going?" said Gerry.

"Not so bad, Gerry," said Cara who ran through the room. "I'm going to feckin' wet myself." And before Gerry or Pat could rise from their seats, she had slammed the bathroom door and they heard the flush of the toilet.

Gerry looked at Pat, who stared at the bathroom with his jaw back on the floor. His future fortune had been flushed away. Then Pat turned and shrugged, sitting back down.

"I guess, that's the way it was meant to be. The Lord decided for us."

For a few seconds, they sat in silence and sipped their tea before they heard another flush. The latch opened and Aunt Cara walked back out.

"Which one of ye dirty animals left a shite in the toilet?"

CHAPTER

8

1979 passed, and Gerry wasn't sure if it was the Pope's blessing or the packet of ten postcards that arrived in his house one day with the image of the tea shop — a mighty photo, in fairness to it — but the tea shop was busier than ever.

In the summer months, the picnic table was constantly outside, and the cyclists with their flat bony arses and their frogs' legs would be there every week, but the Stephen fella wouldn't be about. Gerry had gathered from the others that he was doing bigger hills in Switzerland and France and wherever else. Nowadays, word about the tea shop was getting around and even a few of the football team would call up during the week for a cup of tea and a chat with Gerry or whoever else was there. The rumour had also gone around that the Pope had blessed the tea shop.

Of course, no one would believe Pat Storey when he was in the pub, and Gerry knew that what had happened in the tea shop, stayed in the tea shop.

Gerry wasn't a man for getting in other people's business, or for letting others in his. He never told anyone how the Pope had also blessed his tea shop's bathroom with something else.

And Gerry also noticed that he was getting newer customers who would drive by in the summer from such exotic locations as Mullingar and even as far away as Dundalk.

A couple of English people had passed by too and seemed to be very happy with the tea and the view. He often found himself thinking of Jimmy, and over the years, he was lucky to get a letter — maybe two a year — as he imagined life got busy over that side of the water, what with their fast food and their non-stop, as Jimmy had often said.

Then one evening down the house, he walked in from checking the sheep in the lower field and found a bag of cakes left on the counter. Alongside was another letter. He made himself some bacon and cabbage — not his favorite, but the cabbage was going off and he had to get rid of it, so he ate it — and then in front of the fire that evening, he took out the letter.

Oct '80

Well, Gerry,

How's it going? Not so bad out here at all. The autumn leaves are falling on my time here in Boston, and what a time it has been, Gerry. It's a sad time to be leaving; the city is alive, and the Boston Celtics and that new player I told you about in my last letter, Larry Bird, are cleaning up. They're like the Kerry team of the basketball world.

And Jaysus, Gerry, is he some lump of a man, but he moves across the court with grace, and yet he's a mean bastard when he wants to be too. We could've used him in Ballyduffy. He'd make a good partner for you in midfield should he ever wish to change his line of work. The insurance job went well, and then I ended up falling in with another fella that works for a bank, suit and ties and all that nonsense as you know yourself, but sure it's got to be done. And he only went and got me a job in New York, down on Wall Street, Gerry, although I hear there's not too many walls about the place. Needless to say, it will be something else, and I'm looking forward to seeing New York. Funnily enough, Thomas Murtagh from Carrickbay has a nephew in New York, and through one of the lads with St Mikes, I'll be staying with him for a while until I get on my feet.

Nice to have a Kerry man all the same. And by Jaysus, they're a special team this Kerry team, aren't they, Gerry! They could go on to do five-in-a-row I bet, unless something special trips them up in the last minute of a final.

Every now and then, I think of what might have been, but with this knee injury, it wasn't my destiny.

How's all back there, Gerry? How is the farm and did you ever get the cottage sold? Knowing you, I'd say you made some job of it. How's Aunt Cara and Brendan? It's mad how time passes, Gerry. Nearly five years now, and I'm still waiting on that green card, so unfortunately, I haven't been able to leave America for a trip home. But I plan to once I get it. I'll send you a letter with my new address once I'm all set up.

All the best and have a nice day, Gerry,

Jimmy.

Jaysus, who's this Larry Bird fella then? Gerry thought. *The Kerry team of the basketball world! They must be some outfit. Wall Street? Funny auld name but sure, another part of the world for Jimmy to see.* And they'd plenty of football teams in New York, even had a big field there, Gerry thought, although McHugh Park was grand all the same. Gerry placed the letter in his box in the top drawer before bed. In his next letter, he'd tell Jimmy all about the teashop.

———————•✳•———————

And so, the following summer, Gerry felt a little restless for the first time in his life. Perhaps it was the fact he wasn't playing too well for Ballyduffy, or the inevitability sinking in of Jimmy's future in America, but Gerry found himself alternating nights between the tea shop and his bed down the house. Maybe, in the back of his mind, Gerry had held a thought of Jimmy's return to the house, and to the forward line of Ballyduffy, but it was becoming as far-fetched as it ever was. Truth be told, Gerry was reaching that time in a man's life where no matter if he slept in the tea shop or in his own house, the beds were still lonely. And yet despite the attention of some of the ladies in the town, including Dymphna and Kathleen O'Connor – who by now had also come to realize that Jimmy's future lay in America – he felt unsettled.

But the tea shop kept his feet on the ground, and more and more visitors would come each year. Funnily enough, following a concert in Dingle, the

Dubliners, the famous Irish folk band, had stopped by one evening on the way to Limerick, spending the evening singing songs, drinking tea and eating cake. Gerry turned a blind eye to the bottles of whiskey that they had brought in with them. "To make the tea stronger," the one with the raspy voice had said. And they played songs for their entourage and for Gerry, and for the only other customer in the tea shop that day: Pat Storey. And just like before, nobody believed Pat when he told them that the fiddle and the bow that now hung on the wall beside the picture of the Kerry team had been left there by the Dubliners.

Then in 1983, four years after the Pope had taken a shite in the bathroom, Gerry's life would be forever changed. But before we get there, you need some back story on the Rose of Tralee.

So, that town out on the coast road, where Gerry first sold the cattle to Thomas Murtagh, and to which numerous people got lost on their way, was also home to the largest beauty pageant in Ireland, would you believe? A tradition as old as time itself in Ireland — older if one believed Pat Storey — was the Rose of Tralee festival based on an old ballad about a woman called Mary who, because of her beauty, earned the name 'The Rose.' Over the years, the festival had grown.

In the beginning, it was only the local Kerry women who competed, then it expanded to every county in Ireland, and then yet farther, with 'Roses' from as far afield as Australia and New Zealand. And of course, with all the Irish people who had emigrated over the years, America would often have five or six entrants, each representing their city.

A San Francisco Rose, a Boston Rose, for example. And it wasn't just a beauty contest. No, the Roses would sing or read poetry or dance, all celebrating Irish culture.

And so it was that last year, just before the festival, a red Datsun had come over the hill from Limerick and stopped right outside the tea shop. A man came into the shop dressed in a tuxedo, men also participating in the festival in the form of 'Rose Escorts', assisting the Roses, ensuring they were safe, and seeing that they got to and from the festival in one piece.

There was even a prize for the hardest working Rose Escort who'd be invited back each year.

On this occasion at the tea shop, the man was followed in the door by a lady with blonde hair and a red dress, and although it didn't touch the ground like the red robes of the cardinals, she still was one of the most striking images Gerry believed he had ever seen.

And the girl too, looked very stricken with big Gerry McCarthy who stood behind the counter. Gerry had never seen anything like her, and her accent from up the country — Monaghan direction, he guessed — sounded sweet to his ears. But unluckily for him, the Rose Escort explained that they were late for the festival and asked for directions to Tralee.

And despite the woman's eyes, which told a story that she wouldn't have minded staying, the red Datsun left, and Gerry sat back down on his stool.

Summer passed and once again, Ballyduffy struggled. Johnny Murtagh was flying fit for Carrickbay, and Gerry had a tougher time than usual running after him. They ended the game with a black eye each, but Carrickbay had hammered Ballyduffy.

But there were green shoots, Gerry thought; Ballyduffy's minor team had a bunch of seventeen and eighteen-year-olds who won the county championship for the first time in near twenty years. They even had a few players who had made the Kerry minors as well, so the future was looking good, and next year promised to be even better.

After a few cyclists had left one Saturday evening, Gerry found himself alone in the tea shop with Pat Storey of all people. "I'll have another cup of tea before I head to another pub, Gerry, probably O'Brien's," said Pat, sitting on the stool.

For a man over seventy, he looked fitter than ever, Gerry thought.

"Not a bother, Pat," said Gerry, as he poured Pat a cup of tea. "Drink as much tea as you like."

"I was in the bookmakers earlier, Gerry, and I threw a pound on the Boston Rose. She's the favorite this year," said Pat.

"That's right; it's the Rose of Tralee weekend. I forgot," said Gerry.

"You wouldn't get a radio in here, Gerry," said Pat, looking along the counter.

"I thought about it, Pat, but haven't pulled the plug yet," said Gerry.

"You're probably better off without it, sure. Nothing but stories of murders and kidnappings to take your mind off the peace and quiet up here," said Pat.

He was probably right, Gerry thought. The rain bounced off the roof above. The heavens had just opened, and Gerry looked out the window as the rain poured down. Although it was late evening, the sun was still up, but was now hidden behind a dark cloud. Then Gerry saw a light reflecting off the signpost for the tea shop. A car must have been coming up the hill, and in no time at all, two red Datsuns had pulled in at the side of the road.

The door opened and a fella in a tuxedo ran in, his hair soaking wet, and he wiped the raindrops off his shoulders. He was followed by others including another woman in a red dress with blonde hair, but she wasn't the one Gerry had seen the previous year. These were Rose of Tralee contestants. Another two escorts ran in the door laughing in their tuxedos, and then came the Roses: another in a red dress, another in a maroon-coloured dress, both wielding their bags above their heads to stave off the rain. Gerry saw that familiar rise on Pat's eyebrows.

Gerry glanced up again as another fella came in, one who held the door open for the final rose to come through. She walked in the door in a beige dress, a white sash hanging over her shoulder that said, 'Rose of Tralee.'" Gerry stopped drying the glass with his tea towel, and stared, the Rose looking up at the tea shop, also towards him.

She had dark hair and the bluest of eyes, as blue as that point where the Atlantic Ocean touched the sky on those days where a cloud wasn't to be seen. She had full red lips, and Gerry couldn't look away. He'd never seen anything like her. Not in O'Brien's, not in McMurphy's, not on his nights out in Dingle. If she'd been a postcard, she'd have been a picture of a thatch cottage sitting on the top of a hill, with a green valley behind it and a blue sky and the ocean in the distance. She was the most beautiful woman he'd ever seen.

"Y'all right?" said one of the escorts in the tuxedo.

A Dub.

"Not so bad, though that's a dirty day out there now," said Gerry, who couldn't help but look again at the woman in the beige dress.

"Ah it's terrible, big summer storm. We can't see a thing when we're driving. Might have to sit here for a while if you don't mind." The man looked back towards the group and said, "cups of tea, everyone?"

A resounding yes came back.

Then the woman in the beige dress approached the counter, and even Pat Storey seemed more awake than usual.

"Hello, do you have anything stronger? I've never heard of a tea shop, so I'm not sure whether it's undercover for a pub? Just thought I'd ask," said the woman. "Gina, by the way."

Gerry blinked. She had the sweetest accent he'd ever heard. The woman held out her hand, and Gerry's own began to shake a little before he gripped hers. He swallowed when he noticed that she didn't look down; her blue eyes hadn't left his.

He felt something inside him that he'd never felt before. In his chest and in his stomach, and in other parts too. But he felt it most in his heart.

"Not so bad," said Gerry.

The woman's head tilted to one side and her eyebrows furrowed. "Not so bad?"

Her face seemed to say, *what question is he answering?*

Gerry released her soft hand and stood back a little, combing his hand through his hair.

"Sorry, sorry. I'm Gerry, Gerry McCarthy, and to your question, I suppose I have an auld bottle of whiskey somewhere."

Pat Storey turned to Gerry in surprise, licking his lips and rubbing his hands, and the others in the tea shop cheered. Gerry knelt down and reached into the back shelf, bringing out a half empty bottle of whiskey which the Dubliners had left behind them.

But at that moment, he supposed it was half full.

He poured some whiskey into everyone's tea. Gerry didn't fancy one himself. It was a tea shop after all and he was behind the counter, not on the other side, but Gina took the bottle of whiskey anyway, and didn't she pour some into Gerry's cup.

That's when the party started.

The girls were all Americans and had just come off the stage in Tralee; they were now on their way back to Thurles, halfway between Dublin Airport and Tralee, and that's where they intended to stay the night before flying back to America tomorrow in the afternoon.

And to Gerry's luck, the rain still poured down outside, the kind of rain in which you wouldn't want to drive the country roads of Ireland.

The other Roses were from Miami, San Francisco, and the one with blonde hair, she was a Boston woman, the same age as Gerry. But Gerry couldn't keep his eyes off Gina. She was the New York Rose and had won the contest. Gerry couldn't agree more with the judge's decision. However, Pat Storey let the Boston Rose know he had put a bet on her, telling her he was surprised she'd not won, causing laughs amongst them all.

The jokes flew and the craic was had, until the half bottle of whiskey was gone. But then, sure, didn't the Boston Rose run out to one of the Datsuns and bring in another bottle. She had bought it in Tralee and had been planning on bringing it back to America, but Pat Storey told her she could get a cheaper bottle in the duty free at the airport. *And he would know too,* Gerry thought. And to a barrel of laughs, more tea and whiskey was had.

Then the party tricks came out. The San Francisco Rose sang an auld Irish ballad, whilst the Miami Rose brought in a bodhran — an auld Irish drum — from one of the Datsuns, and she played some tunes on that. Even the escorts got in on it, all Irish fellas from up the country.

One of them sang 'The Wild Rover' and they all joined in, whilst Gina's escort, Conor — the fella who had held the door open as she walked in — did the most unusual dance, ending with him doing the splits to a round of applause.

It was an odd sight for Gerry. He'd never seen a man do the splits before, let alone one in a tuxedo and in a tea shop of all places, but he couldn't help but laugh along with everyone else.

"Now it's your turn, girlfriend," Conor turned and said to Gina.

She was seated on the stool right in front of Gerry.

What happened next would stay with Gerry for the rest of his life. He watched as Gina glided straight across the stoned floor with as much grace as His Holiness, and she stood in front of the photos on the wall. Gerry's eyes widened and his heart thundered.

Jaysus, he thought, *she knows the Kerry team too!*

But then she pointed above the picture, to the fiddle that hung on the wall, and she hopped up on one of the chairs which wobbled a little, bringing down the old fiddle and the bow which the Dubliners had left. She handled them as if they were her own instruments, turning to claps and applause from everyone else, except all Gerry could hear were the beats of his heart in his chest.

Gina placed the fiddle in the spot between her swan-like neck and her shoulder, closing her eyes as the bow touched the string and beginning to play a kind of music Gerry had never heard in his life. He had only heard the likes of traditional Irish folk — the diddly-dee kind — and he loved it. But this, this was something from another world and another time. This was magic.

Gina swayed from side to side, and her fingers, on those graceful hands, moved along the fingerboard, her bow dancing across the strings with a poise and an elegance that Gerry had never known existed. For the next three minutes, Gerry's world stopped.

He couldn't hear the sound of the rain outside, or the hiss of the teapot, or the thoughts in his head. And then Gina opened her eyes and smiled at Gerry, and the bow came down to a round of claps and cheers, and another set of splits from Conor.

From then on, the party continued into the wee hours as another of the escorts took the fiddle, and together with the bodhran from the Miami Rose, played some Irish traditional music. Pat Storey even got in on the act, singing an auld song called 'The Parting Glass.'" But through it all, Gerry only had eyes for one woman. During a verse of 'Black Velvet Band', knowing that everyone had a drink in front of them, Gerry took a step outside for some fresh air.

The rain had stopped, the clouds moved on, and the stars were out.

He looked down across the valley at the moon, which sparkled across the Atlantic Ocean in the distance. Even that sight wasn't as beautiful as the Rose of Tralee, he thought. He took a breath, and the next minute, heard the sound of footsteps.

"Darn, I was going to try to scare you," Gina said, and her tiptoes turned into a hop.

Gerry knew well that at this time of the morning, and after a few whiskeys, tiptoeing sounded quieter in your head.

"I don't scare easily now," he said.

"Maybe I'll get you someday," said Gina.

"What was that song you were playing? Never heard it in my life."

"'Valse' by Johann Brahms. It's an old classical piece of music. My mom had me learn the violin from a young age, useful when your grandad is an Irishman," said Gina. And out here, at the top of Drumbarron Hill, her laugh was as pretty as the sound of that violin to Gerry.

"It was beautiful," he said. He rested one arm on the gate of the field and turned to Gina.

"It is. Pat's song was beautiful too. I think I heard it once before in the pub with my grandad, but never like that. Pat's got a great voice. Do you sing, Gerry?"

And Gerry felt like telling her that his heart was singing as loud as it could then and there.

"No, us McCarthy's were never the most musical."

"Well, Gerry, I could never build this tea shop. I love it, it makes me feel cozy. Or maybe some of that's the whiskey."

Gerry imagined part of it was the whiskey, but he couldn't look away as Gina's eyes turned back towards the tea shop.

"You should see it in the daytime. It's quite beautiful. I think so anyways," said Gerry.

"Is that your way of asking me to stay until the morning? Very smooth, Gerry McCarthy, very smooth," said Gina.

"No, sorry, not at all. I didn't mean it like that. Sorry," said Gerry. His eyebrows raised and he held his breath.

"Got you! I told you I'd scare you," said Gina, and her white teeth shone in the darkness as she smiled.

Gerry laughed and leant back again against the gate of the field. He smiled, shaking his head before his eyes caught Gina's. And they wouldn't leave. Whether it was for a second or for a minute, Gerry couldn't tell. The silence surrounding him and this star of a woman, who had by sheer chance entered his tea shop, wasn't awkward or scary. It didn't make him want to make a joke, or to say anything at all. It felt peaceful. And amidst this moment of silence, Gerry noticed Gina coyly lick her lips, and so he took a step forward, and then another. And just as he bent down to meet her lips, a cow in the field let out a loud moo.

"Would you shut up, Penny?" shouted Gerry at the white cow not too far from the gate.

The next moment, Gina had her hands around Gerry's neck, and the two were making out like lovers do underneath the stars.

And that was that for Gerry McCarthy, a very simple and straightforward man. From that moment on, there was only one woman who could ever have his heart.

The sound of laughter carried around the corner when the door of the tea shop opened, and Conor came out, saying, "Look at you go, girlfriend, that's the Rose of Tralee right there."

Gina and Conor danced for a second before Conor said, "Me and Donal have sobered up, so we're going to get going. We'll have you all back in the hotel in Thurles in an hour and a half."

And Gerry's heart sank on the inside, but on the outside, he remained standing tall. Then Gina turned around. "Hey Gerry, do you know the way to Thurles?"

Gerry nodded. Other than hotels, Thurles had a racecourse, and he'd been there once before with John McHugh and the rest of the Ballyduffy football team on a team bonding day. Conor was right, he thought, it was about an hour and a half away.

"I do," he said.

"Hey Conor, maybe Gerry will leave me at the hotel in the morning? We will be there before we have to leave for Dublin."

Jaysus!

When Gerry saw Gina's smile, his heart soared and his foot began to tap, before he said, "Sure, I can do that."

Conor eyed Gerry, and then he whispered something to Gina, and the two of them laughed.

With that, they headed inside, and they all said their goodbyes, Pat Storey getting a kiss on the cheek from the Boston Rose as they walked out the door.

And Conor made Pat Storey get in Gina's seat, and he gave Pat a lift home before Conor and the others continued their way to Thurles in the early hours of the morning.

Then, Gina and Gerry were all alone in the tea shop. Gerry learned things a Kerry man didn't normally learn that night, and he sat in places of the tea shop he'd never sat. And the counter, he was right, it was plenty sturdy.

In the morning, as Gina lay beside him in the bed in the top room of the tea shop, Gerry listened to her breathing and felt her body against his as the air gently entered and left. He'd never felt so happy in all his life. They had stayed up until all hours, talking and whatever else.

Gina lived in New York and she was finishing college, in music of all things. Her mother was Italian, and her grandfather a Mayo man from Castlebar, and she was his favorite granddaughter, and her dad worked in one of those banks like Jimmy in New York.

She told Gerry all about St Patrick's day there, and about the New York Yankees, although to Gerry, baseball seemed more like farming; standing around a field looking at cows didn't sound all that different. But now, he had to wake her.

Gerry kissed her head and gently woke her up before doing what he was best at — and no, not what you're thinking — and he put the kettle on to make a cup of tea for them both. Then they walked outside and sat on the rock, looking out at the blue sky and the ocean.

"Do I have to leave?" said Gina, staring down the valley with the cup of tea in her hands. "I swear, it's the most beautiful view I've ever seen."

And as Gerry sat frozen in time, his eyes watching Gina scan the valley where Ballyduffy appeared unruffled, unaware of the beauty sitting at the top of Drumbarron Hill beside him, he thought, *I disagree.*

"It's not always like this. The rain comes in hard and fast when it does," said Gerry.

"But then you can put on the fire in here and it's just as nice," said Gina, turning to look at the thatched tea shop. "Your tea is pretty good too, Gerry."

"That's the practice," said Gerry.

Gina laughed and kissed him again.

"I forgot to ask you last night, but do you enter these sorts of things a lot?" said Gerry, causing Gina to laugh some more.

"What do you mean, Gerry?"

"The Rose of Tralee. Do you go to other competitions? Your mother's Italian; are you doing a competition there?"

"Hell no, Gerry. I knew nothing about this until my grandad told me one day that he'd entered me. After I learned I had been chosen, I mean, who can turn down an all-expenses trip to Ireland? And my mom is Italian-American. It's her grandparents who are Italian, Gerry."

And although Gerry thought it was a bit weird that Gina's mother was from two countries, he said, "I wouldn't mind one of those trips. The only thing I remember my pa winning was best turned-out cow at the Tralee spring agricultural fair. He got a bale of hay for that, but sure that didn't last too long."

"I love it, Gerry — a bale of hay! I think it was all a joke to my grandad in the beginning, but I think he'd be proud of me. Never in a million years did I think I'd win. And that's where it all started. And look at me now. It brought me here, to meet you."

Gerry laughed before taking a sip of his tea. In his mind, she would win any competition she'd enter — in Tralee, America, Italy, the whole lot. Then Gerry said the words he'd been dreading from the moment he woke up.

"I think we need to leave now if we're to get you there on time."

Gina looked at her watch, "We've plenty of time though, Gerry? Conor said it was ninety minutes to Thurles."

And even though Gerry knew this meant an hour and a half, what Gina didn't know was that a tractor would take double the time.

"Well, I'll go down and get our transport," he said.

Gerry cycled back down to the house, and Gina had never laughed as hard as when Gerry landed up the hill in his red tractor, which he had bought from Uncle Brendan the previous year.

"It'll be a tight squeeze," said Gerry who held Gina's hand as she stepped up in her bare feet and beige dress from the night before. Gerry laughed too, more mesmerized by this girl as even the tractor wasn't a bother to her; Gina even put her hand on his leg once he'd climbed aboard.

"You see much more up here," Gina said, and Gerry wasn't sure if she meant the tractor or Drumbarron Hill, but nevertheless, she was right.

And so, they set off on their journey to Thurles.

They went past countless green fields with countless cows and plenty of sheep for those who struggled to fall asleep at night. Gina waved at every farmer and other folk out walking the country roads, ones who waved back as the tractor rolled by at a snail's pace. They took the new bypass around Limerick, which was a blessing to Gerry because he didn't want to leave her late, although deep down he did, even if he didn't know it yet himself.

And Gina would nudge and laugh at the beeps behind, which Gerry, like any farmer, had drowned out by now. Although, he'd get a chuckle when Gina would burst out laughing whenever a car passed them by and a middle finger would appear out the window, or a shout could be heard saying, "Get off the feckin' road." Yet still they carried on.

Gerry had given Gina an auld navy and blue Ballyduffy football jumper of his that was in the tractor, one that he would normally wear to training on the colder days, and it suited her, he thought. She was still the finest picture he'd ever seen. At one point, as they climbed a small brae not far from Thurles, Gina looked behind her at the line of cars stretching as far as she could see.

After Gerry had asked directions from a Thurles man with a walking stick and a sheepdog, they found the hotel, and sure enough, Conor was in the car with the others.

They were all ready to set off for Dublin. Gerry could see the smiles and the laughs at the tractor that came down the street.

"Come on Gina. Jacinta helped to pack your bag, and we have to leave now if you're to make your flight," said Conor.

Gerry got out of the tractor and helped Gina down.

They kissed, and as she got in the door of Conor's Datsun, she held up one of the postcards in her hand, and with his Ballyduffy jumper still on, said, "I'll write to you."

Gerry waved, and he didn't know what to feel. His heart was full, but at that moment, there was an emptiness as the red Datsun took off through the streets, the tires leaving a spin mark on the road. Gerry hopped back on the tractor, and just before he set off, he whispered to himself, "Well, she has my address."

And so, Gerry left the main street, heading back out the road to Ballyduffy, but not so long after leaving Thurles, a line of cars stood on the other side of the road at a standstill.

Seeing no one behind him, he slowed down, ushering a man in a silver Datsun to roll his windows down.

"What's all this then?" asked Gerry.

"Some hoor in a tractor holding everyone up, and now they've lines to get in the racecourse," the man said.

"You're a Kerry man?" said Gerry.

"I am. Killarney. And yourself?"

"Ballyduffy." And then Gerry looked over his shoulder, and there was a beep as a car was approaching. So, Gerry asked the man, "What's on in the racecourse today?"

"Munster National's being held here this year. Good luck to you," the man said, his line of traffic beginning to move more freely.

The Munster National, thought Gerry, *the greatest horse race in this part of Ireland.* Sure, he'd be a fool to miss that seeing as he was right here. So, Gerry turned the red tractor around, no mean feat when you'd both lines of traffic beeping at you and throwing middle fingers your way, but he did it, and in no time at all, was in the racecourse with the red tractor parked up.

Gerry went and bought himself a pint. The smell of Gina's perfume was still lingering in his nose, but he had a drink and walked out towards the paddock. He stood beside two Limerick men, who were chatting about the horses walking around,

"Behind some bastard on a tractor the whole way here; missed the first few races," said one.

"Must've been some eejit, holding up the roads on Munster National day. The next race is the big one," another said.

Gerry paid no heed to the tractor comments. Sure, he was lucky; he'd only just made it in time for the big race. He made his way out towards the racecourse proper and stood against the banister, watching the jockeys and their horses make their way towards the start.

The jockeys had all different coloured shirts and silks and helmets — blues and oranges, and blacks and reds, and there were stars and stripes and the whole lot.

But Gerry's eyes were attracted to the black horse, and the jockey with the white helmet and the green and gold horizontal stripes.

Kerry colours!

Then he saw the number, and it was number eight. *A great number!* Sure, wasn't it his number that he wore for Ballyduffy football team. He stared as the horse walked past, and he even looked up at the jockey and said, "Good luck to you now."

Then the horse stopped right in front of Gerry, and sure didn't the horse's tail go in the air, and it took a shite right there in front of him.

Jaysus, thought Gerry. *Finding a shite like this could be good luck.*

So, he turned, looking for the bookmakers and their boards, and he ran through the crowds towards the betting ring. He found the one with no line and stuck his hand in his pocket to pull out a five-pound note, then said to the bookmaker, "Five pounds on number eight please."

The bookie smiled at Gerry before looking up towards his board.

"Are you sure now, big fella? That horse is a hundred to one."

Gerry scrunched his face and shook his head. He knew enough to know that he'd have a better chance of winning the lottery than winning on a hundred-to-one shot.

"How about you pick another horse?" the bookie said, pointing up at his black board with the white chalk. Gerry looked up and scanned the board, which had tirty different horse names, and numbers and odds. And then he stopped at number eight.

The man was right; number eight was a hundred to one. But that wasn't what Gerry was looking at. The horse's name was 'His Holiness.'

Gerry rubbed his eyes. Then he looked up at the blue sky above. He thought of Cara, his superstitious Aunt, remembering her words. "No such thing as coincidences, Gerry."

Gerry smiled, pulled out his five-pound note again and said to the bookie, "Number eight, five pounds on him please."

The bookie sighed and handed Gerry his ticket.

Gerry found himself a spot right up against the banister on the racecourse before a woman, even older than Aunt Cara, touched his arm and said, "You wouldn't let an auld woman stand in front of you, big fella. Won't see a thing back here."

She's right, thought Gerry; he stood back and let the woman in front of him.

Gerry looked out as the horses lined up at the start. Then he saw the auld woman looking at his large hands holding his ticket from the bookie, and then she looked up at him.

So, to be polite, Gerry asked, "Who did you bet on?"

The woman smiled, then looked down at the ticket in her hand. "I've a fiver on His Holiness."

Jaysus, thought Gerry again, and he knew he was right; auld women had the back door to God. And sure, didn't they both watch and scream and shout as the Kerry colours of His Holiness jumped over the final fence in the lead, beating the favorite by a length on the line.

And you could hear a pin drop in Thurles racecourse apart from Gerry McCarthy and this old woman, cheering as they walked together to collect their five hundred pounds each.

"Jaysus, big fella. How'd you pick that one out? You must be happy," said the bookie.

"A load of shite," said Gerry with a smile on his face.

After bidding the auld woman goodbye, Gerry hopped in his tractor and headed for the road to Ballyduffy. He took his time, and with a full heart and a pocket full of money, he didn't hear any of the beeps behind him.

CHAPTER

9

The week after Gina left, Gerry hopped in the tractor, and to beeps and everything else, drove to Tralee one morning, heading to Kelly's music shop. They had fiddles and guitars and bodhrans and tin whistles — the whole lot — but Gerry was looking for something in particular for his tea shop. He walked around the store on his mission, but wasn't really sure what to get; the McCarthys had never been big music people.

"How's it going?" said the shopkeeper.

"Not so bad. How's it going with you?" said Gerry.

"Not so bad. What can I help you with?"

Gerry explained to the man what he was looking for, and after this, he scanned the radios, picking a few up and then setting them down again, and then he looked at these things called 'stereos', among which Gerry couldn't really tell the difference.

Finally, he decided they weren't what he wanted. Then he spotted something, and he paid with some of the five hundred pounds from His Holiness. And the rest of the money, he would place in his tin together with all the letters from Jimmy. "For a rainy day," Gerry would mutter to himself. And he left the shop and raced across to the tractor beneath a shower and black clouds.

Once at the tractor, he placed a record player and three records inside.

There was a record of the Dubliners, which would be useful for customers if they wanted some music, and plus, Gerry liked their songs. Another of Johann Brahms, and Gerry had made sure it had 'Valse' on it. The third had been a suggestion from the shopkeeper, and Gerry liked the name: Wolfgang Mozart. *Very European,* he thought.

But Gerry would come to find Wolfgang's music like something from another planet.

It was as if Wolfgang had access to the strings of Gerry's heart, and it reminded him of Gina every time he would put either that record, or Valse, on the record player in the tea shop.

The football was going well. Those young boys in the Ballyduffy team were starting to come good. Michael O'Brien, a relation of Toe who owned the pub, and Seanie Egan, were two lads approaching twenty, and they were both on the Kerry team as well.

Things were certainly looking up in Ballyduffy, although Gerry knew it might be a year or two too soon to make a run to win the Championship. He knew the young boys would need time to settle into the team, and time was one thing Ballyduffy had plenty of.

Then in the middle of a summer in which Ballyduffy had won half of their games and lost the other half — although they did beat Carrickbay — Gerry was about to close up shop when a white van trundled over the hill, and Gerry could hear the van moving fast. It screeched to a halt, and so Gerry stood for a moment as the three lads got out. He turned his head and behind the van was a big silver trailer, the kind that could be used to move large animals.

"How's it going?" said one of the men. He had black hair like Gerry's, and a poor attempt at a moustache, in Gerry's mind. Gerry noticed his accent: *must be Donegal,* he thought, *from close to the north of Ireland.* And he had a red Manchester United jersey on, and one of the others wore a red Liverpool jersey. The third wore a black jumper, and he was the quietest of the lot.

"Not so bad," Gerry said.

"Is that your field?" the man in the United jersey asked, pointing to the cows behind the tea shop.

"It is. What can I help you with?"

"Would you be able to keep a horse in there for a few days? We'll pay you

---

a few bob."

Gerry looked at the trailer behind the van and then heard the horse neigh.

Then he looked back towards the field. It would be no harm, he supposed. Cows and horses got along, and Gerry didn't mind horses either; the McHughs had a couple, and Gerry had ridden a few when he was younger, so he'd be well able to look after one.

"And how much will it cost you?" said Gerry.

"We'll give you a hundred pounds. But keep that to yourself," said the man.

And Gerry blinked. *Jaysus! One hundred pounds to leave the horse in my field for a few days. These men have lost their minds. But if that's what they're willing to pay!*

"Sure, I can do that," said Gerry.

The men led the horse out of the trailer, and it was the finest looking horse Gerry had ever seen. Muscular, dark brown, with a white blaze down its face. And Gerry looked down at the horse's fetlocks above the hooves; they made it look as though he wore four white socks, and Gerry chuckled. *They'll not be white for long with all the cow shite in that field,* he thought.

After Gerry had closed the gate — and the horse trotted and jumped and looked well in itself, and he had one hundred pounds of notes in his pocket — the men jumped into the van. Before they were about to leave, Gerry signalled them to roll down the windows, and he asked the man in the United shirt, "What's the horse's name?"

The men looked at each other, then the main man said to Gerry, "Why do you need to know its name?"

Gerry shook his head. *These lads haven't a clue,* he thought.

"Well, if the horse runs off and I've to run after it, I'll need to know its name to call it back."

And the men looked at each other for a few seconds, and then the man with the United jersey spoke to Gerry. "Sugar," he said.

Gerry nodded, and the van sped off down the hill as fast as it had arrived. And then, after Gerry had walked the field and made sure Sugar and the cows were all right, he headed back down the hill where he put his one hundred pounds in with all the other money in his dresser.

"For a rainy day," Gerry whispered.

Then he walked back out to the kitchen table, and in his rush to take off his wet coat and his soaking wellies when he'd entered the house, he had missed two letters and the bag of cakes sitting on the table.

Gerry felt his heart go faster than usual as he sat down.

One of the letters was from Jimmy; he knew that writing. The other writing was pretty and elegant, and Gerry's hand trembled as he opened that one. It carried a sweet scent of perfume too, the alluring floral aroma of none other than his Gina.

April 12, 1984

Hey Gerry,

I hope you receive this letter ok. I was a bit concerned when you didn't have a zip code or a postcode, but I trust that you provided me with the correct address. How are you doing? And Pat Storey, I hope he is good too?

What a wonderful time we had there. I haven't stopped thinking about it, Gerry. Every day since I've been back in New York, all I think about is you. I even asked Grandad if there was anywhere in New York to get tea, and he suggested a few places, but they weren't the same. And that tractor with the long line behind us, HA! The memory makes me laugh as I'm writing this. I hope your counter's still intact. I was a little worried that night!

My family were very proud, especially my grandad, of my winning the Rose of Tralee. But since I've been back, I've been a little unsettled to be honest. New York is like it always is, non-stop, with lots of people and things to do. I'm in my last few months of college and enjoying my music, but what I'll do after that, I'm not sure. Mom and Dad are telling me to get a job in Dad's bank but I'm not sure that's what I want for my life.

Conor wrote me a letter. He is good. I don't think he's been down in your direction, but he's joined a dance studio up in Dublin, and he appears to be enjoying it. With those splits, he's flexible enough for dancing, that's for sure!

I'm not sure how long this letter will take to arrive, but I'm planning on taking a short trip to Ireland once I finish college, and I'm hoping it will be ok to visit you and stay for a little. I fly out on July second.

I can't wait to see you,

Gina.

Gina O'Dea,
115 Murray Ave,
Port Washington NY 14250,
USA.

Gerry sat back in his chair. And then he stood up and poured himself a cup of tea, before sitting back down. He could hear Gina's New York accent in his head as he re-read her letter. His heart thumped and his knee was going up and down as if it had a mind of its own.

He knew that unsettled feeling Gina had spoken about, and it didn't feel good, and he hoped she was feeling ok. She'd missed him too. All year he had hoped for this letter, and it didn't disappoint. Gerry smiled, then shook his head.

"Sure, how could the tea be the same over there?" he whispered.

Gerry jumped, spilling the tea on his trousers. "Ah shite!" He ran and got a cloth from the drawer and wiped it away, then rushed to the wall and looked at the calendar. He bought a farmer's calendar every December, and flicked the page over to the new month, something he had forgotten to do this morning.

"Would you look at that?" he whispered. The new month had a picture of a dark brown horse with a white blaze.

Then Gerry shook his head and got to work; Gina would be here tomorrow of all days, and the place needed to be cleaned top to bottom. *She's used to staying in hotels in Thurles,* Gerry thought, *and so a hotel is what she gets when she comes here.* For the rest of that day and into the early morning, Gerry swept and mopped and brushed and cleaned. And then he went to his room and looked at his sad single bed beneath the window. *She couldn't sleep there,* he thought.

He walked up to the other room with his mother's dresser and the empty wardrobe where Pa used to hang his only suit. And he looked at the double bed. The bedsheets were made and hadn't been touched in years. So, Gerry stripped the bed and washed those sheets, then he redid the bedsheets. Once it was perfect, he stepped back, looking around and smiling to himself.

"It looks like a hotel now," he whispered.

He walked back to the kitchen and Jimmy's letter was still there, sitting atop the counter.

But Gerry had had enough excitement for one day, so he put Jimmy's letter in the silver tin and would take it out once his heart stopped racing.

———— • ✹ • ————

The next morning, Gerry arose bright and early. He opened his Ballyduffy football bag, the one with the navy and blue stripes, and placed a load of clean tea towels and other towels inside, and made his way up to the teashop. He emptied the bag and put it behind the counter, placing the clean tea towels in one of the shelves, and a fresh towel in the bathroom. A few cyclists came by, full of excitement as apparently, that Stephen fella in his green Lycra shorts was improving at a rate of knots in his tours around Europe.

And once they left, Gerry went outside to the field to check on Sugar the horse, and the cows, and they all looked as though they were fine.

The rain began to fall — not heavy rain — just light rain, mist-like and good for the skin. But Gerry went inside, not wanting his hair to be wet and dishevelled once Gina arrived.

Gerry washed each cup in the tea shop, three, maybe four times.

In moments like this, he was glad there was no clock in the place. He couldn't even put on the record player as his heart was beating too fast. So, he sat behind the counter on his stool and waited amongst the silence. Then the door of the tea shop opened. Jaysus, here we go, thought Gerry. He held his breath. Then as the light shone through into his shop, he stepped off the stool.

"How's it going, Gerry?"

Gerry sat back down as Pat Storey walked through the door with his cap and walking stick.

"Not so bad, Pat," said Gerry, and he chuckled to himself.

"I'll have one of those teas please, Gerry," said Pat.

Gerry poured Pat a tea and for the next hour, they chatted. And Gerry was happy to have him as the time flew by.

"Is that your horse out there, Gerry?" said Pat as he took a sip from his cup.

"No Pat, just minding it for a few days."

"What's its name?" said Pat.

"Sugar."

"No thanks, Gerry, I'm fine with the tea the way it is," said Pat.

"I meant the horse, Pat," said Gerry. "Sugar is its name."

"Right. Odd name for a horse. But I suppose a horse called Sugar out the back of a tea shop isn't the oddest thing we've seen," said Pat, taking another sip of his tea.

And he was right too, thought Gerry.

"It's a beautiful animal. Fine muscular horse. I'd say it would win a few races in its day," said Pat.

"I suppose it would, Pat," said Gerry, and right that instant, the door opened and wearing a beige coat, with her dark hair and her blue eyes and full lips came Gina, walking in the door.

Gerry's jaw hit the floor and he was silent. He watched as she wheeled in a black suitcase and sat it beside her, saying, "Hey, Gerry."

Gerry's heart melted and not a word would come out. He thought back to that moment where he'd told the Pope he was a midfielder for Ballyduffy, and he shook his head. Then he walked around the counter, and kissed Gina like he'd never kissed any other woman.

"Who needs sugar when you have that?" whispered Pat.

Then he looked out the window as a car turned and headed off up the hill.

"Hey Pat," said Gina, who hugged the auld man sitting on the stool with the few strands of hair on his head.

"How's it going, Gina? Back again? Can't keep away from auld Gerry here?"

"Back again, Pat. And yes, you could say there was something I had my heart set on," said Gina, and she turned and looked at Gerry with a smile that melted big Gerry McCarthy's heart.

Gerry took Gina's beige coat, and her suitcase, and put them to one side as she took a seat on the stool beside Pat, and the three of them had a cup of tea.

"How'd you make it here anyway?" asked Gerry.

"I flew into Shannon Airport and took a taxi from there. It didn't take long," said Gina in that sweet New York accent. And Gerry supposed she was right. In a car, it wasn't that long to Shannon Airport, maybe an hour.

After a while, Pat left, and Gerry and Gina were now alone in the tea shop.

Then, she kissed Gerry, and looked at him with those blue eyes, and Gerry felt those feelings again all over his body and in his heart. He went outside with a sign that said 'Closed', and then on his way back inside, he locked the door, and drew the curtains.

And you're all wondering what happened next, ye filthy animals.

Well, the two of them were very much in love, and in between whatever did go on behind closed blinds and doors, they ate a few cakes from Aunt Cara and indulged in yet more tea, Gerry even pouring a little whiskey in. Times like these were to be celebrated, and he'd never felt more like celebrating than he did right now with his Gina at his side again.

And when it began to get dark and they got hungry, Gina put on her coat and opened the door. Then, Gerry lifted Gina's suitcase and thought, *what the hell could she have in here?*

That case weighed more than all the clothes and wellies in Gerry's house put together.

But alas, he was more than happy to help, and he rolled it out behind him before one wheel fell off and broke. So, Gerry had to use his big arms to balance the suitcase on the other tree wheels as he tried to roll it on its side.

"My, that horse is so beautiful," said Gina, and she stood at the gate looking into the field. Then she reached into the pocket of her beige coat and took out an apple that she had bought in the airport and had forgotten to eat. Sugar rushed over and stood with its long face, with that white blaze, head hanging over the gate, munching the apple out of Gina's hand.

"Is he yours, Gerry?" said Gina, patting Sugar's neck. "He's magnificent."

"No, I'm just looking after him for someone."

"For how long?"

"I don't know. Until they come back to get him, I suppose," said Gerry, and Gina laughed that same laugh that she'd had that night last year when the moon and the stars had been in the sky, and Gerry's heart rushed again.

For the next few days, Gerry would only keep the tea shop open for a couple of hours in the afternoon as he and Gina would lie in the double bed late in the mornings, and he would make her breakfast one day, and she'd make him dinner the other day. Spaghetti Bolognese was a recipe of Gina's mother, and Gerry had a tough time keeping the funny strings in his mouth.

And they laughed like Gerry had never laughed before.

He took her into O'Brien's pub one night, where Pat Storey was the first man to say hello, and the others all welcomed Gina to Ballyduffy. She had a few pints and even Aunt Cara came out to give Gina a hug and to say hello, although she didn't stay long as her two hips had been bad these past couple of years, and she didn't make it up the hill to the tea shop much anymore.

But before she left, she whispered to Gerry, "I have a good feeling about this one, Gerry." And Gerry's heart leapt out of his chest because he had begun to believe in superstitions too.

Then Gerry took Gina to McMurphy's.

There, Seanie O'Shea played the fiddle and songs were sung, and then Gina got up and danced. A few of the fellas came up to Gerry and said, "Jaysus, how'd you get a looker like that?" Gerry stood with his pint in his hand and watched Gina dance, and he thought the same.

"Hey Gerry, this photograph. Is that your father?" Gina pointed to a photo on the wall of the bar.

Gerry stepped closer and stared into the auld black and white picture. It certainly was.

"You never told me he was a champion?" said Gina.

"Oh, he was. He was captain that year. They say he was some player," said Gerry.

He stared into the photo of his father holding the Championship trophy high above his head, with the village folk of Ballyduffy cheering around him. He could almost hear them.

Gerry read the words someone had written in pen on the side of the photo: *Pa McCarthy, captain of the Ballyduffy team, lifts the Kerry Junior Championship trophy, 1938.*

With all the times and all the drinks he'd had in McMurphy's, he had forgotten this photo.

Then his eyes glanced to another image on the wall, a picture of two men in welly boots standing beside two calves. "Jaysus, it's him again," he whispered.

Tralee Fair Prize Calf 1949 – first place: Pa McCarthy, Ballyduffy. Second place: Thomas Murtagh, Carrickbay. And when Gina asked what he was looking at, they both laughed at the story about the time Gerry had refused Thomas Murtagh's money to buy Penny the cow.

Gina and Gerry sang and danced until closing time, which was quite the feat, Gerry thought, as it was known in these parts that the Americans were lightweights when it came to a few pints. But then there was Irish blood in Gina.

They latched arms and walked out onto the road under the stars where the moon shone down like a spotlight. And as they walked past O'Neills', even that sheepdog's bark didn't bother Gerry as it normally would. When they reached his house, Gina stopped and turned to look at Gerry, wrapping her arms around him. In the moonlight, he could still make out those vivid and beautiful blue eyes. "I'm falling in love with you," she whispered.

Gerry felt it too in every bone of his body, from the top of his six-foot-four-inch frame, to the ends of his shovel-like hands; oh, he felt it too. And as he was about to open his mouth to respond, Gina pulled back, ran over to the ditch, and got sick all over it.

That's her American side, he considered.

Gerry held her hair back, and once they went inside, he made sure she had plenty of water before she went to bed, even making her a ham and cheese sandwich so that the bread could soak up the remaining alcohol before she fell asleep. As Gina slept, she snored, and Gerry lay with her in his arms, just watching.

And he knew love like it was meant to be known when Gina farted in her sleep, and Gerry chuckled for a second, then thought, *sure, we all fart, and even the Pope shites.*

Then he kissed her head and fell asleep, never mentioning a thing about it.

However, Gerry wondered if Gina knew that he was falling in love with her too, and perhaps it was about time he told her.

———— • ❋ • ————

One of the days near the end of her week in Ireland, Gerry brought Gina in the tractor to the beach outside Dingle, well over an hour away. Now, there were many beaches in this part of the world, each wonderful in their own way, but that beach was the most beautiful with its golden sand, and dunes with light green rushes, and the waves would crash in your ears. Gerry had prepared a picnic, and they sat on a blanket on the beach with a beer in their hands.

"Ma used to take Jimmy and me down this way when we were younger," said Gerry.

"It's beautiful, Gerry, it really is. I don't know how you do it on your own. You have the farm, not to mention the tea shop."

"It isn't easy, but it gets done," said Gerry.

"You must think of your family a lot?"

Gerry looked at Gina's kind eyes and then out towards the blue sea, where the waves broke one after the other.

"Well, I'm usually up just before dawn, then out at the animals, and I get to the tea shop for around eleven, ten on a Saturday if I know Stephen's going to be about.

"Then in the evening, if there's no one around, I'll close up the shop and do some more work about the farm. So you could say I'm tired when I get home, to be honest. Unless I have the football, because I'm a Kerryman and I can't be missing that."

He paused again to look out at the blue sea, tilting his head a little to catch the sky before he continued, "So, I don't have much time for thinking about them. But sometimes, I can't help thinking about them, of course." *And thinking of you as well,* Gerry thought but kept that to himself. Gina joined his gaze, her blue eyes looking towards the horizon.

"I love this place, Gerry."

"The beach?"

"The beach, the tea shop, Ballyduffy. When I was a little girl, Grandad used to take me into Manhattan, and we would eat iced cream looking out towards the Statue of Liberty. We'd sit together and he would tell me stories of what lay across the Atlantic Ocean. He grew up in a similar place in Mayo, surrounded by the green fields and the sheep. Last year was the first time I'd ever been to Ireland, and I got to visit his village for a day. It's very similar to here.

"I mean this past week has been magical." Gina looked down, then her eyes rose to meet Gerry's and she continued. "You know, he would really like you. He sees things for how they really are, and that's one of the reasons I love him. Life is very different in New York, let's just say that." Gina took a breath, and Gerry noticed her hand picking up and dropping sand.

"What do you mean?" said Gerry.

"I don't know. It's always 'what are you doing with your life? Where are you going?'"

"Sure, how are you meant to know that?" said Gerry.

Gina chuckled then said, "Do you have dreams, Gerry?"

"When I sleep, I do," he joked.

"I once dreamed I was going to be the best violinist in the world. But then it felt like I had this weight on my shoulders. It wasn't the violin! I just feel so much pressure to succeed. I'd love to continue with my music, but Mom and Dad say it isn't a career. My dad wants me to interview with his bank next month. I suppose it could be good, but I don't know if it's what I want. I don't know Gerry; guess we'll see what happens."

Gerry stared into Gina's eyes. He didn't know much about careers. He supposed it was just another word for life. But his life was the farm, and now he had the tea shop. And he supposed for his career to be complete, the only thing missing was sitting right in front of him.

"What does your grandad say?" said Gerry.

"He says if it doesn't work out, I can always come play the violin in his pub. But I don't know any of that diddly-dee music," said Gina, putting her head into her hands and shaking it.

It made Gerry laugh.

"The way you play, I'm sure you'd pick up the diddly-dee in no time," said Gerry.

"You really are one of a kind, Gerry McCarthy. Come on, enough moaning out of me; let's try the water."

So, they tried the water of the Atlantic Ocean, which, although freezing, was known to be great for the body. Now, Gerry wasn't the best swimmer, but he could dangle arms and legs, he supposed, and he watched Gina as she swam in the water like one of those golden fish. And didn't she look great in her bikini too, thought Gerry.

He had learned that Gina had grown up not far from a beach too, and that she had trained to be a lifeguard when she was younger, and Gerry felt safe enough to dip his head under the cold water for a bit. Gina learned all about the cold of the Atlantic, soon jumping into each of Gerry's large footsteps on the sand as they headed back to their spot, wrapping towels around them.

They sat down on the blanket. The beach was empty now both left and right, as far as Gerry could see. Then he heard the crack of a can, and Gina squeezed between his legs to sit there.

He wrapped his arms around her.

Beneath the gentle breeze, Gerry could hear his heart thumping. And with Gina's back pressed up against his chest, he could feel her heart beating, and after a few moments, he felt their heartbeats blend together. After a little while in which the two were silent, Gerry took another sip of beer, then he felt an urge in the back of his throat to let Gina know how he couldn't tell whose heart was beating because they were one.

"Gina."

"Yes, Gerry."

"I was thinking about what you said last night."

"What's that noise?" asked Gina, interrupting Gerry's thought.

Gerry looked along the beach. Then he heard it.

"Someone's shouting," said Gina. She leapt to her feet. Then she pointed. "There."

Gina bolted down the beach towards the water, and Gerry sprinted after her. There was a head bobbing up and down out in the deep, shouting for help, much too far out for Gerry to offer any kind of assistance at all. He felt helpless, hopeless, standing there watching a person drown.

Gina dived straight into a wave as Gerry made his way slowly through the water, venturing as far as his six-feet-four inches would take him before the waves started going over his head. But he jumped, and he saw that Gina had caught the person swimming and was pulling them in. And Gerry could see now that it was a man, and the man's arms were moving, which meant he was still alive, thank God.

They took the man in, and the water was still above Gerry's knees when the man was able to stand on his own, hunched over, trying to gather oxygen into his lungs. Gerry smiled at Gina, who also was breathing heavily after her heroics. *She's some woman,* he thought.

Then the man, who was elderly and frail and probably shouldn't have been out that deep, turned and said, "How's it going, Gerry?"

Jaysus!

Gerry swept his hand through his wet hair, then looked along the beach, and about ten metres from where the water met the shore, weren't there some clothes, a hat, and a walking stick.

"Jaysus, Pat, you nearly died there," said Gerry.

"But didn't His Holiness send an angel to look after me," said Pat Storey, and he turned to Gina and said, "Thank you."

Gina glanced at Gerry and the two of them laughed until their bellies were sore. They helped Pat to where his stuff was lying on the beach and left him alone to change out of the very auld pair of white Ballyduffy football shorts that Pat was wearing.

"I've never met anyone like him," Gina said to Gerry as they walked back towards their blanket and got changed. The wet dark hair fell down the front of Gina's beautiful face and Gerry thought of what Pat had said, then of his Aunt Cara and her superstitions.

Maybe His Holiness did bless the tea shop.

"Didn't know you came down this way, Pat?" said Gerry once Pat came over with his hat on.

"They've a new bus that runs through Ballyduffy on Fridays, Gerry, so I've been coming down here for a swim this last while. Helps that the bus is free for over seventy-fives. And the water's good for the ticker too," said Pat. "Well, it is as long as you don't drown in it."

They laughed again, Pat occasionally stopping to hunch over almost double and cough his lungs up. He prodded the walking stick into the sand. They all headed together to the car park.

"How are you getting home, Pat?" said Gina.

"I'll wait for the bus, Gina."

Then Gina looked up at the dark clouds that wouldn't be long coming in. "When does that come?" she said.

"It comes when it's time," said Pat as he slowly began walking towards the green bus stop.

Gina looked at Gerry again, then called out, "Come on Pat, you're coming with us."

Gerry looked back towards his auld red tractor and giggled, thinking, *it'll be a tight squeeze, but where there's a will, there's a way.* He helped both Gina and Pat into the tractor, so that now all three of them were sitting as comfortably as they could. Gina put her hand onto Gerry's leg, and after the tractor struggled to start for a moment as it was very auld, Gerry finally got it going, and the three of them rolled through Tralee, and up the coast road to Ballyduffy.

And when a man in a blue Datsun sped by on a tight corner on which he shouldn't really have passed the tractor, and he beeped, didn't auld Pat Storey shout, "You feckin eejit, get of the road!" and then he flipped the man the middle finger.

For the next half hour of the trip home, anyone who drove past and beeped, Gina and Pat flipped the middle finger at them, and they all laughed.

And Gerry would have flipped the finger too, but he had his two hands firmly on the wheel because there was an angel of God in the tractor beside him, and he had to get her home safe.

CHAPTER

10

The day came by that Gerry had been dreading all week, bringing with it a sense of lonely déjà vu from the last time he'd had to wave goodbye.

He gently woke Gina with a cup of tea. Despite it being early, and a few hours to Gina's flight from Shannon Airport, Gerry had learned that week, that sometimes Gina took a little longer to get ready than he would've ever thought possible.

At least compared to his memories of living with Pa and Jimmy.

The week had gone faster than any week he'd ever had in his life. A week where his mind and his heart surfed by on an endless wave, as if he was in some strange cocoon with Gina, and it was only his body that was left behind and present in this world.

He had felt something similar before, but very different in other ways, when Pa died. A strange feeling of being far away, distant and alienated, yet somehow, your body was still here.

Only this time with Gina, he was far away in paradise. But Gerry still hadn't found the right moment to tell Gina how he felt and now she was heading home.

Gina, too, was a little quieter than her usual outgoing and charming self. She showered and dressed, and all the while Gerry sat and watched her, trying not to think about how long it would be until he could set eyes on her again. Then, with the heavy black suitcase with the tree wheels standing beside her, and her beige coat on and a pair of jeans, the most beautiful woman Gerry had ever seen was finally ready. He lifted the suitcase up into the tractor and placed it in the same area that Pat Storey had sat, and Gina squeezed in beside.

And sure, she didn't need Gerry to give her a hand up this time.

"I don't know how you'll manage that suitcase all on your own," he said to Gina.

"Well, I managed on the way here, so I'll manage just the same on the way back."

"Yes, but now, it only has tree wheels."

Evidently, she hadn't considered that. "Then I'll have to take you with me, Gerry."

He laughed loudly, saying, "I wish you could. Or I wish —"

But he never completed that thought, not daring to speak it into the air between them.

After that, then the tractor, which was a little rusty and slow this beautiful summer morning, chugged along up Drumbarron Hill, and Gerry parked it up on the side of the road beside the tea shop. *The cyclists will be around anytime now,* he thought.

So, after he checked on Sugar, who had been here for more than a week now, Gerry and Gina went inside the shop, and Gerry lifted one of the stools and brought it behind the counter. Together, they both greeted the cyclists as they arrived. Gerry brought the tea outside, and Gina brought the cakes, and the cyclists all had smiles on their faces when they were greeted by this New Yorker with the beautiful eyes and the accent.

One of them whispered to Gerry after Gina went inside, "Jaysus, Gerry, how'd you get a looker like that?"

And Gerry shook his head and said, "I don't know, but thanks be to God. And the Pope."

"Will she be staying around?" said the cyclist.

Gerry turned and looked through the window as Gina was wiping the countertop.

"I don't think so. Her flight is this afternoon."

And Gerry sat quiet for a moment before he nodded and wished the cyclist a good day.

Time was getting short, and Gerry knew it would be more than an hour's drive to Shannon. And although Gina could've taken a taxi, Gerry had given her his word that *he* would be the one to drop her off. He wouldn't have wanted it any other way, no matter how much work he had on his plate or how busy the tea shop was. And secretly, Gerry had planned to tell her how he felt once they had got to the airport. He had rehearsed it all in his head. "Gina, I want you to take something with you and hold it tight until I see you again. I've felt this from the moment I first saw you and I will feel it for the rest of my life. That is, I love you. And I'll miss you every day."

Or something along those lines were what he had in his mind.

And he had thought often that week how he'd never told Pa how much he loved him. Or he'd never told Jimmy that. Jaysus, he couldn't even remember telling his ma that. But he'd been young and assumed he had. But from what he recalled, he'd never told anyone how he felt.

Gerry put the 'closed' sign on the door and he turned to see Gina standing in front of the gate, rubbing her hand down Sugar the horse's nose. She stepped back and looked down the valley and out towards the ocean. She sighed, a sigh she never tried to conceal. And from his angle, Gerry could see a sparkle in her eyes. And he, too, felt something behind his eyes.

But as Pa always said, 'leave the water to the wells.'

"Come on — it's time," said Gina as she turned and kissed Gerry, then hopped up into the tractor. Gerry dragged his feet, and any thoughts he decided to keep out of his head. It was a bendy, auld road to Shannon Airport after all. He turned the keys and started the ignition, and the auld tractor chugged, then it stopped. So, Gerry turned the ignition once more, and the tractor chugged again, only for a shorter time now. And then it stopped. And the third time Gerry went to turn the ignition, the tractor was dead. Well, it was an auld one after all.

"What's wrong?" asked Gina.

"It's auld, sometimes needs a boot," said Gerry, and he hopped down, played with the engine for a minute or two and gave a hefty kick to the tires. Then he resurfaced to try again. He banged his hands on the steering wheel. The tractor sat silent and still; it wasn't going anywhere.

"It's no use," he said. *Jaysus, what timing*, he thought.

"It's ok, don't worry. I can get a taxi," said Gina.

Gerry's eyebrows raised and he thought, *how would you get a taxi around here at noon on a Saturday?*

He looked back down the hill; his rickety bike was down at the house.

And even if he could make it into the village by foot, there would be no guarantee of getting a taxi either.

Ballyduffy wasn't an airport after all.

Gina, after a week of spending every moment with Gerry, was now able to read him well. She also knew there would be no taxi. So, as she did at the beach that day, her quick thinking came up with an idea, and she said to Gerry, "Sugar."

She must be joking, thought Gerry. But when he turned back around to say something, Gina was already out of the tractor and walking over to the horse.

"Jaysus," he whispered to himself.

He hopped out of the tractor, lifting out the suitcase with the tree wheels and carrying it over towards the gate. Gina had found a piece of rope, and she'd hopped over the fence and fastened the rope around Sugar's muzzle like reins. *And she knows what she's doing too,* thought Gerry.

She turned and laughed at the sheer madness of it all, and Gerry giggled too. Then she stopped when she looked down at the suitcase beside him.

"Oh! I forgot about that," said Gina.

Then she shook her head and finished fastening the ropes. Gerry opened the gate as Gina led the horse out, Sugar swishing his tail as he passed Gerry.

And didn't he take a large shite right there, in front of Gerry.

"It's the only way," said Gina, who smiled and clutched her nose for a second.

Gerry, being a farmer all his life, didn't know a bad smell from another as he'd been brought up with the smell of cowshite and sheep shite and slurry all around him. But he looked down at Sugar's fetlocks that used to be pristine white as if freshly laundered. "Would you look at that?" said Gerry, and he chuckled to himself. Sure enough, the white socks were now dark brown.

"Now, what about the suitcase?" said Gina.

"Well, we're not going to get that on a horse," said Gerry.

"I know that. Have you any other bags, and I can put in only what I really need to take?"

Gerry smiled. When he'd first seen that suitcase, he knew it would be trouble.

Now Gina had seen the light. And then he remembered.

"I do," said Gerry. "Let's tie up this fellow first."

So, Gina tied Sugar up outside the tea shop, and Gerry carried in that feckin' suitcase, and went to the top room and brought out the navy and blue Ballyduffy football bag.

He gave it to Gina.

"It will have to do," she said with a smile. "It will match the sweater you gave me last year."

Gerry chuckled to himself when he realized a sweater was a jumper. And he was amazed by how quickly she sorted out what she needed and didn't need, and then the Ballyduffy bag was zipped up, and Gerry slung it over his shoulder.

"Oh, I'll sort that suitcase out later," he whispered to himself as he closed the door.

As he walked over to Sugar, Gerry knew they had a bumpy ride ahead.

The road to Shannon was rough and full of potholes at the best of times, never mind travelling astride a large horse with no saddle. But before he got on, Gina used that magic brain of hers and said, "I have to sit on the front as you've got the bag."

"All right, so," said Gerry, and after Gina hopped up on the back of Sugar — who seemed very relaxed, as if used to people riding him all the time — Gerry jumped up and wrapped his hands around Gina. "We'll have to be quick," said Gerry. The moment he had finished the words, Gina said "Yaa," and the horse took off on the road to Shannon.

"Used to ride a bit when I was younger," said Gina, and Gerry knew that, because it showed.

And by God, Gerry thought, Sugar was the fastest horse he'd ever sat on in his life.

They ran out the bendy country roads, this horse faster than Gerry's auld tractor by a long way. The farmers out with their walking sticks would wave, and they'd never forget that summer of 1984 when an angel and a big fella passed by on the fastest horse ever seen.

And then, after a while, Gerry nearly fell off the side of the horse when those birds of the skies thundered not tirty metres above their heads. They had arrived at the airport.

"Are you ok? Did that plane scare you?" said Gina over her shoulder.

"I don't scare easily," said Gerry with a wry smile.

And Gina laughed, because Gerry was terrified. Oddly, the horse seemed calm as ever.

They pulled up to the front doors of Shannon Airport, and Gerry didn't notice the gaping mouths on all the comers and goers as he hopped off Sugar.

He held Gina's hand as she slipped down off the horse too, and she kissed him.

Now, it's time, thought Gerry when they stopped kissing and Gina stared into his eyes. He saw a glimmer, the seed of a tear, wiping it once it bloomed.

"Gina, I've been wanting to say something all —"

The sound of a whistle erupted in their ears. Then it sounded again, the shrill sending a shiver darting up Gerry's spine.

"Come on now. Out of here with the horse. This is an airport, one of Ireland's finest and you'll be holding up the flights," said the security man in a light green coat. He whistled again and pointed with the walkie-talkie at a sign which said *No Drop Offs - Passengers Only.*

"Sorry sir, all I need is two —" protested Gerry.

The security man whistled again.

"It's only a horse. Maybe it's flying with me," said Gina.

The man whistled again, and his face went redder.

"When pigs fly, so can your horse. I need you to go or I'm calling the Guards right now. Three, two…"

"Ok. Ok. I'll write to you, Gerry, ok?" said Gina, taking the bag from Gerry. "And make sure Sugar gets some water."

She kissed him again. Then, as she was going through the revolving doors of the airport, she turned and shouted out, "I love you, Gerry McCarthy."

And like that, she was gone inside the airport.

The whistle blew again in Gerry's ears.

"Now I'm serious. If you're not gone in three, two —"

"Ok, I'm gone. Good luck to you now."

You feckin' eejit.

That was the moment where Gerry's heart split. Not all the way, but halfway. Half of his heart had been filled with this unfathomable bliss that he'd never known could exist, then the other half was in tatters. She loved him, but did she know how he felt?

No matter how many times he'd thought it, felt it, his words remained down the well. He hadn't told her, and who knew when he would see her again?

Then, as he looked back at the doors of the airport and the security man who was speaking into his walkie-talkie, he remembered why Jimmy had told him to lie in bed that morning before he'd left for America, and maybe Jimmy had been right all along. The wells behind his eyes filled up before Sugar let out a large *nay* right beside Gerry's ear.

The piercing shriek of the whistle blew in his other.

"That feckin eejit," Gerry whispered in the direction of the security guard. Then he said, "All right Sugar, let's find you some water."

He hopped on and they walked away from the airport and along the roads.

It had been a long journey for the horse and sure, there'd be nothing left but silence back in Gerry's house. And for the first time, he thought that there wouldn't be just silence in the house, there'd be an emptiness. A similar, but very different emptiness to when Pa and Jimmy had each left in their own ways. And none of the three ways felt good, but for some reason, Gerry felt very heavy on the horse, and so, they took their time.

The beeps from motorists soon returned, but Gerry didn't mind.

He stopped into Slieve, a town just over the border in Limerick on the hunt for some water.

Slieve was just like Ballyduffy, a sleepy town where the streets were empty. However, as they walked through, Gerry spotted what he'd been looking for. There was a fountain in the centre, glorious water rising from the spout before falling again. Gerry tugged the reins, and he tied the horse up in the shade so he could have a break from the sun. Gerry sat there on the side of the fountain for a few minutes and watched Sugar drink until he was full.

Just before Gerry went to untie Sugar to leave, he heard a voice. "Hold on there, big fella."

Gerry turned, and wasn't there two policemen, or Guards as they were called in that part of the world, in their navy uniforms walking towards him.

Sugar lifted his tail and made a shite right there as if on cue.

Did that feckin eejit call them on the walkie talkie?

"How's it going?" he said.

"Not bad sir. Just want to have a look at this horse of yours here," said one of the Guards, who had bright red hair under his navy hat, and his hand on his nose.

"Not a bother; fine-looking animal so no wonder you want a look at him. Are ye horsemen yourselves?" said Gerry as he held onto the rope that had tied Sugar up.

"Aren't we all in these parts?" the Guard said with a chuckle. Then he said, "A famous horse was stolen a while back in Kildare, and we've been told to keep an eye out. He's worth a few million so as you can imagine, he's quite high on our list of things to do."

Jaysus, a few million! And who would steal a horse? thought Gerry, and sure Kildare was outside Dublin, a long way from here. Gerry watched as the Guards looked at Sugar's face, and then his body, then finally down at his legs and then his fetlocks, which happened to still be covered in dried-in cowshite, which wouldn't you know, was the exact same colour as the rest of Sugar's body. Except for the white blaze on his face, obviously.

One Guard looked at the other and shook his head.

"Carry on sir, this isn't the horse," said the Guard.

As the Guards walked by, wafting their hands under their noses, Gerry asked, "What's the name of the horse you're looking for? Just in case I see it," said Gerry. Because he was sure that whoever its owner was would like to have their horse back.

"Its name is Shergar," said one of the Guards.

"Ah, this boy's called Sugar," said Gerry as he patted Sugar's neck.

"Odd name for a horse," said the Guard, who raised his eyebrows and then shrugged. "Good luck to you now."

Gerry watched as the two Guards continued their walk down through the town. Then Gerry hopped on top of Sugar, and as he pulled the reins to head on his way, he looked back at the shite that Sugar had left behind, feeling sorry for the man who would have to clean it up.

Sugar and Gerry passed the border and into Kerry, then climbed the far side of Drumbarron Hill, the Limerick side. As they walked, a pheasant, a type of wild bird in these parts, with its colourful brown and white feathers, flew not ten yards over Gerry's head. And Gerry's heart dropped. Thoughts of Gina also up in the sky – soon, anyway – filling his mind, and he looked up to see if he could see those other birds, the vast metal ones.

He patted the horse's neck. "What a woman she is, Sugar," he whispered.

As he came over the peak of the hill, and could see the Atlantic far off in the distance, he thought of America, and of how the two closest people in his life both lived across that ocean.

Gerry sighed, feeling something in the back of his throat.

But then he spotted something up ahead. Right outside his tea shop was a white van, and behind the white van, one of those silver trailers that were used to transport large animals.

When Gerry got closer, he gave a wave to the two men standing outside his tea shop. There was a man in a Liverpool jersey, and another in a black jumper, and as Gerry got closer, the third man, with the poor moustache and a red Manchester United jersey, came around the corner from the field. Gerry noticed the men were all holding large rifles that looked just like the one Pa had.

He remembered it was still under his bed.

"How's it going now?" said Gerry as he pulled up and hopped off the horse.

"Where have you been?" said the man with the United jersey.

And Gerry walked over with Sugar and gave the man the rope that was leading the horse.

He pointed at the red tractor behind the men.

"Sorry about that, lads, the auld tractor gave up on me there this morning, and I had a special parcel to drop off. Have ye been waiting long?" said Gerry.

The men looked at each other, and their shoulders slid down their necks a little, and they began to laugh. What Gerry didn't realize was that these men knew all about delivering special parcels. And the man in the United jersey put his gun down to one side and said, "Not too long now. Cheers for looking after him. He's a special parcel himself."

And he nodded to one of the other men to take Sugar and lead him into the back of the trailer.

Gerry watched Sugar go and wished him well for the memory that he had been the one who'd managed to get Gina O'Dea safely to Shannon Airport.

Then he turned to the fella in the United jersey and pointed at his gun,

"Up shooting pheasants, was it? Seen one a while back there. They're some animals too."

The man with the United jersey raised his brows before looking down at his gun. Then he smiled and said, "You're right, big fella. They are. Now good luck to you."

And he held out his hand and looked down at Gerry's own as he shook it, and then hopped in the car and that was the last Gerry would see of Sugar.

That evening, Gerry would have to walk down Drumbarron Hill, and what was he trying to balance behind him but the suitcase with the tree wheels.

And Gerry used words and curses that I'll not use here, the whole way down, but he didn't leave the tree-wheeled case behind. This was Gina's, and he knew she'd be back for it someday.

And once in the house, Gerry put that suitcase up in Pa's bedroom, which he now supposed was his own, placing the suitcase in the wardrobe.

But it was a feckin' battle to fit it in, and when it was in, didn't he close the wardrobe doors, because he couldn't be staring at that or he wouldn't get any sleep.

Gerry sat down at the table with a plate of potatoes and some sausages. It had been one hell of a day and he was famished. He wondered if Gina had got another apple in the airport before her flight as he couldn't imagine you were allowed to eat on an airplane. And for the first time in a week, his heart had calmed. Then, as he looked at the chair at the other side of the table, he remembered he still had Jimmy's letter to open. So that night, as he rocked in his rocking chair in front of the fire with thoughts of Gina swirling around his mind, Gerry opened Jimmy's letter.

Mar '84

Well, Gerry,

How's it going? Not so bad here at all. Let me tell you, that winter we had was the worst in one hundred years they say; minus forty it was some days, Gerry, and not a hot water bottle in the house that could be filled fast enough. But although it's still chilly, the worst is over and spring is on its way, and St Patrick's Day's around the corner, and they say they have a right auld party for it here.

New York. Where do I begin, Gerry? I've never seen or dreamt of a place like it. There's so much to do, so much to see, and the women, Gerry! Jaysus, they're some of the most beautiful I've ever seen. And they seem to have a bit of a fascination with the Irish accent, which does me no harm at all, but more about that later. And by God is it a non-stop kind of place. A real 24/7 city, and the trains that run underground that take you all over the place, go all night long. I tell you Gerry, McDonald's isn't even fast enough for this place.

I'm working at this bank and by God, it's fast there too. I've the shirts and the ties on every day and it's grand stuff, and sure I'm making a bit of money along the way, thank God. But they always take me out for golf, Gerry. And I know we used to swing those auld clubs of Uncle Brendan's the odd time in the fields, but over here, if you turned up in wellies, they'd feckin' shoot you. We used to get dressed up for weddings and funerals, Gerry. I'll have to add golf to that list. At least I can have a pint while I play, I suppose.

Anyways, I moved out of Thomas Murtagh's nephew's place and I'm now living with a woman, would you believe, and oh, Gerry, is she beautiful. She's Mexican American, and she has beautiful, tanned skin and dark eyes, and truth be told I'm falling for her. But I suppose it's early days. She has to get used to me.

And how is everything in Ballyduffy? What is this I hear about a tea shop? I don't know whether to believe it or not, but if you tell me it's true, then I'll know it's true, and by God I'd be proud of you. I'm proud of you regardless, mind you.

Apologies for the lack of letters, Gerry, but this new job is keeping me more than busy. I hope to be better with them.

All the best,

Jimmy.

James McCarthy,
150 E 78th St,
New York, NY 10075,
USA

Gerry put the letter down on the table and the wood crackled in the fire. *He didn't mention the Kerry team,* Gerry thought. And Gerry didn't know if that was a bad omen or a good one.

"I suppose I'm on my own now," he whispered.

Then he thought of the Kerry team, and an image of Gina popped into his mind, and the thought of her made him feel warm inside, and the fire made him feel warm outside, and then he looked down at the letter again and said to himself, "I think this Kerry team will win three championships in a row."

CHAPTER

11

A ug '84

Dear Gina,

I hope your plane landed safely in the President's airport and that you were able to get an apple along the way.

The tea shop is going well. I upped my order of milk with the local shop to twenty cartons a week from ten. I haven't had any spoil yet so you could say that's a good thing. Aunt Cara and Uncle Brendan asked about you. So did Pat – he wishes you well.

I took your suitcase and put it in the cupboard so it will be here for when you come back.

Sugar's left us, but we'll always have that trip together. Funnily enough, I ran into the Guards in Slieve (another town just across the border in Limerick) and they thought Sugar might've been this other horse that was worth a couple of million pounds. I laughed quietly to myself, though I suppose the two names could be mixed up easily enough!

Anyways, for a moment, I thought about that feckin' eejit with the whistle and how he interrupted what I was wanting to say to you. I wanted to say that I feel the same as you do. Or I hope you do.

Hope you meant it, I mean, because I know you said it before you ran off inside!

I wanted to say that I love you too, Gina.

Gerry scrunched up the page and threw it in the fire. He walked into the kitchen and poured more tea, then rested with his knuckles pressed against the countertop. His sigh swirled amongst the silent air of the house, together with his one regret. He still hadn't told Gina how he felt. He'd wanted it to be perfect, that one moment that they would remember forever.

He sighed again when he heard the crack of the fire. There was more warmth in there than there was in the words of his letter.

"I wanted to say that I love you," he whispered and then cringed.

It didn't sound anything like he wanted it to or had imagined it to. It wasn't *perfect.* He thought of Jimmy over there, across the pond like Gina. Would they ever come back to Ballyduffy? He shook his head. He didn't like thoughts like this.

He grabbed another page and wrote a new letter, saving the last few lines for when he saw her again, and hoped by then he'd have some better words to say to her. I'm no Jimmy, that's for sure, he thought as he read the rewritten letter once more and folded it up, ready for posting.

-----------•✳•-----------

Thoughts of Gina filled his mind that winter, and Gerry waited for word of when she would come again. He found himself sleeping on the narrow side of the double bed – the side he slept on when Gina had lain beside him. And some nights, he didn't wrap the covers around him, just like those times when Gina pulled them across to her side.

Christmas passed with no sign of Gina, and it was late January when her letter arrived.

October 6, 1984

My new role in the bank has been a lot of work, Gerry, more than I could ever have imagined! But we have fun too. We do a lot of client dinners in the nicest of restaurants, and I am going to a conference in Miami in the last week of January, which means I get to escape the winter for a little. . .

I'm sorry, but with the new job, I can't get the vacation time at Christmas like we had planned. I am surprised I can get Thanksgiving off this year! But I promise we will find the time soon. How is . . .

Gerry looked at the final four words of the letter – I love you, Gerry. And he smiled. Yet he felt a heaviness inside his stomach. He hoped they'd find the time soon, but he thought of his tea shop, and understood that when starting a new job, there'd be a mountain of pressures and whatnot to get things up to scratch before it became second nature. He looked at the calendar – January 28th – and was happy for Gina. She was somewhere warm, even if it wasn't inside his arms.

When spring of 1985 arrived, Gerry was awful pleased to get some good news and a break from waiting for another letter. Rumours had swelled around the town about the return of a very special person in the history of Ballyduffy's football team.

Joe McGettigan was a man from outside Dingle, a regular-sized Kerry man, and a regular-sized sixty-year-old too, although perhaps he was a bit fitter than most men his age, and still had jet-black hair, with not a strand of grey to be seen. Simply put, Joe was the greatest manager in the history of Ballyduffy football club. It was near twenty-five years ago now since Ballyduffy had won a championship and Joe had been the manager at that time. In fact, that team won three championships in five years, and Joe had been at the helm for each of them.

There was an air of excitement around Ballyduffy those January and February months before it was confirmed. Gerry, now tirty and not a young lad anymore, thought about the new generation with Michael O'Brien and Seanie Egan, two young forwards who could get plenty of goals, and he knew this could be a very special year.

So, Gerry arrived down for training that night at the beginning of March.

Winter had hung around a little longer than usual, and there was a nip in the air beneath the floodlights that evening, the kind of night you could see your breath moving in and out of your lungs. The rest of the team were standing around in their shorts and their navy and blue Ballyduffy training jumpers, and Gerry was there in his t-shirt, seeing as his jumper was in America with Gina. But Gerry didn't mind; he was glad she had something other than Miami to keep her warm. And anyways, this was the first night that he would get to meet Joe McGettigan.

And he was very much looking forward to that.

Since McGettigan had been confirmed as manager, Gerry and John McHugh and a few of the younger lads had heard many stories about him from the older fellas. Pat Storey had said one night, "He could motivate a dead man to get out of his coffin, Gerry."

This was the level of reverence the town held for Joe. Gerry had heard that although Joe wasn't a master tactician, nor had he the best drills in training, Joe could get men to walk through walls for him. In Ballyduffy's eyes, Joe was Moses reincarnated in the way that he could split the water of a man's mind, hiding his worries on one side, and his negative thoughts on the other.

In that way, you could walk right through them.

And that first night at training underneath the floodlights, didn't Joe walk out from the dark side of McHugh field, and over towards where Gerry and the lads were standing. He was wearing a white tracksuit top and matching bottom, and didn't he have his own stone tablet brought down from the mountain itself: a white clipboard. But first, Joe arrived, and the lads fell silent, Gerry watching as Joe looked around at them all in their blue and navy jumpers.

Then he stopped when he saw Gerry, pointing. "*That*, lads, is what we want, right there," said Joe in the kind of voice Gerry imagined a general would have before a war.

And Gerry tried to clench his jaw, but his teeth were clattering together with the cold.

"What's your name, big fella?" said Joe.

"Ger . . .Ger . . . Gerry McCarthy."

"Well, Gerry. You're our new captain for this year," said Joe, and then he turned to the rest of the group. And Gerry felt his eyebrows rise, and he started hopping from foot to foot to get the blood flowing around his body before the shivers came over him.

"Look at your captain, lads," said Joe, looking around the circle at the others and pointing at Gerry, "Already chomping at the bit, ready to go, and *that's* what I want from the rest of ye."

And he was right, Gerry thought, he was ready to go inside for a cup of tea at any point now.

"Now go on and do tirty laps to get warmed up," said Joe.

And Gerry took off at the front around the field as he needed warming up more than anyone else. Then Joe shouted across the pitch, "Look at your captain, lads, leading by example. He's like feckin' Shergar the horse, he's that quick."

Gerry kept running because he was still colder than the others, and he had never met Shergar, but still knew for certain he wasn't as fast as Sugar the horse.

Once the tirty laps were done, which was a lot more than Gerry or any of the others had ever done for a warmup before, Joe turned and said, "Now ye're warmed up, I want ye to do tirty laps more. But I want them done at twice the pace of the first round."

Gerry and the others were mightily warmed up by the time they'd these done, and they came into a huddle in the middle of the field where Joe McGettigan stood amongst them, asking them all their names before laying out what he wanted from the team for the year ahead.

"You see this, lads," said Joe, holding up his white clipboard with the black markings on it. "This is our stone tablet."

And Gerry blinked because he knew it wasn't stone, but listened anyway.

And Joe continued amongst the silence of the group. "I tell ye boys, ye listen to me; ye trust in me, and I tell ye, we will make it to the Promised Land together."

Gerry blinked again, looking at this man standing underneath the floodlights of McHugh Park in his white tracksuit, and he thought to himself, *he's feckin' Moses reincarnated.*

"And Gerry," said Joe, pointing at Gerry who was just starting to get cold again and had begun to hop from foot to foot, "You are going to be our roamer. You're like a feckin' horse, and look at him lads, he's trotting again, and *that* is what I want out of all of ye. Now a round of applause for your new captain."

And the lads clapped, and Gerry trotted to keep himself warm, also feeling a flutter in his stomach at the fact he was now captain for the first time.

Then Joe said, "Now Gerry, lead them off for another tirty laps."

And for the rest of March, and the beginning of a bitter and unusually cold April, Gerry led the team around McHugh Park in shorts and t-shirt, with the sound of Joe McGettigan's encouragement echoing in his ears.

By now, Gerry had written to Gina, and to Jimmy, to tell them the news that for the first time in his life, he'd been made the captain of the Ballyduffy team. And he told them about Joe as well, and the way the man had a spirit about him that Gerry had only ever felt from a couple of other people who'd visited his tea shop. The tea shop was fine too, of course, and he worked away during the day, even deciding to run up that bastard of a hill a couple of times a week to work. And he thought, I'm going to be in the best shape of my life when Gina comes back again.

———•✱•———

One day in the tea shop, Pat Storey was telling Gerry another of his fabled tales from the high stools. "I was in McMurphy's some time back and was chatting to Paul Feeney. You might know his daughter, Mary? She'd be close to your age, I'd say Gerry. Anyways, Paul and me, well, we'd gone through the Guinness and moved on to the whiskey when he starts to tell me about the Grand Ewe Prize of '71. Do you remember that one, Gerry? Your pa always entered a ewe in it?"

Gerry nodded and thought back to his father and the Tralee Agricultural Fair; it had been like Christmas in summer to his pa, and he and the boys had gone every year.

He remembered seventy-one as well, the most controversial of competitions.

"So that ewe of Toe O'Brien's won it that year. And Jaysus, Gerry, the accusations that were thrown about that Toe had drugged his sheep and that's why it stood there so majestically. I was at it myself and that ewe of his was a picture."

"I'm sure he has a picture in the bar of himself and the ewe; I think I remember seeing it somewhere," said Gerry.

"Exactly, it's behind the bar for God's sake. The cash prize was two hundred pounds, and a wealthy man likes to show off his wealth, Gerry. Now, Gerry, you'll never guess what Paul told me. I always knew there was some truth to the stories, but I never thought it was this one.

"So, you know the rules, Gerry – only Irish sheep allowed. And no drugs, but, sure, that should be a given. Anyways, Paul told me he was standing beside the winning pen after they had handed out the prize, when the summer rain started like it does in these parts. And Toe and that cousin of his looked very flustered as they raced the ewe out of the pen and into a trailer.

"When Paul looked down, there was a trail of white on the grass like the lines of a football pitch leading from the pen into the back of that trailer."

Gerry nodded. He knew the lines of a football field all right. But this was highly unusual in the venue of the Tralee Agricultural Fair.

Pat continued, "So he followed the lines and climbed up into the back of the trailer and peered in at the sheep with the crown on its head. Shocking it was."

"What was it, Pat?"

"White paint was running off the sheep's coat. He cornered Toe's cousin about it a couple of years later. Toe had bought the sheep from the North of Spain, and it was too tan. He would've been found out! So, they covered it in a lick of paint and bolted before the rains came."

Jaysus!

Gerry shook his head and thought of Toe O'Brien. He wondered how many other stories of wheeling and dealing there were, containing Toe. Then he thought of Pat and the tales from the high stool and a strange image came into his mind. Gerry pictured himself a few years older, sitting on the high stool beside Pat and Paul Feeney, with empty pint glasses and shots of whiskey in front. He shook his head. He missed Gina and had to tell her he loved her.

———— • ✳ • ————

The rest of the summer would pass with win after win for the Ballyduffy football team, and in one stretch of games, Gerry went on a hot streak and scored five goals in five games from all his roaming. Gerry would send more letters than he ever had to Gina and Jimmy, keeping them updated with how Ballyduffy were getting on, knowing they'd both be very interested. And although Gerry hadn't heard from Jimmy in a while, Gina had written.

August 23, 1985

I may be crazy, Gerry, but work's letting me take a day's vacation and so I'm coming to Ireland for Thanksgiving weekend, Gerry. I really am crazy! I can't wait to see you. . .

And, despite not having a clue what thanks she was giving and for what exactly, Gerry felt warm inside at knowing that he would soon get to see Gina again. And a few days later, another letter arrived, and Gina, by now knowing Gerry very well, wrote the exact dates that she'd be arriving.

Gerry was very much looking forward to that late November weekend, even though he wished it would be for a little longer. In her letter, Gina had even explained a little more about Thanksgiving, and how they typically would have a turkey for dinner, and it sounded to Gerry a bit like Christmas Day only a month earlier, and he would ponder on that a little longer.

The tea shop was going great too. It turned out the pictures on the postcard were a big draw, and they'd been published in a few other magazines. Gerry was happy for that man with the camera all those years ago, and he wondered had he ever fulfilled his goal and become the biggest publishing house in Europe? The tea shop had more customers than ever, and over the years, Gerry had gathered up quite a bit of money from his little business.

And Gerry, being the smart man that he was, had opened a Credit Union account to save this money for a rainy day. Despite knowing that his silver tin in the top of his dresser still had all the letters, and the money from His Holiness's winnings, and the one hundred pounds from minding Sugar, Gerry knew that it rained quite a bit in this part of the world.

It didn't hurt to keep two pots of savings for rainy days.

In late summer, Ballyduffy would end up in the semi-final of the Championship, unbeaten, and against their archrivals, Carrickbay. The game was attended by a hell of a crowd of four hundred people, and Gerry had never played in front of so many spectators before.

Ballyduffy won by one point, and even though Gerry didn't score any goals, neither did Johnny Murtagh, and that was what mattered. And when Joe McGettigan came up to shake Gerry's hand after the game, didn't he whisper to Gerry, "Jaysus, Gerry, you went through some work today! You're the donkey we're all riding into the Promised Land."

Gerry stood there, fully believing he was going to play in a championship final, and that Ballyduffy were going to win.

A couple of weeks later, however, Gerry and the Ballyduffy team would hear that their opponents in the Kerry Championship final would be Lismore, a team two hours south of Tralee and more worryingly for Gerry, they had 'the Boomer' on their side.

The Boomer, whose real name was Shay, didn't only play for Lismore, but he was also a star on the Kerry team. A once-in-a-generation footballer, and he'd won all those All-Ireland Championships for Kerry. That year,

Boomer would score a goal in the final against Dublin, for Kerry to win back-to-back titles once again.

And because the Kerry team liked to celebrate with a few pints and their trips to Tramore racecourse like everyone else, the Ballyduffy-Lismore final had been pushed back three weeks until the end of October so the Kerry team could have their fair share of pints. Gerry completely agreed; it was only fair, and he was as big a fan of the Kerry team as anyone else.

However, those first few weeks in November were very sad times in both Ballyduffy and Lismore. Father Michael — the parish priest of Ballyduffy — had woken up dead the morning before the rearranged game. And in these parts, respect must be paid to the parish priest who had done all the baptisms, confirmations, weddings, and funerals of the town, and so the game had been delayed and pushed back to the middle of November. Then, in O'Brien's, the Friday night before the final on Sunday, Gerry heard that the parish priest of Lismore, Father Patrick, had also died of a heart attack, and in those parts, respect must also be paid in the same way.

When Gerry heard the new date for the rearranged final was now Sunday, the twenty-fifth of November, he put his pint down on the counter of the bar and ran out into the road as fast as he could, past that yapping bastard of a sheepdog, and home to his house. And when he turned the lights on and looked at the calendar, he thought, *Jaysus, that's the day after Gina arrives.*

She'd be there to watch him play.

————— • ✸ • —————

The week before Gina would come for Thanksgiving and for the football final, Gerry had never been as anxious. Sleep had been hard to come by lately, and he had been having bad dreams about the Boomer from Lismore. But that wasn't the main cause of his worries.

He had decided that seeing as Thanksgiving was a special time of year for Gina, and seeing as this could be the year Gerry could emulate his father as captain of the Ballyduffy football team, was it not the most perfect opportunity to tell Gina that he loved her with his whole heart and that he wanted to figure out a way to be together forever.

So, Gerry knew this Thanksgiving — whatever it was — had to go as smoothly as it could. However, he'd asked in the shop in Ballyduffy each week, and they still had no turkey.

"They'll not be ready until Christmas, Gerry," said Ger Sheehy, the shopkeeper.

Gerry made good use of his new tractor that week because he drove to Tralee, and he drove to Dingle, and he even drove to Carrickbay, all in a bid to find a turkey.

And each shop he went into said the same thing, "No turkeys until Christmas, Gerry."

He was out of luck, but not out of hope. So, when Aunt Cara said one day, "It'll be grand, Gerry. These things always sort themselves out," he finally got a bit of sleep.

Aunt Cara's superstitions were always right on the money.

---------••✱••---------

Gina flew into Shannon Airport that Saturday in November, and even though her flight didn't land until after four, Gerry wanted to get there early. And when he arrived at the airport at noon, he realized it was because the new tractor he'd bought from John McHugh Sr was a lot faster than that auld one. So, Gerry parked up the tractor and walked inside those doors of Shannon airport for the first time. He took a seat by the windows, watching those thundering birds of the sky coming and going, and he waited.

The previous night, he had been down at Aunt Cara and Uncle Brendan's, and Uncle Brendan had told Gerry a little more about Thanksgiving.

Brendan had been to America when he was much younger.

"You've no turkey, Gerry? It's pretty important to have a turkey on Thanksgiving," said Uncle Brendan.

"They've none 'til Christmas. I'm not sure what I'll do," said Gerry.

"Ah, sure as your aunt says, these things always sort themselves out. And just in case it doesn't, you may want to bring some flowers to the airport to meet Gina!"

So, Gerry sat in the airport with his white lilies, which were the only flower Ma had ever had inside the house, and his leg bounced and his foot tapped as he waited for her plane to arrive. It'd been 499 days since he'd seen Gina, and this was going to be the biggest weekend of his life.

"Gerry!" shouted Gina.

She ran and jumped, wrapping her legs around him.

Gerry's knees went weak at the feel of her lips on his, but he didn't want to drop her as she was as precious to him as the flowers in his hands.

"I love them," said Gina. "Thanks for coming to get me."

"You're very welcome," said Gerry, and he had the biggest smile on his face until he saw the big silver suitcase Gina was pulling behind her – with a peculiar set of wheels – which matched the sparkly silver earrings he had never seen her wear before.

"I don't know what happened to that case, Gerry. It didn't have this scratch when I put it on the plane," said Gina, and she stared down at the big scuff that was on the side.

But that wasn't what Gerry was worried about; that was just optics. The suitcase had only two wheels where it surely should've had four. Gerry dragged and pulled that lump of a suitcase through the airport and out to the parking lot.

"I like the new tractor," said Gina, and she hopped in as if she'd grown up with tractors all her life, and her face glowed with the biggest smile. Gerry placed the big suitcase in the tractor with them, and they headed for Ballyduffy. The sky was blue when they came over the Limerick side of Ballyduffy, and Gina whispered, "I nearly forgot this view, Gerry. It's crazy how time flies and things change, yet some things stay the same. I've missed you."

Gerry lifted his eyes off the road for a second. Today, he really appreciated that view of the green fields and the valley and the Atlantic Ocean, and he really appreciated who he could share it with. "I've missed you too. It's great to see you," said Gerry. *I want to see you every day for the rest of my life*, he thought. And he kept those words close for when the time was right.

After they got home and they had settled in, having a cup of tea, of course, and after they'd done whatever else two lovers would do who hadn't seen each other in a long time, Gerry made Gina dinner: spaghetti Bolognese. Although Gina smiled and laughed as she ate it, Gerry knew it was nowhere near as nice as the one she had made before, but he felt she was grateful for his efforts. And that night, the night before the biggest game of his life, Gerry used up some of his roaming energy because he was only a man after all, and not a saint.

And he hoped he'd taken Gina to the Promised Land.

CHAPTER

12

The next morning, Gerry sat up in the bed sweating, Gina's naked body lying beside him. But he wasn't sweating for any of the reasons ye filthy animals are thinking about. No, he'd had another bad dream, the worst one yet, a nightmare about the Boomer. Gina continued sleeping beside him, and he recalled something called airplane-lag from her last visit, and that she would probably need to sleep in for a bit longer. As Gerry watched her sleeping and the smell of her body filled his senses, he calmed a little, replaying the bad dream he was trying to quell.

The scores were tied with only one minute to go, and Boomer had gotten the ball and was running from the halfway line towards Ballyduffy's goal. Boomer was going faster than anyone else because he was a flying machine, and no one could stop him apart from Gerry.

But when Gerry tried to make his legs go faster to try and catch Boomer, Joe McGettigan started running alongside him in his white tracksuit, and he was shouting at Gerry and pointing at his clipboard, saying, "I know what you did last night, Gerry. Wasted your energy, Gerry!"

In the dream, Joe was repeating this over and over again, and all the while, the Boomer was getting closer and closer to the Ballyduffy goal, and Gerry's legs were getting heavier and heavier, falling further behind.

And then five turkeys started flying around Gerry's head, and he had

CHAPTER TWELVE

woken up in a sweat.

He lay there for a moment longer before kissing Gina on the head. Then he got out and pulled on his trousers and his jumper. In the panic of the five turkeys flying around his head, it had given him an idea. Gerry quietly knelt on the floor, and looked under the bed.

He brought out Pa's auld gun. And he looked for bullets, but could only find one under there, and he sighed; *I'm under pressure now.*

Gerry snuck out and taking one last look back at Gina, he closed the door gently behind him.

He put on his coat and his wellies at the door, slinging the gun over his shoulder before he looked at his blue tractor. Then he thought of Gina in the bed, still sleeping.

He knew his new tractor was fast, but it was also loud, and so he looked at his auld bike, and he hopped on and began cycling up the Drumbarron Hill. Now, it was late November and winter had started early in Ireland that year, and Gerry's hands were freezing as he cycled.

Regardless, he pushed through it, knowing he hadn't much time.

And when he got tree-quarters of the way up, much farther than he'd ever gotten before, he pushed the bike the rest of the way with his cold hands and the gun still over his shoulder.

Once at the tea shop, Gerry hopped onto the bike again and he cycled up over the peak of Drumbarron Hill and a little down the far side towards Limerick, where he stopped and put his bike in at the side of the road. It was still early on a Sunday morning, not a sound to be heard except for the wind in Gerry's ears. He hopped over a green gate into one of the empty fields.

It looked as if it went on forever.

Now, in that dream that Gerry had, with the Boomer and the turkeys, one of those turkeys didn't look like the others. It wasn't as plump as the others, nor as feathery, and Gerry had remembered that he had seen one of those skinny looking birds up this hill a couple of years back. And, although this wasn't his usual way of doing things, he thought that desperate times were allowed to call for desperate measures, because today was Thanksgiving and he still had no turkey to cook for his beloved Gina who'd come all this way to visit him.

Gerry walked around that field — which he realized were a few fields connected and split by bushes — with just the one bullet in his gun, knowing he only had a single shot.

124

Up ahead, emerging from the undergrowth, he spotted what he was looking for.

A pheasant had come waddling out, and Gerry had to move fast. He ran forward and put the gun up and the aim to his eye, and he had the bird in his sight! And he went to pull the trigger. Nothing happened. His fingers wouldn't move — they were too cold.

Jaysus, of all the feckin' times!

He quickly tried again but still his hands were too frozen, and the pheasant could fly off at any time. So, he put the gun down, and rubbed his hands and blew into them.

And whilst he stood and watched the pheasant, he blinked. Its plumage seemed to have lost its brown colour and was turning a little grey. And it walked in circles repeatedly. And then it walked towards the bushes but seemed to meander into a tree stump and fall backwards. As the pheasant stood back up again, Gerry didn't know what to think. Was it drunk?

"Its wings are broken?" he whispered to himself, reaching a more logical conclusion.

Then he heard a loud moo. Out of a gap in the bush ahead came a giant of a brown cow. Only Gerry was a farmer, and he knew by the look of this fella that it was no cow. He saw the raging red eyes of the bull as it started to charge towards him. Gerry dropped the gun and he sprinted. He only just made the gate and jumped right over the top of it as the bull thankfully stopped.

"Feck sake; what am I going to do now?" Gerry said.

He had dropped his gun, and had no turkey in his hands.

But at least now, my hands are warm again, he thought.

And after a while of waiting around so he could go and get his Pa's gun back, the bull got bored and walked off into another field.

"Gina!" Gerry whispered.

She'd be waking in the house soon and worrying as to why he wasn't there. He hopped over the gate and sprinted as quietly as he could back to where the gun lay.

The bull had trampled all over it on its way after Gerry.

Gerry lifted the rifle and once he had cleaned it, he looked ahead and couldn't believe his eyes. There was a pile of feathers. *Jaysus,* he thought. Quickly and quietly, unsure if that bull could come out again, he ran forward and found the pheasant lying dead in the grass, trampled by the bull. And

Gerry looked up at that clear blue sky and thanked Mother Nature.

She had been on his side today.

Gerry took the bullet out of his gun and put it in his pocket, and threw the gun back over his shoulder. He lifted the pheasant by its legs, and he ran out of the field and hopped on his bicycle, flying down Drumbarron Hill like he'd never flown down it before.

He went past his house with the blue tractor, and past the O'Neills' farmhouse where that sheepdog shot out in his usual manner and nearly knocked Gerry off the bike, and he went through the main street of Ballyduffy town, past O'Brien's and McMurphy's, and the butchers and the shop, until he pulled up at Aunt Cara and Uncle Brendan's house.

Gerry knocked once on the door, then he walked inside and said, "How's it going?"

"Well, Gerry, you're here early?" said Aunt Cara, who walked out from the kitchen holding a cup of tea. Then she saw what Gerry had in his hands. "That's a pheasant, Gerry."

"I know it is. But it will have to do," said Gerry.

Aunt Cara put the cup of tea down and nodded before coming over and lifting the pheasant off him. "We make do with what we have, Gerry, don't we?" she said. "But I tell you what, let's keep this between ourselves, why don't we?"

"Thank you," said Gerry.

"No bother, Gerry; I'll see you back here after the game, so?"

Gerry nodded and hopped on that bicycle again. And as he began to cycle, he felt a little bad inside because he knew that he was breaking a commandment over this holy Thanksgiving weekend. Then he shook his head and thought, *no one will know the difference between a pheasant and a turkey.* But now, when Gerry had one worry sorted, another popped into his mind. He wanted to get back to Gina before she woke up, aware that it could be daunting waking up in an unfamiliar place alone. And that Sunday morning in Ballyduffy town, wasn't John McHugh coming out of the butcher's after getting some sausages for his mother. And across the street, Joe McGettigan, wearing his famous white tracksuit, was in the grocery shop, getting oranges for the team for half time. Gerry came cycling through the town as fast as he could, and Joe McGettigan blinked when he saw Gerry fly past, and he shouted across to John McHugh,

"Look at your captain, John, he's in the feckin' tour de France; he's that fit and ready to go."

And Gerry was gone in the blink of an eye on that auld bike, and back to the house at the bottom of Drumbarron Hill. As he walked in the front door and took off his coat and his wellies, he headed for the top bedroom and opened the door gently. And on opening, Gina turned around and opened those bluest of eyes. And she said, "Morning love; what did I miss?"

And Gerry blinked, then he went over, kissing her head.

"Oh, a few things, but nothing too important."

"Are you excited for your game? Thanksgiving Irish football Gerry. It's like a fairy tale." She climbed out of bed and kissed him. "You'll do great and Ballyduffy will win. I can feel it."

Gerry's heart rushed inside his chest as those words echoed in his ears, and his foot began to tap. "I sure hope so," said Gerry. Of course, he hadn't told her about the Boomer.

The championship final had been scheduled for O'Se Park, the big stadium in Tralee. He sat in the tractor on the way along the coast road in his shorts and t-shirt with his wool hat on his head and Gina wrapped up beside him. She was wearing Gerry's Ballyduffy jumper underneath her beige coat to keep her warm. Gerry pictured Pa and Jimmy in that big stadium, roaring encouragement from the sidelines, and he knew he'd miss them today.

Then he heard Gina shout in his ear, "In Giants' Stadium, they've over a hundred thousand fans on Thanksgiving football day. The energy's incredible, Gerry. Wonder what this is like!"

Gerry nodded and smiled when he saw Tralee Park up ahead, and that great stand, where up to two thousand of the most passionate fans could fit, and he knew Gina would know all about energy today.

With seconds left in the game, Ballyduffy were winning by one point. But then the Boomer got the ball and began a run. This was surely the last play of the game, Gerry thought, and he took off after him as fast as he could. But the Boomer was a Kerry great, and he'd played for years at the highest level of football in Ireland, and he didn't just look as fit as a gazelle — he was as fast as one too. Gerry chased as Boomer closed on goal; if he scored, Ballyduffy would lose.

The stadium fell silent in Gerry's ears as the thrust of air in and out of his lungs was all that he could hear inside his head. Time seemed to slow as he tried to match the Boomer's strides. Then, from the stand, he heard Gina's screams of, "Go Gerry!"

He got a little closer to Boomer. The Boomer, less than twenty yards from goal now, brought his leg back as he prepared to shoot.

"The Promised Land, Gerry," came a roar from the sidelines, and as the Boomer connected with the ball, Gerry dived and stretched all his six feet and four inches, and he blocked that shot.

The final whistle blew, and Gerry looked up towards Drumbarron Hill far off in the distance as the cheers echoed around the stadium. He whispered to himself, "That one's for you, Pa."

As the six hundred or so Ballyduffy fans rushed onto the field, Gerry shook hands and felt pats on his back, then Gina pushed her way through the crowd to plant a kiss on his lips.

"I've never seen a game like it. Look around, Gerry. I've never seen people so passionate. It was like it was life and death out there. It's just so different. *So* different."

There was a strange look in Gina's smile, but before Gerry could think about it, he was grabbed around the neck. He turned to see Joe McGettigan pull his forehead down to meet his, Gerry seeing the intensity rushing through Joe's brown eyes not two inches from his face.

"Welcome Gerry, how does it feel?" said Joe amongst the cheers and celebrations all around.

"It's a little awkward on my neck, Joe," said Gerry.

"You're right. Sometimes, the place we find ourselves is a little awkward, Gerry. Do you feel you've found the Promised Land?"

Gerry nodded, feeling a lump in the back of his throat as the thoughts of Pa and Jimmy, and of his mother all those years ago, started circling through his brain.

He walked up the steps of the stand at Tralee Park and lifted the cup — the first man in twenty-five years from Ballyduffy to get his hands on that trophy — the raucous cheers from the fans filling him with all kinds of feelings inside. He had made it. But as he pulled the cup down from over his head, he glanced at Gina and saw that same strange look from earlier.

And her words echoed in his ears. "So different."

But another slap on the back and a shake of a hand brought him back into the moment for which Ballyduffy had been waiting a quarter of a century.

———————•✱•———————

After he left the changing room with the cup in his hands as it was customary for the captain to do, he heard a familiar voice call him back. "How's it going, Gerry?"

Pat Storey came around the corner in his hat and with his walking stick, and a Ballyduffy flag.

"Not so bad, Pat."

"Come here. I meant to ask you something earlier, but with all the celebrations I forgot all about it," said Pat.

"Go on Pat," said Gerry.

"Did I see you cycling through the town earlier this morning with a pheasant hanging over the handlebars?"

Jaysus, Gerry thought. He glanced up at Gina who was just out of earshot in his tractor, and she waved down at both Pat and Gerry with a wide and radiant smile.

"Pat, would you like to come for a Thanksgiving?" said Gerry, quietly.

Pat's eyebrows raised, then he looked back up at Gina on the tractor and gave her a wave.

"Ah, I see. But you'd need a turkey for that, Gerry?" Then Pat took his hat off his head and shook it out before putting it back on again, then said, "But I suppose they're all big birds at the end of the day, Gerry."

Pat winked at Gerry and walked towards the blue tractor, and once again, Gerry had three in the tractor – four if he included the championship cup that somehow squeezed in.

———————•✱•———————

"How's it going now?" said Gerry as he walked in the door of Aunt Cara's house at the bottom of the town. He sniffed the air.

"It smells a bit like chicken, Gerry. Which is no bad thing," said Pat Storey, who walked in the door behind him together with Gina.

"I suppose turkey does smell like chicken, Pat," said Gina.

Gerry and Pat looked at each other, then Aunt Cara popped her head out from the kitchen and raced down the hall with her arms open, before giving Gina a hug.

"Welcome, Gina. Welcome, everyone; and Pat, nice to see you — plenty to go around. Come here, Gerry," said Aunt Cara, who hugged him. "I hear you stopped the Boomer right at the end. Uncle Brendan said it was as good a block as he had ever seen. Unfortunately, his brother, Michael, had a heart attack in the stand as the whistle went, so Brendan's on the way to the hospital with him."

"Jaysus, is he all right?" said Gerry.

"He'll probably die. But sure, he lived a good life and he said at the end that it was as good a day as any to go out, and he never thought he'd see Ballyduffy win a championship again," said Aunt Cara, turning and leading the others through to the dining table. "So, we've you to thank."

Gina had a horrified look.

"Michael must be eighty-nine now, Cara?" asked Pat as he walked into the kitchen and took a seat at the table. "Mighty smell you have here."

"Eighty-eight Pat and thank you. The big bird should be ready shortly. Now Gina, come on in! Would you like a drink?"

Aunt Cara ushered Gerry to help pour drinks for everyone before making room in the middle of the table for the championship cup.

"Where will we put the pheas — the big bird — if the trophy's there?" asked Gerry.

"Good point, Gerry. Take the trophy to the sink and give it a rinse, and we'll put the big bird in that," said Cara.

Gerry looked at Gina, who laughed, and then at Pat Storey who raised his eyebrows before he went and filled the cup with the big bird, and they all sat down to eat.

"How's all in New York?" asked Pat.

"It's great, thank you for asking. New York never stops."

"Nor did Gerry in the match," said Pat.

"Very true; he was great, wasn't he?" said Gina.

"He was indeed."

"And how is the job going, Gina? I like your earrings by the way," said Cara.

"Oh, thank you. Yes, I got them a while back. It's going great. It's very busy. I don't get much time off, but it's exciting. I got to go to the Hamptons a couple of weeks back for a company break and we were out on the yachts. It was stunning."

Gerry wondered how nice the Hamptons were, and if the ocean there looked as nice as the Atlantic from his tea shop. And if the water was warmer. Gina spoke so fondly of it, and he wondered did the buildings sparkle like her earrings? For some reason, he felt his foot tapping of its own accord again for a few seconds before it was too tired to tap any further.

"Well, that's great stuff," said Aunt Cara. "And how about the violin? Gerry says you're quite the player."

"Oh, you should see her," said Pat.

Gerry smiled at Gina with pride.

However, he noticed she shifted in her seat. Then she took a drink.

"Hmm, it's going ok too, thanks. This is delicious, Aunt Cara. Thank you."

"It's tasty stuff all right. Thank you. Did you enjoy the game, Gina?" asked Pat.

"It was amazing. Very different. What an ending."

There was that word again, thought Gerry, and he tapped the table with his fingers this time before taking a drink.

"Had you ever seen Gaelic football before?" said Cara.

"That was the first time. But I know my grandad is a big Mayo fan."

Gerry and Pat caught eyes. Their eyebrows raised and Gerry couldn't help but let out a chuckle.

"What's wrong with the Mayo team?" said Gina.

"Well, they're Mayo, Gina. They haven't won in decades," said Pat.

Seeing the confused look on Gina's face, Cara interjected, "You see, Gina, it's said there's an auld curse that's been put on the Mayo team."

"A curse?"

"Yes, a curse was placed on them by a priest, so they won't win another title until the last team that won it — I think it was 1948 or 1949 — well, until every member of that team's died."

Gina joined in Gerry's and Pa's chuckles.

"But surely you don't believe that?" said Gina.

"Stranger things have happened," said Aunt Cara before lifting her glass of wine.

The strangest Thanksgiving dinner that Gina would ever have, was filled with laughter and stories and pheasant, which although a little tougher than the regular turkey she was most likely used to, was still delicious, especially after a long day standing in the cold watching football.

After dinner, Gerry and Gina washed and dried, finding themselves alone in the kitchen. Despite the moments of strangeness that Gerry had felt, he put it all down to his exhaustion from the game. Now, seeing Gina's smile, he decided this was the time.

He looked around the empty kitchen in which he and Jimmy had spent many hours whilst they were growing up, when after school, Aunt Cara would cook for them and take care of them when Pa was trying to make ends meet with the farm.

"Gina."

"Yes, Gerry."

"I've been wanting to tell you something for a long time. And you know, this house is a place that holds a lot of memories for me. It's a place of love."

Gina tilted her head as she stared into Gerry's eyes.

Gerry continued, "And I was going to write this lots of times but —"

Just then, the sound of laughter came in the door as Cara was followed by Uncle Brendan and then Pat with his walking stick.

"Now, ye didn't have to clean up," said Cara.

"We insisted," said Gina. She turned from Gerry and smiled at Aunt Cara. "Honestly, this was so lovely. It's a little home away from home. I'm just going to use the bathroom."

And Gerry watched her go and felt a pine in his stomach. Her words felt both good and sad in his heart, but once again, his perfect moment had been dashed.

"She's something special, Gerry. She didn't even seem to mind the pheasant. I'll just wrap up a few sandwiches and you can take them to the bar with you for the rest of the lads," whispered Aunt Cara.

With that, Gerry, Gina, and Pat Storey walked through the town which was packed with cars on either side of the street, except the patrons were all inside O'Brien's or McMurphy's. A cheer erupted as Gerry walked into O'Brien's and held the trophy up for all to see, and when he put it down, John McHugh, with his fresh black eye from the game, said, "Are they sandwiches?"

"They are, John. Turkey sandwiches," said Gina, and Gerry tried to avoid looking John in the eyes as he placed the cup on the bar.

That night, the drinks were on the house in all the pubs of Ballyduffy, and when Gerry and Gina made it to McMurphy's, Gerry stopped by the photo of Pa with the same championship trophy all those years ago, and amongst the madness and the music of the bar, he had a moment of silence to himself and said a prayer.

Then whiskey shots and the Guinness flowed, and by the early hours, everyone in the bar was very grateful for the 'turkey' sandwiches inside the cup.

With that, Gerry and Gina walked out the road beneath the stars, which seemed to shine brighter than ever over Ballyduffy. However, Gerry looked up again, and the stars had all blended into a blur, and it wasn't easy to focus his eyes on any particular one.

Then he realized that between the exertion of the game and the pints and the whiskeys, the crisp cold air had managed to make him drunker than he'd thought he could've been.

He looked down at Gina and she was holding onto him for dear life as the free bar had come home to roost. He remembered an old saying of Aunt Cara's, that there's nothing free in this life.

"We'll get you home, Gina," said Gerry.

"Home where, Gerry?"

Gerry stopped and his eyes followed Gina as their arms unlinked and she continued to stagger ahead.

"To my house," said Gerry as he caught up with her again.

"Exactly. *Your* home, Gerry."

They walked in silence for a bit and through drunken scattered thoughts, Gerry blurted out something that he'd thought of earlier that evening but had never said it.

"How's your violin coming along?"

"Jesus, Gerry, I don't even know where it is."

"Are you ok, Gina? You seemed a little bit off earlier? A little different?"

"Well, this place is so different to my life. My career. My home —" She paused, then sighed. "I'm fine, Gerry. Sorry, I've just had a lot to drink and it's really cold."

"Oh, of course, sorry."

Gerry took off his jacket and wrapped it around her as they continued their walk past the sheepdog and tonight, the only thing Gerry could hear were their steps on the road.

CHAPTER

13

"Jesus, Gerry, we have to go."

Gerry felt a hand push his shoulder and he blinked a few times before opening his eyes.

"What's wrong?" he said.

"We slept in. We have to go, or I'm going to miss my flight," said Gina.

She paced around the room and put on a pair of jeans from her suitcase before placing a black t-shirt over her head.

"You could, you know?" said Gerry.

"Know what, Gerry?" said Gina. She continued to pace and gather her things into the suitcase.

"Miss your flight."

Gina stopped. She held a bra in her hand, the remnants of her makeup on her face, and her hair stuck out in numerous directions. Then she smiled.

She sat on the bed beside Gerry and kissed him.

"You know I'd love to, Gerry. But I've got to get back to my job."

"Surely they wouldn't mind if you missed a few days extra. Working non-stop is no good for anyone. You need your rest too."

Gina smiled again. But this time, she rose to her feet.

"If only, Gerry. That's not how things work where I'm from. Come on, we need to go."

Gina continued getting packed and in no time at all, they were both on their way to Shannon Airport. Beneath the rattle of the new tractor, which with its mighty strong engine didn't make conversation the easiest, Gina rested her arm on Gerry's leg like she always did, and he put to bed whatever strange thoughts had entered his mind on the drive.

When he pulled up at the front of Shannon Airport, he helped her down and lifted her suitcase. Then he got one of the trolleys and placed the unbalanced suitcase on top for her.

"Thank you, Gerry. For everything," she said, then she kissed him.

"Gina."

"Yes, Gerry."

He held her two hands in his and stared into her eyes.

"I love you too. I'm sorry if I haven't said it. I love you with everything I've got. I've been waiting for the perfect moment, and I've been interrupted each time. And if I see that eejit with the whistle around here, I'll shove that whistle somewhere he won't be looking for it," said Gerry, and his head twisted left and right before he heard that beautiful laugh, just like he'd heard it that first night beneath the stars.

And now, slightly flushed from his words, he turned back to Gina.

She sighed. Then smiled and shook her head.

"I'm sorry, Gerry. I love you, too. I've been a little tense this trip. I've a lot happening at home with my career and everything. I love you. Thanks so much. It really is like a fairy tale when I'm here with you, it's just that fairy tales —" Gina stopped, then looked down at her watch. "Forget it. Ok, I've got to run."

Then she kissed him, and that terrible feeling intruded once more into his heart when she turned to wave before wheeling her bastard of a silver suitcase through the sliding doors. And as he drove back to Ballyduffy, those little looks and comments Gina had made were replaying through his mind. Her comments about her job. The Hamptons. The yachts.

What's 'so different'?

CHAPTER

14

One day in January, after closing the tea shop, Gerry stared across the valley — where a layer of light snow had turned the whole place white — and all the way out to the blue ocean in the distance, and for the first time in his life, Gerry wondered what New York was like. He had read the letters from Jimmy, and had heard the stories of the Giants Stadium and the New York Yankees, but never before had he wondered for himself about this city across the Atlantic. He pondered if he should make a trip that way. It would only be fair to Gina. Well, hadn't she had made many trips this way.

He made a note to let her know his thoughts in the next letter.

Time went slower than usual that winter. It was only natural, Gerry thought, a hangover from the championship final and his Thanksgiving with Gina. Nevertheless, it didn't make him feel any better on those quiet nights in the house when he'd give anything to have her here.

On his arrival home one day, Gerry found a letter sitting on the table.

It was the first from Jimmy in some time, and the first time Aunt Cara had made it up his way in a while, seeing as her hips had been hurting more in the cold weather they were having.

After making a cup of tea and enjoying one of the ham and cheese sandwiches she had made, Gerry sat down in the rocking chair with

Jimmy's letter.

Feb '86

Well, Gerry,

Hope all is well back home. Sorry about the lack of letters again, Gerry, but work has been crazy and I didn't even get Christmas off this year. That kind of busy. But, it's going, and I'm finally making the kind of coin that makes it all worthwhile, thanks be to God.

Ballyduffy, Gerry! What a story! If they'd told me ten years ago that Gerry McCarthy would be the man to lift the championship for the first time in twenty-five years, I would've thought they were mad. But I'm proud of you, Gerry. And Ma and Pa, I thought of their faces when I heard the news. They would've been mighty proud too. I missed it too Gerry, that feeling of being in the changing room with the rest of ye, something you never forget. Alas, sure it is what it is.

The legend of Joe McGettigan lives on. I heard he had a stone tablet for ye boys? Also heard the Boomer couldn't keep up with you; you must be flying fit, Gerry. Wish I could say the same for myself. The work on Wall Street doesn't lend itself to winning championships, unfortunately. Perhaps, I'll get back into it this year. New York has a few teams that would have me, I'm sure.

How is the tea shop, Gerry? Would you believe I saw a photo on a popular magazine they have out here called the National Geographic? It was an article about wild Ireland, and didn't I turn the page, and who was standing there at the top of Drumbarron Hill, with a shovel in his hand, and the most beautiful cottage, and view of the valley and the ocean behind him! Jaysus, it was a sight, Gerry. I had to go buy one of those magazines myself and I cut the picture out and hung it up. You've done well for yourself, brother. I couldn't be prouder of you. To think that's my brother in the pages of a big magazine like that.

Maria and myself are still doing well, thank God. She's mighty beautiful

*and kind, Gerry. And what about this Gina? One of the Connelly brothers
wrote me, says she was the prettiest woman he's ever seen walk into
O'Brien's. I wish you both very well. How does she handle farm life? Not
too many New Yorkers I know that I could see sitting in a tractor or making
their ways around the cowshite! Maybe we will see you out my way soon!*

All the best, Gerry, chat to you soon.

Jimmy.

James ^{Mc}Carthy,
150 E 78th St,
New York, NY 10075,
USA.

Gerry tossed and turned that night in bed. He thought of Jimmy and his
work and his coin, but thought it was very strange that he worked on
Christmas Day. Ma or Pa wouldn't have let Jimmy away with that. And Jimmy
had stopped playing the football out there, or else he never even started, and
that was very unlike the Jimmy he remembered. But then again, Gerry
thought about the tea shop and this National Geographic magazine, and he
was sure Jimmy probably thought the same about him. And just like Gina
always said, it was so different out there.

Regardless, over the weeks and months that passed, whether it was the
letter, or whatever else, the winds seemed to turn in Ballyduffy for Gerry.
A wild dog had managed to get into the bottom field and killed three of
his prized ewes one night, and when he told Aunt Cara about this, she
said, "That's a bad superstition there, Gerry. I'd keep an eye out for any
more of those."

Then it was confirmed that Joe McGettigan, having reached the Promised
Land again, would be retiring from coaching the Ballyduffy team.

With Joe leaving, Gerry felt like he had lost a piece of himself as well.
Those legs of his weren't as keen to trot during training, and he had stopped
roaming the field, returning to a midfielder whose job would be to catch the
ball under the new manager.

Ballyduffy too, struggled. Be it the hangover of that night in O'Brien's
with the pheasant sandwiches and the trophy, or all the drink that had

followed in the next week or two, but whatever it was, they lost their first few games of the league and ended up getting hammered by Carrickbay, with Johnny Murtagh scoring three goals in the process, and getting the better of black eyes with Gerry.

And despite his letter to Gina in which he even hinted at his desire to go and visit her in New York, he had heard nothing back. Even though he knew the letters were never the most rapid method of communication, together with the lack of urgency of the postmen who often came by his tea shop on their trips over the hill, it felt longer than usual. However, he would shrug his shoulders and chalk it down to the restlessness he felt inside.

During those months, it was only the tea shop that kept his mind occupied.

There were more visitors coming from everywhere.

The National Geographic magazine must be big enough in Europe too, thought Gerry as more and more Europeans from places as far away as Scotland and France had made it to his shop, often standing outside to take pictures of the view and the cottage.

In light of the photos, Gerry would take a trip into Tralee, where he'd bought fresh paint so that in those summer months, the cottage looked a fresh white, and the Kerry colours of the doors and windowsills were gleaming come September time where Kerry were in the final for the third year in a row. Despite losing by seven points at one stage of the game, Kerry won the final, this time beating a team called Tyrone from the north of the country.

However, as Gerry watched the final whistle blow on the television in O'Brien's, and the camera zoomed in on the Boomer, Gerry thought he looked a little less fit, and that beard of his had a grey hair or two where once it had been all black.

Whilst he took a sip of his Guinness and the cheers reverberated around O'Brien's pub, Gerry couldn't help but get a sinking feeling in his gut that maybe he wouldn't see this great Kerry team again, and it would be a long time until they'd win another All-Ireland. But being the good-hearted man he was, Gerry took a drink of his pint and kept that thought to himself.

And the celebrations went on into the early hours once again.

On Thanksgiving weekend, which Gerry had marked on his farmer's calendar beneath a picture of a black sheep for November that year, Gerry called down to the post office for a chat with Patricia, a fifty-something woman with blonde-grey hair, who had worked in the post office for as long as he could remember.

"How's it going, Gerry?" said Patricia from behind the counter.

"Not so bad, how about yourself?"

"Not so bad, just taking it easy this week. Things will heat up again soon for the busy Christmas season when all those cards are being sent. I suppose that's why you're here is it, Gerry, to send off an early Christmas card to your lady, Gina, in New York? Very smart of you, Gerry, getting in early like this, beat the rush," said Patricia.

Gerry blinked because he was surprised Patricia knew about Gina and his letters to her, as he would typically place them in the green post box on the main street.

"Not exactly, Patricia. I was wondering if there was any post for me lying around anywhere?"

"From Gina is it, Gerry? Or would that be from Jimmy? His letters seemed to have slowed down over the last few years, I suppose. There used to be tree or four a year from what I remember, and now, I only recall one in the last eighteen months or so.

"I'm sure you wrote to him about you lifting the championship cup last year, Gerry? I'd say he was excited to hear that," said Patricia.

Gerry nodded before rubbing his hand through his black hair. *Jaysus,* he thought, *Patricia knows of every letter I've ever sent.* And he wondered to himself how many letters she dealt with in a day, and it was clear how she kept herself occupied.

"Do you get many letters coming through here, Patricia?" asked Gerry.

"Yes and no, Gerry. I suppose we've the usual, the government ones, the taxes, the death notices, and whatever else, you know. But they're easy to make out from the front, and I don't waste my time with them. They go in this tray over here." Patricia stood up from her seat and pointed to a pretty full box of brown letters on the table behind her. "I call that the death box, Gerry. Not much life goes on in there!" said Patricia with a chuckle.

Gerry's eyes darted to another box on the table, much emptier, just a couple of letters with white envelopes and one or two with brown envelopes lying inside.

"That's the life box, Gerry. For the more interesting stories, if you get me. That's where I would have seen your Jimmy's letters, with his bad handwriting. And there's others from about the town. Did you know ever since he went to Spain five years ago on his holidays, Toe O'Brien keeps sending these letters to some woman called Alejandra in Barcelona?

"And from the feel of them, Gerry, there's a few notes in there — money that is, Gerry. And funnily enough, Mary Feeney — she'd be around your age, perhaps a little older, hangs around with one of the O'Connor sisters — well, doesn't she be getting letters from fellas from all over the place as far away as Switzerland and Italy, after her trip through Europe a few years back.

"Sure, we see it all in here, Gerry, keeps me on my toes, you know," said Patricia, laughing.

Gerry chuckled too. She reminded him of Aunt Cara, and he could only imagine the badness she would get up to if she worked here.

"You're sure there's no letters in that life box for me so, Patricia?" asked Gerry.

"Afraid there's not, Gerry. I went through that box just this morning. I'm waiting to see if this Alejandra writes back to Toe before the holidays. He normally sends her something close to Christmas. Anyways, I'll be sure to have Gerard drop out any letters from Gina or Jimmy as soon as they come through."

With that, Gerry bid Patricia a good day and headed back out the road towards home at the bottom of Drumbarron Hill, hoping for a letter to come by from Gina soon.

———— • ✳ • ————

In the lead up to Christmas, the restless feeling inside of Gerry had only gotten worse. When he told Aunt Cara all the bad superstitions he had seen throughout the year, she had a worried look, although she did say one evening that "normally, you get a good sign amongst the bad. I'll light a candle in church tomorrow just to make sure there's a little light out there flickering for you."

One night, Gerry arrived home from checking the sheep in the bottom field to discover a letter from Gina on the table. He opened it right away without taking off his wellie boots, ending up with shite all over the kitchen floor.

His heart sank when he started to read. It wasn't so much due to the content or the lack of enthusiasm, it was the first line. 'I'm sure you wrote, Gerry, but I waited, and nothing came.'

"Those damn postmen," whispered Gerry to himself, and when he saw the date on Gina's letter, August '86 in the top right-hand corner, he shook his head and started to write out a letter then and there, knowing he'd be waiting on Patricia to open the post office in the morning.

Gerry apologized for his previous letter not arriving, and told Gina that he missed her, and how Ballyduffy had not had a good year at the football, and how a few of his sheep had been killed, and other bits and pieces that he could think of.

Then, he wrote at the bottom of the letter:

I would like to come to New York to see you, Gina. I know that your job is very busy, and you don't get a lot of time off, so please let me know when would be best, and I'll write it on my calendar.

Christmas day was spent down in Aunt Cara's, where Pat Storey had been invited by her again; she found his company great fun, and Pat too remembered how much he enjoyed Cara's cooking. Not having anyone to cook down in his own house the way she did, he very much looked forward to it. After dinner, as Aunt Cara was having a nap, Pat turned to Uncle Brendan and Gerry, and said in his dry tone, "Turkey and pheasant are pretty much the same, so," causing a stream of laughter around the table.

However, there was a certain distance in Gerry's eyes and Uncle Brendan was astute enough to understand where his mind must be at.

"Your aunt told me about the trouble with the postmen, Gerry," said Uncle Brendan.

"We all make mistakes and lose things, I suppose," said Gerry.

"That's true. And what are you doing now? Last Thanksgiving was when she was last here?"

"It was."

"A year can be a long time in a young woman's life, Gerry. Are you planning to see her again?"

Gerry rubbed his hand through his hair and looked up from the table, catching the eyes of Pat Storey. "I am. I'll head out to America once I hear a date from Gina."

"Jaysus Gerry, that's great. And only fair. She's been here tree times now, I suppose," said Pat before taking a sip of a Guinness.

"A bit of advice, Gerry. You'll only get one woman like that in your life.

Make sure you do everything you can to get her, and to keep her," said Uncle Brendan.

"True that," said Pat, who took a long sip of his drink, and his eyes stared over the top of the glass at nothing in particular.

At that moment, Aunt Cara came into the room and there was silence. Then she said,

"And what are ye three gobshites talking about now?"

———————— ·✳· ————————

As the winter passed and Easter approached, Gerry had received and exchanged letters with Gina. One evening, he stared at the calendar on the wall, flicking forward to the image of the nicest looking brown bull he had ever seen. His eyes glanced to where he'd made a big 'X' that day after driving his tractor to Shannon Airport to buy himself a ticket. July first, 1987 — the day he'd see Gina again — this time across that big Atlantic Ocean.

A couple of strange feelings fluttered and lurched inside. The one of love, he knew; he had known this feeling from the moment she'd walked in the door of the tea shop that day nearly three years ago now. The other, though, was a strange and uncomfortable feeling in his stomach, the one that made his leg jiggle and foot tap, and made him rub his hands through his hair.

"Maybe it's the thought of the airplane," Gerry whispered to himself.

Just then, he heard a knock at his door, turning to see Aunt Cara walking through. She had a walking stick with her these days; however, she looked a lot better than she'd been recently.

"How's it going, Gerry?"

"Not so bad. And yourself? Are you sure you're able for the walk out here?" said Gerry.

"Don't be silly, Gerry. If I don't get on my feet, I may as well dig the grave myself."

Gerry couldn't help but copy his aunt when he saw Cara's wily smile appear on her face.

"Anyways, I'm hopeful they'll have a hip replacement for me in the next six months. I baked an extra batch for the tea shop, Gerry. How's it going this week up there?" said Aunt Cara.

"Not so bad. Had a lovely woman stop by with her little boy, from Barcelona of all places. I thought she was lost, but she was looking for

O'Brien's. I suppose she fancied a pint instead of a cup of tea," said Gerry.

"That's very interesting, Gerry. Anyways, before I forget, maybe you can take a seat."

Gerry stared for a moment at his aunt.

"Don't look at me like that, Gerry, it's nothing to be scared of. Sure, make a tea there for us if it helps that worry on your face."

"I will," said Gerry, and he had a feeling in his stomach which he wasn't sure was bad or good, but it was different, to use Gina's word.

"I came up here to give you something, and I don't know why I felt now was the time, but Uncle Brendan was telling me about your chat at Christmas and I suppose, if not now, when?" said Cara.

As he poured her a cup of tea, Gerry watched over his shoulder at Aunt Cara pulling out a seat at the kitchen table. And when he turned, he paused to gently place the cup down in front of her, next to the small square box that she'd laid out on the table.

Gerry sat across from her, his eyes never lifting from the strange small box.

"What's this, so?" said Gerry.

"Open it and see for yourself."

Gerry sat back, then took a deep breath and reached forward, gathering the padded box in one hand and prising it open it with the other.

His eyebrows rose and he stared up. Aunt Cara gazed back.

"It's a wedding ring, Gerry."

"I can see that, but Cara, you shouldn't have."

"Jaysus, Gerry, I'm not asking you to marry me!" said Aunt Cara, letting out a large barrel of laughs, causing Gerry to chuckle along too although he did feel a little red under the collar of his shirt. Cara continued, "Gerry, do you remember that day we cleaned out Pa's room all those years ago now? This was in one of the boxes I took with me, but I couldn't bring myself to sell it to those bastards Kelly's in Tralee; they would've sold it on for three times the price.

"You see, I remember this, Gerry. This is your mother's wedding ring. Pa brought me along to pick it out, sure; he wouldn't have known much about that sort of thing. You know, I don't know what it was, maybe it was my superstitions, but I thought you might want to have this at some point, so I kept it, and it's yours now."

Gerry's eyes went back down to the ring as he took a loud sip of tea.

"No need to slurp at me, Gerry," said Aunt Cara.

However, Gerry wasn't angry at all. In fact, he was stunned. Aunt Cara's superstitions had shown themselves again. Gerry had been mulling over Gina for weeks now, and that foot tapping and the hands brushing through the hair were his nerves. Gerry had realized that he wanted to ask Gina to marry him, and he had decided New York was going to be the place to do just that.

He had gone over and over the scenario in his head, remembering that first letter from Jimmy all those years ago now, recalling the tiny stamp with the statue of the lady holding the ice cream in her hand. Gerry had an image of dropping to one knee in front of Gina with that lady in the background. Gina would be in a good mood there because the sight of ice cream did that to people, and she would be more likely to say yes in the statue's presence.

"Thanks Cara. This sure is something," said Gerry as he gazed down at the familiar gold band in the box, picturing Gina's adorned and delicate hand in front of him, wearing it.

"Anyways, any word from Jimmy? I received a letter; said he's doing some work with the farmers of America for this bank of his. Seems to be doing all right, he says, and making more than a bit of cash. But I don't get the sense he has much time to spend it. All he ever seems to be doing is working.

"But then again, I'm sure when he heard about ye lifting the championship last year, he was plenty sad and homesick. He'd have been so proud of you, Gerry, when he heard."

Aunt Cara took a long and noisy slurp of her tea.

Gerry nodded and drank too, all the time staring down at the auld wedding ring.

He even had an image of his ma's hand pop into his mind with that same ring on, laying down a cup of tea for Pa. Ten years now since Pa had died, twenty since his ma, but the thoughts of them were never far away.

Then he thought of Jimmy. He hadn't told his brother he was going to New York, and he wouldn't be telling him either. A copy of Jimmy's address was on his letters, and when Gerry was there, he and Gina would surprise him. And perhaps Gerry would get to meet Maria too.

That night, and for many nights after, as July first approached, Gerry would sit in front of the fire and re-read Gina's letters, and re-read Jimmy's letters, all the while picturing this place called New York in his mind. He didn't imagine many green fields or cows, but he knew there were people there, more of them than Gerry had ever seen in his life.

And he would pass that wedding band of Ma's from hand to hand when he pictured the scenario over and over in his head.

One morning, whilst bringing some feed for the cows in the top field, he had decided to practice getting down on one knee. So, when he saw Penny the cow in all her elegant beauty standing there in the field staring at him, he thought, *sure no one better to practice on. She can't say no!*

And when she let out a loud moo as he knelt down, he even took it as a good sign.

——————•✳•——————

The day before his flight, he found himself down at Aunt Cara's where she had made some sausages and potatoes, knowing he wouldn't have them for another week until he got back.

"Is your suitcase all packed, Gerry?" she asked.

"Suitcase?" said Gerry with a confused look. "I have my Ballyduffy training bag ready to go with everything I need."

Gerry thought about Gina's black suitcase with its tree wheels in his wardrobe and of whatever she must have inside it, because it hadn't been much needed last time she had stayed.

"A light packer, Gerry. Good man yourself. What time is your flight?" said Uncle Brendan.

"It's at tree in the afternoon. So, I'll probably leave around ten because you wouldn't know what traffic could be like on the road to Shannon."

"Good idea, Gerry," said Aunt Cara.

"You could get stuck behind some auld tractor, and you wouldn't want to be late," added Uncle Brendan.

"Exactly. Now you go on, Gerry, and get an early night. You'll be needing all your energy for when you get there," said Cara. And she winked at Gerry, making him wince. Then Cara continued, "For the airplane-lag of course."

Gerry gave his aunt a kiss on her cheek, and he hugged Uncle Brendan before he cycled through the town and back out to his house at the bottom of Drumbarron Hill.

That night, he would leave his Ballyduffy bag by the door with the box with the wedding ring tucked safely inside a side pocket, and with the passport that Patricia in the post office had recently helped him get, in the other side pocket.

Just before bed, he took a glass of whiskey which he needed to help him sleep, and he dreamt of Gina's dark hair and the feel of her head against his chest, knowing he would soon be there.

CHAPTER

15

Gerry woke before the cock crowed, and he went and checked the sheep in the bottom field, and the cows in the top field. He gave the tea shop a quick clean, then closed the door and hung a sign he had made months ago on the outside: 'Closed: Off to America for one week.'

Ever since he had booked his flight a couple of months ago, Gerry had reminded his regular customers that come the first week of July, the tea shop would be closed. Pat Storey wished him well and told Gerry to say hello to Gina for him, and if he were somehow to encounter that pretty Boston Rose with the blonde hair, to tell her he said hello to her too.

The cyclists were also very happy for Gerry, all remembering the stunning New Yorker that day, the one sitting behind the counter with him. In fact, they'd often asked when she would be back. And John McHugh had kindly offered to tend to his livestock whilst Gerry was gone.

After returning to his house, he showered and took a quick cup of tea, then it was nearly ten o'clock and time to go. He closed the front door, loading his Ballyduffy bag up into the tractor and hopping in, thinking of how different it would be to drive to Shannon in a tractor without Gina alongside — but knowing he would be with her soon anyways.

It would take more than an hour to get to Shannon, Gerry thought, and he turned the tractor around and headed out of his gate. As he was driving, walking up the lane at a snail's pace but seemingly trying to move faster than his walking stick would allow, came Pat Storey. Gerry slowed, turning the tractor off before sticking his head out the window.

This was plenty unusual for Pat to call by Gerry's house, unthinkable at this early hour.

"How's it going, Gerry?

"Just about to leave, Pat. I was going to ask you the same thing."

"Gerry, I have some bad news for you," said Pat. He took off his hat and held it against his chest. He leant on the walking stick, huffing and puffing to catch his breath, a hand on the hat.

Then he drew a deep breath and said with a huge effort to speak, "Your Aunt Cara passed away in her sleep last night. Heard it in the shop from Father Finnegan, the new parish priest. I'm sorry to be the one to tell you, Gerry, but I'd say Brendan hasn't made it out this way."

Gerry froze and looked down at Pat's red eyes. It was as though his own heart had stopped, and the blood was running suddenly chilled in his veins. He swallowed.

For a minute or two — Gerry wasn't sure how long — both he and Pat Storey were in silence. Even the sheep in the field didn't make a noise, and that bastard of a sheepdog in O'Neills' farmhouse down the road had fallen oddly silent for a change, as if in mourning too.

"If there's anything you need Gerry," said Pat Storey.

"Thank you. And Uncle Brendan?" asked Gerry, tears coming to his eyes.

"I'd say he's down the house, Gerry."

"Ok Pat. I've got to go. Thank you for coming out here."

"Good luck to you now," said Pat softly.

Gerry sped off as fast as his tractor would go, leaving Pat Storey standing rigid there with his hat in his hands as he watched him drive away. Gerry clenched his jaw and kept his glazed eyes on the road, trying to hold back all the tears that still wished to leave.

It was hard though, and his mind raced a lot faster than his tractor, thoughts and memories of Cara and of all the times she'd come to his house, and he'd been to hers.

Then, thoughts of his flight to see Gina. But at the forefront of his thoughts was the kiss he'd planted on his aunt's cheek last night. And, of course, he thought of the ring. She had delivered it because... perhaps because she had known she didn't have long left.

He walked in the front door of Aunt Cara's to find Father Finnegan in black, with his white collar, sitting on a chair in the kitchen. Gerry paced into the room and Father Finnegan stood up and shook his hand. Gerry watched as Father Finnegan looked down at his hands, and then over to his side, in the direction of Uncle Brendan who sat at the kitchen table, still in his cream pyjamas. Gerry had never noticed before just how cream those pyjamas were, but he also noticed Uncle Brendan looked like a ghost, with his two hands wrapped around a cup of tea.

As Gerry sat down, Brendan didn't lift his eyes to acknowledge him. He just stared out of the window.

"Brendan," said Gerry softly.

Brendan came back to the room at the sound of his nephew's voice, and he turned and smiled. Gerry could see the redness in his eyes, and the paths where the streams had flowed down his cheeks not much earlier.

"Gerry," said Uncle Brendan.

He lifted one hand from his cup and placed it on top of Gerry's. Gerry sat still and quiet for a few moments as Brendan turned again out the window. Then he looked at the old photograph of Aunt Cara and Uncle Brendan hanging on the wall. He swallowed, his eyes drifting to the other photos, zeroing in on an old black and white photo of Aunt Cara, Pa, and Gerry and Jimmy when they were both kids. *I must've been twelve or thirteen there,* thought Gerry. He felt those wells fill behind his eyes again and a pain in his heart he hadn't felt in a long time.

And as Gerry looked around the kitchen, thoughts and memories filled his mind of Jimmy and himself grabbing a sandwich here after school. Or the cooker, where Aunt Cara would be making a stew and filling a lunch box so that they could bring some home with them for Pa. And Gerry smiled for a moment when he thought of the time when Aunt Cara hit Jimmy around the back of his ear in front of everyone on the street for skipping school one day, and Gerry and Jimmy knew never to mess with her again.

He listened to the sound of Uncle Brendan's wheezy breathing, and other than that, he'd never remembered this house so silent.

"Do you want a cup of tea?" said Father Finnegan, bringing Gerry back into the room.

"Yes, please, Father," said Gerry. "Brendan, would you like some fresh tea?"

Uncle Brendan, lost in his own thoughts and memories, nodded as he stared at his cup.

"Gerry, you have a flight to catch," whispered Brendan. His voice sounded sore to Gerry, the kind of voice when someone's been up most of the night.

"Don't worry about that. I'll look after that," said Gerry.

"You should go. You'll only get one woman like that in your life," whispered Brendan.

Gerry turned back to the photos of Aunt Cara on the wall and his eyes moved down to the table where out of the corner of his eye, he saw Brendan reaching for the last tissue in a packet.

"It's ok, Brendan. I'll go at some point," said Gerry.

The moment Pat had told him about Aunt Cara, Gerry had known that he wouldn't be going to America today. Despite the ache in his heart to see Gina, this was where he needed to be.

As Father Finnegan arrived with two cups of tea, Brendan looked out the window and said, "I've known her my whole life. We got married when I was twenty-five."

"I'm sorry."

He watched as the tears began to roll down his uncle's face again and Gerry handed him a tissue from the new packet that Fr. Finnegan had all of a sudden placed on the table. And Gerry's heart ached, although a strange thought of priests and their ability to always have a packet of tissues to hand at an apt moment popped into his mind. And Gerry grabbed a tissue just in case as he knew that thought sounded like something Aunt Cara would've said. He managed a smile at the thought of how her face would have creased up before letting out a stream of laughter.

"When you've been together as long as we have, Gerry, it feels like you've lost a part of yourself. More. It's as if I've lost the front door of my house," said Uncle Brendan.

Gerry sat in silence for a while longer with Brendan and thought about those words. How, after a day out and about, Brendan would come home and Cara would be here, and inside this house, no matter what the day had thrown at them or how tough the world was outside, they had each other. And he kind of knew what he meant. Father Finnegan made some more tea, and he brought out another packet of tissues from God only knew where as visitors began to arrive.

Gerry walked to the grocery store and bought a few loaves of bread, and plenty of ham and cheese, and began to make sandwiches, all the time thinking *is this how Aunt Cara would have wanted me to make them?* He tried to make them look like hers, and they almost did. Almost.

That night, Gerry's tea shop skills were put to use and he made cups for everyone who came by to shake his hand, and to shake Uncle Brendan's.

Gerry hadn't thought about the time. Suddenly, it was near midnight, and he grabbed another tissue just in case, knowing 'his' flight would be landing in New York right about now.

He slipped outside into the back garden. The air was cold, but all the stars were out in force in the sharp air. Gerry stood there looking up at the stars and the moon, and he sighed.

Gina would be waiting for him, and he had no way to let her know what had happened. He made a plan that first thing Monday morning, he would be outside the post office waiting on Patricia to arrive, and he'd be clutching onto a letter explaining his absence and looking for a new date to go see the woman he loved. Truth be told, it was this feeling inside of him which kept him from breaking down too, because he knew how much love Aunt Cara and Brendan, after more than fifty years of marriage, had still held for each other.

And he felt sure that it hadn't faded, not even for a moment of that time, until the end.

That night, after the visitors had left and Father Finnegan had said he needed to go home, and that he would be back with some more packets of tissues in the morning, Gerry, Uncle Brendan and Pat Storey – who had asked Brendan if he wouldn't mind – remained in the house with Cara's casket. And all those memories of Pa's death came back to Gerry.

That feeling of sitting in the house with Jimmy and the casket the day before the funeral. The quiet, the tick of a clock, the boil of a kettle, the only sounds that filled the air.

The heavy eyelids and the dry eyeballs, and yet no ability to find an ounce of sleep.

In the following days, Gerry would leave his tractor parked outside Uncle Brendan's; his Ballyduffy training bag had plenty of clothes and whatever else Gerry needed, and he slept in the spare room. On the day of the funeral, he would carry the coffin together with others from the town, and he would walk home from O'Brien's that night with Brendan side by side after many tales and pints in Aunt Cara's memory.

———————•✸•———————

"What about Gina, Gerry?" said Uncle Brendan one day as he sat at the kitchen table. Gerry was making a dinner of potatoes and bacon for the two of them. He'd hardly been away since Cara passed, trying to keep Uncle Brendan on an even keel, getting him past the worst at least.

"I haven't heard anything yet. But Patricia made sure to give the letter the express stamp, so I'm sure I'll get something soon."

"And would you not let me book a new ticket for you to go to New York? You could surprise her."

A hiss of evaporating water drowned out Gerry's curses. He grabbed a tea towel and wiped whatever water remained on the oven. Uncle Brendan continued, "I feel terrible, Gerry. I'm sure Gina would love it too. At least let me do that to make it up to you."

"You've nothing to feel terrible about. The timing wasn't arranged by you, Brendan. You've enough on your mind to be worrying about me," said Gerry, and he lay down the pot of potatoes on the kitchen table.

He knew that by staying with his uncle, he had done the right thing.

Anyways, Gina had always said how busy she was in her new job, and he knew how important that was to her and he didn't want to intrude if he could get in the way of that. Well, this was what he would tell himself. Despite wondering about a spontaneous trip for a couple of weeks now, he had made up his mind that he would wait for Gina's reply, and perhaps he would get to experience Thanksgiving in America later this year.

"You know, Gerry, I'm fine down here by myself. I'm sure you must be missing the feel of your own bed," said Brendan, as Gerry put some potatoes out on his plate.

"It's not a bother. It's good for me too. I like being here. Now, you need to eat. I noticed you left half your lunch behind."

"I did not."

"I seen it in the bin," said Gerry, who caught his uncle's look down towards the plate. "Anyways, the tea shop and the farm are fine. Did you open Jimmy's letter?"

"I did. He passed on his condolences, of course, and I could see he was very upset by it. Tries not to show it, you know, like we all do. But it was there all right. Said he was sorry he wasn't here for me — for us. Aunt Cara had a right soft spot for him. And for you, you know?" said Uncle Brendan. "Jaysus, I forgot to give you her letter, Gerry."

"What's that?" asked Gerry.

"Cara – you know what she's like." Brendan glanced towards the small statue of Jesus Christ on the windowsill as he rose to his feet. "Her superstitions and whatnot, but she wrote you a letter a while back and told me to give it to you if something would ever happen to her."

Brendan sighed and looked at the photos on the wall, then returned from the bedroom with a letter in his jittering hand. There was an apprehension in Gerry's stomach at the thought of Aunt Cara, anticipating her own demise, still sitting and turning her thoughts to him. It was moving, yet also made him sad. After Gerry had cleaned up after dinner and Brendan had gone off to bed, he sat down at the table and opened it up.

Sometime in 1987.

Well, Gerry,

If you're reading this, I'm probably hovering above you rather than hovering over your shoulder. Time heals all wounds, Gerry, and I'm sure it's tough but I thought, seeing as you never had someone to really lean on over the years, that perhaps with my passing, you might be in need of a shove or two to get you going again.

But first, let me say that you've aways reminded me of my brother, and like Pa, you weren't one for talking much but I hoped you could always feel like you could talk to me. And if you're ever stuck, I'll be here listening should you want to talk some more.

I remember you asking me once in the tea shop why I gave up nursing so young to help look after you lads, and I suppose I never really gave you the full story. The good Lord doesn't mind a little white lie, Gerry if it's part of a greater good! But the truth was that I wasn't young, Gerry; I was near forty. I don't know, maybe after your mother died, I knew Pa needed a bit more help that he was letting on. And sure, if I wasn't around, your Uncle Brendan would leave the house without any shoes on. God bless him.

And I know what you're thinking, but there's no need to thank me, Gerry; if anything, I needed it more than ye did. It was around the same time that I finally accepted that I couldn't have children of my own. Those first steps can sometimes be the hardest, Gerry. Ye were the breath of fresh air I needed. And I suppose, Uncle Brendan and myself, we always looked at ye both as if ye were our boys. So, thank you.

Now that the sappy stuff is out of the way, I want you to make sure of two things for me. One, I want you to follow up on that letter to Gina. I've good superstitions Gerry, but superstitions only go so far. And two, I want you to take the opportunity to visit your brother in New York. Now, I'm not saying it has to be done tomorrow, as I know with the tea shop and everything else (including making sure Uncle Brendan doesn't forget his shoes) that you're a busy man. But when the time is right, it'd be good for the both of ye, Gerry.

And by the way, that tea shop is as fine an accomplishment as any man from Ballyduffy ever achieved! We were always so proud of you. Not just for the tea shop, but for the man you became, Gerry. A good man.

Take care Gerry, and I'll see you again, but hopefully not for a while yet,

Aunt Cara
X

PS, if you wouldn't mind going into the top drawer in my room and in the back, there's a small tin with a few bob. Take a little for a pint for yourself, but if you could give the rest to Father Finnegan and the church just in case, I'm in purgatory, Gerry. It never hurts to grease the wheels of the gatekeepers!

In his mind, Gerry pictured the sparkle behind his aunt's eyes and the smile sitting on her face despite the essence of what she was writing, and why. He looked at the photos on the wall, then glanced up at the ceiling when he felt a warmth under his collar. He held his quivering lip as steady as he could, and he held that feeling as his chest constricted. She'd been the one constant in his life, and he loved her so much, and would make sure he fulfilled all of her requests.

And Gerry waited for a reply from Gina. Some weeks, he waited every hour of the day. Other weeks, he kept himself busy, building another picnic table for the tea shop, so now he had one permanently outside, and one inside. Or he put a fresh lick of paint on the tea shop, going as far as painting his house down at the bottom of the hill, all to keep his mind occupied. However, even on those days, the nights were long and lonely, and sleep was hard to come by.

Jimmy had also written to Gerry to apologize for not being there, and from his letter, Gerry understood that those kind memories of Aunt Cara from his younger years had been recalled by Jimmy too. However, when he hadn't been here for the longest time, there wasn't much to apologize for, Gerry thought. As time passed, life went on whether Jimmy was there or not, and plenty of life had passed by in the eleven years since Jimmy had departed.

Soon, Thanksgiving arrived, with no football for Ballyduffy, and no letter from Gina.

So that night, after Uncle Brendan had gone to bed, Gerry sat on the chair in the kitchen, the same one he'd sat that day he was meant to go to America, and he wrote another letter to Gina.

Again, he apologized for not arriving. He wrote how he had moved down to Aunt Cara's for the time being. And he asked once more for a date where he could come see her.

However, as he tried to fall asleep that night, he had a strange feeling in the pit of his stomach. Ever since Gina had started working in that bank, she didn't have many holidays, and with Thanksgiving now passed, he was unsure as to the next time she'd be free.

The next day, Gerry went to the post office to see Patricia, and to get one of those express stamps for his letter to Gina in America.

As Gerry walked in the door, he was surprised to find a long queue in front of him. As he looked over the heads of Mary Feeney and Clare McHugh, he could see that Patricia was a little more flustered than usual behind the counter. Gerry watched as she walked back and forth, from death box to life box, lifting letters here, setting others down there.

And after Clare McHugh left and Gerry got one step closer to the counter, he couldn't help but overhear as Mary Feeney raised her voice. "I never received a letter from Italy," said Mary.

"Well, if you never received it, how do you know there was one?" said Patricia, glancing over her shoulder before turning back to flick through some letters in the death box.

"Because I received another letter asking why I'd never replied to the last one, so don't give me that shite, Patricia," said Mary.

"Jaysus, Mary and Joseph, well haven't you got the letters from the Swiss man to keep you busy in the meantime?" said Patricia, her voice loud and agitated.

Gerry had to keep a smile from his face when Mary Feeney turned around in shock. He could see Patricia, too, had stopped flicking through the letters, one of her hands covering her mouth.

"Sorry, about that, Mary," said Patricia and she walked back to her seat behind the counter.

Mary Feeney lifted her bag and stormed past Gerry out the door without a look or a hello.

"Well, Gerry," said Patricia. And Gerry watched as she lit a cigarette once she sat down at her stool. And he looked down towards the letters on the counter, and towards the boxes behind her on the table, and back up towards the *No Smoking* sign high on the wall to the right. And he couldn't help thinking about what might happen if Patricia were to drop that cigarette.

However, he could see from the frown on her face and the gleam of sweat on her forehead, that today wasn't the time to air his concern. Particularly as he needed her help.

"How's it going?" said Gerry.

"Awful sorry to hear about your aunt. Cara was a great woman about the town, always helping ones out and whatnot. There was some crowd about her funeral. As to myself, Gerry, not great, to be honest. Same shite these last few years. People are coming earlier and earlier with their Christmas cards, and those feckers up in headquarters in Dublin won't let us hire any extra help for the next few weeks. Then you have the likes of Mary Feeney running in here complaining about her missing love letter from Roberto in Italy. You'd think she'd be busy enough. I heard in the pub the other night that she and one of the Egan brothers are a thing.

"And I kept my lips shut as who am I to say anything about Roberto, or Sebastian from Switzerland for that matter?"

Patricia took a long drag on her cigarette, and Gerry watched as she blew a large flume of smoke up in the air and it drifted towards the *No Smoking* sign.

"Well, I suppose to be fair to her, there may have been something important in the letter," said Gerry.

"Jaysus, don't you start. And don't be so naïve either. You know one of the letters from Roberto arrived here already opened. Likely checked for cocaine or heroin or one of those other drugs once it arrived in Dublin. You know they do that up there, Gerry? Open the odd letter, especially if it came from a strange, far-off place with a history of crime."

Gerry scratched his head before asking, "And how would they know if a place had a history of crime if it was far off and strange?"

"The television, Gerry. Sure, you're always hearing about murderers and drugs and that on the television from these places. And Italy, Gerry, they have mafia and all sorts out there, so I don't blame those up in headquarters. But sure, that letter had nothing dangerous in it, unless you were a priest I suppose, Gerry. Filled with raunchy stuff, so it was. Made me blush as I read it.

"Those Italians know a lot more than any Kerryman I've ever met," laughed Patricia, who with one more enormous drag finished her cigarette. "Now, Gerry, what can I help you with? Gina or Jimmy?"

And Gerry's eyebrows raised. *Jaysus,* he thought.

"Well, I need this letter to go to New York as quickly as you can get it there," said Gerry.

"Not a problem, Gerry. Slide it across there and I'll give it the double express stamp."

Gerry paid his fee and watched as she placed it on the table with a bunch of other letters. Brown and white envelopes, but reds and greens too, and Gerry realized she was right, and people had started their Christmas letters early. When he turned, he was surprised to see another long line behind him as Toe O'Brien and John McHugh's aunt stood waiting for Gerry to finish. Gerry gave a nod and wished them good luck as he left, heading back out the road towards his house at the bottom of the hill. That night, Gerry would look at the calendar on his wall, at a picture of two beautiful black sheep in a green field. And he would mark today's date.

CHAPTER

16

1988 started off with one of the wettest winters Kerry had had in as long as Gerry could remember. In the top field one morning, as he was checking the cattle, Gerry looked down at his wellies which were overflowing with water. He wondered if the Atlantic Ocean had left the seabed and decided it was moving in next door. The bottom field had got a real soaking one week in late March, and Gerry had to move the lambs in the swirling rain all the way up to the top field, which, although it was a grand size, did look a little crowded with the sheep and the cattle making do with each other's company.

The thatch of the tea shop had been damaged on one particularly bad night too, when the wind howled outside and tried to creep down Gerry's chimney into the house at the bottom of the hill. As a result, Gerry had to close off a small part of the bottom room of the tea shop. However, with the weather, he wasn't getting as many visitors as usual, so the space wasn't needed. Gerry paid a visit to his credit union, very pleased that his rainy-day fund came in just as he had planned, and he was able to acquire some more thatch in Tralee.

In spring, Gerry returned to his own house after Uncle Brendan urged him that he still had his own life to look after, and Gerry was convinced that he was back to himself.

Or as back to himself as could be, he supposed.

He wasn't sure what it was, but he felt six-foot-three and not six-foot-four.

But truth be told, Gerry had retreated inside himself. The death of Aunt Cara, the one constant in his life from as long as he could remember, had struck him harder than he could ever have known. He was still in mourning and his gusto had left. His aunt had always been the one who pushed him, and he had placed that wedding ring inside the top drawer beside his letters.

And when he heard the stories from the cyclists and the visitors to the tea shop, the world outside Ballyduffy seemed a lot bigger. *Very different to here,* he thought.

Nevertheless, his yearning to see Gina still forced him once a week into the post office where Patricia would say, "None from Gina or Jimmy this week, Gerry," and he would try to hide the disappointment in his eyes and the ache in his heart. Now that the busy Christmas period had passed, Patricia would make Gerry a cup of tea, and he would sit and listen as she told him more stories of the post office and the mess that seemed to be headquarters in Dublin.

Gerry didn't mind spending that little bit of time once a week as Patricia's husband, John, had died a couple of years earlier, and he knew well the silence of a quiet house.

And he knew it especially after a wet winter like this one.

Then, one day in late July, on his way to visit Uncle Brendan, Gerry popped into the post office as Patricia was leaving and about to close the door.

"Well, Gerry, how's it going?"

"Not so bad, Patricia," said Gerry.

"Just closing up," said Patricia before she turned and looked at Gerry in his Ballyduffy shorts and t-shirt. "Game tonight, Gerry?"

"Yes. Playing Kellmere later this evening," said Gerry.

"Kellmere — they're an odd bunch, Gerry. I know the lady works in the post office down there. They call her 'the tortoise' because you know that auld story of the hare and the tortoise, and they complain the letters are always slow in getting there. Mad for their nicknames, they are. But sure, it's hardly her fault, Gerry; she's just a cog in the machine like the rest of us."

Gerry felt his shoulders loosen a little. "Any letters for me today, Patricia?"

Patricia paused. Then she opened the door back up and said, "Would you

believe it; a letter from Gina arrived today. I was going to have Peter O'Malley
— that's our new postman — leave it out in the morning. But seeing as you're
here, come on in."

Gerry stood still outside the post office, all turned to mush.

After more than a year of waiting, Gina's letter had finally arrived. And
despite the thunder of his heart which ordered blood all around his body, his
legs refused to budge.

After all those sleepless nights, his weekly trips into the post office, now
that it was here, his body was frozen — all except for his foot which had
begun to tap.

Patricia, who had walked inside and over behind the counter, stopped,
and said, "Well, Gerry, are you coming in or not?"

Gerry remembered where he was and nodded, before following her in.

She fumbled through a box of letters, taking some out, putting some back
in, leaving others to one side, then she said, "Here we are."

She handed Gerry the letter and he clasped onto that pristine, sealed
envelope in both his hands as he read each letter of his name and his address.
He knew that elegant handwriting.

"Come on now, Gerry, I have to close this place up sometime, you
know?" said Patricia, and she let out a large laugh to herself as she ushered
Gerry out the door. "Out you go!"

Parked on the main street of Ballyduffy, Gerry climbed into his tractor,
and his hand shook as he gently opened the letter.

May 1, 1988

Dear Gerry,

*I hope everything is ok with you and in Ballyduffy. I still think about your
beautiful smile, and your beautiful village most days. The Atlantic Ocean I
see from this side does not have quite the same beauty as from the tea shop.
I hope Pat Storey is good and still swimming. Aunt Cara and Uncle Brendan,
I hope they are good also, and I still think about the wonderful Thanksgiving
we had. Nearly two years now, Gerry.*

*It's crazy how time passes. I am very grateful for everything that
Ballyduffy has shared with me, and I will cherish those memories for the rest*

of my life.

I don't really know how to say this, or what to say really. It's been over nine months since I sat waiting for the Shannon flight to arrive in JFK. When you didn't appear, I thought something bad must have happened. I waited for a letter, and I waited some more. When nothing came, it was then I realized that perhaps I pushed you too much, that perhaps my thoughts of us working out were idealistic. I'm like that sometimes, Gerry, and very often, life isn't a dream, is it?

The whole long-distance thing was not easy at the best of times, but our moments together made it worth it. When I didn't hear anything after that day in JFK, I realized maybe it wasn't meant to be.

By the time you receive this, I will have moved into Manhattan. I have recently met someone. He works at another bank, but he has known my dad for a couple of years now. He is nice and well mannered. He is very New York, but my mom and dad like him, and we have similar friend circles so that's good I suppose. Anyways, I don't know why I'm telling you this, but maybe it's to let you know that I have had to accept we aren't meant to be, Gerry, and despite the pain that has been in my heart, I hope this letter helps the both of us find some closure.

My memories of you will always stay close,

Gina.

And after receiving a letter like that, what else is there really to say? Maybe a few of ye have been in Gerry's shoes, maybe a few of ye have stood in Gina's shoes, but all of ye understand how Gerry was feeling at that moment. Sick as a dog, that's how he was feeling.

He read the letter again and again as a tractor and the odd Datsun drove by, beeping and waving at big Gerry McCarthy who took no notice of the sounds, and whose eyes were focused on the elegant letters and words in front of him.

For a few minutes, his heart raced hard in his chest before it followed his stomach in dropping to his feet. Those ducts behind his eyes were overflowing now, but being Pa McCarthy's son, he tried his damn best to keep the water to the wells.

And when a single tear did escape to land on the page, leaving a smudge on the letters *JFK,* Gerry noticed other smudges on the page too.

They surely were remnants of Gina's tears scattered here and there on the notepaper. Or maybe it was his imagination running away with him.

Then he heard the patter of raindrops on his windshield as if the sky shared his broken heart, the heavens opening onto his tractor. A harsh and fast summer storm was passing through Ballyduffy, and Gerry sat there in his tractor, watching the raindrops falling all around the empty street. He thought of how the sound of rain in this part of the world could be peaceful and calm the mind.

Or it could be sorrowful.

Then he realized that the day on which Gina had waved as she passed through the doors of Shannon Airport, the first half of his heart had torn. Now, the other half of his heart had broken.

So, Gerry put the letter into the side pocket of his Ballyduffy football bag and drove to see Uncle Brendan to make sure he had everything he needed.

"Are you ok, Gerry?" said Uncle Brendan.

"I'm grand. Have to rush now, or I'll be late," said Gerry.

Gerry left to face the boys of Kellmere that night, and he decided to ignore the new manager's tactics, roaming over that field as far as his legs could take him. And with twenty minutes left to play, he pulled up with a cramp as he hadn't trained enough to be a roamer, and of course, he had to be replaced.

Back home later that evening, Gerry took the longest shower he had ever taken. He thought it might have been as long as one of Gina's, but he shook his head. *Nothing could be as long as one of those.* But he let the water fall all over his body, the thoughts hurtling through his head.

The feckin' postmen had lost his letters. Had they lost others of his before? His fists clenched and he banged one against the tiled wall of the shower. But Gerry being a big man, he'd always been taught to control his anger, and with a few deep breaths beneath the hot shower, he calmed himself. Now, he was picturing Gina's face, then her fragrant head lying on his chest and her lips on his, and that moment when she'd told him beneath the stars that she was falling in love with him. There came that lump in his throat again, and luckily, the water coming down from the showerhead was good enough to disguise any of those tears that had escaped the wells behind Gerry's eyes.

That night, after he put the fire on, instead of the potatoes and sausages he had planned to eat, Gerry just had a cup of tea. He took out Gina's envelope with the letter from his Ballyduffy bag and laid it on the table beside his rocking chair as he took a sip from his tea.

The fire cracked and burned, and he felt the heat on his face and his body. He looked down at the letter, then back at the fire. And as he stared into the flames, he thought of all the other letters in the silver tin in his dresser. He reached for Gina's newest letter from the tabletop, and he knocked the teacup over, splashes of tea flying high in the air and on the page.

"Ah shite," whispered Gerry. Then he put the letter onto his chair as he reached for something to wipe the table. After everything was cleaned and he'd drunk a couple of shots of whiskey, he placed that tea-covered letter in the silver tin with the others before he'd decide what to do with it.

That night, Gerry would try harder than he'd ever tried to sleep, and not even the thoughts of all his sheep in the field could help him now.

CHAPTER

17

The next few weeks were filled with days that passed without a thought. Gerry was on autopilot in his walks around the fields, where he tended to the sheep and the cattle as closely as he had done in years. In the tea shop, he kept up his appearances, although Pat Storey would say, "You're quieter than usual, Gerry." His other regulars could sense it too, that something had changed in the big man behind the counter, that, despite his smile and his manners, Gerry's blue eyes were distant and seemed to have lost some of their sparkle lately.

And when the odd cyclist would ask if everything was ok, Gerry would smile and nod and say, "Everything's fine; sure, with a view like that, how couldn't it be?"

In the evenings, when he closed the tea shop, Gerry would sit on that rock outside the front, and he would watch the sunset come down over the Atlantic in the distance.

In the beauty of those sunsets, he could feel Gina within him, and his heart would burn with the thoughts that somewhere across that ocean, she was in the arms of someone else. In moments when the gentle breeze swept by his neck, he would think of the flick of her dark hair on his chest as she slept. And Gerry being a good man, despite how much it pained him to not be with Gina, he hoped that her new man would always be good to her and that she was happy.

One evening when he arrived home, he looked up to see a letter which the postman had left on the kitchen counter. From first observations, he could tell Jimmy's messy handwriting, but that wasn't all. The white letter was leaning against a brown package about the size of a shoe box.

Gerry took a seat and picked it up.

It was a parcel of some sort and Gerry held it to his ear and gave it a shake, but there was no sound of anything inside. His eyebrows rose.

He opened the box and lifted out a strange black rectangular object. It was bulky, and there were a few compartments. Gerry fiddled with it, and at one end he pulled out a long skinny antenna, the kind he had seen on the top of the television in O'Brien's pub.

Then he flipped down another compartment at the bottom end of the object and saw a series of buttons with numbers on them from zero to nine, and then a few more. It was the oddest contraption he had ever placed his eyes on. He lifted a sheet from inside the box and read it,

"Motorola Dynatec. Mobile phone. Place and receive calls from anywhere, and at any moment of the day. Well, Jaysus," said Gerry.

Why in the world would I ever want someone to be able to call me any moment of the day? Sure, don't I speak to enough folk up in the tea shop all day?

Then he put the odd phone back inside its box and lifted the letter.

July '88

Well, Gerry,

I appear to have become one of those people who says they'll do something, but always fail to do it. I can blame it on work, and of course, it has me busy, but to be honest, I should be better at making time for these things. Thoughts of Aunt Cara have been close at hand lately. It's brought up some of those auld memories of Ma and Pa, and I suppose I've been keeping myself busy so that I don't have to think of those things. Alas, the price I pay for living in this great country is those times and places I've missed and left behind me.

And so, in lieu of my lack of letters, Gerry, please find a small gift that I

got for you. A colleague at work bought one a while back so I had to join him, and this is the future, Gerry.

It's remarkable now, but if I were to hazard a guess, I'd say they'll have television screens on these in the future, and you'll be watching television everywhere you go. People will never lift their eyes from it, I'd say.

Anyways, it's been some amount of time Gerry, what is it now, eleven years? Perhaps, you'll have to take a trip out this way sometime. It would be great to see you.

All the best Gerry,

Jimmy.

James McCarthy,
150 E 78th St,
New York, NY 10075,
USA

Gerry placed the letter down on the table and turned back towards the strange box. *A television of the future is in here?* His eyebrows raised across his forehead once more. Sure, he'd lasted this long without a television, so he could do without it some more. And he couldn't see how you got a television out of that rectangular brick thing anyway. It had no screen that he could see.

And with that, Gerry, having had nothing to eat all day, made himself some sausages and drank a glass of whiskey, falling asleep in front of the fire with the letter and the phone still sitting on the kitchen table.

———————— • ✳ • ————————

"Jaysus!" said Gerry the following day whilst out with the sheep. After counting them and ensuring they were all there, he had thoughts of that strange device sitting on his kitchen table. *Maybe this is a sign,* he thought.

"Jimmy always knew best," he said quietly to himself as he rushed in the door, remembering his obligatory removal of his wellies, not wanting mud everywhere.

He lifted the phone out of the box and ran into the bottom room to where the chest of drawers lay, and in the top drawer was the tin with all the letters Gina had ever sent him.

He stood and rummaged, sweet memories flashing through his mind. He had read these over and over so many times, he knew exactly what each of them said.

The one where her friends had taken her to Atlantic City for the weekend and she won at the casino. The one where she'd had to repair a string in her violin. Another when she said she'd got caught daydreaming of him whilst sitting at her desk in her new job, and her boss had asked her why she wasn't working and was just sitting there like she had all day to daydream.

Then there was the one where she'd revealed thoughts of Gerry that were the property of two lovers.

Another letter when she'd visited the Hamptons for a work barbeque at the weekend, even missing a violin practice with an old friend.

"There it is," said Gerry. "That's the one."

He held the letter up to his face, the letter where she'd written down her number should there ever be such a thing as a phone in these parts. He pulled out the long string — the antenna — and began to punch in the number with less difficulty than he would've imagined. And he waited.

And he waited.

And he waited some more, staring at this strange device in his hand.

Now, to take a step back for a moment, how long would you wait?

You have never known a phone in your life, and you're not hearing anything back, how long would you wait? A few seconds? A minute? Well, Gerry, being a patient man, and knowing what was waiting down the end of the line, stood there for the best part of ten minutes waiting for a sound from the machine that he had realized after minute four should be held closer to his ear.

And that was when he'd typed in the number again. He could hear the device make a sound each time he pressed a number, but then there was nothing except a dull, faint, constant hum. After trying a few more times, he finally realized there was something he was doing wrong, so he hopped in his tractor with the letter and the phone.

"How's it going, Gerry?" said Brendan, when Gerry walked through the door.

"Not so bad, Brendan. Not so great either, I should say," said Gerry as he walked down the hall and into the kitchen, stopping to bless himself as he walked by the photos of Aunt Cara.

The smell of stew hit his nose.

"What's wrong, Gerry? Are you all right? Would you like some stew?" asked Uncle Brendan.

"No, I'm grand; thank you though. Will you take a look at this?"

Gerry lay the phone out on top of the table.

"What is it, Gerry?"

"Jimmy sent it. It's a Motorola Dynatec. I press the buttons and nothing, nothing happens."

"Hold on there Gerry, a motor dynamite? What? Have you got yourself mixed up with any fellas from the North?"

"No. Sorry, Brendan. Jimmy sent it, says it's a mobile phone. But it just won't do anything."

"Oh right. Odd thing that. But if it's a phone, why don't you try the operator?"

"The what?"

"The operator. Maybe they have to connect you or something. It's zero, zero, zero," said Uncle Brendan.

And Gerry looked at him as if to say, 'how the hell do you know this?' But he tried anyways.

"Nothing?"

"Well, try calling nine, nine, nine? That's the emergency number. If that doesn't work then we — ah, wait, Gerry." Brendan paused to think as he turned and began to stir his pot of stew. "Gerry that thing won't work for a few years yet. It was a special they had on the news a while back. They said in America, that these people were able to call each other when they walked down the street. At first, I was confused; I thought sure, that's not so special. I can call across the street to you if you're walking down it as well. But then I understood. They said the same thing won't be in Ireland for another few years yet."

And with that, Gerry sat down again and stared out the window.

After a few moments, Brendan walked over with a bowl of stew. "You know, Gerry, they said we'd have phones down here by now. They even set one up in Tralee a couple of years ago. But then they were out fixing the lines so much with the wind and the rain that they eventually gave up on it. Sure, we're in Ballyduffy, Gerry. Dublin's a long way from here."

"How did I not hear about this phone?"

"I'm not sure, Gerry. I think people around these parts soon realized it wasn't worth the hassle when it never worked. And sure, I heard Mary Langan say it cost an arm and a leg one day, when she had to use the operator to place a call to Dublin — never mind America."

Gerry looked up from his tea.

"If that's what you were thinking," said Brendan as he took a seat at the table.

And with that, Gerry's talking mood soon subsided. However, he listened as Brendan told him stories about Aunt Cara and the auld days. He spoke of how much things had changed over the last few years, and of all the shows and the news he watched on television now that she was gone. And when Gerry heard this, his appetite disappeared.

When it was time to drive home, Gerry kept his two hands on the wheel as the phone rattled about his feet somewhere inside the tractor. And when he came to turn into his house at the foot of Drumbarron Hill, he put the brake down, and turned off the engine.

He looked up at the road that seemed to climb forever, and he thought of Dublin. Mary Langan could call Dublin. And for a few seconds his heart rushed, and his mind went as fast as it could. Then he took out the letter folded gently inside his pocket with Gina's number on it.

March 1987. More than a year ago now. And he thought of her last letter with the words: *By the time you receive this, I will have moved into Manhattan.* With someone else.

And when the rain started to fall and hit hard on his roof, he sat again in silence, staring at the bastard of a hill in front of him.

———— • ✼ • ————

Whilst his heart was torn, Gerry being the proud man he was, he shook off the cloud that had been hanging over his head and over the next couple of months, he had got in the habit of running up Drumbarron Hill every day. And he would do double checks on his sheep and his cattle to ensure no wild dogs were getting anywhere near them.

In autumn, when the evenings got dark and lonely, Gerry would even start putting a new fence around the fields, realizing the auld fence was from Pa's time, and plus, it would give him something to do, all the while keeping thoughts of Gina far away.

Thanksgiving rocked around again, and this year, Gerry and Uncle Brendan decided not to have any celebration because for the first time in his life, Gerry didn't feel too thankful, and he would instead find himself sitting on the high stool in O'Brien's pub that Thanksgiving Sunday.

After his eighth Guinness, Gerry looked around the bar at the professionals surrounding him. Pat Storey was down one end, and he gave Gerry a nod as he took a slurp of what Gerry guessed had to be his eighty-eighth pint. And there were others, too.

There were a few of the professionals who'd eaten the triangle sandwiches at Pa's funeral, and a few who'd replaced those other professionals, the ones who'd passed away since then.

"Will you have a shot of whiskey, Gerry?" said Toe O'Brien from behind the bar. "Tom Reilly there bought it for you."

Gerry looked across to Tom Reilly who nodded back. Gerry stared at Tom's red nose and his droopy eyes and understood that this wasn't the first shot of whiskey Tom would have had that evening, nor did he think it would be his last. Gerry looked down at his drink.

Why not? he thought.

So, he threw his head back and let it go.

Then, he knew he had to buy Tom Reilly one back. And then Tom bought another for Gerry, and one for Brian O'Shea as well, another professional sitting a few seats down.

And then Brian bought Tom another shot, and one for Gerry too. And Gerry being the proud man, he bought them back their shots and so the night went.

The men talked the kind of talk that comes out at those hours. The buoyant moments — the stories of great football teams and players and games they'd seen over the years — followed by the more sombre moments, not to be mistaken with sober as the whiskey would hit in waves, and like all waves, they crashed before another wave of buoyancy came again.

And in those sombre waves, they'd chat of people who had passed: relatives, folk from the town, other professionals from the pub down through the years. And after those moments of buoyancy had gotten so large like a tidal wave of whiskey-filled laughs, the crash would only be larger, and the sombre stories of heartbreak and lost love would linger in the air of the bar for the seven or eight hangers-on still there in the early hours. When one of the auld fellas mentioned that championship win, and the night they'd enjoyed in here that Thanksgiving not two years ago, that last tidal wave of Gerry's crashed, and his sea of thoughts went quiet.

Gerry felt a hand on his shoulder. He looked around at Pat Storey, who used his walking stick like a third leg to keep him up against the bar. "Well, Gerry," said Pat in a low voice as the other fellas in the pub continued chatting and laughing around him.

"How's it going, Pat?" said Gerry.

"Not so bad, Gerry. I've had a couple all right," said Pat, who chuckled. "You look like ye have the weight of the world on your shoulders, Gerry? Not a great way to be. I take it Gina hasn't been around in a while. Always knew when Gina was around by the grin on your face."

"Ah now, Pat, you could say that all right. Strange how that was what came to your head," said Gerry in a quiet voice.

"Well, sure, what else weighs like love on a man, Gerry? You know, I once sat here like you did. Granted, my shoulders weren't as big as yours."

Gerry smiled, then nodded.

Pat continued, "Ah, Gerry. I was in love once too, you know. May she rest in peace. I lost her to a spritelier fellow, let's say. Why do you think I drink? But I'll tell you one thing for free, best bit of advice I ever got. Best thing I ever heard. Well, I'll tell it to you as long as you buy me another pint because I'm all out of change."

Gerry chuckled when he heard the gasp of laughter in his ear.

"Go on then, another please, Toe," said Gerry.

"Just the one, Gerry?" said Toe.

Gerry looked into his half pint of Guinness which seemed to move from side to side. "Just the one, Toe."

"You're a good man, Gerry. I'll get you back," said Pat.

"What were you going to say there, Pat?" said Gerry.

"Ah that's right. Well, Gerry, as I was saying, I'll tell you one thing for free about love. You see, it's like an anchor, Gerry. The tides come and go, high tide and low tide. And that anchor may be pushed around a little, but it stays there, unmoved. You know, true love doesn't ever leave; it's there somewhere, always. In stormy seas, we just mightn't be able to see it right now."

And Gerry swallowed the remainder of his pint. He felt like saying, 'Pat, enough of your drunk talk and your stormy seas' but by now, it was near tree in the morning, and Gerry wished them all good night and could barely see the door in front of him as he walked out.

The street in front of him was dark and cold. His vision was blurred, the images and memories of Gina surrounding him like ghosts as he staggered out the road. And at one point, once he had passed the sheepdog at O'Neills', he stumbled over a loose rock, and with countless shots of whiskey flowing through his veins, he missed his step, falling into the ditch and rolling a little before coming to a stop. Gerry felt the cold, wet grass on the back of his head, the breath that left his lungs on each movement of his chest also lingering for a moment before disappearing, and he would reach with his hand and try to catch it.

That air felt like all he had left, and when he looked up at the dark sky above, even the stars had left him. He thought some more about Gina and that first night they'd kissed, with the moon bright in the sky across the Atlantic Ocean. He thought of Jimmy, too, and of that night all those years ago when they'd fought and tumbled into a ditch not too far from this one.

A tear rolled down his cheek, but even after all that whiskey, Pa's words echoed once more in his ears. Gerry wiped the tear away, clenching his jaw so another wouldn't get away.

Then farther up the road, there came a commotion from the sheep in his field, odd for the middle of the night. So, he climbed out of the ditch and walked at a brisker pace, if at times from side to side, along the road to where the sheep were gathered up tight against the fence in an unusual manner. Through his blurred vision, Gerry made out a dark shape in the field, and he heard a deep, snarling growl. The wild dog had returned.

He jumped in and made roars and noises and chased the dog away.

"For now," Gerry whispered to himself.

He made his way into his house, where he was pouring a glass of water when he heard that same commotion from the field of sheep again.

"That bastard dog," Gerry said.

He went into his bedroom and bent down under the bed, taking out that auld gun of Pa's. The rain erupted from the heavens, one of those winter storms where every crevice of your body felt wet, and as Gerry staggered along the road, the rain and his glass of water had made his steps a touch more linear.

All the while the bleats from his sheep grew louder as he carried the gun towards the field.

He opened the gate and walked in, letting the bleats guide him, the dark and the rain, not to forget the whiskey, having made his eyes less than useful. In the far corner, the panicked sheep huddled together, and Gerry could just make out the dark figure of a dog snarling in front.

He ran across and roared, and the dog scrambled in the opposite direction before Gerry heard a loud whimper. And then another. The screams of an animal which had hurt itself.

Gerry followed the whimpers, finding himself standing in front of a ring of barbed wire that he had yet to place on the fence around the field. And in the barbed wire was the wild dog that had been tormenting Gerry's sheep. The dog's leg had been caught, and each time it moved, Gerry could hear the whimper, the yelp of pain.

"This is the bastard here," said Gerry.

He lifted his gun and aimed towards the dog. This bastard had killed a couple of Gerry's sheep a while back, and now he had him. The wind picked up in Gerry's ears as he placed his finger around the trigger. The dog looked up, still snarling, still clenching its teeth in between each whimper of pain whenever its leg moved. And Gerry stared into the dark with his finger ready to pull, when his hand began to shake. For some reason, he just couldn't fire.

Despite staring death in the face, despite the pain that was shooting around its body, despite the fear it must have been feeling, this bastard of a dog still had all the fight left in it. Gerry dropped the gun to the ground, feeling about, searching there on his hands and knees for the clippers that he had left against one of the posts.

Gerry made sure to stay out of reach of the dog's teeth, and he said, "Calm down, you bastard," before he clipped the wire and set the dog free to run off into the dark, the whimpers following with it. Gerry lifted the gun and once he checked the sheep, he headed back home.

Hopefully, that blasted dog, having had a painful enough experience with the barbed wire and the fear from the sight of a gun, wouldn't be coming back this direction anytime soon.

Once inside, Gerry made the fire and changed out of his soaked clothes. He made a cup of tea, and with the tea and the fire, slowly felt himself warm from the inside out.

He sat in his thoughts, and for a long time, they were only of one person: Gina. Then he thought of all the people lost down the years: Ma, Pa, Jimmy, and he thought of Aunt Cara.

"Why did she have to die, then?" whispered Gerry through his whiskey-stench breath.

All the while, Gerry felt the cold steel of the gun between his fingers and his palm. He lifted it up to his lap and rubbed his hand along it. Pa had left the one bullet in it, and Gerry had never seen much sense in getting any more. He thought again of Gina and how much he missed her, and how this year, more than any, had been the loneliest he'd ever experienced.

He turned the gun towards himself, so that now, he was staring down the barrel, staring into the dark chamber, just as that wild dog had. The bullet was in there somewhere, somewhere in that dark and his thumb grasped around the trigger. He began to breathe lighter and faster, just like that dog had been breathing through its pain, and he felt the cold metal of the trigger around the inside of his thumb. That was all Gerry could think about as the thoughts escaped him and his mind stopped. Then Gerry looked into the fire, and he clenched his jaw.

He put the gun back down.

———— • ✳ • ————

The next morning, Gerry woke early, and after less than five hours sleep, and with a head that weighed like a ton of bricks — seeing as Gerry was now tirty-two, and whiskey drunk down like that was very uncommon — he headed back out to the bottom field and finished putting the barbed wire around the fence. And he thought of that snarling dog for a moment, facing its death, and still having that stubborn, bastard look in its face, before Gerry shook his head and gripped his hammer and focused on his work. Though it took him an entire day, and despite the pain of the hangover, Gerry felt lighter than he had in many months.

And that night, after he had made himself a hearty dinner of potatoes and sausages, and after he had taken the bullet out of Pa's gun and placed both the bullet and the gun under his bed again, Gerry had the best sleep he had in as long as he could remember.

CHAPTER

18

From the moment he'd freed that wretched dog, Gerry found his way back to the Gerry McCarthy he knew best; his sheep and cattle were well looked after, and that following spring, one of his best cows, a white and brown one, didn't it win the best-turned-out cow at the Tralee spring festival. Gerry had even stood for a photo with it, a red ribbon saying '1st Place' on it.

He had come to realize something that he'd already known deep inside, that he was very grateful for this wonderful little tea shop he had created for himself. Over the winter, he'd replaced a few of the tables and chairs that had seen some wear and tear throughout the years, and he had gone into Kelly's shop in Tralee one day and bought himself a new photograph of the great Kerry team, one with the Boomer in his heyday standing in the back line.

Gerry replaced the old photo on the wall of the tea shop with this colour one, filled with the green and gold. And one day in summer, Pat Storey would stare at that picture, and he'd say, "Jaysus, Gerry, I still don't know how ye beat the Boomer," and he smiled and shook his head.

Gerry too, laughed and thought back to that wonderful day where he'd lifted that championship with the words of Joe McGettigan in his ears. That day, with Gina calling out his name, had been one of the happiest of his life and although the grief and pain were still hidden deep down in the back

CHAPTER EIGHTEEN

chambers and valves of his heart, it was a great memory.

At times here and there, and never more than a month apart, he'd have a thought of Gina. Something would always remind him of her: someone in the tea shop mentioning a relative took a trip to New York, or when he was down at John McHugh's farm and had seen that he'd bought a new horse, a dark brown one with a white blaze. And Gerry wished her nothing but the best because he knew if anyone deserved the best, it was Gina.

Jimmy's letters would arrive six months apart at best.

He seemed to be making more of an effort, thought Gerry, despite the fact that each time Gerry popped by the post office to Patricia, his heart did stop for a moment before his eyes would catch sight of the familiar ragged handwriting of Jimmy.

Sept '90

Gerry, what about that Ireland team? I watched the quarter final game in a pub here in New York, O'Dea's you call it. It was that packed you could barely turn a sweet in your mouth. And despite the loss, sure didn't they do us all proud! It was great. I tell you, if we ever get a chance to go to a game together, I wouldn't miss it for the world. And sure, with the way Kerry are going, it's nice to be able to cheer a team that are making us proud.

Sorry I forgot to mention Gerry, I may have gotten ahead of myself a little when I sent you that phone a couple of years back. I sometimes do that. I read a report in work that said it'll be another couple of years yet until the network is built out. We had the opportunity to invest in building it out too, a foreign investment for us here, but I said things usually take a lot longer than they think in those parts of Ireland like Ballyduffy and the rest of Kerry; it's not Dublin, you know.

When Gerry read it, he couldn't help but think again of Gina and of the hope that had sprung into his heart when he'd thought Jimmy had opened the door to her once again with the Motorola Dynatec. "It is what it is," Gerry said, thinking of the box with the phone that he had flung into the back of the wardrobe, right beside Gina's auld suitcase.

Funnily enough, Gerry had closed the tea shop for all the Ireland matches and he would be in O'Brien's pub like everyone else, squeezed around the television. The whole town would be there, and Pat Storey would have his usual seat at the end of the bar, and Gerry would nod over, and before you knew it, everyone would be singing and cheering the Irish team on.

After one of the games where Ireland had won a penalty shootout, Gerry ended up with Kathleen O'Connor, Dymphna's sister, back in the kitchen of the house at the bottom of Drumbarron Hill. They stayed together for a few weeks and a couple of months after that, but Gerry knew his heart wasn't in it, and so he told her. And to be fair to her, she took it well, and wished him the best of luck. A couple of years later, didn't she marry Gerry's pal John McHugh, and Gerry had the good shoes and the good suit on as best man, and he wished them all the luck in the world from the bottom of his heart. However, that best man's speech was better left unsaid. And at the wedding, didn't Gerry end up with the chief bridesmaid, Dymphna O'Connor, and they both agreed it was a one-night thing after a few too many drinks.

When he returned home the following day, his mind was on Jimmy again.

May '92

Jaysus, Gerry, John and Kathleen. I never would've picked that one out all those years ago. But I couldn't be happier for them both. They'll make a good pair. And yourself, Gerry, I know the whole thing with Gina was hard on you, but have you given thought to anyone else?

What about Dymphna? How is she keeping? She was always great craic now, a bit mad, but sure aren't we all at times? Would you never think about asking her out? Plenty of women over here, Gerry, should you fancy a trip out. It would be great to see you.

Here, I meant to tell you, I've a few changes over here myself. I've joined a new bank, Goldberg and Greenman, and we're helping out the farmers in the Midwest with some things which I've been brought in to assist with, which is great. And Maria and I, well we decided to part ways a few months back. She was a lovely person Gerry, but these things happen, you know. I've met someone new, Rachel's her name. She's four years younger than you and she does a bit of modelling for magazines and whatnot.

Mighty beautiful, Gerry. Early days, but she could be the one.

And this Kerry team, Gerry – the less said about them the better. I fear for this summer.

Jimmy must be busy with this new job thought Gerry on reading the letter; he knew how tough it was to run a farm. But Gerry was happy to hear Jimmy had found his way into a place that had the green and gold of Kerry. And Jimmy was right; this Kerry team was going through a dry patch and there was no sign of the keg being replaced.

Gerry would wish his brother well, and with a model and everything, too! He whispered to himself, "he knows how to land on his feet." However, each time a letter arrived, he still wished it could be from someone else.

The farm was fine, but what Gerry really enjoyed were his days in the tea shop. He was getting folk from all kinds of places now, even America.

An American cyclist was travelling around Ireland for a couple of weeks and sure, didn't he hear from that fella Stephen about Ballyduffy hill.

The American would be staying for a weekend in Tralee and cycle up that hill three times. And Gerry would have chats with him in the tea shop, the man filled with this positive energy.

One night, Gerry would hear in O'Brien's that the American — or Strongleg as he had become known — had been in there, also overhearing something from Pat Storey about the American leaving a stereo or something behind in the bathroom. Gerry sipped his pint. He thought of Gina and the violin, and sure he knew full well the power music could bring.

It made sense that the stereo could help the American get up the hill faster if he wished to.

A fella from as far away as Brazil stopped by too, with a long beard and a backpack. He was walking around Ireland, and when he heard that, Gerry thought, sure why the hell not? The fella was great fun and full of life, and he told Gerry all about Brazil. He said that they'd a big mountain too, and that it had a big statue of Jesus Christ. And Gerry thought, *isn't that something, but did the Pope ever leave a big log of a shite on it?* From the fella's stories, it sounded to Gerry that the Brazilians weren't too different from the Irish and enjoyed a good time, and the fella left Gerry a Brazilian flag with its green and gold colours and the world in the middle, and Gerry stuck it on the wall in the bottom room, along with the picnic table.

Then in 1993, one of those strange occurrences happened at the tea shop.

Gerry and Pat Storey, who at eighty-four years of age was still out on the roads with his walking stick, were chatting about the Kerry football team late one Friday evening.

"If I see them win an All-Ireland again, I'll be lucky, Gerry," said Pat in a loud voice as his hearing aid had partly broken the previous year and wasn't the best.

As Gerry stared out the window at the drizzle coming down, he saw a couple of black vehicles come to a halt outside his tea shop. They were jeeps, with blacked-out windows.

"I wonder who this is, Pat?"

"What did you say, Gerry?"

Then Gerry said louder, "I said, I wonder who this is?"

Pat turned from his stool as the door opened, and in walked the strangest looking fella Gerry had ever seen. He wore a black leather jacket and his trousers were black leather, too. He had long black hair and when he approached the counter, Gerry peered as hard as he could into the man's thick black sunglasses, but all Gerry could see were his own two eyes peering back.

The strange fella wasn't the only one; another three guys came in, and one was even carrying a set of sticks that he kept tapping against his leg. There were another couple of people too; however, they looked more like the regular folk Gerry would have around the tea shop.

"How's it going?" said Gerry.

"I'm doing great. How are you, man? We were wondering if you have any tea going?" said the fella with the black sunglasses.

A Dubliner, thought Gerry.

"I do, for all of ye?" said Gerry.

"Yeah, why not? Pretty cool spot you have here."

And Gerry looked around his tea shop, which had a buzz and energy in the place at that moment. *Maybe these guys have something about them,* he thought.

When one of the men asked if they could bring in a bottle of whiskey from the car, Gerry supposed it was a Friday night, and when he responded *why not,* Pat Storey raised his eyebrows and said, "Did I hear that man's got a bottle of whiskey, Gerry?"

Gerry chuckled and nodded. So did the fella with the sunglasses. And so, the evening went, one of those famous tea and whiskey nights again in

Gerry's tea shop.

It turned out these fellas were musicians and had played a concert in Cork the night before, and they had decided to take a trip around the coast before heading back to Dublin.

After a few more whiskeys, one of the fellas, who was wearing a hat that looked a bit different to Pat Storey's, headed out to the jeep and brought in a green guitar. Then the musicians started playing, and sure, Pat Storey told them to turn it up because he couldn't hear a thing.

And Gerry couldn't believe how loud they were, the stones of his tea shop rocking. *By Christ, is it good music,* Gerry thought. He listened to the fella with the sunglasses as he sang, and Gerry realized that man was telling stories, and the music was just playing along.

And Gerry knew this man was right in what he said, because he also only knew one love, his mind drifting across the Atlantic Ocean again.

And sure, wasn't Pat tapping along with his walking stick as well.

As the fella sang, Gerry poured more whiskey in the tea, and he thought that it sounded as if that whiskey had got caught in the back of that man's throat, so raw and powerful was his voice. And after, they had a chat, and even though they were Dubs, they were nice people, and the fella with the sunglasses told Gerry he could keep the guitar if he liked.

Gerry couldn't believe it. Once they'd said their goodbyes, Pat said, "What was that fella's name? The one doing the singing, was it Bon Bon?"

And Gerry shook his head because he didn't know either; the music had been that loud he couldn't really hear. "I think so Pat. Something like that."

"Well, I hope he finds what he's looking for," said Pat.

And Gerry did too. He and Pat closed the tea shop and walked down the hill together before Pat insisted on walking the rest of his way home, despite Gerry offering a ride in his tractor.

———— • ✳ • ————

The very next day in town, whilst Gerry was leaving the shop after buying his groceries and wondering where in the tea shop he would hang the new green guitar, Pat Storey walked down Main Street. And Gerry stopped when he saw the look in Pat's eyes. When Pat took off his hat before he began to speak, Gerry dropped the bags of groceries.

"Brendan?" whispered Gerry.

"He's gone to the hospital in Tralee, Gerry. I was out for a walk when Father Finnegan stopped me on his way to your house."

"What happened, Pat?"

"He didn't say. But – Father Finnegan's going there himself."

"Thank you, Pat."

On his way to the hospital, Gerry thought of all those birthdays and confirmations when he and Jimmy were younger, when Cara and Brendan would come by their house, and bring a cake that Cara had baked or some other small treat for the boys, naughty treats Ma and Pa would scowl at, saying, "you're spoiling them." And when he'd gotten older, knowing that Christmas was a time of year not to be alone in the house, they'd always have invited Gerry down to theirs, where a turkey would sit and drinks would be taken, and games would be played.

When he arrived, Gerry rushed into Brendan's room. Brendan was talking.

"That's the first time I've ever seen you in a hurry if it wasn't on a football field, Gerry."

Gerry panted as he sat down on the chair beside his uncle's bed. Brendan had a tube up his nose and one in his arm and he looked a little like the grass in the top field after two weeks of non-stop sunshine.

"Brendan."

"Ah, would you stop looking at me like that, Gerry. If your aunt was here, she'd clip you around the ear. One of the nurses said I look like a Kerry jersey," said Brendan.

Brendan laughed and coughed until he was red in the face and then lay back against the pillow, Gerry waiting for the yellowy-green colour to return.

"Now. Father Finnegan was in to see me off before I go," said Brendan, his words slow and his breaths slower. "So, I got a letter from your brother. Said he'd written to you, and he still hadn't heard back yet. But that wasn't all, Gerry. He said he'd told you about the game, and that he invited you over for it. And I'm telling you now, I want you to go to New York."

It was true. Jimmy had written to Gerry not so long ago, and with a lot of things going on with the tea shop and the cattle, he hadn't gotten back to him yet.

And deep down, it was because Gerry still hadn't made his mind up.

Brendan continued, "You promised your aunt and now you'll promise me, Gerry."

"I promise," said Gerry, and he held a glass of water up to Brendan's mouth.

"Good man. Ye are like sons to me, and to thank ye for everything you've done, I left ye a gift in the house. One for you, one for Jimmy, and you can bring it with you to New York. Grief is best shared, Gerry. Don't worry about me. Cara will be whipping me into shape in no time."

Brendan died the next day. A couple of days later, Gerry carried that coffin with others through the town and laid it next to Aunt Cara's in the graveyard. And he bought two bunches of white lilies, and placed them on the grave. One for Aunt Cara and one for Uncle Brendan.

CHAPTER

19

Jimmy sent his condolences and Gerry knew that despite being across that ocean, the pain Jimmy was feeling wouldn't be too far from his own. Jimmy had added in his letter that he had gotten two tickets for the World Cup game between Ireland and Italy later in July in Giants Stadium of all places, and when Gerry set eyes on Uncle Brendan's gift — a green Ireland jersey with the number eight on the back — Gerry wrote back. "I'll see you in New York," he said.

Yet, in that moment, Gerry thought of Gina, and then of that day a few years ago, when he'd been leaving to go to the airport and Pat Storey had come blustering over the hill to deliver the news that Cara had died. Now, he felt all the pain that it brought up inside him again.

How would it feel to travel to New York for a different purpose, and for his Gina not to be there waiting for him at the other end?

————— • ✱ • —————

When the day came, Gerry lifted his Ballyduffy football bag and placed it in his tractor, just like he had done that morning so many years ago except this time, Ma's wedding ring wasn't in its pocket. With his passport and some dollars which Mary Feeney in the post office had helped him exchange, Gerry drove over the hills and towards Shannon Airport.

The game was tomorrow, and Gerry had placed his sign, 'Closed, gone to America for the weekend,' on the door outside the tea shop. Pat Storey and others had asked why he wouldn't stay for longer, and Gerry had replied, "I'm going to see my brother and to the game, and sure, neither of those takes a week." And when they heard that, they shrugged and agreed, knowing that Gerry still had a business to run on the Monday morning when he returned.

So, Gerry, his two hands wrapped tightly along each handrail, climbed the steps aboard his Aer Lingus flight to New York with care. He bent his head down as he entered the door, and walked along the aisle to spot his seat in 8-C. And he looked down at the man on the inside by the window, who was a right bit smaller than Gerry; and he felt a little bad that the man would have a tight squeeze against him for the next however many long hours.

"How's it going?" said Gerry.

"All right; what about you?" said the man.

"Not so bad."

Gerry could tell from the man's voice that he was from Dublin, and as Gerry put his arm, with his shovel-like hands on the armrest, he didn't really mind anymore that the man's flight would be uncomfortable. Gerry looked around the plane, then he clasped his hands together and whispered, "Lord Jaysus, please let us land on the other side like we are sitting here right now."

His foot began to tap, and once the plane started to roll on the runway, he noticed his hands were sweaty and he was breathing faster than usual, clutching onto that tiny armrest as if his life depended on it. Then he passed out, ignoring the squirms of the man beside him, and then he woke up. And sure, wasn't the plane empty, except for Gerry and the Dublin fella still sitting beside him, with a frown on his face.

The air hostess, daubed in her red lipstick, touched Gerry's arm and said, "Sir, we have arrived in New York. It's time to vacate the plane."

Gerry looked again down the cabin and whispered to himself, "Jaysus, that was fast." So, he thanked her and told her she had lovely white teeth, because she did. And he got off the plane.

The Dublin fella, with all his fluster and hurry, ran around Gerry, and once he was far enough away, sure didn't he turn and give Gerry the middle finger.

But Gerry didn't mind; he was in America.

And so, Gerry followed the lines and the signs through the airport. "John F. Kennedy, eh?" he whispered to himself. *A great Irishman,* he thought. He lined up in front of this thing called 'border security,' and it made sense. He knew all about the invisible border in the north of Ireland. The border patrol officer, with a thick bushy mustache and an accent reminding Gerry instantly of Gina, eyed him with a stern look, then glanced at his green jersey. "Business or pleasure, sir?"

Jaysus, thought Gerry, *that's an odd question.*

And being a passionate sportsman, Gerry paused for a moment before saying, "Well, I suppose if Ireland lose the game, it's not really pleasurable, is it?"

The border patrol man laughed, his mustache jiggling up and down.

"I get what you mean. I'm a Knicks fan, and if they lose tomorrow, don't know what I'll do."

Even though Gerry had no idea what he meant, the man shook his head and laughed some more before he stamped a piece of paper and let Gerry by.

Gerry turned back and wasn't the Dublin fella walking in a different direction, with a load of security men beside him. Gerry realized that only now was he in America.

"Hey, Gerry," said a voice as Gerry walked through the large sliding doors into Arrivals.

Gerry scanned the hordes of people standing on either side of the entrance. All cultures and races, some old, some young, some on their own, some families, some with flowers and balloons, and some with signs with people's names. It all seemed more than a bit odd; surely, if you were waiting on someone, you'd know their name by heart or that would be a bit weird. Or who knew, maybe it was their own names they were holding up. Just as bizarre either way.

Then, for a nanosecond, he wondered if Jimmy would be holding a sign that said 'Jimmy McCarthy.' Would he even recognize his brother after eighteen long years?

'Hey, Gerry, over here,' said the voice, and Gerry knew whose it was, even if it did have a hint of Gina's accent in it. Gerry set eyes on his brother, who stood in a pair of shorts and with a navy-blue polo shirt on, his hair slicked back with gel. Although he looked like how Gerry imagined one of those boater boys in Dublin looked, at least he was wearing Ballyduffy colours.

"How's it going, Jimmy?"

Gerry dropped his bag on the floor, and went to shake Jimmy's hand before Jimmy grabbed him and hugged him, and Gerry couldn't help the smile that broadened across his face.

And amongst all the hustle and bustle of an airport a million times busier than Shannon, the two brothers held each other close, in silence. Through the squeeze of his brother's arms, and the sigh that Jimmy exhaled before he let go, Gerry knew that the ghosts of Aunt Cara and Uncle Brendan, as well as Ma and Pa, were here somewhere amongst the hordes of passengers in JFK.

"I'm good, Gerry. You're still a great big hoor, I see. Do you want a hand with that bag? It's a grand bag – is that the one ye got for winning the championship?"

"It is, and no, I'll be grand — sure, it's not like one of those suitcases. I travel light. And I'll never buy one of those suitcases with the wheels on, let me tell you now!"

"You travel light and fast, Gerry. You're only in until Sunday?"

"That's right."

And although Gerry could see a flash of disappointment on his brother's face, Jimmy said, "Well, we will have to make the most of it, so."

"Hold on a second there. Let me see your hand again," said Gerry.

Gerry saw the smile come across Jimmy's face, the same smile that could charm a room. The same smile and twinkle in the eye that Jimmy had always shown when they were kids, whenever he'd been caught doing something wrong. A smile that could win anyone over.

"Rachel and I got married last Thanksgiving. I'm a taken man now, Gerry," said Jimmy.

And Gerry stopped for a moment, and he blinked.

He smiled back at Jimmy, but he tilted his head to the side. The eyes spoke volumes.

"It was only a small ceremony, Gerry. Now come on, I want to hear all about this tea shop?"

They chatted about Ballyduffy as they walked through the JFK terminal, and Gerry looked around at the large M, and the Burger King, before deciding to try a burger from each one because he hadn't eaten anything since Ireland. And despite the fact that McDonald's was faster coming out, and he liked the name of the Big Mac, he found the Burger King to be more to his liking., which turned out to be controversial, because Jimmy thought the opposite.

"Taxi!" shouted Jimmy.

Gerry couldn't believe it when out of the shadows came a vivid yellow cab, and he learned they would take it to Jimmy's house in Manhattan and the whole way there, Jimmy would point out this building and that building, Gerry even pulling down the window and sticking his head out, unable to see the tops of the buildings from inside the car.

The noise of the place was something else. At one point, when the cab was stuck in traffic for the umpteenth time, Gerry listened to countless people walking by, some chatting amongst each other, others speaking on their mobile phones which looked just like the one back in Gerry's house, if a little smaller. And to think, his own was still only useful as a doorstop.

The honks of the cars brought Gerry back to those days of driving the tractor around Kerry on his way to Tralee or Dingle. And for a moment, the city appeared to fall silent except for his heartbeat when a brown-haired woman with a fine figure and a beige coat came walking down the street towards them. But when she got closer, Gerry realized it wasn't her.

Besides, he had promised himself not to think about Gina for the weekend. And so, he made that promise to himself again right there.

Once they arrived at Jimmy's building, Gerry followed his brother into the elevator, and his head twisted and turned to take in the magnitude of everything surrounding him.

"It has a grand view of Central Park, Gerry," said Jimmy.

And when Jimmy pressed the button for fifty-four and the light came on, Gerry saw that there were numbers up to eighty-nine, and he laughed to himself, knowing that his younger self would've pressed all the buttons from fifty-five to eighty-nine for a laugh.

Jimmy's apartment was plenty new and shiny, thought Gerry, everything gleaming from the marble floors to the bright white sofa that could fit five or six.

The whole place was like something out of a magazine.

"Rachel designed most of it," said Jimmy.

"Very good; it's all very new. Where's Rachel? Now that she's a McCarthy, I'd love to welcome her to the family," asked Gerry.

"She's out for brunch with her friends right now, but we're going to meet up for dinner later. Now Gerry, is there anything you'd like to see whilst you're here?" said Jimmy.

Gerry took a walk over to the window and down at Central Park and it looked quite nice, but he couldn't help thinking that it looked like the park sat imprisoned by the gates of tall skyscrapers all around. However, it was still mighty green, if not as green as the fields around Ballyduffy. It would do. This was a city after all. And different, sure enough.

"Well, I wouldn't mind seeing that big statue that's on the stamps. And I suppose, I've heard of this place with all the lights, that would be something," said Gerry.

"You read my mind. Don't worry, I've them on our list. But first, let's hit up a bar for a pint like auld times."

The afternoon passed with sightseeing around New York, interrupted with pints in bars such as McSorley's, Sullivan's and the Mean Fiddler. And there were lots of Irish fans around, who, like Gerry, had made the way over to New York for the game. As the late afternoon temperature rose and the beads of sweat appeared on his head, Gerry lamented the jeans he had on as they were stuck to the inside of his legs, and he made a note to wear his shorts tomorrow.

Down along the southern part of Manhattan, as Gerry and Jimmy lined up for the boat that would take them to the Statue of Liberty, Gerry mulled over what a beautiful sight it was. That torch in her hand looked nothing like an ice cream, and Gerry thought again of those damn postmen and their stamps. He thought of his plan to propose to Gina here too, and like the ice cream, that plan had also gotten burned to flames.

But Gerry felt alive and light in the heat, and the sweat of his jeans didn't bother him as much with the fresh breeze coming off the other side of the Atlantic Ocean.

He stood in amazement at how large the statue was in the distance, and at that moment, regretted not having a camera. So, he paid someone five dollars to take a picture of him and Jimmy, and although he knew he was the fool for paying that amount for a simple photograph, he wanted it as a memory. And then Jimmy paid another five dollars for a photo too.

The tour guide with the microphone told them all the history of the statue, and something deep inside Gerry was alight and burning quietly like that flame.

He felt filled with liberty and freedom, and there was something about America that gave him spirit. Maybe it was all the noise and the people, but there was an indisputable energy about the place, and when he was standing on top of that statue looking at the skyscrapers littering the sky, he felt as though it had cast its spell over him. And in his conversations with fellow tourists and visitors, Gerry suddenly found himself with more words than ever before.

Later that evening, around seven, Jimmy and Gerry ascended another elevator in a building called the Liberty Tower, walking into a restaurant on the ninety-first floor where Jimmy had reserved a table right by a window. Gerry nearly tripped over the chair when he saw Jimmy greet a woman already sitting there. It turned out to be Rachel.

Jaysus! She looked like one of those women Gerry had seen in adverts on the television in O'Brien's pub at half time, in whatever game he'd been watching! With her light brown hair, greenish brown eyes, and tan skin, she was quite the picture, he thought.

"So nice to meet you, Gerry," said Rachel. Her voice sounded like Gina's, but a little more *something*, and Gerry couldn't quite find the word to describe it.

Rachel stuck out her hand and Gerry looked down to see she was wearing two rings.

One was a gold wedding band which looked like Ma's but was very new and shiny, just like Jimmy's apartment. The other boasted the largest diamond he had ever seen, like a lightbulb on her finger. Then he noticed he was staring, so he shook himself.

"How's it going, Rachel? Very nice to meet you too."

"How was your flight over? I've been telling Jimmy we will have to take a trip over sometime," said Rachel.

Gerry looked at her dark red blouse and sparkly earrings, reflecting the evening light, and then he looked to the seat beside him where she rested her grey leather bag. That, too, seemed quite sparkly somehow. He didn't know why, but he couldn't really picture Rachel in the bottom field with the sheep, never mind the top field with all the cowshite.

"It went a lot faster than I thought it would. Now tell me, how did you meet this gobshite of a brother?" said Gerry.

As Rachel spoke about something to do with an art gallery and photos, paintings, or something, Gerry thought about the rocks outside his tea shop, and then kept catching the light reflecting off her ring like a laser beam of some sort. Now, he realized that the word he had been looking for was 'polished.' Rachel spoke a lot more polished than Gina, and truth be told, he wasn't sure he preferred it. However, this was Jimmy's wife, so he was cordial, and despite the airplane lag beginning to wash over him like waves on an ocean, he smiled and laughed and told her his stories of the auld days in Ballyduffy from when he and Jimmy were growing up.

At one point, he looked out the window and over towards herself — the Statue of Liberty — in the background, and couldn't help but look right past and towards the line where the sky met the Atlantic Ocean. He found himself thinking of Gina and picturing himself in her position.

"Gerry; hey Gerry," Jimmy's voice brought Gerry back into the room.

"Sorry, I drifted off there for a second."

"I know you did, must be the jet lag. Rachel was just saying she has to go," said Jimmy.

Gerry stood up, and then looked down at Rachel, who gave him a handshake and a smile, and said she would see him later.

"She has a friend's birthday party tonight, so it frees us up for a few pints," smiled Jimmy.

They left, and after ascending high into the sky for something to eat, they were now descending into a hole in the ground, on their way to find a bar.

As they walked down the steps, a blast of heat hit Gerry in the face and the thick jeans started to stick to his legs again. Soon, they were standing on the platform waiting for one of those subway trains to deliver them to Times Square.

Gerry looked around wide-eyed at the amazing architecture, experiencing an extraordinary sense of pride when Jimmy told him that the New York subway had actually been built by an Irishman. However, that pride diminished a little when Jimmy said the fella was a Corkman. Kerry and Cork folk didn't get along. Nevertheless, it was quite the feat.

Once they got on a train, Gerry blinked when a fella in a red and blue basketball shirt began to sing, and he stood and listened to the most powerful, soulful voice that he had ever heard. And Gerry loved the words the man was singing too when he spoke of sunshine on cloudy days. And being from the west coast of Ireland, Gerry knew all about the cloudy and rainy days. The fella took off his hat and said, "Any change, brother?"

"No, please keep doing what you're doing, it's great," replied Gerry.

Jimmy laughed and placed a couple of dollars in the fella's hat.

"What was that song you were singing?" asked Gerry.

"What, you don't know *My Girl*, brother? Have you been living under a rock?"

Gerry blinked. He lived at the bottom of Drumbarron Hill, and he supposed a hill to be made of rock, so the fella wasn't far wrong.

"I'm sorry, I don't know who your girl is. Who is she?" said Gerry.

And the fella smiled then winked at Gerry. "Never you mind, brother. Have a nice day."

Jimmy seemed to be having a great time, and Gerry saw him laughing together with an auld woman sitting on a seat across. And when the train ground to a halt at the next stop, the auld woman whispered to Gerry as she was leaving, "He was singing 'My Girl,' by the Temptations. You should check them out sometime. Have a nice day."

Gerry understood now why they had laughed, and he chuckled too, and said, "Thank you, you also have a nice day. And I will. I'll check it out."

As the woman left, Gerry made a note to get that record for his tea shop once he got home.

In Times Square, Gerry could hardly bring himself to speak. He stood amid this strange land, his eyes wide open and his head turning from side to side.

"It's some sight," said Jimmy, beside him.

Gerry nodded, continuing to struggle to take in everything he was seeing, something new to look at in every spot. And the strangest thought popped into his mind. He thought of Rachel's diamond ring, and all the light and the sparkle of it, and he wondered if it would sparkle here, because he'd never seen a place more lit up at night in his life. The billboards and the banners, and the video loops and screens with all their brash colours and images, were non-stop.

"It's just like your letters said," said Gerry. *And like Gina said too,* he thought.

"Yeah, Ma and Uncle Paudie knew what they were talking about, Gerry. It's a little quieter in winter. But not much, I suppose," chuckled Jimmy.

Then Gerry stopped looking around, and he turned his head back and peered above. Up past the lights of the offices that climbed like a staircase into the sky, past those billboards with their adverts for the new movie — which from what Gerry had gathered seemed to be about a nice man from Alabama who liked to run to different parts of the world — Gerry's eyes continued past the McDonald's sign and up into the night sky. He paused, his eyes tensed and staring harder than they ever had since he'd landed here in this magical country.

"Ye don't get to see the stars too often then?" said Gerry.

Jimmy followed Gerry's gaze.

"I suppose I don't, Gerry."

And in among all the noise and the thousands of people around the place, a small pocket of silence cut in between the two brothers from Ballyduffy.

Then Jimmy said, "I remember that night like it was yesterday. If only I'd had one pint less, I'd have caught you with that right hook and it would've been you on the ground."

Gerry let out a loud laugh before the silence returned for a brief moment.

"Some chance. Now come on for another pint."

For the next few hours, Jimmy and Gerry went into a couple of Irish pubs around New York, Gerry regaling Jimmy with stories all about the tea shop and the tales he had heard from Pat Storey. He also let Jimmy in on the stories of the Pope, and the Dubliners, and then of the green guitar, and finally, he told him about Gina in a quiet voice.

And, although that conversation only lasted for a few short seconds before Gerry changed the subject, Jimmy must've known not to ask any more questions.

"Jaysus, Gerry, I believe everything you're saying. It's mad. I'm sad I missed the craic now. I'll have to take a trip back. Between you and me, that green card never came, so that's why I never made it yet, but I'm hoping if I play my cards right, it will be here soon," said Jimmy.

Gerry watched as Jimmy took a sip of Guinness and he could see a tear in his brother's eyes. After all these stories, all these memories that he'd missed out on, including Aunt Cara's and Uncle Brendan's funerals, Gerry also knew not to ask any more questions.

Despite the many years and all the physical distance that had kept the brothers apart for so long, they could still read one another's minds, knowing when to talk and when to be silent.

After a moment, Gerry asked, "How's the job going? Are there any other Irish working with you?"

"It's grand. And yeah, there's one, Gerry, would you believe. A Dub!"

Gerry shuffled in his seat, "And how do you put up with him?"

Jimmy laughed and lifted his glass to his mouth, before he said, "One thing I've come to learn Gerry, is that when you branch out, you realize that we're all part of the same tree. I suppose, back home in Ballyduffy, be it with Carrickbay, or Tralee, or Dublin, you have to fight the next branch over for a bit of light and space. Or whatever else."

Jimmy took a long sip of his pint and Gerry joined him.

Gerry had a chuckle at the thought of the Dub who rushed off the plane and wondered if he ever did make it to America. Then he thought of Carrickbay and all the fights with the Murtagh's down the years. And he told Jimmy the stories of Joe McGettigan.

"You don't play any football out here, Jimmy?"

"Work has me too busy for football, Gerry, but how do you think I got those tickets for tomorrow? You know, I'm sorry about leaving you alone with, well you know, Aunt Cara and Uncle Brendan, Gerry. If it's any consolation, I felt as alone here, too," said Jimmy.

"It's ok. Life gets busy. I get it," said Gerry.

And nothing was said for a few minutes as the brothers sipped their pints in silence.

"Jaysus, they were always about, you know," said Jimmy.

"Yeah, they were."

"Looking back on it, I'm not sure what Pa would've done without them looking after us two. I suppose you weren't so bad. I probably gave them a few sleepless nights. God knows where we would've ended up without them. I know they're together somewhere up there."

Jimmy took a long sip of his pint as he glanced at the ceiling.

"Sorry to hear about Gina too, Gerry. You never know. New York's a big city, but the world's smaller than you think sometimes. If it's meant to be, you'll cross paths again."

Gerry nodded. And he took a long sip of his pint, then ordered two more.

Near midnight, Gerry yawned as that airplane lag had come over him fully now, and so with a big day tomorrow at Giants Stadium, they went back to Jimmy's apartment where Gerry slept in a spare bedroom in the most comfortable bed in which he'd ever slept in his life.

Well, after he had thrown the extra five pillows down onto the carpet.

———— • ✹ • ————

Gerry woke early, *something to do with time travel,* he thought, and so, he went for a walk around the neighbourhood which was mighty nice and quiet at that time in the morning. Seeing as he was awake, he thought that he may as well get himself some breakfast. To Gerry's luck, up ahead was a place that was open, and it turned out to be a coffee shop. Gerry thought back to Jimmy's comments from years ago about there being coffee shops all over America, and said to himself, "That Jimmy man could always tell the future."

Gerry entered the dinky donut store, casting his gaze around for a seat where he could eat his breakfast, but to his surprise, there were neither seats nor tables in the place. The customers in the line in front would get their drinks and their breakfast and take it with them — and leave!

How did that work, then? He couldn't imagine it was very comfortable eating his breakfast while walking back down the street.

"Jaysus, it's not like they're late for Mass. Sure it's Saturday," whispered Gerry.

Regardless, with three teas and three donuts, Gerry left and headed back to Jimmy's apartment where Jimmy had awoken.

"I've the feckin' butterflies, Gerry. It'll be some game," said Jimmy, and when he saw the teas and donuts in Gerry's hands, he said, "Thank you. You didn't have to."

"Not a bother; we'll need a good cup of tea before the game. I've one for Rachel too."

"Well, it's an extra one for you then, Gerry. She's just away out. The foundation she's involved with has a meeting this morning."

Gerry thought about the foundation of his house, and then the auld foundation of the cottage that was the tea shop, and he thought Rachel didn't seem to be the building kind of person. But what did he know? His mind drifted to the game, and he took a sip of tea.

"Jaysus," said Gerry.

Jimmy noticed the grimace on Gerry's face, and he said, "Not like the tea back home, is it?"

Gerry nodded, then decided to take another drink. Even though it tasted like cowshite, he'd paid for it, so he may as well drink it. And after a shower and a brush of the teeth, Gerry put on his green jersey, and his white Ballyduffy football shorts.

"Love the jersey," said Jimmy when Gerry walked into the living room.

Jimmy had the same jersey, only with number fourteen on the back, his auld number for Ballyduffy. "Uncle Brendan was some man. God rest his soul."

Now they were ready for a day they'd remember for the rest of their lives.

As they walked to the subway, which would take them in the direction of Giants Stadium, Gerry noticed the heat in the air, and was glad he didn't have any jeans sticking to his legs today.

And when someone shouted from across the street, "Who likes short shorts?" Gerry looked down at his Ballyduffy football shorts and smiled and shouted back, "They're very comfortable. I'd recommend a pair for this heat." And the man who shouted over didn't know whether to laugh or cry, or any other reaction, really. He just kind of stood quiet and shrugged, before walking off in the opposite direction, much to Jimmy's enjoyment.

They hopped off the subway close, but not too close, to the stadium. Gerry, a giant of a man where he came from, looked out at that stadium stretching far and wide into the sky, and he thought this stadium was for different kind of giants; he'd never seen anything like it.

Jimmy led Gerry to a pub close by — Molly Maguires — and even though there were still a couple of hours to go until kick off, it was jammed with green jerseys, just like the kind the McCarthy brothers were wearing. And Gerry drank a couple of Guinness with his brother, just like the days of auld when they would watch Kerry together on the television in O'Brien's.

There were Irish fans there from everywhere: Galway, Mayo, Dublin obviously, and even a few men in blue Italian jerseys in the pub as well, drinking and laughing, and the butterflies were flying all over the bar in anticipation of the game.

In the midst of a sip of Guinness, Gerry's hand shook and nearly spilled some of the black stuff over his green shirt.

"What's that feckin' noise?" he said.

He had been startled by a beeping sound coming from somewhere. It wouldn't stop ringing in his ears. He looked around the bar for whatever was making the noise. "Jimmy, do you hear that sound? It'd drive you mad."

Gerry turned around and looked down at Jimmy, who had a small device in his hand. It looked as though he was watching something on it, or reading something, and Gerry realized the noise was coming from that very device. Then Jimmy pressed a button, and Gerry saw the lightness in his brother's body leave, and he seemed to sink down into his stool.

"Jaysus, Gerry. I have to go into the office," said Jimmy.

Gerry blinked because it was a Saturday, and he knew the bank in Tralee

CHAPTER NINETEEN

was closed on a Saturday. But he took a sip of his pint and let his brother continue telling him all about it.

"It's a pager, Gerry. Terrible things; they can get you at all times. I got rid of my phone, but they still get you with this," said Jimmy, who took the last sip of his Guinness and continued, "I'm sorry Gerry, I have to go. Here, take my ticket and give it to someone else. Meet me at seven-thirty tonight at the Lobby restaurant, and we'll go out for drinks.

"You take the subway to Grand Central later, and it's only a couple of blocks from there. Sorry again, Gerry. I didn't expect this. I feel like shite for leaving you all alone."

Jimmy handed Gerry his spare ticket, and Gerry watched as number fourteen walked out through the sea of Irish jerseys. He didn't know what to think. He supposed it must be something very important for Jimmy to leave now, and so he finished his Guinness and walked outside, and decided to head a little closer to Giants Stadium. He was here on holidays at one of the biggest games in the history of the Irish team and those butterflies hadn't followed Jimmy out the door.

It was easy to know he was walking in the right direction because there were droves of people, more than he had ever seen around Ballyduffy or Tralee or any other part of Kerry he'd been to. There were probably more spectators in this one street than would even fit into Ballyduffy. And there were more of those blue Italian shirts milling about now too.

Gerry had met a few Italians in the tea shop over the years, and he knew they were great people full of lively animation and loud voices, and he sometimes thought they talked through their hands. And wouldn't you believe, there were a few supporters dressed up with those long hats that the cardinals had worn when they'd walked into Gerry's tea shop that day.

Gerry smiled as he walked past, saying, "Good luck to you, now," though he didn't mean it.

He stopped in another bar closer to the stadium, O'Donnell's, and sure, wasn't it packed. He stood at the counter and had a pint.

Then he felt a tap on his back and the sound of a woman's voice saying, "You wouldn't let an auld woman stand in front of you, big fella? I won't get a drink back here."

Gerry's jaw touched the floor when he saw the auld woman behind him, and the flashback came into his mind of that day in Thurles racecourse when His Holiness had won at one hundred to one. The auld woman said, "Ah it's yourself! If that's not a sign we are going to win today, then I don't know what is."

Gerry bought the auld woman a pint, soon learning her name was Rosie, and it turned out Rosie had also kept her winnings from His Holiness for a rainy day. When it hadn't come, she decided to use the money to fly to New York with her son for the game. She supposed she hadn't too long left to wait for any of those rainy days to arrive. And even though she was from Cork — which made Gerry raise his eyebrows for a moment — today, they were all Irish.

"You haven't a spare ticket, do you?" asked Rosie.

"By Christ," whispered Gerry.

He threw his head back and looked to the skies, but all he saw was the ceiling of the bar, and all the flags of the counties of Ireland were hanging there. And sure, wasn't he standing under the Kerry one. Gerry felt the spare ticket from Jimmy in his pocket and he knew for certain that auld women had a backdoor to reach God.

So, as Rosie's son had a ticket for another part of the stadium, Gerry and Rosie went to the game together, and hadn't Jimmy gotten them great seats, right near the touchline, behind the Irish dugout. They could even hear the players and the managers chatting, they were that close. When the Irish coach turned around, Rosie gave him a wink, and Gerry thought the coach looked a little hot under his collar, but he wasn't sure if it was the heat or something else.

When the game began, Gerry cheered and screamed at the referee just like everyone else.

He looked up into the stands of the giant stadium, unable to believe the noise in the place. And in between the green, white, and orange of the Irish flags, he would see the green, white, and red of the Italian ones, realizing they weren't so different.

Gerry listened as Rosie roared out curses and bad words at the referee that I'll not use here, and although the Italians had this one player who was the best in the world, the one that they called 'the Divine Ponytail,' Gerry was sure that the Italians didn't know His Holiness was on Ireland's side today.

Would you believe Ireland scored early, and a beautiful goal it was.

And the little fella who'd scored did a cartwheel and the fans celebrated. Rosie turned to Gerry and pointed at his green jersey, saying, 'You picked the right number again, Gerry.'

Gerry looked down and then over at the player who had done the cartwheel. The little fella that scored was wearing number eight as well.

With a few minutes of the game remaining, Gerry looked to his right, and auld Rosie, all seventy-five years of her, was taking off her green shirt and standing in a grey bra!

Gerry blinked a couple of times before he asked, "What are you doing?"

"The Italians are coming, Gerry. We need to waste some time. I'm going to streak," and she started taking off her bra.

Gerry looked at the clock and there was only a minute to go in the game. He stopped her, and said, "No need to do that, Rosie. Isn't His Holiness on our side?"

He watched as a wave of relaxation came over Rosie's face, and she stopped and put her shirt back on. *Maybe we all have doubts,* thought Gerry. Then he heard the sound of the final whistle in his ears, and he hugged her. Ireland had won the greatest victory of all time.

As they were leaving the stadium, Rosie said she had to go meet her son, adding, "Even though I live in Cork, Gerry, I was born in Tralee. I wanted to see your reaction, and sure, didn't it make me laugh. Good luck to you now."

Jaysus, thought Gerry as she walked away into the crowds. *Rosie from Tralee!*

CHAPTER

20

A fter another celebratory pint of Guinness in one of the bars, Gerry
supposed it was time to go meet Jimmy; he had forgotten all about
him in the magic of the game and the celebrations, and he began to
make tracks across New York towards the restaurant where they would
meet.

Gerry boarded the subway down to Grand Central just as Jimmy had said,
and once he arrived, he walked the rest of the way, stopping to ask if he was
heading in the right direction.

The Americans were good to Gerry, and would wish him a nice day, and
when they heard his accent, they'd ask if he was Irish and if he knew their
great-grandfathers or their great-grandmothers. And for Gerry, normally a
man of few words, maybe it was the few beers he'd had earlier at the game,
or maybe it was the liberty and freedom that he was still feeling inside his
bones from that statue, but he was in a talkative kind of mood and would
humour them all.

So, he'd ask a million questions as to see if these great-grandparents were
from this town or that town, and if they knew this man or that woman. To
be honest, a lot of the time, the answer was no, but Gerry didn't mind; these
were nice people, and he wanted them to find what they were looking for, as
they were helping him find his way to The Lobby.

When Gerry saw a sign for the restaurant up ahead, he noticed two men who would have looked right at home in that Giants Stadium standing at the door in their black coats. It seemed a little odd as he was in his shorts and jersey. Gerry walked up and shook their hands, and said, "Hello, I'm Gerry McCarthy. Ye fellas must be plenty warm?"

And they laughed and laughed some more when Gerry looked down at their hands as he was shaking them. These fellas' hands were bigger than his, and he could only imagine them wrapped around a football in McHugh Park in Ballyduffy.

The men introduced themselves as Darnell and Big Mike, and Gerry could see why he was called Big Mike since he stood even a good bit taller than Gerry. Big Mike looked at Gerry's green shirt and his shorts and said, "Were you playing a game, Gerry?"

Big Mike's infectious, wide smile had the same effect on Gerry.

He replied "No, I was just supporting."

"Who are you supporting in the basketball tonight, Gerry?" said Darnell.

Gerry didn't know who was playing, but he thought back to his letters from Jimmy all those years ago and said, "I know the Celtics are like Kerry, and Kerry are the best."

Big Mike and Darnell looked at each other and they laughed.

"An Irish, Celtics fan," said Big Mike with a chuckle. "A real stereotype right there Gerry."

At that very moment, a car drove down the street with its windows down and music so loud it felt as though Gerry was at a concert of some sorts, and he nodded back to Big Mike.

Clearly, Big Mike had heard the stereo as well.

After Gerry had told them he was meeting Jimmy McCarthy, Big Mike smiled. "Get out of here, he's a lot smaller than you, Gerry."

Gerry smiled; he could tell Big Mike was joking about telling him to get out of there.

So Big Mike brought Gerry into the restaurant, and it was nothing like the pub he had come from earlier. For starters, Gerry's green Ireland jersey shone out like a light in the dark restaurant, and the seats at all the tables were filled with men in suits and the odd woman in a fancy outfit that Gerry would normally have seen at a wedding or a funeral.

A fella in a white shirt and a black bow tie, said, "Hey, Big Mike," then he nodded at Gerry.

"Hey Pedro, this is Gerry. He's going over to Jimmy's table," said Big Mike.

"Hey Gerry; good game today," said Pedro.

Gerry nodded and he followed Pedro to a rectangular table where he caught eyes with Jimmy, who was wearing a dark suit with a green tie.

Jimmy rose and walked around the table. "Hey Gerry," and he shook Gerry's hand before whispering in his ear, "we're running a little over time. Won't be much longer, I promise."

Jimmy turned to the rest of the table and said, "This is my brother Gerry."

The others waved and Gerry waved back before Pedro nodded to another fella in a white shirt and black bowtie, who was similar in height, although this fella had a mustache. Gerry thought it suited him well, the man fetching a chair for Gerry to sit at the end of the table.

The fella with the moustache asked, "Do you want a tea or coffee? Or some wine, sir?"

"A tea would be great please," said Gerry.

And the fella nodded, whispering, "Good game today for Ireland."

Gerry smiled as the fella walked off and he wondered: if this restaurant was called The Lobby, were those guys in the bow ties lobbyists?

Then Gerry looked around the table at the others, who had either a glass of red wine, or a tea or coffee, in front of them. Three people sat on the right of the table in dark suits, with protruding bellies that looked as though they'd eaten plenty of cakes in their day.

On the left side was another man with a dark suit and a balding head right next to Gerry, and then an aulder woman with grey hair and a blue outfit. Next to her was Rachel, and at the top of the table, directly across from Gerry, sat Jimmy. They caught eyes and Jimmy smiled, before he turned to chat to the man to his left, who had a purple tie on, the others in reds and blues.

The man with the balding head sitting next to Gerry turned and said, "Hey Gerry, nice to meet you, bro."

And Gerry looked at the man's suit and tie and smiled back.

Then the man asked, "I hear you're a capitalist, Gerry?"

And if Gerry had held a cup of tea, he would have spilled it in shock.

"I'm sorry, but you're very mistaken. I am from Kerry. Dublin is the capital," said Gerry.

The man blinked for a moment before he burst out laughing. And he was still laughing when the fella in the white shirt and the bow tie came back and placed a cup of tea in front of Gerry, whispering in Gerry's ear, "I put a little something in it, sir. I think you will need it."

Gerry lifted the cup and smelled it before taking a sip. *Jaysus,* he thought, *the fella's put whiskey or something in it.* And after the tea experience of breakfast time, Gerry thought this fella must've known how bad the tea was over here, so he must have put in a little something to help the taste. "I'll have to thank him later," Gerry whispered to himself.

Once the man with the balding head had stopped laughing and had wiped away a tear with his napkin, he turned to Gerry and said, "That's a great one, bro; you're a funny guy, Gerry. I mean, I hear you have a business of some sort?"

And Gerry took a sip of his tea, and he thought of his tea shop and supposed he did.

"I do," said Gerry. "And what about you?"

"Our business is lending money," said the man.

"So, you're a bank?" said Gerry.

"I work for a bank, but not just any. An investment bank," said the man.

Gerry rubbed his chin; he hadn't any clue what this meant.

"And what do you do there, so?" said Gerry.

"Bro, we do all kinds of crazy shit. Right now, we're working with Jimmy's bank on these deals. It's making us millions," said the man.

Gerry nearly spat out his tea. *Jaysus,* he thought. *Millions.*

A different planet from the five hundred pounds he'd won that day on His Holiness.

"Jaysus, fair play to you. Must be a great business you have; you must do a lot for the community for them to value you so much," said Gerry.

And the man with the balding head blinked for a second before he burst into laughter again. Only this time, a little shorter. Gerry couldn't work out why, so he added, "I suppose making all that money, you must pay a lot of taxes?"

And it was like a lightbulb went off in that man's eyes. He leant in closer to Gerry and said, "You're asking the right questions, Gerry. Love it, man. See that guy sitting across from me?"

Gerry looked at the man to his right, engaged in a conversation with one next to him.

"That's our tax accountant, Gerry. All I can say is this: he makes a few strokes with his pen, and all that money flies around in circles before dropping into our pockets, and out of the tax man's reach."

And Gerry blinked. Over the years, his tea shop had been a moderate success, he had made profits and a little bit of money, more than enough for the simple life he led. And Gerry didn't enjoy paying his taxes at the end of the year any more than the next man did.

But pay them he did. It never would have occurred to him to do anything else. And for whatever reason, his mind began to race away with itself in that moment. He thought of Pat Storey that day down at the beach when Gina had saved him, and of the free bus that would come and go on Fridays.

He thought of how Pat was nearly ninety-two now and those swims had probably added another few years onto his life. And he thought of all those years in the tea shop where Aunt Cara couldn't walk up the hill because her hips were so bad… and the pain she'd endured, and the joy on her face when she had finally got a replacement in the local hospital.

Gerry looked again at this balding man's beady eyes and the smile on his face, and he couldn't believe what he was hearing. So he decided to ask some more.

"This may be rude, but you said millions. Did you make more than a million last year?"

Gerry noticed those beady eyes open wide, and a sparkle that reminded Gerry of the ring on Rachel's finger came over the man's eyes. He leaned in and quietly said to Gerry, "More than a million, Gerry. How about thirty-nine of them?"

Gerry's jaw hit the floor for a second. Then it clenched, and through his clenched jaw, Gerry asked, "And how much tax did you pay on that?"

The man lifted his glass of wine and winked at Gerry, before he looked at the tax accountant and said, "With our guy's magic wand — none."

And for some reason, Gerry felt a burning inside of him, and he looked around at the rest of the table and their suits and their watches which shined when the light hit them. So, he turned to the man again and asked, "Jaysus, you did well for yourself. But surely, you'd think if people knew about these things, they'd go to the courts, or the law or something, and get them changed?"

"I love how you're thinking, bro. You're asking all the right questions here. Well, here's the thing, Gerry. You see that man beside the tax accountant? That's the judge."

"He's at your table?"

"Put it this way, bro..." The man bent a little closer. "He takes the crumbs off our table. But it's enough to get him to keep ruling on our side."

Gerry shook his head in disbelief. At that moment, Gerry heard the bark of that bastard of a sheepdog from the O'Neills' farmhouse in his head for some reason, and so he asked, "But surely, there's some watchdog or something that keeps an eye out for this kind of stuff?"

"I love it, bro. You're following the trail. You mean the regulator or the SEC? He's normally here when we do these things, but he's at a golf event with one of our competitors today."

Jaysus, thought Gerry. He looked around the table and couldn't believe what he was hearing. But there were others there, and so perhaps it was the strange kind of whiskey in his tea that was setting fire to his stomach, but he thought he'd ask some more.

"Ok. Well, surely, then, if the Government knew all this with the taxes and the judges and the watchdogs, they'd do something about it?"

"You're like a mastermind, bro. Maybe you can come work for my bank someday. Well, Gerry, you see that guy up there in the purple tie?"

And Gerry looked up at the aulder man with the grey hair, currently engaged in a deep discussion with Jimmy.

"That's Senator Scott. He's on the banking commission and everything. Jimmy and I, we like to keep him sweet, you know. Take him out to fancy dinners, golf, barbecues. That way, he may say a few things out loud on the world stage, but behind the curtain and the screens, he knows we're here, if you get me?" The balding man took a sip of wine and let out a satisfied, "aah."

Gerry looked again at the Senator's purple tie and for some reason, he thought of that day one spring when he'd been painting some markings on the sheep. He had mixed up the red and blue paint, and ended up with purple markings, and the other farmers had laughed.

Then Gerry asked, "Can I ask... You know, to get all your millions in the bank — before you guys make your own — like, where does that money come from? Like, I get that I have a bank account and ye have our savings and that, but that's surely not enough for all this stuff that ye do. You know, it's never made sense to me."

"Love it, Gerry. The key question of all. You see that woman next to me?"

And Gerry looked at the aulder lady with the grey hair who was chatting to Rachel, smiling.

"Don't be fooled by how quiet she is. That's Ms. Loudly. She works for the Central Bank, Gerry. I mean they're great people. They've always got our backs when we do something silly or get something wrong. And in the good times, they look after us as well."

"I still don't understand; what do you mean?" asked Gerry, rubbing his chin.

"Good question. It's all very complex and that's how we like to keep it. Therefore, the uninitiated don't ask the right questions like you do, Gerry. She has the ability to create money."

"What do you mean — create money?"

"Well, it's a magic money tree, Gerry. It's all to do with loans. The Central Bank loans to my bank. I lend to other banks, and other banks buy this stock, and that loan, and you see, it all gets complex quickly. But what it really is, is this: she gives us money, and we buy things with it."

And Gerry wasn't sure if he got it, and he didn't have one of those magic money trees, but he thought he'd ask some more. "Well, can't she give the rest of us money, so? And wait, if these are loans, don't ye have to pay them back at some point?"

And the man with the balding head burst out laughing again.

"You're a great guy, you really are. Extend and pretend, Gerry. They put new loans on top of old ones, and everybody knows they'll never get paid back. Really, it's just new money for us, and we can buy more things with it." The man laughed before continuing, "To your other question. No, That's the amazing thing — it's only for us."

"You mean like a club?"

Gerry noticed the man looking around the room of this dark restaurant.

"Think of it like this: it's for those people in this restaurant, Gerry, not for those outside."

Jaysus Christ, thought Gerry, looking for the first time in detail at the dark suits all around. At each table were deep discussions going on, and at the head of the table was always one fella in a suit. Some had grey hair, others short brown, but they all looked like clones of each other; and so, Gerry turned back to the balding man.

"But surely, the people outside… I don't know, even the police or the army or something would stop all this?" asked Gerry, and for the first time, he felt a little raspiness in his voice, but whether it was the whiskey or the exasperation of the conversation, he wasn't sure.

"Gerry, if you're worried about any of this, don't be. Just invest with Jimmy. The people don't care. I'm sure you've heard of pensions. Well, the people are given these pensions and so they think when they retire, they'll have plenty of money and it keeps them in line."

And Gerry blinked as he was unsure about something the man said.

"What do you mean, they think when they retire, they'll have plenty of money?"

"Oh, come on, Gerry, you know. Say a fireman or a teacher retires, and for the next ten or fifteen years, they have one hundred thousand saved for retirement —"

Gerry blinked and shook his head; one hundred thousand was a lot of money in Ballyduffy.

Then the man continued, "— these people think that one hundred thousand will make them rich. But when it's time for them to retire, that one hundred thousand might be good for two, maybe three years because the cost of things goes up. Inflation, Gerry. How long have you had your business?"

And Gerry thought back; he'd been at the tea shop now for quite some time.

"Seventeen years or so," said Gerry.

"Well, think of something you need for your business to run and the cost of it. I bet it costs a lot more now than it did seventeen years ago."

Gerry shook his head at the thought. Hadn't the price of milk kept climbing year after year? And then he understood what the man was saying, and it all made sense.

"So essentially, ye stay rich because you've already bought all the stuff with her free money, and I'm sure that stuff goes up in price too, and then the rest stay poor?" said Gerry.

The man laughed.

He looked over at Jimmy and then back at Gerry, and he said, " *We* stay rich, Gerry."

Gerry had never felt that fire inside him burn as much as he did at those words, but he had a question come to his mind. "The lady there to your left, the Central Bank, she gives you the free money and you buy things with it. What kind of things do you buy?"

"Love it, bro, finally. You want some tips, don't you?" the man laughed, before continuing, "Well, we buy stocks in companies, art, farmland — we're actually starting to look at —"

And Gerry interrupted as he remembered in one of Jimmy's letters, he'd mentioned something of working with the farmers of Midwest America.

"I know Jimmy mentioned something about the farmers, all right. What about those?"

And the biggest smile of the entire conversation came across the man's face as he took another sip of wine.

"That's where I made the millions, Gerry. Great times. Ok, and stop me anytime, as I'm sure Jimmy has told you most of this before. Because we have all this free money from the Central Banks, and they have our backs, we can go and buy farmland from a farmer for five times what any of the other farmers can afford it for. And it's like a painting or a piece of art, Gerry, in that once we pay that price, the rest of the farmland is now worth five times more than it was.

"Why? Because we said it was, and that way, we are the only ones who can afford the farmland."

Gerry's foot tapped under the table, and he sat back in his chair with his hands on his thighs. Then he asked, "Do you work on the farm then, is it?"

And the man made his loudest, most grotesque laugh of the entire conversation. When he calmed down, he said, "No of course not, bro. The farmers rent the farm from us, Gerry, and they work on it. It really is genius. Then, every year, or couple of years, we increase the rents. Where do you think I made my money last year?"

Gerry's hands began to shake when the man laughed. He looked up at Jimmy, who took a moment to turn away from his conversation with the Senator.

Jimmy smiled, raising a glass of wine towards Gerry, before turning back to his conversation.

"And does my brother do this too?"

"Of course, bro. He didn't make as much as his boss — he's not here tonight, by the way. Jimmy's here in his place but I'm sure Jimmy had a good year too. You want in on it as well, Gerry? I'm sure I could cut you in on a deal if you'd like?"

And with that, Gerry felt the anger reach boiling point. He rose from his chair with his fists clenched and his hands shaking. He looked down at this balding man, with his beady eyes and his shirt and tie and he said, "You sir, are the worst human being I've ever met in my life."

Gerry didn't realize, but his voice boomed out around the restaurant. And it wasn't just his own table that was now silent and staring at the big fella in the green Irish jersey.

Then that balding man rose to his feet, and squared up to Gerry and said, "You can't say that to me. Who do you think you are?"

He pushed Gerry in the chest, but Gerry only took a step back before he swung his right fist, knocking that balding man flying in the air.

At that very moment, one of the lobbyists — the fella with the moustache who had poured the whiskey in Gerry's tea — was walking behind with a tray of wine glasses, and the balding man landed on him and sent all those glasses flying.

However, the lobbyist had managed to catch one of the glasses of wine.

But when he looked down and saw the balding man on the floor, he looked back at Gerry and winked before subtly pouring the glass of red wine out on top of the balding man.

The next minute, Gerry felt Big Mike's hand on his shoulder.

"I'm sorry Gerry, we're going to have to take you outside." Big Mike then bent down and whispered into Gerry's ear, "Come on. I'll take you through the back way."

Gerry was still staring down at that man on the ground, but his fists had unclenched, and he had started to breathe a bit deeper and slower. Then Gerry saw Pedro point at the other lobbyist who had poured the drink over the man, and said, "Hey Zeus, go in the back and get changed. I'll get someone else to clean this up."

Gerry caught eyes with the wine-covered lobbyist with the moustache as he smiled, before the fella whispered something to Big Mike. The next minute, Big Mike ushered Gerry through the restaurant towards the kitchen.

"Hey, Big Mike, wait up," came a voice.

Gerry and Big Mike turned to see Jimmy, his arms out to his sides.

"What was all that about, Gerry?" said Jimmy with a frown.

"Tell me you're not involved with all that stuff?" said Gerry.

"Come on Gerry, no need to…"

"Tell me you're not involved with all that stuff?" said Gerry again, his blue eyes firmly fixed on his brother's.

Jimmy put his hands in his pockets. His weight shifted from foot to foot and after a moment, he said, "It's not what it seems."

"Tell me then, Jimmy? Tell me how it really is."

"If you ask another question, I'll give you another answer," said Jimmy.

Gerry turned to Big Mike and he nodded, and Big Mike put his hand again on Gerry's shoulder and continued ushering him out through the kitchen. Gerry felt that anger in his stomach leave, and a feeling of disgust had now entered. Then the strangest of things happened.

As Gerry was walking through the kitchen, where the chefs all in white and the lobbyists in their white shirts and black bow ties were collecting and returning plates of food, Big Mike's hand left his shoulder. Gerry looked over to see the lobbyist they called Zeus, with his moustache, and his shirt covered in red wine, and he was smiling.

And the others in the kitchen were smiling and laughing too. And they all stopped what they were doing, and started banging their knuckles together, as if they were clapping their hands.

Big Mike said to Gerry, "We can't clap because it's too loud and they'd hear us out there. Hey Zeus, I got to get back out front. Gerry, take some food with you before you go. It's very nice to meet you, man. You won't be allowed in this place again, but I work on Thursdays at a club on Seventh Avenue called Lolita, and you'll always be allowed in there.

"You'll be a VIP too. Anytime brother."

And Big Mike, with his giant shovel hands, shook Gerry's hand, and headed out. Then the man they called Zeus approached Gerry. "That was so cool, man. We've all been wanting to do that for years. My shift's ended, so come with me, Gerry; I'll get you food and drinks someplace else. We have to celebrate. Did you like the little something in your tea?"

And Gerry looked down at a smiling Zeus, and around at the people in the rest of the kitchen, who were still smiling, and he said, "Of course! It was great."

Any anger, or thoughts of Jimmy, left his body as he walked through the kitchen and out the back door into an alley, where he followed Zeus some more. And Zeus told him stories of other people in that restaurant that he'd wanted to punch over the years.

"One time, there was a vice-president of the United States in there, and he was a real A-hole. Don't believe what they say on TV, Gerry."

Gerry stopped still and smiled. He knew that a 'TV' was a television, and he felt he had met a kindred spirit in Zeus. And Gerry looked down at Zeus and thought what an odd name it was. Then he listened closer to the slight accent in his voice, which sounded European, and he thought about those days in school all those years ago, about the myths of the Gods and the hammer, and realized that Zeus was European, and from Greece.

I've never met anyone from Greece before, he thought.

After they had walked a few blocks, they arrived at an apartment building — which didn't look much like Jimmy's — and walked the stairs up to the eighth floor.

"You need a drink after that, Gerry. See?"

Gerry nodded, and when he looked over the edge of the stairs, and all the way down to the ground floor, he could definitely see.

The door of Zeus's apartment opened, and Gerry couldn't believe the noise in the place. As he walked down the hall, there were men singing and guitars playing. Although the apartment wasn't much bigger than Gerry's house, the noise and the smell of whatever food was cooking made it feel bigger. On entering the kitchen, Gerry guessed there must have been fifteen people squeezed in it. And he laughed, when they all cheered to welcome the large Irishman in his green jersey.

"It's Papa's birthday," said Zeus. "He's seventy today. The years have flown by, isn't that so, Papa?" Zeus nodded to the auld gentleman sitting at the end of the table with a very large hat on his head. The man gazed back, tipping the hat and breaking into a gap-toothed grin.

Gerry looked around the room. There were three other men in large hats sitting there too, and two had guitars, and the other a set of odd-looking items in his hands which made a noise when he began shaking them. There were a couple of auld ladies around the oven to whom Gerry was introduced; they were Mama and Aunt Mariana. There were others too, including Rosa, who Gerry guessed was about tirty, and quite beautiful with her dark eyes and dark hair. And Rosa gave Gerry a look that he had only ever seen a few times before.

"That's my sister. You touch her and I kill you," said Zeus with a smile and a laugh.

And Gerry wasn't sure if he was serious or not, but Zeus's laugh was infectious, and Gerry couldn't help but laugh along.

The band played more songs, and Gerry gazed around the room at their dark hair and dark eyes and tanned skin. And he listened as they talked amongst themselves in their language and when he saw a green, white, and red flag on the wall, and he looked over at Zeus again, he suddenly realized how silly he had been. *They're Italians.* They even had their own Italian whiskey, which Gerry would take a few shots of, and he was also grateful for the limes or lemons which appeared.

Rosa had even been so kind as to show him a trick.

"It don't taste so bad with salt," she said, and Gerry liked the sound of her voice.

But then he caught Zeus staring at him with a look that said he'd meant those words earlier, before he smiled at Gerry with his eyes, and made him laugh some more.

Mama and Mariana brought out the strange food they'd been making called tacos, and they looked nothing like the spaghetti that Gina had made him, but they were delicious all the same.

Zeus and Rosa and the others would laugh when Gerry rushed for a drink as he took a bite, the taco burning the mouth off him, with strange spices he'd never tasted before.

And when Papa passed Gerry another small shot glass of that Italian whiskey, sure, the others laughed harder as the drink only made his mouth burn more.

For the next couple of hours, Gerry would sing and laugh and have more of that whiskey, and he would keep looking around the kitchen when Papa and Mama and the others kept saying "see," and Gerry would nod, because he could see how nice the evening was, and how he had found a little home away from home.

When Gerry looked at a clock on the wall and it was nearly ten o'clock, he said his goodbyes because he had a plane to catch tomorrow morning. And sure, Papa gave Gerry his great big hat and Gerry was thankful, because he could see out the window that it was beginning to rain.

On his way out, Gerry thanked Zeus again, and he looked at a sign along the wall in the hallway which said, 'Mi casa es tu casa.' *Was that the name of a place, or the words of a song?* He just wondered it because the words sounded nice when he whispered them to himself.

So, Gerry walked down the street in his green jersey and his big hat, and the rain fell; however, it was only a light sprinkling, so Gerry decided he would walk a little farther, seeing as the streets were very busy with cars that weren't moving anywhere fast.

He walked a couple of blocks and had missed many subway signs, when he heard a lot of shouting and cheering. And so, he went over to see what the commotion was.

Gerry asked a fella standing by the door in one of those navy blue and red basketball shirts, "What's going on in there?"

"It's the fourth quarter. The Knicks are up by three," the fella replied.

Gerry looked inside and there were lots of people in those navy blue basketball shirts, screaming at the televisions. *Well, seeing as I'm here, I may as well have a look,* thought Gerry.

And to Gerry's luck, amongst the sea of blue jerseys in the bar, sitting right in front of Gerry, were two very auld fellas in green Irish shirts, just getting up to leave. As they turned, one of the men, who had grey hair and thick grey eyebrows said to Gerry, "Great game today, wasn't it?"

A Mayo man, thought Gerry.

"Great day, I tell you. Is that a Mayo accent?" asked Gerry.

"It is, boy. Castlebar." And the man looked down at Gerry's white Ballyduffy shorts and laughed, then said, "And you're a Kerry man. I don't need to ask you that."

Gerry was impressed. "You're right. I'm Gerry. Nice to meet you."

"Nice to meet you, Gerry, I'm Dan. Please take our stools. Good luck now, Gerry," said Dan, turning to whisper something to the barman.

Gerry wished them well, and he sat down and asked for one of those Italian whiskeys, but the bartender didn't understand, so Gerry had a Guinness instead. He looked up behind the bar, and they had more televisions in here than he had ever seen in his life. And each screen showed the basketball game, and the people of the bar cheered for every point.

Then a fella sat down on the spare seat next to Gerry and said, "Hey, Zeus, is it?"

Gerry turned, and the man, dressed in a white t-shirt, pointed at Gerry's hat.

"No, I'm Gerry. But I know Zeus, and where he lives, if you need to reach him?" said Gerry.

The man laughed for what seemed like a long time, and Gerry couldn't understand why. Then Gerry remembered the big hat on his head, and he took it off and placed it on the bar, imagining the people behind him couldn't see; that would've been very rude of him.

"You're a funny guy, Gerry," said the man, and he ordered himself a pint of Guinness too.

Gerry looked a little more at the man sitting beside him. He sat taller than Gerry, and the man had blond hair and blue eyes, and his hands wrapped around that pint of Guinness as if he could hold anything in them. Gerry asked, "Are you Irish by any chance?"

The man laughed and he said, "No, Gerry, but I'm a Celt," and he winked, and took a sip of his Guinness.

And oddly enough, when the team New York were playing — Houston — scored a rocket of a shot, the bar was silent only for this big fella beside Gerry celebrating.

"You got to cheer against the Knicks, Gerry," he said, and Gerry laughed, because if this was Dublin playing, he would've done the same.

So, Gerry sat with this man as the time ticked endlessly down in the basketball game, and Gerry's eyes opened wide at how high the players could jump. He thought many of them could make great midfielders for Ballyduffy.

"Are you a basketball fan, Gerry?"

"I'm more a fan of the Kerry football team. But I suppose they're going through a dry patch right now. 1986 was the last time they scaled those heights and steps of greatness," said Gerry, and he took a long sip of his Guinness.

"I know all about that, Gerry. 1986 was a good year all right," said the man, who took a long sip of Guinness too.

Gerry noticed the man had a similar look in his eyes, as if reminiscing over the Kerry team himself. Gerry added, "But, that's life; we have the highs and the lows, and the days when the keg is filled and the Guinness flows. And then we have other times when the keg's dry, and in need of changing," said Gerry.

"I'll drink to that, Gerry," said the man, letting out a great cheer when Houston scored another rocket.

And Gerry enjoyed the rest of the game, and the man was very nice, with a certain grace about him too. And at the end, after the Knicks had missed a shot and lost, Gerry could hear a pin drop in the bar except for the big blond-haired man cheering loudly beside him. After the man had whispered to the barman and paid, he said to Gerry, "Really nice to meet you, Gerry; you're a real good guy."

And Gerry shook his hand and said, "Thank you. And I didn't catch your name?"

"I'm Larry. Now you get home safe, Gerry."

And Gerry watched Larry walk through the crowd, who strangely enough had their jaws on the floor, and seemed to part to let him by. And Gerry knew why, too; Larry was much taller standing up than when he was sitting down. Well, all men were, but Larry was something else.

Gerry turned back to the bar and sure, didn't he have another pint of Guinness in front of him that he hadn't ordered. So, he asked the barman, and the barman said, "Larry paid for it."

And Gerry was thankful and wasn't thankful all at the same time because now he had two more pints in front of him and a plane to catch early in the morning.

The crowds of blue basketball jerseys left, leaving the bar much less full. Gerry walked to the bathroom at the back, past the booths of people remaining. And afterwards, he washed his hands, and on the way back to his stool, up ahead in one of those booths, he spotted another green Irish jersey. And the sight of it stopped him still in his tracks.

And his foot began to tap as if it had a mind of its own again, and he rubbed his hand through his hair. And the whole bar seemed deathly quiet, except for the beat of his heart in his ears.

No — it wasn't just beating, it was thundering. As sure as his name was Gerry, he was about to have a heart attack right here. He was certain of it. Gerry was filled with wonder, and shock, surprise, fear and apprehension, a melee of feelings and sensations. And of memories too.

The person in the Irish jersey had long dark hair and full red lips, and when her blue eyes, as blue as those Italian jerseys in the stadium, rose up to meet Gerry's, he grabbed one of the poles to stop himself from falling over.

"Gerry? Gerry McCarthy?"

CHAPTER

21

"How's it going, Gina?" said Gerry, his voice breathy, knees wobbly. His hands were still wrapped around the pole, although thankfully, his foot had somehow stopped tapping.

"Why are you hanging onto that pole, Gerry?" asked Gina.

Her voice was as sweet, soft, and melodic as when he'd first heard it all those years ago in his tea shop. And her smile floored Gerry — not literally, as he was still clutching onto that pole, of course — but inside of him, all those butterflies from the game had returned.

"I was just checking it, making sure it was sturdy," said Gerry. "You know what I'm like, testing things to make sure —"

He shied away from lingering on the topic.

Gina laughed, and Gerry's heart soared as she walked closer and hugged him, embracing him in an all-enveloping hug as if they had never been apart. Her scent was still the same.

The feel of her against him was the same. How could it be after all these years?

And, although he let go of the pole, he didn't really know what to do when he looked down at her dark hair pressed up against him.

"It's so great to see you, Gerry," said Gina, who also held on for a touch longer than a stranger or mere friend would normally hug someone. "Come meet my friends."

Gerry followed Gina over to the booth where she had been sitting on a long bench seat with two other women, both in Italian jerseys, both with dark brown hair and dark eyes, and they were quite beautiful too, although nothing like Gina. The women had been sitting opposite Gina.

"This is Francesca and Bianca," said Gina.

"How's it going?" said Gerry.

"Nice to meet you. And your name is?" said Bianca.

"This is Gerry," said Gina.

Francesca and Bianca looked at each other, then at Gerry's Irish jersey, then back at Gina.

"*The* Gerry?" said Francesca.

"No, just Gerry. Nice to meet you both, too. I'm sorry your 'Divine Ponytail' didn't work out today," said Gerry, who hadn't noticed the look that Gina had given Francesca.

Francesca and Bianca rolled their eyes and laughed.

"We've been hearing that all day from her," said Bianca as she flicked her head towards Gina and lifted her glass.

Gerry scanned the table with all the empty glasses. It seemed they too had had a great day.

"Come on, Gerry; sit down," said Gina, shifting over as Gerry sat down on her side of the booth.

"You know, I actually spent the evening with my friend Zeus and his Italian family. It was great," said Gerry.

Bianca and Francesca sat forward and smiled, then enquired some more about the party that Gerry had attended. And when he told them about the big hats, and the little guitars and the shakers, they looked at each other and at Gina, and then they leant forward a little more. Then Bianca asked, "What did you eat there? They made you Italian food?"

"Of course. It was delicious, even if it did burn my mouth."

"Yeah, but what was its name?" said Francesca.

"They made me tacos," said Gerry.

And as an ice breaker, it would've saved the Titanic. Tears rolled down their faces amongst the laughter. And when they told Gerry it was a Mexican party he'd been to, he laughed along too at the great memories he'd always take with him of Jesus and his home away from home.

"You have a coffee house, Gerry?" said Bianca.

"No, I've a tea shop," said Gerry.

"You should see it. Gerry made all the furnishings himself. And in the winter, when he puts on the fire, the place is so cozy and warm," interjected Gina.

Gerry's hairs stood on the back of his neck to hear her describing it with such fondness and as if it was only yesterday she had been there. *She remembers it,* he thought. And he watched Gina take a drink of her pint.

"And what about yourself?" said Gerry.

"I work at a prison upstate. I'm the nurse there," said Francesca.

"That's great. My Aunt Cara was a nurse. Ye do a lot of great work for the community," said Gerry.

"Your mother was a teacher, wasn't she Gerry?" asked Gina. "Bianca is a teacher as well."

"Yeah, I teach elementary," said Bianca.

"Very good. Yes, my mother was, but that's long ago now," said Gerry. He turned to Gina and asked. "And what about yourself? Are you still working for that bank?"

"Is she what, Gerry?" asked Francesca.

"This is the first time we've been out together in a year," said Bianca. "And on that note…" Bianca nudged Francesca. "Sorry, Gerry, we have to go; it's been a long day. Very nice to meet you, and you're just like we pictured. Gina, you stay, and we can talk tomorrow."

Gerry didn't see Gina's jaw hit the floor, but he heard the smiles and the giggles of Bianca and Francesca, and they turned to wave as they walked out.

Whilst he watched them leave, Gerry didn't notice Gina picking up a wedding band from the table and slipping it back on her finger. But when she lifted her glass for a drink, his eyebrows rose when he saw it, but he didn't say anything, and neither did she.

"They seem nice," said Gerry.

"Aren't they? They're my oldest friends. I've known them since I was four years old. How long are you here for, Gerry?" said Gina.

Gerry looked at the clock on the wall and it was near midnight.

"For ten more hours."

Gina chuckled and took a sip of the Guinness that she was drinking.

CHAPTER TWENTY-ONE

"Never change, Gerry."

And Gerry didn't really know what she meant but he hadn't planned on changing.

"How is your music going? The violin is still on the wall of the tea—"

He cut himself off. There was silence for a moment. Then Gina took another sip of her pint, a longer one. And Gerry noticed the smile had disappeared from her face.

"I haven't played in a while, Gerry."

"Well, that's ok, Gina. Sometimes life gets busy. I'm sure it's like football, once you learn how to play it, you never forget. Although, it does take a little practice to get back to where you had been."

With that simple line, the smile reappeared on Gina's face, and in the light above the table, Gerry could see more sparkle in her eyes than he had seen on that gigantic diamond on Rachel's finger. However, he missed Gina wiping a tear when she turned her head away.

"How is Aunt Cara?" asked Gina.

Gerry's head turned down towards his pint, and he stared into it for a moment.

He lifted the glass and swirled it around as the image of Pat Storey rushing up his lane flashed through his mind. And the pain he'd felt when Pat said the words. And that night when he stood in the back garden of Aunt Cara's and stared at the stars, wondering if Gina was looking at the same ones, waiting for his plane to arrive. And after seeing Times Square, he realized Gina wouldn't have seen the stars, even if she'd seen his plane. Then he said, "She passed away some time back. Uncle Brendan did too. A lot of change."

The memories of Aunt Cara and Uncle Brendan, and their times together, filled the bar with silence for the pair of them. Gerry took a sip of Guinness before Gina said, "I'm so sorry, Gerry. She was a wonderful woman. Uncle Brendan was lovely too. Even though I only met him the once, I could tell how warm he was as a person. A good man."

"Aunt Cara really liked you too," said Gerry.

So did I.

He felt a twinge inside his chest and a heavy feeling in his stomach. Perhaps it was even that same feeling he'd had when he'd read Gina's letter, telling him how she'd met someone.

"You know, Gerry, I never told you, but I knew it wasn't turkey we had that day."

Gerry looked up and saw a cheeky grin shining through Gina's teary eyes, and he couldn't help but smile along too. Then he burst out laughing, again only for the briefest time.

"I suppose you got me there," said Gerry. "How come you never said?"

"It was so kind. You all went to such efforts to make Thanksgiving special for me. It really was the most amazing trip. I've never forgotten it, Gerry. Whether it was turkey or whatever else, it didn't make any difference. It was the best Thanksgiving ever."

The smell of pheasant came wafting into Gerry's nostrils as he thought of that Thanksgiving Day all those years ago, one of those days that he would consider the best of his life. And for a little while, Gerry and Gina sat close on their long bench seat and took a drink together.

And nothing needed to be said.

And when Gina asked to be let out to use the bathroom, Gerry felt her leg brush against his, causing his already jumpy body to freeze up, and he felt a nervous tingle he hadn't known since climbing those steps to board the airplane for the flight here.

When she returned, Gina squeezed in past Gerry and back onto her seat.

Gerry looked across at the empty side of the booth where Francesca and Bianca had been sitting; neither he nor Gina had shifted across there to get more space between them.

But he wouldn't want to read anything into it. They were two old friends, just bumped into each other again by chance. It was all this occasion was. He thought. Then he took another drink.

"How about Pat Storey? I told all my friends about him too. I've still never met anyone like him. And that day, when we saved him at the beach, and we didn't realize it was him," said Gina.

"Pat's Pat."

And Gerry laughed and Gina joined him as those words said it all. Then he told Gina the story of Pat and the strange band that came through that night not so long ago. It turned out that Gina and her friends had been to a big concert at Yankee stadium with Bon Bon and his band in New York the previous year. And at that moment, Gerry wanted to mention how he had felt, and who he had thought of when he heard those words 'one love.'

But he caught sight of her wedding band again and decided not to.

"I married him in the end, Gerry," said Gina, and she took a sip of her Guinness, and the silence came over them again for a moment.

"I hope he's good to you," said Gerry.

And Gina nodded, but didn't say any words.

Then she took a longer sip, so long that she finished her drink. And she put the glass on the table and said to Gerry, "Where are you staying tonight?"

Gerry blinked, and then he looked down at his glass of Guinness and realized his vision had blurred again as by this stage, he'd had many pints and many of those Italian, or Mexican, whiskeys. He said, "Up near Central Park, fourth avenue and ninety-six. They add to one hundred, that's how I remember it."

And Gina laughed and said, "I live on fourth and ninety-three. Let's take a cab together."

On their way out, they stopped by the bar as Gerry realized he hadn't paid, and the barman lifted Gerry's big hat from behind the bar and gave it to him.

When Gerry asked for his bill, the barman said, "Dan took care of it."

Gerry missed the look that the barman had given Gina, but he felt very grateful for how nice these New York folk were.

Once the cab pulled up at Gina's building, Gerry got out and held the door open for her as similar to himself, Gina had had a long day with lots of cocktails and Guinness, and her feet too were a little unsteady. And to Gerry's luck, the cab drove off, and Gerry didn't understand when Gina said that Grandad had paid for it.

So, Gerry stood with Gina on the sidewalk outside number eight, stranded there and wondering what might come next and what he was to do. He'd just have to walk the rest of the way. But eight was Gerry's lucky number, and sure enough, it had ensured he and Gina had got out of that cab together and been left there. They both swayed a little from side to side by now, and through his blurry vision, Gerry could still make out those blue eyes just as he had seen them all those years ago, and even though they were a little redder just like Gerry's, they were smiling.

And her eyes were getting closer. Then Gerry felt those full red lips on his, and he kissed Gina back just the same way he had under the stars outside his tea shop.

Then Gina whispered, "I don't know. Do you want to come inside?"

Gerry blinked. He thought of the ring on Gina's finger. He looked her in the eyes, and he asked, "Are you happy? With him, I mean."

And Gina stepped back, a change coming over her face. The smile and the carefree attitude for which Gerry knew her had all of a sudden disappeared.

"I think about you every day," said Gerry. "I never stopped. Not for a moment. And you know—"

Gina took another step back, and her hands left Gerry's neck and came down by her sides.

"You can't tell me that now, Gerry. You can't tell me that now."

Her voice rose in a way that Gerry had never heard before. The streetlights reflected off the tears that were flowing down her face. Gina continued, "I waited, and I waited for a letter, and you never wrote. It broke my heart. So, don't give me that. You can't tell me that now."

Gerry stepped forward, but Gina stepped back again. And he went to open his mouth.

He wanted to tell her he had written, and that they'd got lost in the post. That it was the same day that Aunt Cara had died. But nothing would leave his mouth; the spell of liberty and freedom cast by the statue had worn off.

Gina ran inside the apartment building and as the glass doors closed, Gerry shouted "Gina!"

She turned once, but the doors slid shut and Gerry once more stood heartbroken. But this time, he ran to the doors. And as the darkness of the building overtook them and Gina disappeared, he shouted, "She died. Aunt Cara died the day I was to come. She died."

And Gerry stood with his face pressed against the glass at the foot of this enormous building as the rain began to fall, only heavier this time. And he waited. He waited for five, maybe ten minutes. Despite the cover of the large hat he was wearing, the raindrops that landed around him were Gina's tears, and he had caused them. And they reminded him of that day when he'd sat in his tractor after receiving her letter telling him she had moved on. A crackle of thunder echoed down through the skyscrapers, and the sky lit up for a second with a strike of lightning.

Reluctantly, Gerry backed away from the glass.

He staggered a couple of blocks to Jimmy's, surprising himself with how easily he could navigate around this massive city. When he got into Jimmy's, Gerry lay the spare key quietly on the table in the hallway and went straight to bed, closing the door behind him. And after all the drink, all the highs and lows, the heartbreak, and the airplane lag, he fell right asleep.

———————•✻•———————

Gerry missed his alarm. But being a farmer, his body was used to waking early, although an hour late would leave him in a foul mood. He knew partly it was the hangover of the day's drinking, but also seeing Gina had left a stamp on his heart.

After he had closed the front door quietly and was waiting for the elevator, Jimmy's voice came down the hall. He walked out in a navy dressing gown and a pair of slippers, saying, "Gerry, you're not going to leave just like that?"

Gerry stood unmoved, waiting on the elevator to arrive.

Part of his foul mood was the disgust he still felt in his stomach at the balding man in the restaurant, and at Jimmy for being part of it all.

"Thank you for letting me stay, Jimmy," said Gerry.

"Come on, Gerry, don't be like that," said Jimmy, with his arms out.

And Gerry stood in silence and turned back towards the elevator. The bell went off and the doors opened. Gerry turned and said, "Goodbye, Jimmy."

Jimmy ran to the door, holding it open and he said, "Take this."

He handed Gerry a strange paper ticket.

"I don't want your money," said Gerry.

"It's a ticket chit. And it's not mine. It's the company's. Just give it to the cab driver."

It's that filthy bank's, thought Gerry.

"Then I'll take it off those fuckers, so," said Gerry. He smiled and nodded at Jimmy, who chuckled and smiled back as those doors of the elevator slid across and closed.

Once he got outside, the humid heat of the early morning sun hitting him, feeling as though it could be two in the afternoon and not seven in the morning, Gerry knew he had barely enough time to make one stop by Gina's before he'd have to rush to the airport.

And with that, he set off walking as fast as any man could walk who'd downed near fifteen pints and whatever else the day previously, scanning the street for any sign of the love of his life.

But the streets were empty. It was a Sunday morning after all.

Gerry stood outside number eight, and he waited for Gina or for anyone else to come in or out that he could ask. But none came.

And as seven-tirty arrived, Gerry took one last look at those glass doors as he stepped into the taxi, and he knew then that lucky numbers weren't a thing after all.

Once Gerry got on that plane, he sat down beside a skinny fella with long brown hair, and when Gerry heard the man was from Dublin, he made himself as wide as he could and fell asleep, grateful to know that when he woke up, he'd be back home in Ireland.

CHAPTER

22

Acouple of weeks after coming back from America, Pat Storey
arrived through the doors of the tea shop. Gerry had only seen Pat
once since he'd returned, preferring to keep to himself again,
waiting for the scars on his heart to heal and keeping busy tending to his
farm. The farm Pa had looked after, and *his* Pa had looked after. After
learning all about Jimmy's life in America, he felt damn grateful for the sheep
and the cattle and the green fields. Plus, Pat was getting very auld now and
didn't make it up the hill as much anymore.

"How's it going, Pat?" said Gerry.

Then Gerry looked down at Pat's hand, not the one with the walking stick,
but the other. And in it he held a lead and Gerry's eyebrows lifted when he
saw what was on the end of it.

"You don't mind her in here, do you Gerry?" said Pat, loudly.

Gerry rubbed his hand through his hair. He supposed no one had ever
brought a dog inside.

"Not at all. Come in, Pat."

The little black and white puppy with the pink nose sat on the floor beside
Pat's stool. And Gerry thought back to growing up in the house, and how
Jimmy had always wanted a dog, and how he supposed he wouldn't have
minded one either. But Pa, for some reason, would never allow it. And now,

looking down at this puppy, he chuckled. The puppy's tail began to wag, and then it bent itself forward into an awkward shape and looked Gerry in the eye before taking a shite on the old stone floor of the tea shop.

"Jaysus," said Gerry, and he grabbed his nose, much to Pat's enjoyment.

"It's only a shite, Gerry," said Pat.

Gerry thought of all the shites he had known over the years and supposed it was true. Everyone did it. So, he just grabbed some paper towels and got down on his knees, cleaned it up and after washing his hands, poured a cup of tea for himself and for Pat, and they watched the puppy run around the floor after a ball.

"What's its name?" said Gerry.

"Cara."

And Gerry swallowed as he watched the young curious pup sniff all the chairs and the tables.

"That's a good name, Pat. What made you pick that?"

"An old love of mine, Gerry."

Gerry tilted his head and furrowed his eyebrows. Pat took a sip of tea before turning again to the puppy and continuing, "What I never told you before, Gerry, or anyone for that matter, is that me and your aunt were a thing once. A long time ago."

Jaysus! Had he heard that right?

Gerry sat down on his stool and turned to face the puppy. This was a turn up for the books. He'd always imagined Pat as a bachelor, a man content in his own skin, one who helped about the town when he wasn't on top of a bar stool.

"I was twenty-seven, Gerry. We'd gone to the dance a few times together. And you know your aunt; there wasn't anyone else like her. But I went off to London for work for 513 days. And when I came back, she was engaged to Brendan, would you believe it."

Gerry felt a draft over his shoulder, and he looked up at the ceiling to check if Aunt Cara was listening in. Then he heard the puppy bark, and it ran over to one of the stools, gnawing at a leg.

"Come on now, Cara. Less of that," said Pat.

He chuckled, then he turned to Gerry and said, "Let me tell you something, Gerry. Never let work get in the way of love. It might take you a while here and there, but you can always find a job. However, that love might only come once in your life. I learned that the hard way."

ALONG THE COAST ROAD

Gerry sat in silence and listened to those words. Then he pictured Gina's tears. Had he prioritized his tea shop? Was that what stopped him stepping on a plane back when he needed to? Back when she might have been waiting for him? He sighed and looked down at Cara the sheepdog, and he felt more a puppy himself than a forty-year-old man.

—————•✳•—————

Then, one morning, after a night in which Gerry tossed and turned and he smelt the perfume of Gina all around his room for some reason, there was a knock on his front door, which was strange as most people in these places knew the back door was always open.

Gerry rose from his bed and when he opened the door, his eyebrows rose to see Father Finnegan standing there. When he saw the look on the priest's face, he felt something heavy in his stomach. "How's it going, Father?"

"Gerry, I'm sorry to come here. But I don't know where better to go, really. Pat Storey passed away in his sleep last night."

Gerry's face went as white as a ghost before he thanked Father Finnegan for coming out to tell him the news, adding that he would see him down in Pat's house.

Gerry didn't hear the latch on the door when it closed. The ducts behind his eyes didn't fill, and his stomach had returned to its normal place. He took a seat on his rocking chair and stared into nowhere, lost in shock. Gerry wasn't sure how long he sat there for. His mind was empty, and then he heard a strange noise, and wasn't sure if it was inside his head or if the bark was coming from the sheepdog down at O'Neills' farmhouse.

"Jaysus, I wonder is Cara ok?" whispered Gerry.

He got dressed and hopped in his tractor to drive to Pat's house, where Father Finnegan was standing in the hallway, pointing Gerry in the direction of the bedroom to where Pat's body lay. Gerry had never walked as slowly as he did right then, his feet reluctant to put one in front of the other as he headed down the hall towards the bedroom.

Although he'd dropped Pat home a couple of times in his tractor, he'd never been in Pat's house before, and Gerry stood outside the bedroom door and put his hand on the doorknob. It felt cold. Then he heard the puppy barking from inside.

"Cara," he whispered.

And Gerry stopped whispering and felt a lump in the back of his throat when he opened the door and the puppy's head poked out from beneath Pat's bed, then came running over to him.

He bent down to pet the puppy.

The curtains were still closed, and when Gerry spotted Pat's body in the bed, he thought that he looked as if he was in a peaceful sleep. He opened the curtains, and the quiet was only broken by the scrapes from the puppy, trying to bite Pat's walking stick which lay on the floor.

It was then that Gerry decided that from now on, he would be the one to look after Cara the sheepdog, as he supposed Pat would've wanted her to be in a good home.

He gently eased Pat's walking stick from the dog and put it on one side to take home.

Pat was the first paying customer he'd ever had. But it was more than losing a customer, it was losing a friend, a piece of furniture from his tea shop. He thought back to that night all those years ago when his father had died, and Pat Storey had been sitting at the bar telling stories about 'the camel.' And he thought about all the other escapades they'd had with the Pope and Sugar the horse, and then, Gerry thought of Gina. For a moment, he thought of writing a letter to let her know about Pat's death. Through her quick thinking and fast response at the beach that day, she had added ten or so more years on to Pat's life. *She really was an angel,* Gerry thought.

He would help carry the coffin for Pat, and after the funeral, Gerry and a niece of Pat's from Kellmere would be helping to clear out Pat's house and giving whatever items remained to the Trocaire charity. As they were cleaning, Gerry spotted one more thing he couldn't give away.

He held onto that one item. A few weeks later, he would hang the black and white photograph of Pat Storey, and his walking stick, beneath the green guitar in the tea shop.

———— • ❋ • ————

For the next few months, Gerry cursed that dog as all it seemed to do was eat and shite and piss all over the inside of his house. On arriving home from the tea shop, he found the book that had been sitting on his table in the living room — *The Coffee House* — torn to shreds all over the floor. At that moment, he felt like teaching the dog a lesson. But then, the puppy looked at him with its big eyes and turned its head to one side and started wagging its tail.

And sure, didn't Gerry start to giggle.

And he supposed that auld book, with its pictures of the coffee houses in Milano and Paris, had played its part and had its time, and so he threw the scraps of paper in the fire.

Besides, the dog had kept Gerry's mind off the troubles he had. The loss of Pat. His disgust at Jimmy. The cut in his heart which had been reopened after meeting Gina again. One of the nights, when Gerry was thinking about his farm and the blood started to boil inside, he had gone into the dresser and retrieved Jimmy's letters from that silver tin, and he'd been about to throw them in the fire when the puppy barked and took a shite on the floor. And by the time he had cleaned it up, Gerry had calmed down and put the letters back into the silver tin once again.

That winter was to be the longest of Gerry's life, a winter in which for the first time, he was having those unsettled thoughts about the future. He had always been a man to live in the present, never worrying too much about life and how his story had been written for him.

However, with the lack of any letter from Jimmy, which despite the disgust he still held for him, Gerry longed for, he found himself thinking. He thought of Gina again, and of how Aunt Cara had gotten that one wrong. The *only* superstition she had ever gotten wrong.

In the run up to Christmas, he thought of Pat Storey too, and of how Pat had lived his life as a bachelor, and of Pat's many nights around all the pubs of Ballyduffy. And Gerry wasn't sure if that was the future for him too. Gerry said thank you to John and Kathleen McHugh on leaving their house on Christmas day and Kathleen said, "anytime, Gerry," and he felt grateful for the community of Ballyduffy through those winter months.

The one bright spark throughout the spring was that Cara had grown from a puppy and was becoming a good sheepdog. She didn't even bark like the O'Neills' one, although Gerry thought a touch longer when he realized he hadn't heard that bastard of a sheepdog in a long time, and he wondered if it too had gone the way of the land.

The customers liked Cara too. Another couple of Americans, two women in their early twenties, took many photographs of the sheepdog and other photos of the view of the valley from Gerry's tea shop. Gerry even posed for a photo, letting them stand behind the counter and pretending to serve tea to him, and he thought this was great craic, even giving them a couple of cakes for free. Cakes which he now had to purchase from the Daly's bakery in Tralee every week. Even though they weren't as delicious as Aunt Cara's, they still brought a smile to the customers' face when they enjoyed them with a cup of tea.

Then one day in late August, Gerry was standing in the tea shop late one Saturday evening when a summer storm was coming down outside. He stared at the photo of Pat Storey on the wall as he waited for the rain to pass, thinking back to all those chats in the tea shop and of how much he missed his dry and slow tone. "He was a good man, Cara, your auld man," whispered Gerry, looking down to the black and white sheepdog.

Then he heard the rain take a heavier turn on the thatch, so he opened the front door of the cottage and looked outside. The strangest thing happened.

Cara, who until then had been a great sheepdog, always by her master's side and never running off, suddenly bolted through the rain and off down Drumbarron Hill.

"Hey!" shouted Gerry.

He reached for his raincoat which he kept behind the door of the tea shop, taking off after Cara. The water fell so heavily that it looked as though the road was raining up towards the sky itself. "What the hell's that?" said Gerry.

Through the storm, he heard a horn beeping, and it wasn't stopping.

When he turned the bend, his eyebrows rose to see Cara running in frantic circles and barking, not out of surprise or confusion, but out of fear.

Lights flashed on and off in unison with the sound of a loud horn which thundered in Gerry's ears. He sprinted harder than he had done since chasing down that Boomer all those years ago.

"Hello, are you ok?" said Gerry, bending down to look in the window of the overturned car, paying no attention to the glass shattered across the road.

Screams from the girl in the passenger seat rang out above the beeps of the horn. And when Gerry leaned a little closer to the driver, he let out a breath in shock. The driver — wearing a tuxedo — had a cut on his head and opened his eyes. Then he whispered, "Gerry?"

"It's ok, Conor; we'll get you out of here," said Gerry.

Gerry looked over to the woman in a purple dress with the blood streaming from her side, and he realized what he already knew: he was out of his depth. His mind raced as quick as the raindrops that kept falling on the cracked windscreen of the red Datsun.

"Conor, I'll get you an ambulance," said Gerry.

Before Conor could reply, Gerry sprinted down the hill, and he burst into his house and straight into the wardrobe in his room. On top of Gina's auld suitcase with the tree wheels, which he had never brought himself to throw out, was the auld parcel that Jimmy had sent him years earlier. He ripped the box out of the wardrobe, and his hands fumbled, and he dropped the mobile phone on the floor, and shoved the charger into the wall.

Then he found the 'on' button and pressed it for the first time in a few years.

What was a minute felt like an hour, and once the phone turned on with an annoying sound, Gerry said, "Would you hurry up, you bastard of a thing?" And he vowed that if it didn't switch on this time and do something useful, he would be hurling it in the bin that day.

Gerry pressed *nine, nine, nine* and listened for a moment before hearing a voice. Holding the strange device to his ear, Gerry said, "Hello, I need an ambulance."

The lady on the line replied, "You're breaking up sir, an ambulance, was it?"

"Jaysus Christ, a feckin' ambulance. And I need it now."

"Ok sir, and where do you need it?"

"Drumbarron Hill. Halfway up the hill on the Ballyduffy side," said Gerry.

"I'm sorry sir, you're breaking up again. Ballyduffy Hill is the name of the place, is it?"

Gerry lifted the bulky phone from his ear, and he lengthened the antenna and shouted, "Jaysus feckin' Christ. No, Drumbarron Hill, on the Ballyduffy side."

"Ok sir, thank you. I'm sending one now."

"No, send two. And a fire truck as well," said Gerry.

"Ok sir, they're on their way."

Gerry threw the phone on the bed, and ran out into the rain, sprinting up that hill with Cara a few metres ahead of him the whole way. Within twenty minutes, which seemed like a lifetime amongst the screams of the girl and the closed eyes of Conor, Gerry waited by their sides for the ambulances and fire truck to come, feeling helpless, useless, and alone.

Yet he knew full well there wasn't much more he could do.

Once they arrived, the paramedics helped Conor out and put him in one of the ambulances and darted off to the hospital in Tralee. The firemen helped cut the woman out of her side of the car, and they put her in the other ambulance, and it rushed off too. When another ambulance arrived, and they asked Gerry if he was all right and why he had asked for tree ambulances, Gerry thought about that bastard phone and shook his head.

However, he realized now that the phone was good for some things, and later that evening, he would put it back in the box in the wardrobe so that it was there for emergencies.

The following day, Gerry would take his tractor into the hospital in Tralee to check on Conor and the girl, who had been on their way to the Rose of Tralee festival. When one of the nurses there told Gerry that they had been lucky, and that the woman could have bled to death if he hadn't been there, he thought of Cara, and what a watchdog she was.

Gerry smiled when the nurse said that the woman would make a full recovery. Then he went into Conor's room, where he lay on a bed with a bandage wrapped around the cut in his head.

"Hello, Gerry," said Conor. His voice sounded a lot quieter and fainter, compared to the exuberance and energy from that night in the tea shop all those years ago.

"How's it going, Conor?" asked Gerry, taking a seat.

"It could be better. But I'm alive thanks to you. We're *both* alive thanks to you."

Gerry nodded as he didn't know what else to really say or do. And he sat there for another little bit and chatted with Conor, who had clearly been relieved to hear that the woman, the Dublin Rose for this year's festival, would make a full recovery.

Then they sat in silence for a little before Conor said, "You know, she was heartbroken when she never heard from you."

And Gerry knew he wasn't talking about the Dublin Rose. Gerry nodded again. He turned away as Conor's eyelids began to look heavy.

"I loved her. I still love her," whispered Gerry under his breath, his eyes staring down at his feet, assuming Conor had fallen asleep. Then he felt a hand reach over and land on his.

"She wrote to me. She always writes to me at this time of year. She said she met you in New York. You know what, Gerry? I've been taking care of Roses down here for nearly twenty years, and she's the only one who ever won it. She said it was the best weekend of her life," said Conor faintly, his eyes beginning to close again underneath the bandage that wrapped around his head.

"She'd win any competition she'd ever enter," said Gerry, smiling at the thought.

"She said it was the best weekend of her life because she met you. Gerry, go into my bag, and there's a black book. You'll find her number in there, should you ever wish to call her. It's the least I can do."

And Gerry looked towards the black bag on the table beside the bed. And when he looked back at Conor, his eyes had already closed, and he'd fallen asleep.

Jaysus, thought Gerry. His hands trembled as he reached across and lifted the bag. And ignoring whatever else was there, he found a small black book and lifted it out. He flicked through the pages, seeing many names and addresses of people that Gerry had never met. And he assumed there were many Roses in here, yet he was only looking for one.

And then he found her.

Gina Friedman, Manhattan, New York.

His heart began to surge. He knew it was her, could only be her. *Friedman,* he thought. And Gerry was sure that O'Dea had suited her better.

But he knew the name that suited her better than any of those.

Gerry copied the number down and then placed the book back inside the bag and returned it to the side table. Then he said a prayer and his goodbyes to a sleeping Conor.

On his way out, Gerry would learn from the nurse that Conor too would pull through, but that he wouldn't be doing any of those splits again.

Gerry drove a little slower than he would've liked out the coast road back to Ballyduffy, too slow given that now, that he had a number in his pocket that he wanted to call. That he *must* call.

Yet, for some reason, he felt grateful for everything he did have in his life, and especially for his little sheepdog. He wondered if Gina and her would've gotten along. And he thought of how good Gina had been with Sugar the horse, and he never doubted it again.

When he got home, Gerry gave Cara a pat and a treat, and then he went to get the phone from the wardrobe. He began to type the number in, finding his hands a little sweatier than usual.

"Feck sake. What's wrong this time?" said Gerry.

There was nothing but a dull sound that for a moment, Gerry thought was in his head. He tried the number a few more times and then threw the phone down on the bed.

"Feck it."

He sat down on the bed, the little bit of paper in his hands. *Did I make a mistake? Did I take down the wrong number? Is it even her?*

Then Cara, who had followed him into the room, barked, and Gerry stood back up again.

"You little star," said Gerry and he patted the dog once more before lifting the phone once again and dialling a second time.

"Hello?"

"Oh, hello?" said Gerry.

"Hi. Operator," came the voice down the end of the line.

"Hello, operator. I want to call someone in New York. Can you help me?"

"Hello, you cut . . . there?"

"I want to call someone in New York?"

"York, England, transferring now."

"No, no, *New* York. America. The Statue of Liberty," said Gerry.

"Hello. Operator. Can you give me the York region number that you would like to contact?"

"Hello. No, I want to call New York."

"Sorry sir, you're cutting out. Yes, this is York."

Gerry pressed the red button and hung up. "Jaysus Christ," he said, looking down at Cara and shaking his head. "Well, at least I know it works. Come on, Cara, let's go."

With that, Gerry put on his coat, left the front door, and began walking up Drumbarron Hill. And when he got halfway up, he stopped and blessed himself at the place where the grass at the side had been flattened, black tire marks still lining it. He knelt to pat his dog.

"Jaysus, they were lucky you were here, Cara."

Then he walked a little farther, about tree-quarters of the way up, and he took out the phone and dialled the operator.

"Hello. I want to call someone in New York."

"Ok. New York; connecting you now."

And when the phone started to ring, Gerry felt a flutter in his stomach. He was really doing it.

"Hello."

"Hello, Gina?"

"Sir, this is the New York international operator. Can I please have the number you are wanting to connect with?"

"Oh, right. Yes, well, it's tree, tree, two."

"Is that three, three, two?"

"Yes, tree, tree, two . . ." and Gerry continued until the operator said, "Putting you through now. Have a good day."

And for a brief second, he forgot about Gina, and thought instead about all the good memories he'd had in New York that time, and the friendly people who'd all wished him a good day. *It is a good day*, he thought. And as the phone began to ring, he added aloud, *"this* is a really good day." After the phone rang for tirty seconds, he heard a sound and his heart stopped.

"Hi, you've reached Brad and Gina's. We are currently unavailable. However, please leave your name and number and we will call you back. Have a great day."

From the first tone, the first "Hi," Gerry pursed his lips at the man's accent.

And despite not knowing the man at all, and realizing he had no reason to find distaste in him, he did. And he thought, *it is what it is.* Then he began to speak.

"Hel. . . Hello, Gina. This is Gerry. Gerry McCarthy . . . hmm . . . from Ballyduffy. . . hmm . . . Kerry. I don't really know what to say here now, but it would be great to speak with you. I've got a mobile phone now. I'm actually near the tea shop, would you believe? Hmm... Anyways, so if you want to call me back, it's . . . feck. . . hmm . . . feck . . . sorry."

And Gerry hung up. And he started running down the hill again, just a little slower than he had the night before. He burst in the front door and when he reached the bedroom, he headed straight for the wardrobe and pulled out the box.

"There's the bastard number," said Gerry.

He ripped off the piece of cardboard which had the number of his mobile phone, and he started running back up that hill to the same spot where he'd been standing before.

Once he arrived, Gerry, breathing heavily, rang the operator, and was wished a nice day again, and he thought, *ah, would you ever get on with it?*

And then he waited for the pre-recorded message once more. As he waited, he knew exactly what it was going to say, and then what he was going to say. He had to tell her that he'd loved her every minute of every day since he first saw her, and that he had written and was sorry his messaged never arrived, and that her letter to him had broken his heart in two, and that he wanted her to come live with him, or he could come live with her.

If only Brad would feck off, he thought. Then there was a sound. Gerry listened harder. *Is it the wind? Or is there someone breathing in my ear?*

"Hello? Hello?"

Silence. *No, there's breathing, thought Gerry.*

"Hello? Gina? Is that you? It's Gerry. Gina, I wrote, and I'm sorry, they lost my letters . . ."

And then Gerry heard a click. And there was no breathing. He pressed his ear into the phone.

"Hello?" said Gerry.

He switched the phone to his other ear, but there was nothing, only the Kerry wind that was beginning to swirl all around him. *She answered,* he thought. He was sure of it. He called again and the operator put him through, and his foot began to tap, leg jiggling as it always did when the nerves got the better of him.

"Hello?" said Gerry.

But there was only a dull sound. That same dull sound he'd heard years ago when he first tried to use the mobile phone. He called again and got the same result.

Then he asked the operator, and they explained that there was nothing they could do; it was the same number each time, and nothing had changed on their end.

The rain started to fall in Ballyduffy, and Gerry stood still with the phone in his hand and cared nothing about the drops that battered his coat.

Did she hang up on me? She didn't want to talk to me?

Cara barked, alerting Gerry to the fact that a storm was arriving just as it had the night before. Then the two headed off together down the hill as the water began cascading down the middle of the road, washing away all the shite and the mud.

When he got inside, Gerry took off his coat and lifted the kettle towards the sink, and he turned the tap on. *I let her down one too many times,* he thought. *And this is the price I have to pay.* He stared out the window into the early evening, now blackened by the torrential downpour that had squeezed the last vestiges of light out of it. He thought of the streetlights in

New York, and of the way they'd illuminated the glistening tears in her eyes.

He heard her cries in his ears, cries that he had caused and that had pained him every day since. "I waited and I waited… You can't tell me this now."

Then he pictured the letter she'd written to him, and the teardrops on the page. And he heard again her breath on the phone line.

"Ah, shite."

Gerry dropped the kettle. He had poured the hot water by mistake and near burnt his hand. The steam rose from the sink, and landed on the window, hiding the rain outside.

And inside, in his home, it was only Cara and himself.

CHAPTER

23

Gerry never did use that goddamn phone again. He threw it in the back of his wardrobe where it would stay, lying on top of Gina's auld suitcase which Gerry had never brought himself to throw out. He didn't want to bring himself to hurt her anymore, and for some reason, the thoughts of throwing out the suitcase reminded him of how she must've felt when his letters never arrived, and when she never heard from him. And that it was the same way he had been feeling too.

And if he threw out that auld suitcase, somehow, he believed she would sense it and that this would only pile another layer of hurt on top of all the ones he had caused to her.

The sound of her breathing would haunt his dreams for weeks and months after, but he had made a promise to himself after a moment of weakness, when one night he had taken a glass of whiskey and had tried to call, and the operator said, "this number is no longer in service..." Yes, he had promised himself then that maybe it was time to let go, and he'd put the phone away.

One day a few months later in the run up to Christmas, Gerry was sitting behind the counter of the tea shop chatting to Tom Connelly, one of his best pals in the town, and the goalkeeper for the Ballyduffy team. They were chatting about football, and Tom was trying to convince Gerry, now forty-one years of age, to come back and play for another season.

"We'll see," he said to Tom.

Gerry had been thinking over the last couple of months that when playing midfield, a man needed more juice in his legs than when playing goalkeeper, and he had concluded that he had played his last game for Ballyduffy.

Just then, another fella came into the tea shop, a postman with one of their navy blue uniforms that Gerry had been well used to seeing down the years.

Now, he'd never seen this fella before, but he served him a cup of tea and looked over at the fella's table where he took out a newspaper. Gerry was always astute enough to know that whenever a customer brought out a newspaper, they more than likely just wanted some peace and quiet to have a cup of tea and a read. They didn't want to chat when a paper came out.

So, he joined Tom Connelly again at the counter for some more talk about football.

After Tom had left, Gerry and the postman remained in the shop, and when the postman went to use the bathroom, Gerry went over and lifted the man's empty plate from the table, where he'd finished two cakes. Gerry glanced down at the newspaper, and his eyes were drawn to a headline on the side of the page:

Kerry man in New York sentenced to forty years for insider trading.

Gerry's stomach sank. Then the postman ran out of the bathroom and left a couple of pounds for Gerry on the table and said, "Keep it. Jaysus, I didn't realize the time."

"Good luck to you," whispered Gerry, but his eyes never rose from that page.

He picked up the newspaper in his hands which were shaking violently, and he read the words under the headline:

James 'Jimmy' McCarthy, forty-four, from Ballyduffy, County Kerry, was sentenced to forty years in jail in a New York federal court last month on charges of insider trading, illegal immigration. . .

Gerry gasped, and stepped back. His heart was beating and all he could see in his head was that image of Jimmy smiling, handing him the taxi chit as the doors of the elevator closed. Gerry took that newspaper over to his counter and sat down. When a cyclist walked through the door, Gerry's head didn't even manage to lift to greet him. How had this happened?

Gerry thought back to the horrid people around that table in The Lobby, and he heard the voice of that man with the beady eyes and the balding head, and his words, "you're asking all the right questions, Gerry." Gerry couldn't help but get a lump in his throat and a pit in his stomach. Was that part of this?

"Gerry. Gerry. Excuse me, Gerry," said the cyclist, who brought Gerry back into the room.

Gerry shook his head. *Surely not,* he thought; *well, Jimmy and his dealings with the farmers must have finally caught up with him.*

"Sorry, Colin; let me fix you a tea now," said Gerry, placing the newspaper under the counter. That evening, and for many evenings after, thoughts of Jimmy would roam Gerry's mind. One particularly wet and windy night, he went down to the silver tin in the dresser and searched for Jimmy's letters, lifting out the tin and re-reading each letter over and over again.

After, he walked down to the bottom bedroom and looked over to where Jimmy's bed used to be, not six feet from the other. Then he rushed to the bathroom, and got sick over the toilet bowl.

CHAPTER

24

Gerry peered into the calendar on his wall, seeing a picture of a sheep, with two lambs running alongside, a white and a black one. He looked at today's date: Seventeenth of April, 1996. Twenty years to the day since Jimmy had left for America. Gerry took a sip of his tea, and he sat down at the kitchen table. Cara barked, and Gerry remembered it was her feeding time, so he went to one of the cupboards and searched for a bag of dog food. When he couldn't find a bag, he went out to the shed around the back of his house, searching there for the spare bags he would keep for a rainy day. But he rubbed his hand through his hair when he couldn't find one.

"Jaysus, I must've forgot," said Gerry. "Come on so, Cara."

Seeing as it was a beautiful spring day, Gerry and Cara walked into town to the shop. As he strode, Gerry paused for a few moments and peered into his field at all the new lambs that were prancing and jumping around. He chuckled when one came right up to the fence to look at Cara, who barked, sending the newborn lamb rushing away bleating, back to its mother.

He bought a bag of dog food and was carrying it over his shoulder on his way through the town when Mary Feeney came out of the post office and she stopped, and gasped, when she saw Gerry. Gerry paused too because this was unusual.

Mary Feeney wasn't one for being so quiet and uncomfortable looking. "How's it going?" said Gerry.

He could see Mary's foot begin to tap, then she said, "Gerry, I have a letter in here for you. It's from . . .It's from Jimmy."

Gerry's eyebrows raised and he blinked. *No wonder she's uncomfortable,* he thought.

The whole town had heard about Jimmy McCarthy, and when news like this spread in towns like Ballyduffy, the playbook was the same. Gerry had first received the looks, then the silence, then the questions. But over the last couple of months, knowing none of it had been Gerry's doing, people had gone back to their day-to-day lives. And seeing as Jimmy had been gone a long time, he was quickly forgotten again, if not by Gerry.

Mary Feeney went inside, and she came out with the letter and gave it to Gerry before she carried on down the street.

"It sure is Jimmy's writing all right," whispered Gerry, and he carried that letter and the bag of dog food with him to the house.

Gerry chuckled as the tail wagged as fast as it could on Cara, before the dog buried her head into the bowl. Then, Gerry reached for a cup from the cupboard, pausing when he saw Jimmy's navy blue cup beside Pa's. He wasn't sure why he paused, either. That cup had been there for the last twenty years, and he'd never worried much about it until today. But still, there was some uncomfortable feeling inside him when he finally sat down to read the letter.

He opened the envelope and as he unfolded the letter, a photograph fell into his lap. Gerry swallowed the lump that arrived, and he took a drink of tea to wet his dry throat as he stared into his brother's eyes in his green Ireland jersey, with Gerry beside him and the Statue of Liberty in the background. In his rush to leave that morning, Gerry had left his copy of this photo on the bedside table in Jimmy's spare bedroom.

Feb '96

Well, Gerry,

How's it going?

For the first time in my life, I'm stuck for words, Gerry. It's a funny auld game, life. Sometimes you win and sometimes you lose, and I'm afraid I've been losing a lot this past while.

I want to apologize to you for your time in New York. After all those years, to have left things like that will stay with me forever. And that time in the restaurant, I should've had your back like family does, and like Pa would've, and if roles were reversed, like you would've, Gerry. But I didn't and that's my cross to carry. I've always been proud to call you my brother, and I'll tell you again how proud I am of you.

You were right about the whole lot of them, Gerry. And what they did with the farmers, they'll do next to people's homes, and the numbers on the streets will go through the roofs that they will have had stolen from over their heads. When it came to the truth, you could always pierce the veil, whereas clouds would get in my way. At times, I even brought the rain upon myself. I forgot that we're all part of the one tree.

I don't know if you will have seen the news by now, Gerry, but I'm in a place where I'll not be able to leave for a long time. And as I write this, I don't know why I can hear the words of Ma in my ears: "Locked bird syndrome."

Wasn't that what she used to say about Uncle Paudie?

They threw the whole lot on me Gerry. In another place, in another time, I would've gotten a couple of years, but for some reason, they decided to bury all our dealings with me. I suppose they needed a fall guy. Maybe they were afraid of someone asking too many questions, but I'm here now and that's on me. I'm sorry for all that I've done, Gerry, for not being there when you lifted that championship for Ballyduffy, for not being there for Aunt Cara or Uncle Brendan, and most of all, for not being there for you.

Rachel left me too. To be honest, I'd like to say that was due to all this news, but truth be told, she knew all about the green card and if I'd gotten off, she'd have left me anyway.

And the Kerry team. Jaysus, Gerry, the green and the gold of Kerry. When we were younger, we used to want to watch every game, and the joy and the dreams it brought us. Alas, I haven't seen a game in a long time, and the jury's out on whether I'll see one again. I saw the look in your eyes in Times Square that night, Gerry, when you looked towards the sky. Perhaps you were right to avoid the screens and the billboards and look for those stars. I haven't seen stars in years, and if I see them again, it'll be in a different place to where I am now. Goodbye, Gerry, and as I said when I left the house that morning all those years ago, I don't *want to see your face.*

Jimmy McCarthy
Hudson Correctional Facility
500 West Coast Street
Hudson, New York, 15364
America.

And what is there to feel after that? Maybe some of you feel your hearts pine for a man alone in a distant country who got lost along his way. Maybe some of you may feel Jimmy deserved everything he got. But for Gerry, that was his only brother, his next of kin, his only family left in this world, and he sank into that kitchen chair and stared into the photograph.

Then he went into the cupboard, and he lifted Jimmy's navy cup, and threw it against the wall where it smashed to pieces. Gerry placed his hands on the kitchen counter, and he looked out the window, his breath as fast as the heart in his chest, and his thoughts came flying in and out of his mind, one after the other.

What did he mean by his last Kerry game?
He mightn't see a star again? Those bastards at that table.

Gerry felt the pit in his stomach. He thought back to that morning twenty years ago, and to the sound of the footsteps around the bedroom, and the close of the door. He understood what Jimmy was saying, but it didn't make him feel any better.

For the rest of the day, Gerry tried to be present in his tea shop, and to his luck, it was a quiet day. So, he cleaned the counter and the tables and chairs three times that day, all to the sounds of Wolfgang and his other records, which reached to every corner of the auld tea shop at the top of Drumbarron Hill. In front of the fire that evening, Gerry wrote Jimmy back a letter.

And in it, he would tell him not to be sorry — that he was his brother, and they were family. Gerry apologized for leaving Jimmy the way he did in

New York, and for all the times where he also had got too busy or procrastinated on writing Jimmy back a letter.

He told Jimmy about his new sheepdog, Cara, who was as wily as their aunt. And he told Jimmy what Brendan had said to him before he died. That he and Aunt Cara had mentioned that God had never intended for Uncle Brendan and herself to have children of their own, but that even before Ma's death tirty-one years ago now, they'd thought of both Gerry and Jimmy as if they were their own boys, and always would.

After he'd folded his letter and put it in an envelope, he took out an auld bottle of whiskey from the cupboard and poured himself a glass. He sat with his thoughts for a while, staring at the log in the fire, how it burned through and turned to ash, all to provide some energy, some heat for those sitting nearby. Then the strings of Valse, which he had played earlier that day in the tea shop, appeared in his mind once more. And with those strings, the memories of Gina reappeared.

He thought of how he'd left New York that weekend, with the doors of the elevator closing on Jimmy, but also the sight of Gina running away with tears in her eyes that night.

Then Gerry lifted the pen and another piece of paper, and he began to write.

April '96,

Dear Gina,

I haven't been a man of many words down the years, and you of all people know that. At times, this has been a blessing for me, when others preferred to be the loudest in the room, or when those with loose lips told stories they shouldn't have told.

Pa used to say, 'you've two ears and only one mouth for a reason.' However, there are also times when that hasn't been kind to me either. Times I feel I let slip by, times I didn't share what was going on inside of me with those around me.

Over the years, I think back to Pa and how he kept the world shut out, and I've come to understand there are two ways to do that. You can turn off your televisions and stick to what you know; however, the other way is to keep yourself on the inside, so that the outside world never knows what's going on behind the screen. And I've come to understand that like Pa, I have been guilty of this many times.

I think back to our moments together and have these burning questions in my head. Did I show you enough? Did I do enough? I hope through my actions that I did show it, despite my lack of expression through words. And what is "it," I suppose, anyway?

"It" is the scent of your perfume that I still smell everywhere I go, in the oddest of places. Like when the flowers of spring arrive on the side of the road on Drumbarron Hill. "It" is when I hear Valse in a crowded room, yet for a moment in time, it is only you and I present. "It" is the rip I felt inside when you turned to wave goodbye that day in Shannon Airport, and how it stayed with me until you returned. "It" is the thoughts I have every time I look at the blue of the Atlantic Ocean on a summer's day and picture your eyes. And in the winter days, when the dark clouds are overhead, "it" is the feeling of warmth you would bring whenever you'd walk into the room.

There is still something I wish to explain to you, something I ought to have told to you so long ago and never did, for so many reasons. I only hope that you understand.

It is that the morning I was meant to come to America, Aunt Cara passed away. Why as to that day, I've never understood, and the only rationale or comfort I have is when I think of something I heard Pat Storey say a long time ago, that 'True love doesn't ever leave, it's there somewhere, always.' Maybe my letters getting lost in the post – and you see, I did write to you – were all meant for some reason. Maybe it was to shake something out of me that needed to be shaken, or I suppose, maybe, it was to shake something out of you.

I think I understand what Pat meant, that maybe love is like an anchor dropped into the ocean. The boat will stay where it is, and the world will go on around it. But for the boat to move forward, that anchor will have to be pulled up. I'm not sure, and I have doubts some days, but Aunt Cara was a superstitious woman and that seems to have passed to me. Following her death, I can't believe that the only superstition she ever got wrong was that *you and I were meant for one another.*

I know it is selfish to send you this now — you're married — but for some reason, be it a voice inside my head or a wish inside my heart, but that night in New York, I felt you still had thoughts of me. If I'm wrong, I apologize, and I'll not bother you again despite how much I will think of you for the rest of my days.

Yours sincerely,

Gerry.

Gerry McCarthy,
Ballyduffy, Kerry
Ireland.

Gerry put the letter into another white envelope, and he wrote Gina's name on it. Then he wrote her address on it too. Despite how hazy his memories of that day in New York were, he always remembered that she lived at number eight, and her street was tree blocks down from Jimmy's.

That night, Gerry slept in his auld single bed down in the bottom room, and in the dark of night, he would peer in the direction of Jimmy's empty corner. And in his nightmare, he pictured Jimmy's bed in his new location: a prison cell. And Gerry woke from his sleep early in the morning in a sweat.

————•✳•————

Before he would open the tea shop for the day, Gerry and Cara would walk into town again, and Gerry had brought both letters in his hand. And during the walk, he was mighty glad for Cara's company, keeping his thoughts on her when she sniffed the flowers on the side of the road and everything else that caught her scent.

"How's it going, Gerry?" asked Patricia when Gerry walked into an empty post office. "It's been a while since I've seen you here."

"Not so bad, Patricia. How's it going with you? I didn't know you were working here anymore. I've seen Mary Feeney whenever I've been in."

"You're right, Gerry. I only work two days a week now, which is great.

CHAPTER TWENTY-FOUR

Mary does most of the work here now. You could say I'm semi-retired, Gerry."

Gerry didn't see any sign of sweat on her head or a cigarette in her hand. Patricia looked well, and she even had a smile on her face.

"Well, that's great, well deserved," said Gerry.

"Thank you, Gerry. We had some great tea chats in here over the years. It's great though, it really is. To tell you the truth, I was getting a bit stressed there for a while, putting letters in the wrong boxes and whatnot, so I'm glad those bastards in HQ in Dublin saw sense, and sent me a bit of help. Mary's been great."

Gerry smiled back at Patricia. He thought of those letters that hadn't made it to Gina and whether it was Patricia's fault, or one of the postmen who liked to take long tea breaks in his tea shop, or even if the mistake had been made in the headquarters in Dublin or somewhere else across the Atlantic. But it was all neither here nor there now. Water under a bridge. *We all make mistakes,* he supposed.

"Two days a week must be great," said Gerry.

"It's brilliant, Gerry. Between you and me, I leave a lot of the Government letters and the tax notices and that — the death box — to Mary Feeney; and I try to keep tabs on the life box. And here, what about your Jimmy? He got himself mixed up with the wrong sort over there, didn't he? But sure, he'll not be the last, and he sure as hell wasn't the first. Sad news, all the same.

"You know, I always remember that smile of his from when he was a boy. Your mother wasn't much younger than me, and that boy was never out of her arms. He was a very happy child from what I remember, very content, you know, no badness out of him. Anyways, sad about these things. You know, I was surprised when he flew over there all those years ago. Anyways. Well, I suppose his flying days are done for a while now. No offence, Gerry."

Gerry nodded and he tried to smile back and said, "none taken, Patricia." He supposed he couldn't argue with anything she said, no matter how upset he was about his brother.

"Gerry, you haven't been in here a while, but come here until I tell you, Mary Feeney, you know she's engaged now to Brian Egan? Well, she still has all those letters coming in from Italy and Switzerland. She thinks I don't see them, but I do. She even went to Germany there last year to visit her aunt, and sure, isn't some fella Hans sending her letters now. Right on time, every first Friday of the month he sends one, Gerry. Those Germans are awful efficient.

"But who am I to say something, Gerry? And you know me — never one for gossip."

Gerry couldn't help but smile. And he felt a tug on his heart as a memory of Aunt Cara popped into his mind. Then Patricia spoke up again.

"Now Gerry, what can I help you with? I suppose it's Jimmy as I haven't seen anything from Gina in years and I suppose that fizzled out."

Gerry raised his eyebrows, and then he blinked. He held the two letters tightly in his hand, staring down at the both of them, then back up at Patricia.

"Yes, Jimmy please, Patricia. You couldn't give this the auld express stamp?" said Gerry, and he passed across the letter, swallowing a lump in his throat in the process.

"Of course, Gerry. Number seven," said Patricia.

Gerry's eyebrows rose.

"Number seven?" said Gerry.

"Yes, you see after my mix ups, I write down and record the number of letters I process in a day, Gerry. I have time to do that now, you see. Now, what about the other one?"

Gerry's eyebrows rose again, and once more he looked down at the letter in his hands. He grasped it tight. *Number eight.* And in his head, he pictured the glass doors close beneath the large number eight of Gina's building in New York that night. And he thought about how he'd stood outside the next morning, and there was nothing to be seen.

And Gina's phone number ended with an eight as well. Then he heard the click of the phone in his ear, where she had hung up on him. Maybe after all these years, it wasn't his lucky number after all. He looked back up to Patricia and said, "No, just the one today, please."

"No problem, Gerry, suit yourself."

Gerry placed the letter in his back pocket, and he walked out onto the road with Cara a lot slower than he had walked in. And he looked down at Cara's tail flicking from side to side and he shook his head. Because he supposed that if he had a tail, it would've been between his legs right now, years of hurt and failure weighing heavy on his shoulders.

Love's an anchor? It's more like a ball and chain wrapped around my neck, thought Gerry. He didn't think about anything else at all as he dragged his feet up Drumbarron Hill towards the tea shop, where a couple of cyclists were already waiting.

He placed that letter in a drawer behind the counter and set about his day.

CHAPTER

25

Despite the fact the letter still lay in a cupboard in the tea shop, Gerry tried to put into practice all those words that he had written down. Over the winter, he began to get involved with the community, taking up some of Aunt Cara's work with the church, making sure that the children had toys for Christmas, and that the auld and lonely folk were looked after over the Christmas period with food and company. He never thought it might have been because he was forty-two and lonely, but he did it anyway, and it made him stand a little straighter. Christmas passed once more in the McHughs', with John and Kathleen and their two boys, aged five and two — John Jr and James — and Gerry was grateful for their friendship.

Although he hadn't played for Ballyduffy the previous year, he took up running and found himself up in the hills, even out along the coast road towards Tralee a couple of times a month. On New Year's Eve in O'Brien's, Tom Connelly pleaded with Gerry to come back and play.

"Sure, you're flying fit again, and we've a few young lads coming through, Tom Walsh and Joe Sweeney. There could be a championship in here in the next few years."

"I'm done for good, Tom. I'm a supporter now. I'll be on the other side of the fence around McHugh Park," said Gerry. And he supposed he would enjoy it, as being a supporter for the Kerry team wasn't doing him any favours. They hadn't made an All-Ireland final in over a decade, and to make matters worse, Cork had won two in that time, and Dublin had won the previous year, and were now full of themselves again.

When he found himself in the tea shop one day reminiscing over the photo of the Kerry team, he thought again of Jimmy, and wondered how he was doing in prison, having not received a letter back. The strangest thoughts came through his head, but for a man who'd never known anyone else to be in prison, nor had he a television; these were the questions we'd likely all ask.

Was Jimmy ok? Did he have his own room?

Did he have a single bed or a double?

What was the food like?

And Gerry paused a moment, shaking his head, realizing he was mixing a prison with a hotel.

And then the pit, which he had left out of his mind, returned to his stomach once more. This was no holiday for Jimmy; this was going to be the rest of his life, most likely. Gerry thought about his own life. He was now forty-two, and he supposed he couldn't remember all forty-two years, but he knew it was a long time, and that this was no joke. Despite Jimmy's protestations in his letter, Gerry decided then and there that it was only right to go visit his brother.

Then, a postman walked through the door.

"Well, Gerry," said the postman.

"Well, Michael, how are you? What brings you up this way?" said Gerry.

Michael was the postman for the Dingle area, and he'd stop by perhaps once or twice a year at most, normally keeping himself down near the coastal waters where he felt at home.

"I'm covering for a fella in Slieve. He does a few of the villages on the other side of the hill. Load of shite to be honest, Gerry. Every year, those bastards in headquarters ask us to do more and more. Jaysus, there'll come a time I'll be the only postman in Ireland at this rate. Be some chance getting the letters in a timely manner then, I'd say. Rushed off my feet, so I am. Nevertheless, I've got a couple of minutes, so I'll have a tea and one of those cakes please."

Gerry chuckled as he went to get Michael his tea.

These postmen have a hard life, he thought.

"Come here. Do you mind if I ask you a question, Michael?" said Gerry.

He looked over at Michael who was taking out a newspaper, so he'd only have time for the one question.

"Certainly, Gerry."

"I heard a long time ago that they open letters in Dublin to check them for the likes of cocaine and heroin. If they're from a strange, far-off place with a history of crime, that is. Is that true?"

And Gerry saw the shoulders bounce up and down on Michael, and his laugh echoed around the room.

"Jaysus, Gerry, do you think we have the time for that?"

Gerry shrugged and supposed it made sense. The postmen were always late no matter where they went. So, he made the tea and left Michael to himself.

Once Michael had finished three cups and three cakes, he went to the bathroom. Gerry went to clean up when he saw the newspaper wide open on the table. On one page was a large picture of the Dublin team, and a preview of the All-Ireland Championship for 1996, where the newspaper predicted Dublin would win back-to-back titles.

Gerry nearly dropped the plates in shock.

On the other page were death notices from all around Ireland.

"Life and death," Gerry whispered as he looked at the two pages again.

Then, for whatever reason, his eyes scanned down to part of the page on the death notices where he saw the words 'New York.' He read the words:

Dan O'Dea, 97, died in New York last month. Originally from Castlebar, Mayo, Dan was well known in the Irish-American community, owning a number of pubs in . . .

However, before he could read the rest, Gerry's eyes were drawn to the notice below, and he dropped the plates on the ground.

"Are you all right there, Gerry?" said Michael, rushing out of the bathroom.

"Ah – yeah. Yeah," said Gerry, whose eyes hadn't left the page.

"Ok then, I'm feckin' two hours late. Here Gerry, take this and keep the paper. I'll see you again soon," said Michael, who threw a ten-pound note on the table and ran out the door.

Gerry never moved. Nor did he hear the screech of the van take off down Drumbarron Hill. He didn't lift the paper, nor did he lift the plates that lay shattered to pieces on the ground.

He read the notice again.

James 'Jimmy' McCarthy, 45, died in Hudson Prison, New York State, last month. Originally from Ballyduffy, Kerry, Jimmy had been facing forty years in prison for insider trading, amongst other charges. Cause of death: suicide. Listed Gerry McCarthy, Ballyduffy, as next of kin. May he rest in peace.

Gerry stumbled when his knees gave way, knocking over the table and chairs behind him. He stood some more with his hand on a chair, staring into space. All those memories of Jimmy flashed through his mind: the football, the Christmases, the pints. Those days at the beach when they had been boys with Ma. The raised voices from arguments with Pa. Those jokes and stories of America and other parts of the world that Jimmy seemed to know a lot about. The picture he had in his house of the pair of them outside the Statue of Liberty. The sight of his brother with his Ireland jersey and number fourteen on his back. Then the image of Jimmy in his navy dressing gown as the doors in the elevator came into Gerry's mind.

He stumbled again.

He walked across the floor and into the bathroom, where he tried to be sick but couldn't. He stood up and splashed water all over his face and stared into the small mirror, staring for God knew how long. Time had stopped again. And he saw Jimmy staring back at him.

When he heard the door of the tea shop open outside, Gerry dried his face with the towel. He took three deep breaths, and his hand reached for the latch of the bathroom door. However, before he could find the latch, he stumbled back again, gasping for air as he bent down towards the sink to splash yet more water over his face. His hand shook as he placed it under the tap, clasping at whatever water would sit in it, then he took a sip.

"I'll be with you now in a second," shouted Gerry, managing to hide the trembles in his voice. He looked in the mirror again, turned, and opened the bathroom door.

When he looked towards the table with the newspaper, and the chairs on the ground, he stood still. But that wasn't what he was looking at. Standing there, with a black coat on and a pair of jeans, and a Ballyduffy training bag by her side was Gina.

Gerry wanted to rub his eyes, but his arms wouldn't lift. He couldn't move.

"I'm sorry, Gerry," said Gina.

Gerry looked into her blue eyes. They sparkled, but for whatever reason, he thought they looked as though they had passed many tears at some point not so long ago.

Then Gerry fell to his knees, and for the first time in his life, Gerry McCarthy opened the wells behind his eyes and let the water that he had held inside flow out. When he felt Gina's arms around him, he buried his head into her chest, and he let more of those cries out.

Gina too, couldn't help the tears flowing down her face, and some landed on top of Gerry's head cradled against her bosom. After a few minutes, Gerry heard, "I'm sorry" whispered for a second time into his ears.

He got to his feet, and wiped the underside of his eyes.

"Thank you. I don't know what to say. Are you a ghost?" said Gerry.

Gina let out a loud laugh and wiped the underside of her own eyes, before Gerry felt her thumb brush along his cheek, and he assumed she was catching a tear he had missed.

"Do you want a cup of tea, Gerry?" said Gina.

"Don't you worry; I'll make it."

"No Gerry, I insist. Why don't you take a seat?"

And for the first time in nearly twenty years, Gerry was served a cup of tea in his tea shop.

He glanced back over at the newspaper with its picture of the Dublin team and a strange thought came into his head. All those worries he'd had down the years about the Dublin team and the Kerry team, and the Dublin folk who came by with their confidence and so full of themselves, and yet they were all miniscule and unimportant compared to the news on the other page. And he thought of the words, *Cause of death: suicide.*

And he couldn't help his mind thinking about the rope that they had used to lead Sugar the horse, and then thinking about that night with the wild dog caught in the barbed wire, and the feel of the cold steel of Pa's gun in his hands in front of the fire as he'd stared down the barrel.

Then he thought of the words, *Next of kin: Gerry McCarthy.*

He thought back to the final time they'd taken a drink in the rocking chairs and Jimmy had said to Gerry, "If you need anything, you write, and I'll be on the first plane home." And Gerry couldn't help the tears coming down his face because he'd never said the same thing back.

"Gerry. Hey, Gerry," came Gina's voice.

Gerry felt her wipe his cheek with a napkin before she placed another into his giant hands. He looked down, and then over at the teacup. *It looks a little milky,* he thought.

Then he looked up at Gina and another tear dropped.

He always knew she was an angel of God.

Gina's eyes flicked towards the newspaper again. He saw her head drop and that was when he realized something: the auld fella Dan that he'd met in the pub in New York all those years ago was Gina's grandfather, from Castlebar, Mayo.

"I'm sorry, Gina," said Gerry.

"You've nothing to be sorry for, Gerry. It's me who must apologize to you. But we can talk about that some oth —"

"Are you back for good?" interrupted Gerry.

Gina paused and her blue eyes, red like Gerry's, rose to meet his, and she smiled through the pain that was all around the tea shop. And she nodded.

And for the rest of the day, nothing more needed to be said about that. For a while, they sat in silence, Gina's hand resting on top of Gerry's as the memories of moments past filled the room and their minds. Another strange thought came to Gerry's mind: Gina and Jimmy had never met.

That night, down in the house, after Gina had made some potatoes and sausages with what was in Gerry's fridge, Gerry put on the fire, and they sat in those two rocking chairs with some tea and whiskey. And so, Gerry went into the bottom room and brought out the silver tin from the dresser, which had all the letters of Gina and Jimmy that he had kept throughout the years.

On seeing this, a smile came upon Gina's face, and she kissed Gerry, her lips tasting of the tears from the day, although Gerry was never sure if they were hers or his own.

"You never met Jimmy," said Gerry.

"I met him through all the stories you told me about him, Gerry."

Gerry felt the lump in his throat return. Then he said, "Would you like to read his letters?"

That night, Gerry and Gina read all the letters Jimmy had written over the last twenty years. They laughed together, and cried together.

"I said this, too, about New York, Gerry," said Gina, and Gerry chuckled because there were many times like that throughout their letters.

And through heavy eyes and heavy hearts, when Gerry looked down at the final letter from Jimmy from his time in prison, he said, "Let's leave this one for another day."

CHAPTER

26

I t would be a week or two after when Gerry and Gina would sit down and understand the years that they'd been apart. Regardless, Gerry was just pleased that she was here at last, and one day, when she opened the wardrobe and saw her auld suitcase with the tree wheels that Gerry had never brought himself to throw out, she would laugh herself silly – even more so to find that the clothes still fit, and she'd say it was like buying a new wardrobe.

And Gerry would chuckle too, and for the first time, felt a bit of warmth towards that case because it was only then that he really knew Gina had no intentions of going anywhere soon.

"You have a mobile phone, Gerry? For some reason, I never pictured you with one of these things," said Gina.

"You wouldn't know the half of it," said Gerry.

Gina's laugh felt like music in his ears.

The news spread around Ballyduffy that Jimmy had died, and Gerry was surprised when people would start calling to his house. Over the course of a week, the likes of Patricia and Mary Feeney from the Post Office, Toe O'Brien from the pub, and the likes of the McHughs and the Connelly brothers would call out to Gerry's place. Gina had used that magic brain of hers and brought down a couple of teapots from the tea shop one day, and so there was always tea available for those visitors who had made the trek from town.

And they'd all say the same thing: "We're so sorry, Gerry. Jimmy was a good man around here, great craic so he was," and they'd all have a story or two about him.

Peter Connelly, the aulder brother, who was the same age as Jimmy growing up, said that in school, Jimmy was always getting into trouble with the teachers. "Because he knew more than them about the world and how it worked," laughed Peter. "And he used to drive Mr. O'Malley mad. 'Where'd you read that, James?' he used to say."

Gerry caught eyes with Gina. The sound of her laugh filled him with hope, and he was glad she was getting to hear these stories too.

Those from the town remembered Gina as well.

How could they forget?

"It's great to finally meet you. You've quite lovely handwriting," said Patricia, one evening in the house.

"And likewise. Thank you very much," said Gina in response. Then once Patricia was out of earshot, she turned to Gerry and said, "That's a little strange that she would remember my handwriting from the letters?"

"That's not all. She probably knows you better than I do," whispered Gerry, and he gave Gina a wink.

Then one day in the tea shop, after a couple of cyclists had left, Gerry finally asked her how it had come to be that she was here.

"I don't know if I ever loved him. Not like I loved you, anyway. We were very different people. I mean we hung around with the same group of friends through work. However, he didn't really get along with Bianca and Francesca, or my other friends if you know what I mean?"

"I thought your mother and father liked him?" asked Gerry.

"They did. He was well mannered and I'm not sure how to say this — polished, maybe? But my grandad..." Gina paused and chuckled, and Gerry saw the ducts behind her eyes begin to open before she composed herself again. "My grandad, rest his soul, said he was as dry as sandpaper, and that there was more craic in his big toe. He also called him a hungry hoor, which I always laughed at."

Gerry pictured the bushy gray eyebrows of Gina's grandad that day in the pub in New York. He had only met him for a second, but Gina's grandad had known Gerry was a Kerry man straight away, so Gerry knew that man was probably right.

"We drifted apart over the years. We were in counselling when I met you in New York that time, Gerry. I'm sorry again. When I spent that time with you, it made me realize just how unhappy I was. I filed for divorce, and I thought about sending you a letter, but I wasn't sure if it would've been right. Especially after how I'd left that night."

"But you came."

"Because I love you, Gerry. I'd made the decision to come visit, to see if we could work things out. I wasn't sure; maybe you had moved on. But then when Francesca told me about Jimmy, I hopped on the next plane. It's always been you, Gerry. From the moment I walked in here that night, it's always been you. I don't know, but when you didn't write, I thought I'd done something wrong. I hoped you'd come to New York, and that you'd fall in love with it and want to move there with me. Then when you didn't show, it was as if a dream had died."

A tear appeared on Gina's head, and Gerry bent forward and kissed it.

"Can I show you something?" he said.

Gina swept away another tear when Gerry went into a cupboard and brought out an envelope.

"What's this, Gerry?"

"It's something I should've told you many years ago."

Gerry sat in silence as Gina read the letter. And when another tear rolled down her cheek, he thought back to that day in the tractor when his teardrop landed on the initials 'JFK.' They sat in silence for another few moments. Gerry knew Gina had finished reading, but her eyes never lifted from the page. When they finally did, she leaned forward and kissed him.

"I'm sorry I never came. I should have flown over there."

"No, Gerry. It's not your fault. If you did try, I don't know if it would have made any difference. It wasn't the right time for us. I don't mean that I didn't love you. I always did. I think that after I didn't hear from you, I blocked the pain out. I put it away, threw myself into this other life. I was lying to myself, Gerry, and I don't think even you could have helped me see the truth back then."

"I could've tried harder. I didn't take care of you. I can only imagine how you felt when I never turned up at the airport."

"Gerry, you've taken care of things all your life. You took care of your pa, whether you knew it or not. You took care of the farm, the customers in the tea shop, you took care of Uncle Brendan. And you always took care of me when I was here. Maybe it's time that you let someone take care of you for a change."

And Gerry sat back in his chair. Gina seemed to awaken the warm feeling inside him again, a feeling that had been gone for too long. But he had an itch in the back of his mind. He leant forward again and said, "I wrote the letter, and never sent it. Once you never returned my message after I called you, I suppose I —"

"You called?"

"I did. I heard your voice. I mean your breath, and you hung up and I —"

"That bastard," said Gina.

"What?" said Gerry.

"It must've been him. Well, Gerry, it doesn't matter now. I'm here. You know —"

Gina paused and turned to face Gerry. She held his hands together, looked into his eyes and began to speak.

"The one thing about you that I always admired, is that you always knew who you were. You knew what made you happy and content, and you knew what didn't. I get it. In the part of your letter when you said something needed to be shaken out, I think that was on my side.

"I was caught up in a life that wasn't what I wanted. All my life, I'd felt pressured to be successful for everyone else, to achieve something — to conform to something that wasn't me.

"If I wanted to play music, I had to be one of the best in the world for it to be successful, to be worth it. I fell out of love with it as a result, Gerry. I haven't played in years.

"Then they thought I should join the bank, and I had to work the hardest and climb the ladder so my dad could tell his friends about me. Then to get married. I never dreamed of that life, Gerry. I was living a life others wanted for me, and no matter how many rooms your apartment in Manhattan has, or how many fancy restaurants you dine in, none of them made me as happy as those times spent here with you in Ballyduffy. Deep down, there was always something missing.

"When Grandad was dying, he said to me, 'Fuck the lot of them and go with your heart.'"

Gerry laughed at Gina's Irish accent.

He rubbed his thumb along the top of her hands, and Gina continued, "I think he always knew it. He saw how happy I was when I returned from seeing you, and then he'd see the smile disappear from my face over the following months. I think it's fine to follow dreams; I think you just have to make sure they fit inside your soul, or else the dream turns into a nightmare.

"It took me some time to realize what was in my soul. I just wanted an ordinary, decent life, with someone I love. I'm glad I followed my dreams in the end. I'm where I'm meant to be, Gerry, if you'll have me?"

Gerry opened his mouth to speak but then closed it again. Then he leant forward and kissed Gina on the lips. Cara barked, and Gerry looked down towards this blessing of a sheepdog.

"I always had a feeling that Aunt Cara had to have been right. I think deep down, I always believed, although like Rosie from Tralee, I suppose I may have had a doubt or two."

Gina chuckled before saying, "Rosie from Tralee?"

"I'll tell you about her someday. And about everything else." Gerry took a sip of his tea before he continued. "You know, something you said made me think of Jimmy. I've been thinking about him a lot."

"Of course, you have, Gerry."

"I think back to when we were younger. I was only ten when my mother died. Jimmy was that bit older, and I suppose, perhaps it impacted Jimmy that little bit more. I didn't know my mother for very long in terms of what we would call a normal life, but my experience as a son is that your mother will love you and be proud of you no matter what you do. And I suppose with your father, you just want to make him proud, want to emulate him. I think back, and think I did make my father proud, but you know, that doesn't mean I have to *be* him, whether he was a great man or not. Jimmy being that little bit older when my mother died, I can only imagine how it hurt him, and maybe, maybe he felt he had to go over there and all that to make Ma proud.

"And then thinking about Uncle Paudie and those dreams of going to America and whatnot, I just don't really know if they were ever Jimmy's dreams. Whether they fit inside his soul. Or whether he was looking for something after Ma died that he couldn't get in my father.

"Maybe he thought he had to do something or make more of himself to make her proud, whereas I knew she loved me, and she was going to be proud of me regardless. I can't help but think that Jimmy knew everything about the world, yet nothing about himself and who he was.

"And I feel so sorry for him for that."

Gerry looked at Gina and wiped a tear that came running down her cheek.

He drew a deep breath and continued, "That's a part of life: dreams. And with all his gadgets and his fancy apartment and his money and his suits, was he ever really that happy? All the years he was over there, and he didn't get that green card and couldn't come back. And I think, you're over there and you're surrounded by people who love you for your achievements and your entitlements, rather than loving you for who you are.

"I'm not saying there's anything wrong with achieving things. I mean, I think I've achieved a lot in my life with the tea shop and whatever else. But I'd rather be loved for who I am, and I think in Ballyduffy, and in you, I've found that. *You* help me to be happy for who I am."

"Jesus, Gerry, you're making me cry here," said Gina, kissing him through her tears.

After another sip of tea, Gerry continued, letting himself talk as much as he had ever done before, feeling he had to get some things off his chest that he had held onto for far too long.

"Jimmy was always telling me he was proud of me, and you know what? I never said it back. I always thought, sure he was my big brother, and he always knew what was going on, all this stuff about the world. And I never thought, you know. I just never thought."

As the cup in his hand began to shake, Gerry felt Gina's hands on his and she steadied the teacup on the plate, preventing any from spilling. Then he placed the cup and saucer down on the table, and he turned to Gina and said, "You know I look at you, and I'm sorry it took us this long to get here, but I'm so glad we're here now. I think I've learned that when you have the chance, it's important to tell someone that you love them when you do, or to let them know how you feel about them, because perhaps they don't know that enough.

"All those years, I waited for the perfect moment to tell you how I feel. And this isn't the perfect moment. There is no perfect moment. True love is an anchor, it's permanent, it doesn't have moments and there's no need to wait for one. I love you Gina, the person you are… And you can always be yourself — the real you — around me."

Gina smiled through teary eyes, and kissed Gerry.

Then, she moved her chair closer, and he felt her head lean against his shoulder. And there was silence in the coffee shop as the ghost of Jimmy floated around the room.

————·✳·————

A few months passed and Gerry and Gina were finally where they were always meant to be. On the bright summer days, they'd take Cara out for walks up Drumbarron Hill or the surrounding countryside. On those days where the rain blew hard, Gerry would take Cara out for a walk alone, knowing that the sideways rain takes a bit of getting used to in these parts.

However, Gina fit right in.

She'd made friends with Mary Feeney in the post office, sending letters back and forth to friends and her family in America, letting them know that for the first time in her life, she felt at peace within herself and her surroundings, now that she was with her one true love.

And the customers of the tea shop were happy to have a beautiful woman helping, and they were happy too for big Gerry McCarthy, who through years of rain, snow, and sunshine, and whatever else the world had thrown at people, had always offered them all a friendly face and an ear for a chat. They didn't mind the tea either.

One evening, as the sun was setting on the Atlantic, Gina and Gerry sat on that rock outside the tea shop with Cara by their side, watching the sun take its usual course.

It was one of those evenings where the full moon had made an early appearance in the blue sky, as if it itself knew that it didn't want to miss this moment. When Gerry reached into his pocket and got down to one knee and brought out that ring of his ma's from years ago, Gina burst into tears. Then Penny, the white cow, who by now was on her last legs, let out a loud moo.

"Didn't a cow do that the first night?" asked Gina.

"Yes, it was her. Go away and eat some grass, Penny. I'm trying to do something important here," said Gerry, causing Gina to laugh some more.

"Gina, I planned to do this a long time ago, and I've no ice cream here, but I suppose you need milk to make ice cream, and to get milk you need cows, so maybe this is where it all begins. And it all began at this tea shop, and that night when I kissed you under the moon.

"I fell in love with you then, and that never left. It never will. So, will you do me the honor of becoming Gina McCarthy?" said Gerry.

And for the first time that Gerry had known her, Gina couldn't get the words out, but she nodded through the tears and kissed him. And a few hours later, Gerry would understand that Gina felt like the luckiest woman alive, but that she would be sending a letter to her lawyer in America, as she needed to ensure her divorce had been processed.

It would be a good idea, she said, before she took another hand in marriage.

But it didn't matter to Gerry. He thought back to all those years where she'd been across the ocean and he had been here alone, and he felt that after years of soul searching, he had finally returned to the Promised Land.

———————•✱•———————

One quiet afternoon in the tea shop, Gerry sat looking at Gina, who was cleaning one of the tables. He thought back to those feelings of restlessness in his past, considering how much of a stranger they were to him now. He quietly sipped his tea and smiled as Cara followed Gina to another table. Then Gina stopped. She stared up at the wall, and Gerry knew it wasn't the photos of the Kerry team or Pat Storey that she was looking at.

But Gerry said nothing, and he took another sip of his tea.

In the silence, he waited and watched as Gina slowly, and with much more reservation than she'd had all those years ago, climbed up, and lifted the bow and fiddle from the wall. She held the fiddle against her neck and rubbed her fingers along the strings, and it appeared to Gerry as if Gina was welcoming home a long-lost friend. Then she closed her eyes and started to play. And just like before, it felt to Gerry as if a star had exploded inside his chest.

And when Gina missed a note here and there, it was exactly as it was meant to be, thought Gerry; love was a struggle, and you dropped the odd note now and then. But when she finished the song and he saw the smile on her face, his entire body felt that love had succeeded.

And later that afternoon, with the air of magic around the room from Gina's playing, she said to Gerry, "I'd really like to learn how to play Irish music; you know, the diddly-dee kind?"

"Well, I'm sure Seanie O'Se would be more than happy to teach you."

"You think?"

"Yes, sure you're a Ballyduffy woman now," said Gerry with a smile. And as he looked at Gina, he too felt something had awakened inside of him. He thought some more about his late brother. Then Gerry thought of all those goals he had gotten through to create the tea shop, and others down the years. And then a couple of new goals came into his mind.

"You know, I've been thinking. We may have taken the coast road to get here, but I'd like to start a family with you. But we can chat about that. In the meantime, maybe it's time for me to see a bit of the world. Other than New York and Kerry, I haven't really been anywhere. Maybe a short trip would be good."

Gina couldn't help the smile that came to her face.

She stopped what she was doing and took a seat on the stool beside Gerry.

"That's interesting on both points, Gerry. Where would you like to go?"

Gerry looked around the tea shop he had built, before pausing at the green and yellow flag with the world in the middle, which he had been given a long time ago by a friendly man who had came by, one of the many gifts in return for his warmth and hospitality.

"I was thinking about Brazil. They say they have a big rainforest there, and who knows how long that'll be there for?"

"I love it, Gerry. Brazil; why not? However, maybe let's start with something smaller to begin with? How about a trip to Dublin? The All-Ireland Final is on in a couple of weeks' time, I believe? Maybe Mayo will win it for my grandad?"

And Gerry laughed and shook his head. It was true. That cursed Mayo team and Kerry were together in the final for the first time in many a decade. Kerry hadn't won a championship in twelve long years now. And he knew right then that Gina was his good luck charm for life, because there was no way in hell Kerry could lose a final to Mayo.

Author's note

D.G. Craig is the debut author of Along the Coast Road, a magical journey following the life of big Gerry McCarthy - a proud Kerryman.

When not working on his next book, D.G. can be found stalking his two-year-old around the playground and everywhere else on those dreamy adventures only a toddler can have.

If you wish to stay up to date, please follow along at www.dgcraigbooks.com or on twitter @DG_Craig

Printed in Great Britain
by Amazon

35637558R00158